Little Boy Blues

A Camilla MacPhee Mystery

by Mary Jane Maffini

RENDEZVOUS
PRESS

Cover and title page art: Christopher Chuckry

We acknowledge the support of the Canada Council for the Arts for our publishing program. We acknowledge the support of the Government of Ontario through the Ontario Media Development Corporation's Ontario Book Initiative

RendezVous Crime
an imprint of Napoleon & Company
Toronto, Ontario, Canada
www.napoleonandcompany.com

2nd printing 2009
Printed in Canada

13 12 11 10 9   5 4 3 2

National Library of Canada Cataloguing in Publication Data

Maffini, Mary Jane, date—
    Little boy blues

(A Camilla MacPhee Mystery)
ISBN 0-929141-94-6

I. Title. II. Series: Maffini, Mary Jane. Camilla MacPhee mystery.

PS8576.A3385L58 2002   C813'.54   C2002-900189-7
PR9199.3.M3428L58 2002

ACKNOWLEDGEMENTS

This is a work of fiction. That means, of course, that the characters are figments of my imagination. I hope they seem like real people, but they're not. That's probably a good thing. I have taken liberties with some streets and buildings in Ottawa and in Sydney. The Alvin Ferguson Fan Club will never track down Father Blaise's Youth Club, Justice for Victims, Gadzooks Gallery or Alvin's apartment in Hull.

The Bluesfest is real as are the splendid performers mentioned. The legendary Fuzzy's Fries in Sydney is still worth the trip. Once again, I am indebted to Mary Mackay-Smith and Janet MacEachen for their friendship, enthusiasm and sage counsel. Ron Keough has been a tremendous and cheerful source of information. The Ladies Killing Circle Inc. (Joan Boswell, Victoria Cameron, Audrey Jessup, Sue Pike and Linda Wiken) applied its usual bracing and astute recommendations.

I thank my husband, Giulio Maffini, for his support and encouragement, despite the disturbing fact he always knows whodunnit, and my daughters, Virginia Maffini Findlay and Victoria Maffini Dirnberger, for being dangerous and perceptive, yet always helpful. Thanks also to Louise Crandall, Carole Dalgliesh, M. L. Dalley—Missing Children's Registry, RCMP, Barbara Fradkin, Keary Grace, Sergeant Dave Morrison of the Cape Breton Regional Police, Dr. Lorne Parent, George Pike, André "A. J." Sauvé, Micah Shannon and Michael Steinberg, and the guys at Compact Music.

Alvin expresses his appreciation to Cheryl Freedman of Crime Writers of Canada. Once again my publisher, Sylvia McConnell, and editor, Allister Thompson, managed to keep stiff upper lips throughout the creation of this book. Bless them.

Any errors are mine alone.

1985

They were supposed to stay in the house until it stopped raining, Ma told Jimmy and his brother, Allie, before she left for Sobey's. It was hard for Jimmy to wait, because he really wanted to see his baby ducks. He'd been watching those ducks since they hatched by the creek. He was lucky to have seven ducklings in his own park across the street. Jimmy had two big K-Mart bags full of stale bread ready by the door.

As soon as the sun peeked out, Jimmy said, "It's stopped raining. Can we go now, Allie?"

Vince was the one in charge. He was doing algebra homework in his room, so the little kids had to leave him alone and play quietly. He didn't want to hear one word. But before they left, Allie called up the stairs. "We're going to feed the ducks. See ya."

Vince didn't answer.

Jimmy said, "We better tell Frances Ann."

But Frances Ann was off at her piano lesson, so how could they tell her? And Tracy was in her bedroom playing with her Barbies and she had the NO BOYS EVER sign on the door.

Jimmy didn't want to wait for Frances Ann, because she might stop to see her friends. He wanted to feed those ducks.

When they went out, Jimmy had on his yellow rubber boots. He liked the way they squished in the puddles on the way to the park. Allie pointed up to the sign. He said the X meant CROSS, and this was a special crossing for ducks. Jimmy could only read kindergarten stuff, but he already knew about the special duck crossing, because Allie told him every time they went to the park. Allie thought it was funny.

Sometimes a mother duck and babies would waddle to the other side in the duck crossing, and the cars would have to wait. Jimmy and Allie would fall on the grass laughing, because some of the drivers got real mad.

Allie made Jimmy look both ways. Then they raced over on the duck crossing. Allie said the ducks were getting smarter, and now they could read signs. He said those ducks would be so smart by next year there'd be ducks in Jimmy's Grade One class. Allie said the ducks might get gold stars in their workbooks, and then the rest of the kids would quack up. Then Allie rolled down the hill into the park, past the daffodils, all the way to the pond.

• • •

It was already time to go home when the big guys showed up.

Jimmy didn't notice because he was busy feeding the ducks.

Allie said, "Uh oh. Let's get out of here."

Jimmy had a couple of crusts left, and he had been waiting a long time to come to the park, so he said, "I'm not finished."

"Forget it, Jimmy. Run."

"Wait."

"Now."

When Jimmy looked up, Allie was already near the top of the hill. "Wait for me, Allie," he yelled. "I'm coming." But somehow he got some water in his boots and, he couldn't really run fast because of his asthma. Allie knew that. Allie had disappeared over the top of the hill. Jimmy could hear him yelling, "Hurry up, stupid." The big guys chased after Allie but only ran halfway up the hill.

It looked like Allie got away. That was good. The big guys turned around and walked back into the park. They stood next to Jimmy.

The really tall guy in the brown jacket picked up a rock and threw it into the water. The rock hit one of the ducklings. The mother duck squawked and flapped her wings. The other guy laughed, and they slapped each other on the back.

"Get her next." They both had rocks. The guy with the yellow eyes aimed for the mother duck. The rock hit the duck and she sank below the water without making a sound.

"You can't do that," Jimmy yelled. "Leave the mother duck alone."

"Listen to short-arse," the tall guy in the brown jacket said, heaving a rock. The rest of the ducks were quacking and flapping their wings. They must have been afraid.

Jimmy thought another duckling got hit. He couldn't stop crying. "Stop it. You big fat bullies. Leave the ducks."

The tall guy said, "Who the hell do you think you are?"

Jimmy looked around, hoping Allie would come back. Allie was the smart one, and he was tough in a fight. Allie was gone. But Jimmy couldn't let anything happen to the ducks.

"Leave her alone."

"Listen to him, will ya. Thinks he's tough."

The tall guy turned to look at Jimmy. He had a rock in his hand. "He's a dumb little kid with a snotty nose."

"I am not." Vince always said you have to stand up for yourself. And names can't hurt you. Jimmy didn't mind standing up for himself, but he hoped Allie would show up soon.

"I guess we gotta do what he says." This guy had eyes the

colour of pee. Jimmy had never seen anyone with yellow eyes. He was scarier than the tall guy. But Vince always said don't let anyone know you're afraid.

"Don't hurt them. Okay?"

"He's right."

The tall guy looked at the guy with the yellow eyes and said, "What?"

"You heard him. We can't pitch rocks at the ducks."

The guys looked at each other funny. Maybe it was going to be okay. But Jimmy didn't like the mean smile on the yellow-eyed guy's face.

"The problem is, if we can't pitch rocks at the ducks, what are we going to do with these rocks?"

The guys laughed at that.

"You can put them down," Jimmy said. He was glad he'd stood up for himself.

"I don't think so. That would be a waste of a good rock."

Jimmy looked up the hill one more time. No Allie. He started to back away from the guys.

"My big brothers are coming back for me."

"I guess they're coming a bit too late." The mean guy with the yellow eyes raised his arm.

Jimmy was running up the hill when the first rock smashed into his legs. He fell onto his knees. The guys laughed at Jimmy crying and trying to get his breath. "What a sook."

The rocks kept flying. Jimmy's leg hurt so much. A big rock hit his back. Jimmy screamed as loud as he could. "Allie!"

"Look at short-arse cry. Guess you won't tell us what to do the next time."

A rock smacked Jimmy's head. Blood splashed down his shirt. His chest hurt. He couldn't breathe. He couldn't even scream any more.

The tall guy said, "Hey, look, maybe we better stop. The kid's bleeding."

"What are you, a wuss now too? Afraid of a little blood. Boo hoo hoo."

The tall guy sounded scared too. "That's enough. Let's get out of here."

The mean guy said, "You go if you want to, wussy girl."

Jimmy made himself as small as he could when the mean guy kicked him. "Time to play with your ducks."

Jimmy curled into a ball as he was rolled toward the pond.

He could hear the yellow-eyed guy laughing and laughing until he felt the water on his face.

Then he couldn't hear anything.

One

It was one hell of a party. And for once I had something to celebrate. I don't mean Canada Day in the nation's capital, although there was that too. No, this was the imminent departure of my office assistant, Alvin Ferguson, for greener pastures. For some reason, everyone in my large, meddlesome family thinks the sun shines out of Alvin's rear end. That's why fifty or so people were whooping it up on July 1st in my sister Edwina's manicured garden.

By ten o'clock the temperature had dropped from the pleasant mid-twenties to seven degrees, and the wind had whipped the trendy market umbrellas out of the tables. Maple leaf napkins swirled across the lawn. Red and white paper cups bobbed in the pool. Even the hardiest Cape Bretoners snatched up their rum and cokes and staggered into the house. I imagine the neighbours felt some relief.

At some point in the evening, after one Captain Morgan's too many, I had hiked up my long Indian cotton skirt and hopped on one of Edwina's new dining room chairs to propose a toast.

Everyone hoisted glasses, with the possible exception of Edwina, who was keeping an eye on the brocade seat cover.

"To Alvin Ferguson." I held my toasting hand high.

"To Alvin!" The room rang with it.

I gazed around with pride at the gathering. My three sisters had outdone themselves with food and drink. Even after the heavy-duty barbecue, we still had to face dessert. The chocolate dipped strawberries and cappuccino crème brûlée would be talked about for weeks. Edwina's husband Stan was a hit with his favourite joke novelties, if you don't count a couple of killjoys who'd left early after finding plastic roaches paddling in their *pinot noir*.

The crowd was now wedged inside Edwina's home, the ideal place for Alvin's going-away party. Not everyone has that many Waterford crystal wine glasses. I looked around, mellowed by the event. I smiled at my favourite sister, Alexa. Alexa looked wonderful. Marriage to Detective Sergeant Conn McCracken obviously agreed with her. I felt a twinge of guilt. I'm told I'd behaved like a jerk during the preparations for her wedding the previous winter. Maybe it had been jealousy because my own husband, Paul, had been killed by a drunk driver at the age of thirty-one, and now Alexa was getting a second chance at happiness. Maybe because I am the short, stocky, dark-haired sister misplaced in a family of willowy and elegant blondes. Maybe because I can be a pain in the ass.

Whatever.

Alexa seemed to have forgotten all about it. I raised my glass to her, fondly.

"Speech! Speech!" Who the hell was yelling that? I realized I was three sheets to the wind, teetering on an upholstered chair, feeling unusually sentimental and wearing a pair of borrowed high-heeled mules. So a speech wasn't exactly what I had in mind.

"I don't think so," I said.

My father looked up at me. He is the only person in the world who scares me. Even when he's looking up. Even if he's eighty-one years old. Even if he scarcely remembers my name.

"Um, Camilla. I know you're terribly upset to see Alvin go, but he deserves a proper send-off."

"He sure does, Daddy."

"Then, you should do it. The MacPhees are not afraid to show their deepest emotions when it's appropriate."

My deepest emotion over Alvin's decision to leave was unrestrained joy. I wasn't sure I wanted to share that with this crowd.

My father said, "You are equal to the task."

And so I gave it my best shot.

"Alvin Ferguson is surely the most unbelievable office assistant anyone ever had. Justice for Victims will not be the same without him," I began. That meant, among other things, our utility bills would be paid, the collect calls from Sydney would cease, messages would be passed on, outgoing correspondence would not contain coffee spills, and no topless bathers would be painted on our solitary window. It might also mean no more pilfered library materials would land on my desk.

Alvin had lasted twenty-six long months at Justice for Victims only because my father would never let me fire him. I chose not to mention that.

"Hear, hear!"

"I feel confident the management of the Gadzooks Art Gallery will continue to be surprised, no, amazed, when they realize what kind of gallery assistant they've snagged in our Alvin." And by the time they did, I figured I would have had the locks changed at Justice for Victims.

I swayed on the chair. The crowd gazed on expectantly. I noticed some of them were getting a bit fuzzy. Perhaps they'd had a bit too much hooch.

What the hell. Sometimes you've got to let go. Why not tell the truth?

"As many of you know, I owe Alvin my life, and I will always be grateful to him. To Alvin! There's no one quite like him."

I was telling the truth. The truth but not the whole truth. Sure, I'd be dead if it weren't for Alvin. Sure, he could ferret out more information by quasi-legal means than anyone else. But that didn't mean I wanted to be cooped up in a fifteen by fifteen office with someone who sported nine visible earrings, a fresh tattoo, a fondness for bad music and major attitude.

Al-vin. Al-vin. Al-vin. People chanted and waved their Waterford stemware and sloshed their red wine on Edwina's new pure wool cream carpet.

I continued, "Alvin, as you know, risked his own life to put a murderer behind bars."

My seventy-nine year old neighbour, Mrs. Violet Parnell, put down her new high-end digital camera long enough to beat a military tattoo on the frame of her walker. "Bravo, young Ferguson."

Alvin, splendid in a tuxedo jacket over his skinny lizard-skin patterned jeans, stared at the floor modestly.

I continued, "It has been an astounding experience working with him." Working might have been stretching it.

Alexa began to cry. People blew their noses. My father stood proud. Edwina blotted the carpet.

I shouted, "After Alvin, we have nowhere to go but down."

They tell me that's when I fell off the chair.

Two

By Monday morning, when you would think they'd still be doing the dishes after the party, my in-laws and outlaws were massed at the airport security gate ready to begin a three-week jaunt *en famille* through an unsuspecting Scotland. I was half the send-off party. Leonard Mombourquette, my brother-in-law Conn McCracken's partner on the force, made up the other half.

Too bad. Mombourquette always brings out the worst in me, especially if I have a hangover. I think it's his strong resemblance to a rodent, although no one else seems to notice it. But I suppose someone had to bring McCracken's car home.

"Good luck, Braveheart," Mombourquette said, as McCracken disappeared through the security gate.

"He'll need it."

"Better him than me," Mombourquette added, in case I'd missed the point.

"Oh, I don't know. Conn will have a great time with the girls." I'd caught the dead man walking look on McCracken's face as he was frog-marched through security by my sisters. But that was his problem. I couldn't stop smiling. Not even when my iced *latte* dribbled down the front of my silk blouse.

"I can't believe they asked you to look after Stan's new Buick." Mombourquette eyed the blotched blouse as we headed for the parking lot. "Are they crazy?"

"He's worried about vandalism. And face facts, nothing's going to happen to it." I clicked the snazzy remote to open the Buick's door.

"With you driving it?"

"I am not planning to *drive* it. They asked me to park it in the garage at my place. We have video surveillance and on-site security."

I didn't mention the space was available because my Honda Civic had never fully recovered from certain events the previous winter. This time, the transmission was on the fritz. I didn't want Mombourquette to bring up the circumstances of the Honda's troubles.

"And I like to walk." In fact, I needed to walk because of the ten pounds I'd packed on while my broken leg healed.

"I think Stan's out of his ever-loving mind. It's like praying for bad luck."

I didn't care for his smirk. "Speaking of bad luck, you better keep your eye peeled for black cats, Leonard."

Very restrained of me, considering the company.

Half an hour later, I tucked the Buick safely in the garage of my apartment building and looked forward to a tranquil morning. Most people would take the day off in lieu of the Canada Day holiday, which had fallen on Sunday, but I had planned a pleasant stroll to work in my empty office at Justice for Victims. No relatives. No appointments. No Alvin.

It doesn't get any better. I was in an excellent mood, even though I had to change my blouse. It was a sunny twenty degrees, amazingly fresh for July in Ottawa. I had no need to rush. That meant I could linger over my coffee. I slipped into Bermudas and a tee, then joined Mrs. Parnell's little calico cat on my balcony. I enjoyed my jumbo mug of French roast. Mrs. Parnell's cat enjoyed a bowl of milk.

From the sixteenth floor, I get the long view down the Ottawa River. The green roof of the Parliament buildings are just visible to the East. To the West I can see the white sails at the Britannia Yacht Club.

I got a glimpse of tents popping up for Bluesfest. After five years as a widow, it was time for me to get a life. I hadn't quite got the hang of it, but this year I'd kept the Bluesfest program. I'd read it cover to cover. Twice. The blue booklet lay open on the table, waiting to be read for the third time. The pages were dog-eared. I picked it up and stuck it in my backpack.

My phone rang the minute the apartment door closed behind me and the lock clicked in. It rang on and on as I headed down the hall. I figured it could wait. All my clients had my cellphone number.

The door to apartment 1608 creaked open as I strode by.

"Good morning, Ms. MacPhee." Mrs. Parnell leaned on her walker in the doorway, getting ready for a busy day spying on the occupants of the sixteenth floor. "You've had an active morning."

I nodded and tried to keep walking.

"Do you have time for a visit?" Behind her, the lovebirds, Lester and Pierre, squawked.

I had a fifty-five minute walk ahead of me to get to the office. On the other hand, I owe a lot to Mrs. Parnell.

"Afraid not. I've got some catching up to do. How about tonight?"

She blew out a splendid stream of Benson and Hedges smoke. "I'll be waiting."

"Something wrong?"

She sniffed. "Young Ferguson's gone on to greater adventure and glory."

"We both know Alvin's gone on to work in the Gadzooks

Gallery. Avant garde, I admit, but definitely not glorious."

The tip of her Benson and Hedges turned red. "They could have an armed robbery. A heist."

"I don't think Alvin is hoping for a heist and, even if he is, I feel confident his new employers are not."

She leaned forward, bony and angular. A long convalescence will do that to a person. I might have gained ten pounds after my injuries last winter, when we had taken on a murderer, but she'd lost at least that. She looked every one of her seventy-nine years.

"You are correct, of course, Ms. MacPhee. Pay no attention. I'm finding myself yearning for excitement. Aren't you?"

Our last bit of excitement had almost killed us. "No. I'm not. I'm really looking forward to a quiet summer with no trouble."

I was humming "I Got My Mojo Working" as I hit the elevator button.

• • •

Usually the best part of my walk is along the river. It's cool and silvery in the mornings, no matter how scorching the day ahead. The bike path I followed downtown meandered through Lebreton Flats, and I slowed a bit to catch a look at the set-up for the Bluesfest.

Five days to go, and the staging was already partly erected. I spotted a fleet of flatbed trucks near the acoustic stage up on the hill and more trucks by what looked like the Main Stage.

A trailer with a long line of porta-potties was pulling in.

I figured the rectangular tent off to the Northwest was probably the gospel tent.

It was the first time in years I had let myself get close to the festival grounds. The Bluesfest was the last special place I'd been with Paul. Back when it was much smaller, a cosy, sexy, schmoozefest over in Major's Hill Park.

The sight of the tents brought back Paul's memory. I couldn't imagine what the sounds and smells would do to me when I actually went.

But if I was going to get a life, I couldn't think of a better place to find it.

Three

By the time I got downtown, my T-shirt was stuck to my back. The Bermudas chafed my thighs. My feet smelled, and my head hurt. I clutched my iced *latte* from the Second Cup and finally pushed open the door of Justice for Victims. A rivulet of sweat trickled between my shoulder blades. But I was alone, gloriously, wondrously alone.

I decided to get in the mood for the funding proposal by whipping the in-basket into shape. I started with the stack of bills. Quite a few of them had a telltale red strip on the return envelope. Apparently Alvin had been distracted during the previous three months. Half an hour later I confirmed it. JVF was in great shape, if you didn't count the hydro, the business tax, the photocopier rental and the insurance. Our phone bill, now two months late, had an entire sheet detailing collect calls from Alvin's mother in Sydney.

Then I found the note from the landlord outlining what to expect if we didn't ante up the rent, pronto.

To offset the bills, I had practically no income and, unless I was wrong, I had missed our deadline to file for several key grants that keep organizations like Justice for Victims from going down for the third time.

Never mind. I was alone and loving it. With a song in my heart, I answered the phone. The song faded when the automated voice asked if I would accept the charges for a long distance call from someone called Ferguson. I had a damn good reason to press one for yes.

"Mrs. Ferguson," I said, before she could say a word, "Alvin, as you should be aware, does *not* work here any more. I suggest you direct your calls to his new place of business. I will be happy to provide you with that number."

"Hello? Allie?"

I rubbed my temple.

"Who is this?" the voice said.

"Let me make my point again. Alvin does not work here. Not that he ever really did. You can find him at Gadzooks Gallery. Goodbye."

"I need to speak to Allie." You couldn't mistake the hysteria in that crazy woman's voice. No wonder Alvin was always so distracted.

"Sorry. Alvin doesn't work here any more." I enjoyed hanging up.

When the phone rang again, I was ready to press two for no, nay, never. But this time it wasn't a collect call. It wasn't Alvin's mother either.

"Miss MacPhee?"

"Yes."

"This is Tracy Ferguson. Alvin's sister? We are so sorry to bother you, but we don't know what to do. We know Allie has a new job, but we need your help."

I opened my mouth, but nothing came out. I think it was because Tracy Ferguson was someone's sister, and yet, she sounded gentle, nervous and utterly inept. My sisters are more like the offensive line for the Argos. Jump out of their way, or you'll get grass up your nose.

Unless I was wrong, Tracy was the sister who taught elementary school. I could hear her speaking urgently to someone in the background. "It's all right, Ma, you lie down now. I'll talk to her. Okay?"

I tried being reasonable. "As you know, Tracy, Alvin started his new job this morning. Let me get the number for you." I flipped through my desk for the Gadzooks Gallery cards that Alvin had thoughtfully deposited around Justice for Victims during the final three weeks of his employment.

"But that's it, Miss MacPhee. Alvin isn't at the gallery."

"Well, he isn't here. He should be at Gadzooks."

"But he isn't."

"It's an art gallery. They don't answer their phones before ten."

"But they did answer the phone, and they said Alvin wasn't in."

I found myself massaging my temple again. "Well, I don't think you have much to worry about. He'll drift in to work in his own sweet time. Trust me."

"Miss MacPhee?"

"Look, um..."

"Tracy."

"Why don't you try him at home?"

"He doesn't answer his phone."

"Well, he is probably on his way to Gadzooks." How could an entire family be so stunningly irritating?

"But he wasn't at his apartment. We started calling last night. We left about ten messages."

Okay. Tracy might sound like she was ten years old, but we all had to grow up sometime. "Perhaps Alvin spent the night with a *friend*."

"Oh."

"Right."

"It's urgent. Because of my little brother, Jimmy. We can't find him anywhere."

Unless I was wrong, Alvin's little brother was twenty-one.

"My mother is really upset. We need to find Jimmy soon."

"News flash, Tracy. Sometimes young men get distracted and forget about their mothers. He'll be able to look after himself."

"But that's just it. Jimmy couldn't."

Not my problem. I thought someone should tell Mrs. Ferguson to let her baby boy grow up. "Everything will work out."

"It won't!" Tracy's voice rose. "He can't look after himself."

She said something else, but I missed the rest in an explosion of nose blowing.

"Biss BacPhee?"

"Maybe Jimmy felt like a bit of a break." And no wonder.

"He left his medication. He needs that, or his seizures will start again. He doesn't have his puffer. And he left Gussie on the road. He'd never do that."

"Who?"

"Gussie. He loves that dog. He'd never leave her to fend for herself downtown in the traffic. Jimmy has disappeared. He's absolutely vanished. Now we can't find Allie, and we need to tell him."

She had me. Whatever Alvin's flaws, ignoring his large family wasn't one of them.

I couldn't concentrate with incessant calls from the Fergusons. I had no clients scheduled because of the quasi-holiday. Plus the inside of Justice for Victims by this time was one hell of a lot hotter than the Ottawa streets.

"Okay. I'll do what I can."

"Thank you. You know Allie thinks the world of you, Miss MacPhee."

Ah, shit.

• • •

The phone rang as I reached the door. On the off chance it was Tracy calling to say Jimmy had shown up or Alvin calling to apologize for the inconvenience, I shot across the desk and grabbed the receiver.

"I know I am breathtaking, and it's time you realized it, Tiger."

My friend P. J. Lynch sounded too cheerful for a reporter who'd been yanked back from a big-time assignment in Charlottetown to deal with his mother's heart attack.

"How's your mom?" I asked.

"False alarm. They boosted her meds, she's home again, ready to rumble."

"That's a relief. I'll send her flowers."

"Don't worry about it. Listen, I have terrific news."

"It is terrific news, P. J. But I've got to tear off and find Alvin."

"Find him? I thought you were ecstatic to lose him. Sorry I missed that party, by the way."

"I'm out the door. Call you later."

"Okay. But here's the good news."

I knew what made P. J. a first-rate reporter. He didn't understand any part of no.

"Later," I said.

"I have a chance to do a restaurant review this week. Hot new spot. Friday night. Want to come with me?"

"Aren't you covering Nicholas Southern's Right to be Wrong, Let's Bore the Country Senseless from Coast to Coast to Coast Campaign?"

"Very funny. The Right to be Right is a serious movement."

"Sure. Serious bowel movement."

"I won't dignify that. Anyway, he's got some private function

19

that night. Oh, quit laughing, Tiger, it's not that hilarious. Come with me to the restaurant. It'll be like undercover work. You can be part of my disguise."

"Not that I haven't always wanted to be part of a disguise, but no can do. I'll be at Bluesfest. Blue Rodeo opens. I am *there.*"

"But Bluesfest isn't twenty-four hours a day. You have to eat."

"No dice, P. J. I'll eat on the site. Any other time would be great."

"You don't understand, Tiger. I'm stretched to the max with this assignment."

"I hope you're not complaining. This Nicholas Southern thang is supposed to haul you out of crime reporting and onto the national scene. Make you or break you, I believe you said. Or was that the restaurant reviews?"

"Come on, I've the weekend off, at last. You're supposed to be my buddy. Don't let me down."

"Gotta go, P. J."

I knew the longer we talked, the more persuasive he would become. It takes more than rudeness to shake P. J. Lynch. I hung up.

· · ·

I set off to Gadzooks to find Alvin and hold him in a headlock until he called his family. Twentysome minutes later, I hit the far side of the market and strolled up to the small, upscale gallery. Through the plate glass window, I spotted René Janveau, the owner, surrounded by vast, gleaming crystal sculptures.

René knew my name, since I had provided Alvin with an extraordinarily glowing recommendation. I plan to work that off in Purgatory. He kept running his hands through his hip hairdo and spewing anxiety.

I got to the point. "I need to speak with Alvin Ferguson."

"I am afraid that's not possible."

"Well, it's an emergency."

"It certainly is. I have to leave for Montreal, and Alvin is not here yet. Where do you think he is?"

I felt a little throb in my temple. "I don't know. I'm asking you."

"How ridiculous. I am his employer, and I have no idea."

"Well, I'm his former employer, and I have even less." I tried to imagine Alvin keeping the sparkling half-acre of glass free of fingerprint smudges and dust. I failed.

"But I must leave immediately. A major show could fall through if I miss these negotiations."

I shrugged. I had a lot of problems, but this wasn't one of them.

He brightened and gave me a crafty glance. "You look more or less presentable. Would you consider filling in here until he shows up?"

•   •   •

Hull, Quebec, may be another political world from Ottawa, but it's a short walk from the market. I always love walking over the Alexandria Bridge. The breeze blowing up the Ottawa River was the best thing that had happened to me so far that day. But the cooling effects were quickly lost pounding the pavement on the other side.

It was a hot half-hour before I panted up to Alvin's rickety eight-unit building on Boulevard St. Joseph and staggered through the front door. As usual, the faint memory of marijuana hung in the corridor.

I thumped on Alvin's door. Legally, that was better than thumping Alvin himself, which had crossed my mind. I almost hoped he wouldn't answer so I could continue to get rid of my frustrations.

A small child emerged from the next apartment and watched me with great interest. I provided a bad example by giving the door a kick. It swung inward. I hated to venture into Alvin's apartment unassisted. I never knew what I'd find, but I always knew I wouldn't be prepared.

Inside the apartment, the floor had been painted black, the walls an elegant shade of dove. The lighting was museum quality, but the temperature hovered slightly below boiling. I managed to maintain my cool as I came nose-to-nose with a pretty fair papier mâché replica of *The Thinker*, sitting in the middle of the floor. A series of question marks hung, suspended by invisible wires, over his lovely puzzled head.

Alvin's retro fridge had been redone in a bracing shade of fuschia, and labelled *The Pinker*. The toilet which he uses as a planter had a cabbage rose growing in it and a little plaque on the wall behind that said *The Stinker*.

A floor-to-ceiling rectangle consisting of three broad vertical stripes caught my eye. Alvin had thoughtfully added a blinking artificial flame at the base of the painting and a talk bubble that said, "Ouch, that's hot," at the top. It got the label, *The Blinker*.

On the next wall, a Picasso from the blue period. The large eye winked at me, and two seconds later the small one did. The label said, naturally, *The Winker*.

That boy gets me every time.

I did have to ask myself: if Alvin was ingenious enough to create and maintain this display, why, in his time at Justice for Victims, had he never once answered the goddam phone properly?

•   •   •

I found Alvin in the bedroom. I almost didn't spot him under the tangle of sheets. He was curled into the fetal position. His eyes were closed, and I couldn't see any movement. His ponytail spread over the crisp white pillowcase, and five of his visible earrings glinted in the pale glow filtering in from the living room.

Alvin didn't even appear to be breathing. I almost stopped breathing myself. I reached out and touched him. Warm. And better yet, that small rise of his chest indicated that he was alive.

Now that I knew he was alive, I really felt like killing him.

I shook him vigorously. "Are you out of your mind, sleeping in on the first day of your new job?"

Alvin didn't respond. I gave his grey, bony cheek a gentle slap.

I sat back and looked around. Had he accidentally overdosed? I saw nothing in the small bedroom. Unlike the living room, it was simple and neat. Double bed. No clothes strewn. No museum knock-offs. His all-season leather jacket hung on a wooden hanger in the closet, next to his Mickey Mouse scarf.

I checked the bathroom. It was spotless. White towels with the monogram AF were displayed neatly on the towel rack, fresh soap sat in the soap dish, and the bathmat was clean and fluffy. Aside from the Magritte panel reproduced on the inside of the shower stall, it could have been anyone's bathroom. I opened the medicine cabinet.

It contained a toothbrush and a tube of Crest.

I rushed back to the bedroom and stuck my head under the bed. Not even a dust bunny.

Alvin hadn't budged. My cellphone decided this was a dead zone. I was pretty wobbly as I hightailed it to the living room to call for help. Too bad Alvin had painted his telephone black to match the floor. I was about to race into the hallway yelling for help when I stubbed my toe on the missing phone.

911. I stammered out the address. And admitted he was breathing. Yes, I was calm, I insisted. No, I didn't know of any medical conditions. No, I didn't think he had been sick recently. No, I'd found no sign of any drugs. No, I didn't know for sure if he might have ingested anything. No, no pill bottles in the apartment. Yes, I already said I *was* calm.

Extremely goddam calm, in fact.

It didn't take long for the paramedics to arrive. Eight minutes by my watch. Eight hours by my emotional state.

Long enough to notice no light flashing on Alvin's answering machine. Looked like he'd picked up his messages.

•   •   •

As the paramedics were peering under Alvin's eyelids with little lights, he popped his eyes open and sat up.

"What's going on?" he said.

"You tell me," I said, perhaps too forcefully, because the paramedics asked me to step out of the room. "Not a chance," I said.

I found myself being propelled by the female paramedic. She could have bench-pressed some serious numbers. I relied on the Cape Breton solution and made tea in Alvin's grandmother's pink and white china teapot. The tea had reached the bracing black stage when the bedroom door opened and the paramedics emerged. Lines of sweat ran down their faces. "Looks like he's all right, Madame," the male said. "He's making sense. It's probably the heat, but you should check with his doctor."

"He had a bit of a shock. I think he got a phone message

that a family member has gone missing."

"That may be. But it is dangerously hot in here."

"Is that tea?" the female attendant said.

"Would you like some?"

She shook her head. I heard her mutter something like *anglaise, tête carrée.*

I had no idea who Alvin's doctor was.

"You should get him someplace cool and make sure someone stays with him for the next twenty-four hours."

I'd already figured that one out myself.

"And no tea."

When the door clicked behind them, I turned to face Alvin. He clutched a silver-framed photo.

"What happened, Alvin?"

Alvin emitted a low keening sound, raising goosebumps on my arms. He slumped to the floor.

I dropped to my knees beside him.

"Alvin. *Alvin.*"

"He's dead," he whispered.

"What?"

Tears streaked his cheeks and dripped onto the black floor. "Our Jimmy's dead."

"Alvin, he's not dead. Nobody said he was dead. He's missing, and they're worried because he left his medication and what's-its-name, the dog. I just spoke to your family no more than an hour ago, and they are out searching for him."

"I know Jimmy's *dead.* And it's my fault."

Four

Warmth and sympathy don't come naturally to me. But after this tragic news, even I knew Alvin needed a cool spot and someone to look after him.

I arranged for a cab. I called Gadzooks and explained there'd been a death in Alvin's family. I alerted Mrs. Parnell and told her to expect company. Finally, I took a deep breath and tried the Fergusons. Busy.

Forty minutes later, Alvin was settled on Mrs. Parnell's black leather sofa. His breathing was deep and ragged. Vivaldi played soothingly in the background. Every now and then, the lovebirds Lester or Pierre gave a war cry.

The Fergusons' line continued to be busy.

I filled Mrs. P. in on the background. I figured she'd be baffled too. She surprised me. "Poor boy. He's lost his favourite earrings."

"That's the least of his problems."

"Perhaps, Ms. MacPhee. My point is, young Ferguson is meticulous about his appearance. He must be terribly disturbed to have left home like that. Of course, that's one of the symptoms."

"Symptoms? Of losing a relative?"

"Shell-shock."

"You're kidding."

"Not in the least. I saw a lot of it during the war. Many

lovely boys were ruined. We mustn't let that happen to young Ferguson."

"Wait a minute, Mrs. P. Alvin hasn't been in a war. He's upset about his brother. I guess they must have found his body and reached Alvin to tell him. Alvin was too distraught to give me the details. But anyway, I can understand his reaction." My hands were shaky. I far preferred my old familiar Alvin, the gold-plated pain in the arse, to this fragile being.

"This is not the way people act when they hear about a death. They might be shocked. They cry and carry on. Many keep a stiff upper lip. This is much, much worse, Ms. MacPhee. I can tell by the eyes."

"His eyes are closed. And what could be worse than losing a family member?"

"If you had seen what I have, Ms. MacPhee." Mrs. Parnell inhaled deeply. "We must stand by our fallen comrade."

I wasn't in the mood for Mrs. Parnell's endless allusions to World War II. But I did have to admit, it wasn't like Alvin. "You know, I would have thought he'd already be on the plane heading home to comfort his mother. Whatever you can say about him, he's great in an emergency."

"My point exactly. Something else is at work here. Something evil."

Alvin cried out in his sleep. "Forget the stupid ducks." He flailed his arms about, staring wildly at nothing. The framed photo tumbled to the floor.

Mrs. Parnell bent over and picked it up. "Beautiful child. What a shame, to die so young."

I took a look myself. If that was Jimmy Ferguson, he had indeed been an attractive young man. Wide spaced blue eyes, short dark hair, broad forehead, narrow chin, a smile to break your heart. Even the broken glass couldn't hide that. It was hard to believe anyone with that combination of innocence and good looks could have been fished out of the same gene pool as Alvin.

"The main thing is to get him home to Sydney. Fast," I said.

She shook her head. "I am fond of young Ferguson. I'll do anything for him. This is more than grief."

"You haven't talked to him yet. How can you be so sure it's more than grief?"

"I know it when I see it. Young Ferguson has it in no small measure."

"I'll keep trying to get through to the family. They must be devastated about Jimmy, and now they have to worry about Alvin, too."

Mrs. Parnell stiffened. "It's their duty to worry about him."

I took a deep breath and dialed. A little of the Fergusons goes a long way. This time Tracy answered on the first ring.

"Tracy," I said, "let me tell you how sorry I am."

"How sorry you are?"

"Yes. I can only imagine how devastated you must be."

"Devastated?"

"How is your mother?"

"My mother?"

"Yes, your mother." What was the matter with these people?

"She's not too well."

"Of course, she isn't. Please give her my sympathy."

"Your what?"

"I want to assure you Alvin will be home in time."

"In time for what?"

I couldn't believe this girl could be allowed to teach school. Alvin, for all his faults, was at least intelligent.

"Well, for the funeral."

"What funeral?"

I tried to be charitable. The Ferguson family had suffered a great trauma. The family members couldn't be thinking straight.

"Your brother's funeral." I pronounced every syllable.

"What?"

I tried not to scream. "Jimmy's funeral. Again, please let me express my condolences."

She blubbered. "I thought I heard you say Jimmy's funeral."

"I did."

"Did you say Jimmy's dead?"

"Well, yes."

"*Dead?*"

"I am sorry."

She gulped, "Oh, my God."

Okay, so something didn't seem quite right.

"Hello?" I said.

On the other end of the phone chaos erupted. I could hear Tracy shrieking: "Oh God oh my God please no dear God." People were shouting and crying. A dog began to bark.

Someone else picked up the phone, and a man's voice boomed. "Who's speaking, please?"

Was it possible I had something confused?

"Wrong number," I said and hung up.

•   •   •

I reached my father's second cousin once removed in Sydney shortly afterwards. Daddy always said if Donald Donnie MacDonald didn't know about something, it couldn't be worth knowing, even though it might not be worth repeating. Better yet, Donald Donnie and his equally observant wife, Loretta, lived right next door to the Fergusons. Not that they got along.

Lucky me. Donald Donnie answered his phone.

"Checking in," I said after the initial pleasantries were over. "What's the word on Jimmy Ferguson? Have they found him yet?"

He knew what was going on with Jimmy Ferguson all right. Apparently including my latest phone call to the Fergusons, made less than a half-hour earlier.

Across the room, Mrs. Parnell kept a close watch on the sleeping Alvin. She raised her glass to me and blew smoke rings sympathetically.

"Jimmy's still missing," I mouthed at her.

Mrs. Parnell had the grace to look surprised.

"I'm sure the family is in a state. I wouldn't want to disturb them by calling and..." Here I lowered my voice and stepped around the corner into Mrs. Parnell's kitchen.

Donald Donnie said, "Indeed, they're disturbed already. Some wretched creature phoned and told them Jimmy was dead. They're a pretty strange bunch, that crowd, but I can't understand the cruelty of that."

"Really? Someone called them and told them he was dead? Perhaps it was a misunderstanding."

"A misunderstanding! My God, girl."

"Well, I'm glad he's alive."

"We don't actually know he's alive, Camilla." I could hear Loretta jabbering on in the background too.

"We don't?"

"If the police don't find him soon, he might as well be dead. That's right, Mum, I'll tell her. He's in a bad enough way now. He can't look after himself at all at all. Any more trauma, and I can't imagine what would be left of that boy's brain."

•   •   •

When I returned to the living room, Mrs. Parnell looked up brightly. "Little something to take your mind off your trouble, Ms. MacPhee?"

I shook my head.

"Don't blame yourself. In his state, young Ferguson could easily have misinterpreted his family's message."

"I guess so. Anyway, I'll head back to the office and grab a few files. I can work here until we get this thing settled."

"Before you go, you'd better fill me in on young Ferguson's family in case he comes to. Then I'll know what's going on."

"Sure. Seven kids, although it seems like more at times. Five are older and doing well for themselves. My father thinks the world of Alvin's mother. She's been a widow since Alvin and Jimmy were babies, yet she managed to get all those kids through university, except the youngest one, Jimmy. He had some kind of problems."

Mrs. Parnell blew a couple of very impressive smoke rings. "What sort of problems?"

"Alvin didn't talk about him much. I figure everyone in the family pampered him."

Mrs. P. said. "The lovely boy in the picture. When did he go missing?"

"I haven't really got the details. Everything blew up all of a sudden. His sister, Tracy, was very upset on the phone, and then Alvin collapsed. But it must have been after the going-away party last night. The family called to congratulate Alvin. Collect as usual. At first I thought it was strange people would be so agitated about this kid taking off overnight. I mean, Alvin's way up here on his own, and nobody goes nuts about him."

"Hmmm." Mrs. Parnell picked up the photo and squinted at it through a veil of smoke.

I had a thought. "According to Donald Donnie MacDonald,

Jimmy has seizures, and he's not able to look after himself. Some kind of brain damage. And then the fact that he left his dog alone downtown, I guess that's the clincher."

Mrs. Parnell continued to examine the photo. She said, "We need better intelligence before we can develop a plan of action."

My idea of a plan of action was to have Alvin talk to his family and tell them he was all right and maybe drive him to the airport.

Mrs. Parnell jammed another Benson and Hedges into her cigarette holder. "One always needs a plan of action. But more to the point, Jimmy may be all right, but young Ferguson certainly isn't. We need to get to the bottom of that before it's too late." I had to hand it to her, Mrs. P. knew how to convey a fine sense of impending doom.

"Too bad my father's in Scotland. I bet he'd know more about this Jimmy. What do you mean by too late?"

"Ah, these darling boys. I've seen it too often. Things set them off. Some small trauma. Something the rest of us wouldn't give a second thought to. But it takes them inside themselves. Each time gets a bit worse. Then one day, they don't come out again."

What did this mean? That Alvin might never snap out of it?

"Ms. MacPhee, it would be useful to have something of a context. If we know what's going on, then we can think about how to combat it. If young Ferguson wakes up, I'll try to get a bit more out of him without setting him off again."

I stood up. "We have to send him home. Pronto. He'll be better off with his family."

Mrs. Parnell stood up too. She leaned forward. I leaned back. She pursed her lips. I gathered that meant no. "Can he afford it?" she said.

"If he can't, then I'll have to help him."

"Is that such a good idea?"

"No choice, Mrs. P. He needs to be with his family. They'll be able to help him. Like you say, he seems traumatized."

"Perhaps."

"For sure. And listen, we have to contact his family, and I don't want to get their panties in a twist again. So how about this. You call them and tell them he's not feeling well and he'll be in touch. In the meantime, I'll make the arrangements for his flight."

"Not so fast, Ms. MacPhee. Consider this, young Ferguson's family are probably the source of his problem."

Five

P. J. nabbed me on the cellphone before we got any further with that idea.

"I got some good news for you, Tiger," he said.

As usual, the enthusiasm in his voice was enough to make me smile. You can trust him as far as you can throw a piano, but you had to like the guy. "I can use some good news."

"You get your Bluesfest pass yet?"

"No, Mrs, Parnell and I have to help Alvin out with a serious problem. I'll pick up my pass later."

"Don't bother."

"Try not to be annoying, P. J."

"Hey, come on."

"Look, I have a situation unfolding which is giving me grief. I am not, repeat not, in a good mood. So don't pressure me. I am going to goddam Bluesfest. Don't try to talk me into anything else. I have to get off the phone and make airline reservations pronto."

"Pronto? That's my point, Tiger. I got two Clubhouse passes to the Bluesfest."

"What?"

"Clubhouse passes. Two of the suckers."

"You're kidding. Since this morning?"

"Yeah. I won a draw at the paper."

"That's fabulous."

"Hate to tell you, but it's actually bad news. Because *The Ottawa Citizen* is a sponsor, and as an employee, I was not eligible to win."

What was going on here? "That's miserable."

"Actually, it isn't. I knew I wasn't eligible, so I put your name on the entry form. Then I put my own telephone number."

Irritation cancelled. If I remembered the Bluesfest program booklet, Clubhouse passes cost more than two hundred smackers a pop and came with a lot of goodies. I'd planned for the sixty-five dollar full festival pass myself. Now I'd have to dip into my savings to cover the shortfall of Justice for Victims, not to mention springing for Alvin's plane ticket, so saving sixty-five dollars was welcome. "Definitely good news."

"Sure is."

"Why don't you drop by the office and slip the passes under the door? I'll decide who to take." P. J. was born to be teased.

"What do you mean, you'll decide who to take? I thought we'd go together. That was the whole idea. Didn't you say going to the Bluesfest was a sign you were getting a life?"

"Did I? You told me you weren't eligible. You're a highly paid reporter, and now with these restaurant review gigs and this big honking political assignment, you'll be floating in cash. You can buy yourself a pass. I'll take someone who can't afford it."

"Are you crazy? Clubhouse passes are sold out." P. J.'s voice shot up an octave.

"But as you say, the passes are in my name."

"Wait a minute. You didn't buy the tickets."

"You didn't buy them either. Anyway, what are you worried about? You can always cover it for *The Citizen*."

"I wish. I can't cover that and Nicholas Southern's campaign too."

"You keep whining about that. Seems to me a high profile assignment is money in the bank, even if you do have to listen to all that right wing bullshit."

"Yeah well, the paper can hardly give me Bluesfest too."

"That is not really bad news, P. J. Mr. Southern's a big story. You'd better concentrate. Let me know if anything about the New Right starts to make sense to you, and I'll do my best to get you to a deprogrammer. I can fill you in on the concerts afterwards. It's not like you know anything about the blues anyway."

"Hang on a minute. The good news is the story is going well. Southern never shuts up, but he has a life. He's off the road this weekend. I won't have any trouble getting to Bluesfest." I noted the panic in his voice. If P. J. didn't want to be tormented, maybe he shouldn't have sent me a prickly cactus last year when I was laid up in hospital.

"Come on, Tiger, you've been yakking about how much you wanted to hear Blue Rodeo. I thought you'd be happy to spend the time with me," he added.

Time to quit horsing around.

"Bad news then, P. J. You'll have to put up with me for the whole festival. But I have to take care of something important first."

I thought I heard a whoosh of relief.

• • •

"I've been thinking about it, Mrs. P. Alvin's family are profoundly irritating, but they seem to truly care about him, even if it's on someone else's phone tab."

"Perhaps."

"I can't believe they caused him any trauma."

"We must consider it, even if it is unpalatable."

"More unlikely than unpalatable. But why don't I try to get a bit more dope on what's going on before I book his flight?"

I made the call from Mrs. Parnell's bedroom, out of Alvin's earshot. My source was in.

"Camilla," Donald Donnie MacDonald said. "Twice in one day?"

"Sorry to bother you. I need to know a bit more about what happened to Jimmy Ferguson, for Alvin's sake. He's in a weird anxiety state. And you seemed to be the logical person to ask." I didn't mention Donald Donnie lived for gossip.

"Indeed, ask away, girl."

"Fill me in on the situation, right from the beginning."

"I'm not surprised Allie's in a state. The family's in crisis. Jimmy's disappeared off the streets of Sydney on Canada Day in broad daylight. Poof! There he was, gone. Just like that."

"You mentioned Jimmy wasn't quite all right. What's the story?"

"Indeed, it was a tragedy."

"I'm sure. But what was the tragedy?"

"Must have happened about sixteen years ago. Springtime it was. Eighty-four. What, Mum? Oh right, eighty-five."

"What exactly happened?" I parked myself on Mrs. Parnell's king-sized bed. No point in being uncomfortable. I knew Donald Donnie, and this was going to take a while.

"Jimmy nearly drowned. In our lovely little park right across the street. Loretta and I can practically see it from the front veranda."

"Maybe that's why Alvin's so agitated. Did Alvin find him?"

"No. Allie and Jimmy were always together. Allie ran for help, and Loretta and I raced down."

"So was Jimmy all right?"

"Indeed he was not, girl. He never got over the near-drowning. He was left brain-damaged. He has the mind of a ten-year-old child now, when he's at his best. That's why they're so worried."

Mrs. Parnell stuck her head around the corner and leaned on the doorjamb. She must have reacted to the look on my face. She spilled a drop of sherry as she inclined forward to follow the conversation.

"That is terrible," I said. "They'll just have to keep looking."

"Don't talk foolish. Of course, they'll keep looking. Everyone's helping. Neighbours, Jimmy's friends, their parents, total strangers. We've been out ourselves, not that they'd give us the time of day next door."

"I guess they'll have to get the cops to take it seriously."

"Now you're being ridiculous again, girl. Indeed, the police have taken it seriously."

"In that case, they're bound to find him. He can't disappear."

"Well, that's the thing, Camilla. They've found no trace of him anywhere. He's completely vanished. We need every bit of help we can get."

"So we'll make sure Alvin gets home as soon as possible."

"I hear you're no slouch at sorting things out, Camilla MacPhee. You should get your arse in gear and get down here yourself."

• • •

"No wonder young Ferguson's so upset," Mrs. Parnell said.

"It explains a lot." I followed her into the living room.

"Imagine, his brother is missing and doesn't have the intellect to deal with danger effectively."

Mrs. Parnell looked fondly towards her black leather sofa,

38

where Alvin was curled up under the zebra throw. "We have to do something."

"Donald Donnie MacDonald said a near-drowning accident caused Jimmy's brain damage. He said Alvin was there. If that's not traumatic, what is?"

Mrs. P. splashed herself a healthy dose of Harvey's Bristol Cream. "It would be. The symptoms often show up long after the event. Then something triggers the memory, and it's more than the lad can deal with."

"Okay. First we get him home. Then we figure out what's going on in his head."

Mrs. Parnell stood, silent, staring out her window, at the long view down the Ottawa River toward Parliament Hill.

"Some of these boys never recover. The hospitals were full of them, you know, after both the wars. Wasted young men."

"That won't happen with Alvin. He's resilient. Look at how he bounced back from all our problems last winter."

Mrs. P. picked up the photo again. "I believe you are correct, Ms. MacPhee. I think this beautiful boy is the key to our understanding. If this accident is the root of it, young Ferguson obviously never had any help to deal with the trauma."

"Kids often don't talk about things. Let's give the family the benefit of the doubt and find out what happened before we court martial them." I didn't want to inflame the situation by mentioning that Alvin was not the easiest person to understand or by suggesting his family might find him as baffling as I did.

"You are right, Ms. MacPhee. That is the honourable thing to do. But I believe in the end, it will be left to us to find out what young Ferguson's problem is."

I hate it when she's right. "We have to call them and tell them he will be home as soon as possible. As I said, it's better if you make that call, Mrs. P."

She folded her arms.

"We have to," I said. "What if they get news, good or bad, and can't reach him? That would certainly compound his problems, wouldn't it? Don't be surprised if you get collect calls. And you'd better give them my cell number too, for emergency only."

"I suppose we have no choice. We must keep the channels of communication open to the front."

"Right. And another thing, whatever the problem is, Alvin's in no shape to travel by himself. He can't go on a plane like this by himself. And as you say, his family will be way too distracted to worry about him. I'd better go too."

•   •   •

First things first, I thought. Before I headed out, I called my doctor and left an urgent message. The next message was for my travel agent asking about booking the most direct flights to Sydney. I left Mrs. Parnell's number with her. While waiting for the beep, I had a brainwave. Leonard Mombourquette's family were from somewhere in Cape Breton too. I was betting he'd have the connections. It's a gene-pool thing. Worth taking a few more digs about me and Stan's Buick. I tried to reach Mombourquette at his Ottawa Police Services extension and at his cellphone number, but he was holed up somewhere. I left messages asking him to get a line on Jimmy Ferguson's disappearance. In the meantime, I had places to go and people to see.

•   •   •

I needed to know I could get back home fast in an emergency, so I took the Buick. Bonus, it had air conditioning. I wouldn't have been much good to anyone poached. Stan would understand.

I buzzed down to Elgin Street and, despite the afternoon holiday crowds, I found a parking meter. I headed into the inferno that was Justice for Victims and snatched up my briefcase. I jammed the more pressing files into it. If I was going to be unavailable until we got Alvin settled, I could at least pay the overdue bills.

Miraculously, my cellphone rang. My doctor was happy to confirm what I thought: that Alvin should get professional help as soon as possible. "But don't hold your breath," she said. "It takes a while to get in to see someone. Unless you think he should check into the psych ward."

I was hardly qualified to make this decision. "No," I said. "He'll be better off with me and with his family. He can probably get in to see someone faster in Sydney. To be on the safe side, can you try to get him a referral here for when we get back?"

•   •   •

Since the Buick was already on the road, and I still had Alvin's apartment keys in my pocket, I decided to whip over to Hull and collect a few essentials for him. Somewhat belatedly, it had crossed my mind that we should pick up his health card and ID. Not to mention toiletries and clean clothes. That way if we got him a last minute flight, we'd be off in a flash.

I parked the Buick with due care and consideration and bolted into Alvin's apartment. I ignored the *Thinker, Winker, Blinker* and *Stinker* and tried to keep my wits about me.

Where would Alvin keep his documents and ID? Okay, he had a cabbage rose in the toilet. So, not there. I checked the fuschia fridge. It was well supplied with neatly organized oil paints, brushes, acrylics, watercolours and other artist's gear. I noted the inside of the fridge was the only comfortable spot in the apartment. No sign of Alvin's ID and health card. Fine.

I found nothing in the kitchen except spices and condiments and the makings of small, neat meals.

I headed for the bedroom. Feeling a bit guilty about ignoring the tangle of sheets in Alvin's room, I rummaged through the dresser drawers. Because it was Alvin's, I started at the bottom drawer, assuming he'd do everything in reverse. I was right. I turned up nothing of note, unless your interests included underwear in exotic patterns.

The second drawer yielded socks, in every colour you could imagine, neatly lined up following the spectrum. Who knew Alvin had such a rich inner life?

The top drawer held hundreds of postcards, packed together with elastic bands, neatly, as I had come to expect. Most had a telltale Cape Breton tartan design, a piper, or a panoramic shot of some part of the Cabot Trail. Lobster shots figured prominently. Some of the lobsters wore tams at jaunty angles. Others played bagpipes or lounged on beach chairs or were winning big at the casino. No accounting for taste.

I riffled through the postcards, which contained innocuous messages, written in uneven letters. I kept hunting. It would be just like Alvin to hide his documents behind a partly-dressed lobster.

Nothing turned up. I tucked the postcards back in the drawer.

I was hot and bothered by the time I located Alvin's brown and gold Quebec medical insurance card along with his other

ID in the inside pocket of that damned leather jacket. Alvin looked like a deranged raven in the photo.

I grabbed the ID, some underwear and socks in electrifying shades, a number of black T-shirts, the blue-striped pyjamas, the toothbrush and Crest and stuffed them all into his kitbag. I decided to take the leather jacket in case it got cold in Sydney. I added a few basic art supplies, watercolour pencils and a notebook, to keep his mind occupied on the trip down East.

I hesitated as I walked by *The Stinker*. Then I headed back into the bedroom, where I made Alvin's bed. While straightening the sheets, I found one of his missing earrings. The others turned up under the bed. Alvin must have been spinning like a bad stock.

I had a clear conscience by the time I locked the apartment door and slung the kit-bag over my shoulder. On the way out I noticed the row of mailboxes in the front foyer. A small key on Alvin's key chain opened his mail slot.

The mailbox contained the usual pizza delivery ads, an art magazine and a postcard of a lobster playing the fiddle. I turned the postcard over and found the same uneven letters and the same large unformed cursive signature. James Ferguson. Alvin would be happy to get it. I tucked the postcard into my purse. And that made me think again about the rest of the postcards in the drawer. Obviously they were from Jimmy Ferguson. Surely Alvin and his family would want them, no matter what.

I hiked back up to the apartment, unlocked the door, raced to the bedroom and scooped out the postcards. It was obvious from their careful storage that they meant a lot to Alvin, so I thought it better not to squish them into the kit bag. I held on to them until I got back to the car and slipped them into my briefcase. I'd give them to him when the time was right.

• • •

My next stop was back in Ottawa on Elgin Street again, Ottawa Police Services Headquarters. I made my way to the second floor, Criminal Investigation Division. The guy at the desk knew me as Conn McCracken's sister-in-law. Things had greatly improved since the previous year, when every cop on the force had been on my case, and I'd even been tossed out of the building.

This time I waved my way through and headed over to Major Crimes.

"You want me to buzz Lennie?"

I smiled. "I'll surprise him."

When I stuck my head in the door, Mombourquette raised his pointy nose, sniffed and narrowed his eyes. He knew when he was trapped.

"Hey, Leonard," I grinned. "Cat got your tail?"

"Not a good time."

"I'm here now, and we both want me to go away soon."

"We sure do."

"Did you get my message?"

"All of them, in fact."

"Only two. Don't exaggerate, Leonard."

"Here's the deal. I've got a cousin on the Cape Breton force. I made a call. So he gave this information to *me*. All right?"

"Sure, Leonard."

"He did not give the information to you. Understand?"

"Fine."

"Okay, Jimmy Ferguson has diminished capacity. You probably know that. He has never been away from home. He has serious medical problems, including *petit mal* seizures resulting from a brain injury. The family does not believe he

44

can look after himself. He has simply disappeared."

"Yesterday."

"He never came home. They've checked the bus station and the airport, even though it's highly unlikely he could manage to get himself a ticket."

"Maybe they underestimate him." I could relate to that.

"You want to let me finish? Or you know everything already?"

"Okay, okay, keep going."

"They've got a media call out. He was seen by a number of neighbours making his usual rounds from one friend to another. Nothing out of the ordinary. He was also seen on the boardwalk overlooking the harbour, although he's not supposed to be there. No one has seen him since."

"Maybe he became disoriented and got lost," I said.

Mombourquette shook his head. "I suggested that. My cousin set me straight. Apparently everyone knew this boy. It's a close-knit community. The radio stations have been making announcements. Plenty of appeals to the public. They've searched the parks. Everywhere."

"Okay," I said.

"But Jimmy Ferguson has vanished off the face of the earth."

"Right next to the harbour," I said.

"That's it. That's the big worry."

"Could he swim?"

"Wouldn't matter if he had a seizure near the edge of the water. You can't swim if you're unconscious."

"What the hell are you doing to find out if that's what happened, Leonard?"

Six

S top yelling at me."

I stared. "I'm not yelling at you, Leonard."

"Yes, you are."

"Okay. I didn't mean to, and I apologize. Now where were we?"

"We were in Sydney."

"What's the name of your cousin on the Sydney force again?"

"Let me repeat. I don't want you calling up my contacts on other forces and giving them a hard time."

"I'd never do something like that." I couldn't help smiling, because Mombourquette was wearing a soft grey summer shirt and pants, and his whiskers twitched.

"You do things like that all the time."

"Not this time. I have no intention of badgering anyone, but my father will ask me, and you know what Cape Bretoners are like about getting the names of peoples' relatives. He's eighty years old. Can't you humour him?"

"Your father's in Scotland. How stupid do you think I am?"

I really hated to let that one slip by. "He's bound to call me, Leonard."

"I can't stand this."

"There's a way to make it stop."

"Okay, my cousin's name is Ray Deveau."

"Thank you. Now was that so hard?"

"He's the nicest guy in the world, and I don't want you bugging him. Understand?"

Mombourquette's cousin? Nicest guy in the world? Hardly. "Perfectly. What *exactly* did he say? Is Alvin overreacting?"

"They're convinced something serious happened to the kid. I told you, it's not such a big place, and a lot of people saw Jimmy before he disappeared. He's kind of a fixture. Anyway, people would call the police or try to help if he was in trouble."

"Maybe he got himself outside of Sydney. to of the other nearby towns. You sure they've looked everywhere for him?"

"What kind of idiot question is that? They're competent police officers. They don't need you to tell them how to do their jobs."

"All right, I'm sorry. It's an emotional kind of issue."

"So do you want to know what Ray Deveau thinks?"

"Of course I want to know."

"It's been over twenty-four hours. So one of two things. They figure if he's in the area, he's dead."

"But it's summer. He could survive outside."

Mombourquette reached over and touched my arm.

"It was eight degrees Celsius in Sydney overnight. Anyway, this boy won't survive long on his own, no matter where."

"But..."

"Like you said, it's not good to disappear next to a harbour."

"Yeah, but you said the place was full of people. Tourists and musicians and all that. Wouldn't they notice him?"

"I haven't been back since they built this boardwalk, but Ray told me there's a section at the end where a person could drown unseen."

"Did they send down divers?"

"Of course they sent down frigging divers. What is the

matter with you? And they worked with the Coast Guard."

"Why don't you want me to speak to this Deveau guy?"

"I've been a cop for twenty-five years. I've been a detective working major crimes for twelve. Ray's been on the force for, let me think, eighteen, twenty years. It's his home town. So, sure, yeah, I think a word from you would probably clear the whole thing up. Show us dumb cops that we should have looked for him in his closet. Or maybe put out a missing persons bulletin in the local media. We should have turned to you first. Maybe you can clear up all our cases."

"No need to be sarcastic."

Mombourquette scurried away from his desk and passed me in the doorway. He said, "This reminds me, did I ever mention you really piss me off?"

"You and everyone else. Don't go thinking you're special."

"Good-bye, Camilla."

"Wait a minute, you said, one of two things. What's the other?"

But Mombourquette had taken the cheese and skipped the trap.

• • •

The Ottawa River Parkway was clear sailing all the way home. It was quarter to four when I got back to Mrs. P.'s. Alvin was in the bathroom. Mrs. Parnell seemed to feel he had improved.

"But I don't think we should tell him they've found no sign of his brother." Mrs. Parnell kept her voice low.

"He's going to find out anyway. Better if he hears it from us."

"I don't dispute that, Ms. MacPhee. But the point is that young Ferguson is coming out of a disturbed state. If he receives more bad news right now, it could send him back over the edge."

"But what can we do? We can only guess why he's in this state, and we don't know where his brother is. By the way, did my travel agent call back?"

"Indeed she did, Ms. MacPhee. She's tried everything. Unfortunately, they have not a single flight available into Sydney for the next week."

"Be serious. Did you play the compassion card?"

"Naturally. And the poor old lady card too. Apparently they book up early for this time of year because of family reunions and people returning for holidays in addition to the booming tourist trade."

I shuddered, and not just because of the family reunion idea.

Mrs. P. mashed a fresh cigarette into her holder and fixed me with a look. "I know what you are going to say, Ms. MacPhee, and I have beaten you to the draw. I did a detailed check on the travel sites, discounters, the airlines themselves, the works, and there's not a seat to be had. Not a single seat. Not through Fredericton or Charlottetown or Halifax. Not through Boston. Not one. You will have to accept that."

"Oh, great. Now we're in a pickle. He's in no shape to spend a long trip on a train or a bus. We can't keep him here. We can hardly grill the family over the phone about what might have led to this state, and Mombourquette warned me against contacting the Sydney cops. We're more than a thousand miles away, and we can't do diddly about it."

I knocked on the bathroom door and told Alvin I'd brought fresh clothing for him. The door opened a crack, and the kitbag was whisked inside.

Mrs. Parnell heaved herself to her feet. "It is time for us to mobilize our forces," she said.

"If you're thinking what I think you're thinking, the answer is no," I said. "Absolutely not."

• • •

I figured Mombourquette was in his office. I left a message in his voice mail. "Come on, Leonard. This is serious business. What's the second thing? Squeak up."

Of course, I knew in the pit of my stomach what the second thing was. I also knew that most likely the police would be taking a hard look at known and suspected pedophiles in the area.

I heard the bathroom door open. I hung up and turned. Alvin looked a whole lot better. For one thing he'd changed into his clean black jeans, fresh black T-shirt and black leather jacket. He was wearing all his earrings. He moved to the leather sofa and patted Mrs. Parnell's little calico cat.

I saw no sign of hysteria. So far so good.

"Good to see you looking like your old self, Alvin," I said.

I glanced over at Mrs. Parnell. She managed to look inscrutable behind a wall of Benson and Hedges exhaust.

"I'm okay now." Behind the cat's-eye glasses, his eyes were clear and focused.

Mrs. Parnell lifted one eyebrow. Lester and Pierre shrieked.

"Are you sure?" It was tricky dealing with this new fragile Alvin. Threats, insults, all the conversational conventions that had defined our relationship when Alvin was the world's worst office assistant were now inappropriate. I had no idea how to communicate.

He said. "I must have been overtired."

Mrs. Parnell patted his hand. I couldn't get used to her new role as a handpatter either. It was a world gone mad.

"But you're feeling better now?"

"I'm fine. And I want to thank both of you for everything."

My jaw almost hit the ground.

Mrs. Parnell said, "We'd do anything for you."

There were distinct limits to what I would do for Alvin, but it didn't seem like the moment to mention that.

"I really appreciate it. But you know I'd better get going now."

"Right," I said.

"I've got to get home. They need me. Thanks for packing up my things, Camilla. That makes a difference."

"You won't be able to get a flight. Everything's booked."

Alvin narrowed his slanty eyes at me.

"Trust me," I said.

"Is this another one of your tricks, Camilla?"

"What do you mean, another one of my tricks? Look, my travel agent struck out. And before you continue on, let me add that Mrs. Parnell has been on the web scouring every travel service possible, and she had no luck either. Apparently everyone who has any tie with Cape Breton has chosen to descend on the island this summer. The week around Canada Day is particularly popular for some reason."

"What about stand-by?"

Mrs. Parnell glanced at me and shook her head warningly. I took a deep breath.

"I have it on good authority the majority of flights are actually overbooked, and even ticketholders are likely to be bumped. Stand-bys are up the creek. If you want to wait until next week, that might be different."

Alvin stood up. "Next week is too late. I'll take a bus or something." He looked a bit wobbly as he headed back to the bathroom.

I said. "Looks like Alvin's okay."

"Don't be fooled, Ms. MacPhee. This bounceback of young Ferguson's will turn out to be purely temporary."

"He looks fine to me. It must have been the shock of Jimmy's disappearance."

She jammed another B & H into her holder. "It won't take much to push him into the abyss again."

"But he's back to normal."

"If, as you suggest, the news from home is bad, I fear for him."

"Look, I'll go down with him on the bus if we have to. I'll see he gets some professional help."

Mrs. Parnell clutched my arm in her vicelike grip. "You must listen to me, Ms. MacPhee. I know boys. Whatever is behind this will turn out to be something almost too dreadful to imagine."

So what can you say to something like that? "Mrs. P., I think he's come to grips with whatever it is, no matter how dreadful, and he's doing the right thing by going home."

"You don't send them back to the trenches when they're in this state. That's when you lose them forever."

She sure knew how to raise the stakes.

"Come on," I said, "think about all the trauma Alvin's had since he's worked for Justice from Victims. He dealt with those situations very well."

"Ms. MacPhee, this is different."

"So what are you saying? He won't be safe at home?"

"We must not throw young Ferguson to the wolves."

"I don't think you need to worry. I'll get him there. I've already left a message for clients that Justice for Victims will be closed for the next two weeks. I'll drive him if I have to."

"Ms. MacPhee. I hear the call to duty. My decision's made. It will be much better if I go along too."

Seven

Oh, Alvin," I said, when he had emerged from the bathroom. "I almost forgot to mention I picked up your mail. You have a postcard from Jimmy, and maybe it has..."

I wasn't counting on his eyes losing focus and the strange humming moan he emitted.

"Oh shit," I said.

That was lost on Alvin. He collapsed onto the carpet. I leapt to keep his temple from striking the metal and glass coffee table.

"I was afraid this would happen," Mrs. P. said.

"It's not necessary to say I told you so. I realize I should have waited," I said when we had dragged and lifted Alvin back to his place on the leather sofa.

By this time, Mrs. Parnell was perched on the edge of the leather chair, breathing deeply on a fresh Benson and Hedges. "I was not planning to say I told you so. Neither of us knows Alvin's private demons, so we have no idea how to avoid arousing them."

"We know one thing: they involve Jimmy."

• • •

"Don't ask," I said to P. J. when he called. "We have no option but to get Alvin home on the double."

"But that's a crazy idea. This is Monday. The Bluesfest starts this Friday. Even if you left now, how could you drive to Sydney and back by then? You're going to miss Blue Rodeo. And..." Rustling noises followed. "And a bunch of other really really good stuff. Really good. You'll never get here in time."

"Unlike you, I already know who's playing. But I have a situation to take care of, and I'm going to take care of it."

P. J. said, "I thought you were excited about Bluesfest."

"Let me remind you we are having a crisis."

"Yeah, but you want to go to Bluesfest, right?"

"I can't think about it at this minute."

"Yeah, but listen, Tiger..."

"What is the matter with you? We have a terrible situation here with Alvin's brother missing."

"What do you mean, Alvin's brother's missing? You never mentioned that."

"I'm sure I did. He may even be dead."

"You said you had to help Alvin get home. You didn't mention his brother was missing. What kind of thing is that to hold back?"

"Cool your jets. You're not reporting a crime now. Alvin's brother has disappeared."

"That's bad."

"Yes, it is. The police in Cape Breton have done all they can to search for Jimmy."

"Jimmy. That's the brother?"

"Right."

"How old is he?"

"He's twenty-one."

"Get real. It happens all the time. The family goes off the deep end, then the guy turns up with a five-alarm hangover and lipstick on his underwear and can't figure out what all the fuss is about."

"I wish that were the case here, P. J., but it's not. Jimmy's got some developmental problems."

"Oh. That's different."

"I was hoping you'd done a piece on missing kids, and you might be able to tell me what to worry about or how to help the family."

"Maybe he was abducted. Kids like that are vulnerable."

"Exactly. So you can see why I'm not thinking about music right now."

"But we do have Clubhouse passes."

"I don't want to hear it. I have to deal with this. Mrs. Parnell thinks Alvin might be shell-shocked. He keeps going into these trance states."

"Two hundred and fifty dollars each."

"It's not like you paid for those passes." I ignored the choking sound. "You won them, remember? And they're in my name."

"Holy crap," he said.

"So I'll let you know as soon as we get this thing under control. If all goes well, we can get back for Saturday or Sunday."

"I don't know why you're so grouchy."

"Who's grouchy? Do you know anything about post-traumatic stress disorder?"

"What I read in the paper."

"Don't push me, P. J. What about missing kids? Do the cops do a good job in that area?"

"Depends on what cops, I guess. The Mounties have a special section to deal with them. You want me to find out who to talk to?"

"Sure. Got any contacts in the media in Sydney?"

"No, but I can ask around. Lots of people from the East

coast in this business. Plus I can chase down the missing kid angle for you."

"Great. But what I really need is for you to feed Mrs. Parnell's birds and cat. And also to make sure they're not left alone together. So the cat has to stay at my place."

"Feed the cat? And *birds*? Can't the building super do it?"

"Nope. He's on vacation. The replacement's run off his feet."

"I am too. Remember Nicholas Southern and the …"

"Right. So I really appreciate you doing this for me. I'll drop off the keys to Mrs. Parnell's place and mine on our way out of town. You've got my cellphone number, but I'm sure we'll be out of contact for much of the trip. Don't worry about calling me, I'll call you."

"Wait."

"Thanks, P. J. You're a bud."

• • •

"For the last time," I said, "no way."

"It is simply not your decision, Ms. MacPhee."

"The hell it isn't."

"If you don't like it, stay here and attend to your business. I've got my marching orders."

"Look, Mrs. P., it is an eighteen to twenty hour drive to Sydney. We are not going to drive in your twenty-five year old car, and that's that."

"Nonsense. My garageman tells me he's got the old girl purring like a kitten today."

"Yeah right. So maybe he'll volunteer to drive it then."

"Have faith, Ms. MacPhee."

"Really? And what happens if Alvin has an episode in the middle of nowhere, and the car breaks down?"

"We will find a way."

I'd already exhausted my opinions on the notion of Mrs. Parnell pelting across country in the ancient LTD with Alvin as a ticking time bomb in the passenger seat and me snarling in the back seat. It reinforced what I already knew. The woman could be unbelievably stubborn.

"I have a better idea," I said.

"What is it?"

I took a deep breath. "The Buick."

"You'll get no argument from me," she said. "I'm packed, and you've got young Ferguson's kit-bag ready."

At least she could have put up the semblance of a fight.

"Fine," I said. "Can you arrange hotel reservations? I have a few urgent things to take care of." That was code for doing a bit of laundry, washing my hair, picking up some cash, figuring out which files couldn't wait until I got back and throwing my toothbrush into a satchel.

"I'm on the job," she said.

"The sooner we leave, the sooner we get back. Let's get cracking."

"Now?"

"Two hours to get ready and drop the keys to P. J. and to let the traffic on the Queensway clear up."

"Excellent."

"And, one more thing."

"Name it, Ms. MacPhee."

"I am absolutely the only driver."

"Victory will be ours," she said, "however long and hard the road may be."

Eight

The trip to Sydney had shades of the lost weekend about it, without the light-hearted fun.

I felt a twinge about commandeering the Buick, but I believed Stan would understand it was almost a matter of life and death. If he didn't, Edwina would make it clear to him. The plan was to drive straight down to Sydney, deposit Alvin, assure his well-being, get him an appointment with an appropriate therapist and then turbo straight back home to normal life. I would be the only person to touch the steering wheel, so what could go wrong?

We clipped along the 417 toward Montreal, making excellent time, slowing briefly to join the Friday night crawl across the top of the city on Boulevard Metropolitain. From the soft snores coming from the passenger seat, I figured Mrs. P. was dozing. Alvin lay limply in the back seat. I hoped he was asleep, for his own sake. As for me, I tried not to think what could have happened to a boy like Jimmy, last seen standing by the harbour. Except for stops every two hours for coffee and bathroom breaks, the Buick shot through the hot summer night. It gave new meaning to the word boring. You don't hear a slogan that says "See Canada by Dark", and for good reason. I kept busy hoping we weren't heading straight towards a funeral.

At around four in the morning, I pulled into an all-night gas station outside Edmunston, New Brunswick, and prepared to limp stiffly to the ladies room. Mrs. Parnell headed in first. Rank has its privileges. Alvin teetered to the men's. I offered to pick up the refreshments.

When I got back to the car with a Coke for Alvin and coffee for Mrs. Parnell and me, I found she had managed to get herself into the driver's seat. She proved impossible to dislodge, even when I put down the coffee and gave it a real good try.

Sometimes we have to yield to a higher power.

"Let's see what this baby will do," Mrs. Parnell said.

Alvin perked up in the back seat.

"Pedal to the metal, Violet," he said.

Normally, I would have bitten his head off, but I was glad to see him looking like himself. I hung on.

As it turned out, the Buick could get up to one-fifty without so much as a shimmy. I told myself Stan had it coming after all the times he'd put fake dog poop in my briefcase before important court appearances. On the other hand, I didn't feel entirely ready to die. It took a certain threat level in my voice to get slowed down to well over the limit.

"And don't encourage her," I said to Alvin. "We need to be alive to help your family."

"Ms. MacPhee, cut the boy some slack."

"Slow down, or the only cutting will be with the jaws of life."

"Lovely machine, this. Reminds me of the good old days."

"Watch the road, Mrs. P."

"Personally, I would prefer something with a bit more horsepower."

Mrs. Parnell had the cruise control set at one-forty, and I had a hard time keeping my eyes off the speedometer. Alvin was leaning forward, asking excited questions about World War II.

"Mrs. P., I know we agreed to drive right through, but it's better if we take shifts."

"That's what we're doing. You had your shift and now it's mine."

"Yes, well."

"Close your eyes, Ms. MacPhee."

"Why don't you pull off at the next rest stop, and I'll get in the back. You two can enjoy war talk, and I'll get some sleep, then take over driving again."

"Superb idea, Ms. MacPhee. Why wait? I'll pull off right here."

Highway act. Schmighway act. Mrs. Parnell is above all that mundane stuff. I had to admit the Buick had great braking capacity. I settled in the back seat and positioned myself to keep an eye on them.

"Dear boy," Mrs. Parnell said, "we can relax now."

They could chatter on about Dunkirk and Dieppe. I was in charge of worrying about what we'd find when we got to Sydney. And what the hell we were getting Alvin into.

• • •

I opened my eyes to a thunderous roll.

"Keep your heads covered." I dived for the floor of the Buick.

Alvin said, "It's just music, Camilla. Shostakovich is the dude to set the mood."

I stared out the window, stunned by the sight of a Nova Scotia road sign. "What happened to New Brunswick?"

"You slept through it. And you snored," Alvin said. "I'd get something done about that if I were you."

"I slept through an entire province?"

"One and a half. New Brunswick and now a chunk of Nova Scotia," Mrs. Parnell said. "You must have been exhausted."

"I wonder why that would be. But I'm awake now. So I guess it's time to stop and switch drivers."

"No point, Ms. MacPhee. We've broken the back of the journey. We're almost to Cape Breton. One final push over the hills."

"Wait a minute," I said. "Did you two put something in my coffee?"

"You wound me, Ms. MacPhee."

"Every minute counts," Alvin said. "Look Violet, the Canso Causeway."

"Be sensible. You shouldn't drive all those hours straight."

"*Au contraire*, it's a wonderful idea. Reminds me of the war."

I knew what she meant.

• • •

We arrived at the Ferguson home less than five minutes after the Buick shot past the Sydney city limits sign. Mrs. P. and Alvin were elated. I was thirsty after too many bags of pretzels and irritable from seeing my life flash by on the 105 through Cape Breton. The black clouds gathering overhead fit my mood.

Alvin's family knew we were coming thanks to the miracle of my cellphone. As we pulled up to the Ferguson home, several people exploded out of the front door. For added drama, the neighbours appeared on their front porches and applauded. I spotted Donald Donnie MacDonald and Loretta waving. I gripped Alvin's elbow and propelled him forward. I felt him wobbling. "Pull yourself together, Alvin."

Alvin kept his mouth shut, which I thought might be a

good thing. On the other hand, Alvin's mouth had been shut for the entire last leg of the trip, and that was anything but normal. I wondered whether he was slipping. I didn't want to try to explain that to his mother.

The four people who had stampeded from the house stopped and stood on the lawn, composed like a formal portrait. Every one of them was handsome enough to make you blink. A man and two youngish women, all of them obviously carrying the genes of a tall silver-haired woman. I pegged her on the high side of sixty with the kind of features and carriage that could make Lauren Bacall chew her nails in envy. The younger women flanked her. Their hands hovered at her elbows.

A least a half-dozen small children darted in and out. There were those genes again. Slightly slanted sooty-blue eyes, dark eyelashes, crisp chins and cheekbones you could cut bread with, plus the unfair advantage of glowing ivory skin against nearly black hair.

I tried to figure who was who. Tracy was easy. I recognized her voice. The woman closer to my age must have been Frances Ann. Frances Ann had a bunch of kids and was some kind of health administrator.

The only man in the group stepped forward and spoke. "Do you always have to think of yourself, Allie?"

Mary Frances said, "Knock it off, Vince."

I looked around. No one else seemed to find this in the least bit unusual. Alvin's earrings jingled. "I'm so sorry," he said.

Vince said, "We're all sorry. So don't start with the bullshit."

I stepped forward in case Alvin landed in a heap on the grass, but he braced himself. "Camilla, meet my brother, Vince."

The deep blue eyes narrowed.

Ever since Alvin got pneumonia in my service, my name has

been mud with the Ferguson clan. It wasn't enough they had shot my phone bill into the next galaxy for the last twenty-six months, but they got to pretend I was the bad guy too.

I gave Vince my best bonecrushing shake before he could whip his hand safely behind his back. "Glad to meet you."

Vince kept his mouth shut.

"Ma," Alvin bleated.

Mrs. Ferguson opened her arms and Alvin fell into them. The rest of the gang surrounded them protectively. Except for Vince.

Alvin was hugged and kissed and patted. Three beautiful women cried. Alvin blew his nose.

"You have to meet Violet," he said.

I guess everyone had heard good things about Mrs. Parnell. They did everything but bear her on their shoulders into the house. When the front door slammed behind them, I found myself standing alone on the lawn as the clouds burst. Donald Donnie and Loretta lit cigarettes and watched with interest. I nodded grimly when they gave me the thumbs up.

Tracy must have taken pity on me. She stuck her head out the door and said, "Ms. MacPhee? Would you like to come in and have a cup of tea with us?"

•   •   •

The Ferguson home was large, airy and smelled like fresh bread and cinnamon. The three-story house, probably built before the nineteen twenties, sat on a tree-lined street with a wide sidewalk on one side and a park on the other. It featured a bit of gingerbread trim, a neat lawn, a few dozen Siberian irises, plus a porch swing.

The entrance way was soothing faded blue, last painted who

knew when. A row of hooks held the rain gear neatly in the hallway, and the well-placed water-colours on the wall spoke of organization. On the telephone table sat three Daily Missals in a stack. I saw nothing to indicate that Alvin's unique temperament had been nurtured within these walls.

We were herded into the living room, where Alvin remained the centre of attention. "Come on in, Allie."

"Sit here, Allie."

"You want something to eat, Allie?"

"Can I try on your earring, Uncle Allie?"

So much for Mrs. P.'s notion that the family was the source of his problems.

It took less than a minute for a giant earthenware pot of tea and a plate of shortbread cookies to appear. Alvin got freshly sliced homemade white bread and butter. Of course, the anxiety about Jimmy was reflected in the frenetic movements, the race to grab the telephone at every ring, the outbursts of tears, and the hushed conversations with other Fergusons who were out combing the hills for Jimmy. I couldn't miss the muted hostility toward me, but I felt this would be a pleasant place, as a rule.

I guess if you have seven kids and twice as many grandchildren, you'd need two sofas and four large comfortable arm chairs. Books and magazines occupied most surfaces. I spotted an entire collection of P. G. Wodehouse in tattered orange covers and shelves of green-backed Penguins. Plus hardcover novels by Alistair MacLeod, Linden MacIntyre, Lynn Coady and Ann-Marie MacDonald. Giller stickers glistened on book jackets.

The graduation pictures took pride of place over the sofa. High school, university, grad school too, judging by the variety of gowns. Vince made it three times, including one that must have been a Ph.D.

Alvin didn't eat his fresh bread.

Small children raced up and down the stairs and past the adults calling "Uncle Allie watch me! No, watch me."

They all looked so much alike, I doubted even their parents could tell them apart. The dog, Gussie, chased after them, barking. Every now and then someone shouted at Brianna, Ashley, Dylan, Cayla or Brittany, "Cut that out right now. Yes, you." I resolved not to remember the children or their names.

Tracy spoke non-stop to Alvin, her small hands moving in a blur. Like his mother, Alvin stared without speaking out the window at the dark, wet street as if expecting Jimmy to appear from behind a shrub.

Vince didn't say a word. No one else made eye contact with me. That was fine.

Someone pressed a plate of cinnamon buns towards Alvin. He didn't seem to notice them. I ate a couple to be polite then stepped across the room to check out the cluster of First Communion pictures artfully arranged on the top of the upright piano.

I spotted Alvin before his ponytail and earring phase, a scrawny child with a face full of apprehension, wearing dress pants that stopped above his ankles. Frances Ann and Tracy looked like miniature versions of themselves in fluffy white veils, gleaming ankle-length dresses and tiny gloves. The others were recognizable too. Vince's broad grin showed off his missing front teeth.

Jimmy's picture sat in front of the others, a palm frond attached to its frame. A smiling priest stood with his hand on the boy's shoulder. Every few minutes, someone's eyes would light on that photo, then look away. Jimmy's absence hung like a fog, draping everything in grey.

· · ·

All I needed was a hotel with a nice shower and a meal without company. I managed to catch Mrs. Parnell's eye and hiss in her ear. "Where are we staying? I need to shower and change."

"Encountered some obstacles, Ms. MacPhee."

"What do you mean?"

"A bit of a stumbling block in securing hotel accommodation."

"What?"

"Didn't want to dwell on it before we left, in case it slowed down our departure."

"But you said you would make arrangements. We can't sleep in the Buick again."

"Best of intentions."

"How hard can it be?"

No one paid any attention to me as I stepped into the hall. The Ferguson telephone was kept free for calls about Jimmy, so I used my cellphone and blew an hour working my way through the phone book. To hear the responses, they were stacking the tourists three deep in the hallways of every hotel, tourist home and B & B on the island.

Sometime during my search, Gussie, a large, shaggy dog of uncertain breed, had discovered me and laid his or her chin on my knee. That would have been heartwarming, except someone must have been feeding him or her beans.

Mrs. Parnell slipped up behind me. She's the only person in the world who can be stealthy using two canes.

"It looks like we're stuck with the Fergusons for a while," I whispered.

"Step outside, Ms. MacPhee."

I followed her out to the porch. Mrs. Parnell flashed her lighter and fired up a Benson and Hedges.

"Non-smoking household," she said, her tone tinged with disapproval.

"I can think of worse things. Anyway, I'm glad we got him here."

"If you say so."

"He's fine. Not curled in a ball and not hallucinating. Although I noticed a strange undercurrent with the brother."

"Most disturbing."

"The rest of them are obviously fond of him. They're going to look after him."

"Don't count on it, Ms. MacPhee."

"They seem like an exceptional family, even if they don't pay for their own phone calls. Pretty cheap, considering they must have at least fourteen university degrees among them."

"That's not the point. Young Ferguson's family is going through the same trauma he is. They're not in any position to help him. Do you remember what I said about the source of his trouble?"

"I can't believe it's the family."

"Regardless, Ms. MacPhee, we are the only comrades he can count on. United we stand. Divided we fall."

I didn't like the way this was going. My plan was to head back to Ottawa as soon as possible, and Mrs. Parnell was well aware of it.

I thought about Vince and his reaction to Alvin. Maybe Mrs. Parnell was right. Something was going on that we didn't know about. I couldn't abandon him.

"Okay, fine. Time for a plan."

"I already have one," Mrs. Parnell said.

"Why am I not surprised?"

"Mock not, Ms. MacPhee."

"I wouldn't think of it. I'll work on Jimmy's disappearance.

And I'll do my best to figure out how to help Alvin. The family won't be the ideal place for unbiased information. But I'll nose around. What's your plan?"

"We're of the same mind, then. I'll get to know the neighbours," she said, blowing a few fine smoke rings in their direction. "They look like they're ready to talk."

I glanced next door. "They're ready to talk all right. That's Donald Donnie MacDonald and Loretta. I'd better head over and say hello, if I know what's good for me."

∙ ∙ ∙

Tracy picked that moment to beckon me into the kitchen. Mrs. Parnell stayed outside to finish her cigarette.

"Poor Allie," Tracy said.

Vince leaned back against the fifties-style cream-painted kitchen cupboards and folded his arms across his chest.

"Yes. It's good that's he's back here where you can all support each other," I said to Vince.

Vince stared at his feet. Tracy bit her lip.

"It's the worst thing that could have happened," Vince said.

"I know it's awful, and Alvin's in rough shape, but he can help in the search. He's very talented that way," I said. "And we can help too."

"Having Allie back is a disaster," Vince said. "The only thing you could do to help is to keep him out of the way so the rest of us can get something done."

"What?" I'm lucky I didn't bruise my jaw when it dropped.

Vince curled his lip.

Tracy said, "Well, it wasn't a good idea to bring Allie home. He's never been too, what would you say, Vince, sensible?"

"Stable," Vince said. "Or intelligent."

Tracy's hands kept moving. From her hair to her T-shirt to the chair and back to her hair. Sometimes they hovered like moths. "He's especially unstable when it comes to Jimmy. He'll flip out. He'll get Ma in a state. Since you insisted on bringing him back without consulting us, now we have to deal with it."

When I got my breath back I said, "What do you mean since I insisted on bringing him back?"

Vince cut me off. "You called from Ottawa to say you were bringing him home, you hung up, you called again from ten miles out of town and then you showed up with him. What do you call that if not bringing him back?"

"But he wanted to come home. Have you ever tried to stop Alvin from doing something he wanted to do?"

"Even so," Tracy said, adjusting her flower earrings. "It's the worst thing in the world for him."

"It's an unmitigated disaster," Vince said. "He'll go right over the edge when we need to keep our minds on Jimmy."

"Hang on a minute. Let's see if I understand. You called me and insisted that I find Alvin and tell him what had happened. I did that, and now it's a disaster,." I said.

"Well, we had to let him know. But he always flips out if it's something with Jimmy, and that's a problem for everyone," Tracy said.

"Alvin has always been level-headed in his own peculiar way, right up until he heard Jimmy was missing. Mrs. Parnell and I think he's been traumatized in some way. Sorry it's not convenient for you to hear this. But you have not one but two younger brothers, and since you know Alvin goes over the edge, I have to ask if you ever got psychological help for him."

"Bullshit," Vince said. "He can get his act together like anybody else. We're run off our feet looking for Jimmy, and we don't need to be babysitting him."

Whatever that turkey did his doctorate in, I figured it wasn't psychology.

Mrs. Parnell loomed into the doorway and cleared her throat. She gave me a look that said I told you so. By now, I'd figured she was right on the money. This whacko family had to be the source of Alvin's problems.

• • •

Even though they couldn't stand me, I could not be allowed to go to a hotel. Or a B & B. Or a guesthouse. Even if space had been available. No sir. You come to Sydney with a Ferguson, no matter how inconsiderate your visit, no matter how inappropriate your behaviour, no matter how unwelcome your presence, you will be staying in the Ferguson home. Black fog of resentment or not. They made that clear.

I blanched as this sank in. What if I ended up with Frances Ann and all those kids? Or one of the others who kept coming and going but whose names I couldn't even remember. Tracy had a small apartment somewhere on George Street. But Tracy's place was already full of volunteer searchers.

"Of course, you have to stay here with Ma and Alvin."

I said, "You have enough on your plate with everything that's going on."

"Don't be silly," Frances Ann said. "Ma is glad to have you. Especially with Allie here."

Considering the number of times I'd refused collect calls from her in the course of the past two years, I doubted Ma Ferguson was at all glad. But apparently, the entire Ferguson family had the same ability to withstand facts as Alvin did.

Vince laid down the law. "And it will be good for Allie."

I hadn't thought that things being good for Alvin would even interest Vince. "I wouldn't be so sure. We're not always on the same wavelength. But it would be good for him to have Mrs. Parnell here. She has a way with him."

Mrs. Parnell chose that moment to teeter into the kitchen. She flashed me a poisonous look. Perhaps because she was passing right under a prominent No Smoking sign. Alvin loped behind her.

"Thank you very much, young man," she said to Vince in tones reminiscent of McArthur in his finest hour. "But I wouldn't think of being a burden."

"You would not be a burden," Vince said.

"No, you wouldn't," said Tracy. "We'd love to have you here."

"We won't hear of you going elsewhere," Frances Ann said.

I thought smoke would pour out Mrs. Parnell's ears, but Alvin spoke up. "Violet can't handle the stairs here. She'd be better off next door with Loretta and Donald Donnie. You'll like them, Violet. The three of you can sit up all night and smoke like forest fires."

"Really?" said Mrs. Parnell. "That sounds most satisfactory."

"Loretta and Donald Donnie? Ma won't like that." Tracy said.

"Have you lost your mind, Allie?" Frances Ann slapped a dish towel on the counter.

"I told you so," Vince said.

I was proud of Alvin. He paid no attention. "And they have a spare bed on the main floor, so you won't have stairs, Violet."

Mrs. Parnell smiled fondly at Alvin.

"Plus, they keep the liquor cabinet full," Alvin said.

"You're always so thoughtful, dear boy."

"Let's go, Violet. I'll introduce you."

"Wait a minute. They're *my* relatives." I wanted to scream "Don't leave me here with these people." But the door had already slammed behind them as they thumped down the front steps. At the bottom, Alvin paused briefly to flick Mrs. P.'s lighter for her.

I watched them head next door, Mrs. Parnell lurching with her two canes and Alvin loping his lope. Only the set of Alvin's shoulders gave a clue that things were not as they should be.

"See what I mean?" Vince said to Frances Ann.

"Typical," she said.

I'd had enough. "Well, that's great. I'm glad Mrs. Parnell will be among like-minded people. I'll head over too."

"No." Mrs. Ferguson had a tightness around the mouth which I assumed resulted from the Donald Donnie and Loretta switcheroo. "You will stay here. No one can say Fergusons don't do the right thing."

I tried one last tactic. "Do you have enough room?"

"Seven kids grew up here. Only Vince and me now. And Jimmy, of course. You can take your choice of places to sleep."

I know when I'm beaten.

Tracy chirped. "Take my old room. It has the best bed."

I caved. I needed a bath and a snooze so badly at that point, I would have stepped cheerfully into the grizzly section of the zoo, which was a pretty good comparison. But I couldn't see myself relaxing until I had a few answers. Creature comforts would have to wait. I knew where the answers would be.

Nine

Somehow after the tensions at the Château Ferguson, a wall of second-hand smoke would be a small price to pay to relax.

Loretta and Donald Donnie didn't have a swarm of family photos on every wall. But then they'd never had children, or even pets, and they were no beauties themselves. They were somewhere in the gray zone between seventy-five and eighty. Loretta had a few too many teeth and red hair that would be startling on a twenty-year old. It had a surprising tendency to rise straight up. Donald Donnie didn't have any hair but kept his scalp nicely polished. They seemed to favour *TV Guide* over the current Giller winners and things that came out of packages instead of out of ovens. They sure liked company. Gussie followed me over, wagged his or her tail, and managed to get stuck in the door.

"Let Gussie in, though I have to tell you, that dog farts something awful," Loretta said, slipping Gussie a few pretzels.

"We've been having the most interesting conversations," Mrs. Parnell said, lighting up.

"I bet," I said.

"Took her long enough to get over here, didn't it, Dad?" Loretta said, giving me an arched red eyebrow.

"Indeed it did."

"I would have preferred to be here earlier, trust me. What have you done with Alvin?"

"He's tucked in upstairs, resting quietly," Mrs. Parnell said. "We'll let him be."

"I suppose they had you in a headlock. Filling you full of their opinions about poor Allie. If you'd any brains, you'd of jumped out of the window and run for it."

"She's here now, Mum. So, girl. Feel like a slug of something before dinner?" Donald Donnie said.

"I'm okay, thanks. I need to be able to think straight."

"All right, if you think that will help." Loretta found this almost as hilarious as Donald Donnie did. Even Mrs. Parnell flashed an evil grin.

"You doing all right next door?" Loretta deposited a large blue plastic bowl of salt and vinegar potato chips within easy reach.

"They're very kind," I said, lying through my teeth. It didn't seem right to trash the Fergusons when they were giving me a room, even though it came with a high psychological price.

"I never knew them to be kind, did you, Dad?"

"Indeed, I never did, Mum. Are you sure about that?"

"Smart as whips, the lot of them. But kind? That's a new one."

That's where you get when you try a harmless social lie. Caught up in a web of deceit.

"How are they being kind? Exactly?" Loretta said.

"You know, offering food and everything." I now needed to change the subject and fast.

Donald Donnie was shaking his head. "Kind. Isn't that amazing. Must be the shock of Jimmy being missing."

"You know, I think it is." I helped myself to a hefty mouthful of chips so I wouldn't have to invent details of the Fergusons' alleged kindness.

"Loretta and Donald Donnie have lived here for thirty-five years. Did you know that, Camilla?"

I pointed at my mouth and raised my eyebrows to indicate interest. I wished I was home in Ottawa, where I could be rude to strangers without the worry that they could retaliate and squeal to my father.

"They watched all those children grow up." Mrs. Parnell looked from one to the other and raised her glass. Donald Donnie was splashing Harvey's Bristol Cream into it.

"Yes, we did," Loretta said. "Didn't we, Dad?"

"Indeed, Mum."

I had managed to swallow by this time. "You know, Alvin is distraught over Jimmy. We are really worried about him."

"You should be. He's the best of the whole lot. Isn't he, Dad?"

"You know he is."

This was good news. Here we had a double-barrelled source of information that wasn't too crazy about the Fergusons and had a soft spot for Alvin. And they were related to me, however distantly, so they might cut me some slack.

"You know I think I will have a splash of something after all," I said. "Rum and coke if you have it."

Donald Donnie moved with lightning speed to fill that order. "You'll not have had one of those next door. Dry as a Sunday sermon."

"Now, Dad, remember the time of it she had with the husband."

"Twenty years he's been gone, Mum. Surely to God she could have a drink in the house."

"Alvin is really cut up about this. We can't leave him without knowing what's wrong. I bet the two of you could give me some helpful insights," I said firmly.

Mrs. Parnell interjected. "Loretta and Donald Donnie tell me that Alvin was deeply affected by Jimmy's accident, as we suspected."

"Never had an easy life, that boy. Not since that day," Loretta said, squinting as she lit a cigarette. "Has he, Dad?"

"Indeed he hasn't."

"We haven't felt comfortable asking him about what happened, because he gets emotional," I said.

"Well, he would, wouldn't he?"

"I didn't want to ask Mrs. Ferguson, either because she's quite distraught. Perhaps I should speak to Vince when he's got a minute."

"You could, I suppose, dear. But Vince can be a bit of a, what would you say, Dad, about Vince?"

"Indeed, I'd say a gold-plated pain in the arse, Mum. At his best."

"I'll drink to that." I gasped for air at the first sip. If he'd put any coke in that rum, I couldn't taste it.

"Dad likes to say what's on his mind, don't you, Dad?"

"They remember the accident quite clearly," Mrs. Parnell said meaningfully. "I think Loretta and Donald Donnie should tell you all about it. You'll find it most interesting."

"I'll bet," I said, when I'd caught my breath after the solid kick of the rum.

"It was terrible," Loretta said. "More than terrible."

"Must be what, fifteen years?"

"Sixteen. And I remember it like it was yesterday. Well, poor little Allie, he was hysterical, wasn't he, Dad? He came running up the hill screaming like a banshee and bawling his eyes out. He banged on the door for Vincent to come and help. But, of course, Vincent wasn't home, was he?"

"And neither was the mother. Out shopping. Leaving those kids alone."

"You mean, no one was looking after them?"

"Well, they'd never admit it, that bunch with their noses in the air. But Vincent wasn't where he was supposed to be, was he, Mum?"

"No, he was not. I don't give a Jesus what they say. And that Frances Ann was late getting home herself. The three little kids were on their own. But that didn't stop them from blaming Allie. He couldn't have been more than seven years old. It wasn't his fault. Boys will be boys, and anyone who has a brain in their head knows they need an adult."

"So Alvin and Jimmy were alone?"

"And Tracy. She was playing in her room all along."

"And the boys went to the park."

"To feed the ducks."

"And something happened? Do you know what?"

"We'll never know, will we, Mum?"

"You mean Alvin didn't say how the accident happened?"

"The poor little thing was screaming 'Help my brother, he's hurt, he's hurt.' Dad and I came out to see what was going on, then he led us to where Jimmy was with his darling little face right in that dirty water, and Dad pulled him right out and gave him mouth to mouth, and I took off like a shot back here and called for the ambulance. It saved his life, I guess, but he'd been in the water a bit too long, and we weren't fast enough to save him from brain damage."

"No, we were not, Mum. Don't you start crying over that, either. We did what we could."

"Your prompt action saved the day," Mrs. Parnell said. "Wouldn't you agree, Ms. MacPhee."

"Thank God you were here, or he would have died."

"Indeed, surrounded by ducks. Imagine that."

"And what did Alvin say happened?"

"He didn't, did he, Mum?"

"No, he did not. He never said a blessed word."

Mrs. Parnell gave me an I-told-you-so look.

"He didn't talk about it?"

"Not a peep."

"But people must have asked. His family must have wanted to know."

"Oh, they wanted to know all right," Donald Donnie said.

"Indeed. They blamed him. They said he shouldn't have taken Jimmy to the pond. They even punished him, didn't they, Dad."

"But he never said what happened?"

"He couldn't remember. Poor little thing was not himself. Not that anybody noticed because they were all for Jimmy. It was a long time before Jimmy got out of the hospital, and they all saying novenas and Stations of the Cross and lighting candles and all that, but the fact is they had this other child, and anyone could see he was hurting, couldn't they, Dad?"

"Indeed they could."

"Dad told *her* that too. Right to her face."

"Indeed I did. I told her not to blame that boy, because those three kids were home without proper supervision."

"I imagine she didn't take it all that well."

"You're right, girl. Things were never the same between our two houses after that. But it was the truth, and it had to be said. Of course, she couldn't say anything about that to anyone. After all, Dad saved Jimmy's life. But she kept Allie from seeing us, and that was punishment for us. And he used to be here all the time before that. It punished him too. I think he needed to talk, don't you, Dad?"

"Indeed, I do."

"We never had kids, and we were crazy for those little boys."

"Young Ferguson seems on good terms with you," Mrs. Parnell said.

"He is that. A regular here when he's in town, which isn't often enough. Once he was a teenager, he started to visit on his own. Of course, he'd come to the back door."

"Yes, he did. And we were right glad of it. But he never talked about the accident. Didn't want us to talk about it either, did he, Mum?"

"He did not. And we respected that."

Mrs. Parnell blew smoke rings and nodded. I took a spine-stiffening sip of my drink. I was thinking about what a hellish time Alvin had growing up.

Somehow in the course of the next hour, the combination of the rum and coke, the twenty-hour drive, the lack of regular sleep and the worry about Jimmy and Alvin took its toll.

Alvin was conked out upstairs. Mrs. Parnell and Donald Donnie had switched to recounting the glory days of the Canadian army's march through Italy. For some reason, Loretta was encouraging them.

Gussie and I stumbled back to the Fergusons.

•   •   •

Through the back door, I spotted Vince and Tracy busy in the kitchen doing something organizational. I headed around to the front. Frances Ann, more children than I remembered, and some people who had to be Fergusons I hadn't met yet spilled out onto the front porch. Emotions were running high. I didn't feel like running that particular gauntlet for the dubious pleasure of crashing in Tracy's former bed before it was dark.

"Walk time, Gussie," I said.

It was early enough to find plenty of people in the park, kids playing, old people sitting on benches, people strolling through swinging shopping bags. Ducks and feathers everywhere. I couldn't imagine how anything bad could happen to Jimmy there. For one thing, the brackish water looked far too shallow. For another, the kids would never have been out of sight of the large old houses that bordered all sides of the park. I wondered if we'd ever get to the bottom of that old tragedy.

It had been quite a while since I'd been in Sydney, but I remembered the way to the waterfront. Ten minutes later, Gussie and I had crossed the Esplanade, passed behind the fire station and were standing on the end of the boardwalk behind the small playground. My hair was whipped by the wind. I wasn't sure if dogs were allowed, but I was prepared to argue the point with anyone who objected.

Short, sharp waves lashed the stone breakwater that formed the underpinnings of the boardwalk. Gussie sniffed around and whined.

We walked along the boardwalk the way Jimmy might have but didn't find much company. Up the hill was a line of hotels, every goddam unit sold out. Someone must have seen something. Perhaps something they didn't realize was important. Something to ask Ray Deveau about when I met him. Had the police talked to the people in the hotels?

I gazed down into the harbour. How deep? Deep, I remembered that, but the rock base projected out a bit. Could Jimmy have found himself in that water, struggling, unseen, unheard until he died alone and sank into the depths of the harbour?

I didn't find any answers on the boardwalk. I knew one thing: the police, RCMP, media and hundreds of searchers hadn't turned up Jimmy dead or alive. I was an exhausted, virtual stranger in this town without much to contribute. But I could make a difference for Alvin.

• • •

P. J. picked up his cell.

"It's about time," he said. "I thought you'd become another tragic statistic on our highways."

"Don't start."

"Where are you?"

"In Sydney."

"Hey, Tiger, if you get on the road now, you could be back for Blue Rodeo."

"Not a chance, P. J."

"Okay, start tomorrow. Saturday will be great. We can have the day on the site and catch John Hammond and George Thorogood."

"Nice. You've been studying. But listen, I need something from you. Can you get any information about an accident that happened in Sydney fifteen years ago?"

"You must be kidding."

"Mrs. Parnell and I think it's the key to what's the matter with Alvin. Anything I can find out that would shed light on it would help. Even an intro to somebody here in the media."

"You already asked me. I came up empty."

"Try again, can you. Anything at all."

"But *you're* in Sydney."

"Right. And you can't imagine how useless that is. Work on it, okay, P. J.? In between the political thing, of course."

I found the number of the Cape Breton Regional police and started to track down Mombourquette's cousin. Ray Deveau apparently didn't feel he had to work nights. I didn't leave a message. Wouldn't want to ruin the surprise value when I caught up with him.

Gussie and I tramped the streets until I figured it was safe to take a bath and hit the sack without running into any more Fergusons.

• • •

Sunlight streamed through the pink Priscilla curtains in the window and struck the face of the yellow bunny on the dresser.

I sat up and gasped. It took a minute to remember where I was. And to connect the pungent aroma with Gussie, smiling blissfully, asleep on the pink ruffled bedspread.

I limped with my legs crossed toward the one bathroom. Vince, surly and unshaven, emerged from the door next to mine. He reached the door first and shut it in my face. Shortly after, I could hear water running, which was the last thing I needed. I used the time to pace. What was Vince going to do? Spend the morning in the shower?

All the doors were open, beds made, except for mine and Gussie's and the one in the room Vince had come from. Which one was Jimmy's?

The last room was obviously a boy's. Framed photos of school and friends hung on the walls, interspersed with posters of musicians. I checked the photos. Jimmy at a picnic. Jimmy at a campsite. Jimmy with two other boys. I found only school books and children's stories on the bookcase. I lifted the bright and new-looking navy and green plaid bedspread and checked behind the matching pillow shams. The spread was wrinkled where someone, probably Jimmy, had last sat on it. I looked under the blue and green area rug. There wasn't much else to examine: a small television, baseball caps hanging on hooks on the closet door, a wardrobe of jeans and T-shirts, an empty bulletin board. Not neat, not messy. Innocent and uncomplicated. Like Jimmy Ferguson would be.

I whirled when I heard a noise at the door.

Vince said, "Bathroom's yours if you've finished snooping."

I asked myself, why couldn't Vince be the missing brother?

• • •

Tracy was in the kitchen, fresh-faced as ever. "Good morning, Camilla." Her hands blurred between the coffee pot and the mug.

In the dining room, Frances Ann had covered the table with charts indicating which volunteer searchers would be searching which areas. Maps were spread out and colour-coded. The phone continued to ring. So did the doorbell. Within fifteen minutes, four casseroles had arrived from friends and neighbours.

Mrs. Parnell was already installed and reporting that the previous evening spent with Donald Donnie and Loretta had been most congenial.

"Ms. MacPhee, you look like you haven't slept a wink. I had a most excellent night, as did young Ferguson."

Alvin raised a languid hand in greeting. Slow motion. The kitchen was crawling with Fergusons, but no one else paid the slightest bit of attention to me. Which was fine. Except that they were all swilling coffee and no one offered me a cup. I wondered if my tongue would actually have to drag on the ground first.

"No one gets waited on here," Vince said.

I can take a hint. I got my own coffee.

Mrs. Ferguson, wearing a huge flowered apron, was busy heaping a small mountain of pancakes and maple syrup onto a platter to feed the group that was about to head off to search woods on the perimeter of town.

A massive electric griddle with what looked like two pounds of bacon sizzled on the counter.

"Poor Allie is so thin," his mother said.

"Especially since that terrible bout of pneumonia," Frances Ann added.

Vince glanced meaningfully at me.

"He was thin when I got him," I said. You could blame me for a lot of things, but Alvin's ectomorphic state was not one of them.

"What do you think of these posters, Camilla?" Tracy said. "I'm putting them up on telephone poles and bulletin boards all over town. Someone must have seen him. Allie's going to help me. Aren't you?"

Alvin nodded.

"We have to keep busy," Tracy said. "We have to do something."

The posters had a picture of Jimmy that I hadn't seen yet. He leaned against a Mazda Miata convertible, young and strong in jeans and a plain white tee. His arms were folded and he was smiling. He looked like any happy, healthy young man. Handsomer than ninety-nine per cent. Gussie grinned by his side.

HAVE YOU SEEN OUR JIMMY?
Gerald James (Jimmy) Ferguson, aged 21
Last seen July 1st, early evening
The boardwalk behind the Esplanade fire station
Needs medication for life threatening condition
REWARD FOR ANY INFORMATION

A fringe of phone numbers was cut at the bottom of each poster.

"Vince did the poster on the computer. The little kids helped me separate the phone numbers," Tracy said.

Alvin made a choking sound. Mrs. Parnell laid a soothing hand on his shoulder.

Alvin croaked, "People don't even need a picture. Everyone in town knew Jimmy."

"Everyone in town *knows* Jimmy," Frances Ann said, with a touch of anthracite in her voice.

"It's been all over the news since he went missing, Tracy. What makes you think these posters would make a difference?" Alvin said.

"I think they're a good idea." I wanted to comfort Alvin. "Who knows, maybe someone who has been out of town on vacation will get back and see these posters and remember something about that night."

"Evening," said Vince.

"Did you think we would let our Jimmy out alone on the street at night?" Mrs. Ferguson turned to me with the hot spatula in her hand. "We supervised him properly. It was broad daylight. How can a boy vanish off the street in broad daylight, and no one see a thing?"

"Oh, Ma." Tracy wrapped her arms around her mother. Vince's knuckles tightened.

"My point exactly," I said. "Someone will have seen him. They might not know it's important, but they will have noticed some detail. These posters will trigger a call."

Probably many calls, I thought. Of course, most of them from fools or scoundrels, but all it would take was one new lead.

"I'll help you post them," I said. "I'll go with Alvin."

No one paid attention.

Alvin slipped forward in his chair. "He's dead," he said. "Our Jimmy's drowned."

"Shut up, Allie," Vince said.

Mrs. Ferguson sank into the empty seat at the head of the table. She raised her flowered apron and wept quietly into its folds. The burning bacon set off the fire alarm. Gussie howled.

Ten

I was about to open the door and head out when a visitor arrived and created another stir. Mrs. Ferguson half-rose from her seat. "Father Blaise. It is so good of you to come."

"Father Blaise." Tracy seemed overcome. Maybe she was relieved to have a distraction to get Alvin to stop rocking and his mother to stop crying.

"Father Blaise." Vince shook hands in a manly fashion.

Another chorus of Father Blaises rose from the Fergusons who had been polishing off the second attempt at bacon in the kitchen. They wiped crumbs from their mouths as they clustered near the front entrance. Frances Ann stood in the door from the dining room.

I recognized the priest from the photo with Jimmy Ferguson. Father Blaise nodded gravely at everyone. Not being the most church-going person in the world, I was having a bit of trouble figuring out his appeal. He somehow managed to be both pear-shaped and doughy, a Tweedledee-Tweedledum kind of man. Too much nose and not nearly enough chin. If the hair on his head was lank and sparse, he more than made up for it with the stuff that sprouted from his nostrils and ears. His watery blue eyes swam behind coke-bottle glasses. Of course, I'm no beauty myself, but something about the man put me off. Probably his air of easy authority. Father Blaise struck me as an old-style priest. He was somewhere on the near side of seventy, and he looked like a man who expected "how high" to be the answer to most of his instructions.

Only Alvin hung back. I was proud of him.

"Of course, I came as soon as I could," he said.

"It's so good of you, Father, when you were right in the middle of your vacation. Did you drive all the way back from Maine?"

Father Blaise was escorted to the living room. Tracy raced back to the kitchen to make fresh tea and probably bake a few tea biscuits and maybe a layer cake. Father Blaise sat like he owned the place and glanced at the First Communion photos, the palm frond tucked in Jimmy's frame.

"My poor people," Father Blaise said. "My poor dear people. How are we to deal with this terrible thing?" Damned if it didn't sound like he meant it. "Our own lovely Jimmy. He must be all right."

Mrs. Ferguson blew her nose. Father Blaise squeezed her hand. "Dear Mary. I can only believe that God will take care of our lad." His voice was choked, and his colourless eyes got a bit more watery.

Everyone seemed to take comfort from this. I wished I could have shared his confidence. Tracy fluttered into the room with a tray of something new and a dangerously steaming pot of tea. She had the china teapot and the matching creamer and sugar. Cube sugar and silver tongs too. And a package of After Eights. Behind her, Frances Ann carried a second tray with china cups. Father Blaise was getting the full treatment.

The second time they filled the tea-cups, Father Blaise seemed to spot me, although I was doing my best to be inconspicuous.

"I don't believe I..." he said, getting to his feet.

Tracy did the honours. "Father, this is Camilla MacPhee,

who's visiting with Alvin. She's…"

"MacPhee. MacPhee," he said. "They tell me your father was the teacher. Went off to Ottawa to become a school principal, didn't he?"

"Yes."

I don't take kindly to hand squeezes as a rule.

"A fine man, your father, very fine. I knew your mother too, of course, but that was many years ago, before you were born."

"Really?" I said.

"How wonderful you can be here to offer your support during the search for Jimmy. Bless you," he said.

Vince lifted a dark brow. Tracy fluttered. Mrs. Ferguson blessed herself.

Five minutes later, I'd had to revise my opinion completely. That's the problem with letting your biases influence your initial reactions. Sometimes you get it wrong.

That didn't mean I wanted to hang around.

•   •   •

Well, how *could* a kid like Jimmy disappear off the street in broad daylight in a town like this? I kept asking myself the same question as I set off on another stroll to clear my head. Alvin was trapped in the living room for the duration of Father Blaise's visit. Mrs. Parnell had given me a nod to indicate she'd be watching out for his welfare. And Tracy had thoughtfully provided me with a stack of "have you seen Jimmy" posters and a heavy-duty stapler.

Back at the Fergusons', they would be heading into the second decade of the rosary. I stapled my way along Crescent Street towards the downtown area. After the ninth person said hello, I stopped looking behind me to see who they were talking to. People on the street in Sydney are nothing if not friendly. It took a little getting used to. Twice I had to tell total strangers my father's name. I had no trouble at all getting directions to the police station.

•   •   •

"What did you say your name was?" Ray Deveau said pleasantly.

"Camilla MacPhee. I'm a lawyer with Justice for Victims in Ottawa. I'd like to talk to you about Jimmy Ferguson."

"Justice for Victims?"

"That's right. Lennie Mombourquette, who I believe is your cousin, suggested I drop in and say hi. Is this a bad time?"

I found nothing of the rodent about Deveau. He had a sandy crew cut, light blue eyes, pale freckles and a build that indicated he'd played college football quite a few years back. He had a smile that would melt ice. "What's your connection with Jimmy Ferguson again? I didn't quite catch that."

"Terrible thing about Jimmy's disappearance. I'm staying with the family, and they're really ripped up about it."

"And you say you're a lawyer?"

"Right."

"Sorry, and what did you say your name was?"

"MacPhee. Camilla. My family was from Sydney originally, but we've been in Ottawa for more than thirty years. Home sweet home and that. What was your father's name? I bet mine would know him."

"MacPhee? And you're a friend of Len's? That's great."

"More or less. I dropped in to see if there was anything I could do to help."

"What do you mean? Besides what the police and the

volunteer searchers are doing?"

"And I also thought I might pick up a bit of background, so I don't put my foot in it."

"Oh, yeah. How's Lennie doing anyway?"

"Lennie? He's been busy scurrying around Ottawa. Criminal investigations."

"Haven't seen him in years. He called me about this case. I guess he's interested in it for some reason. Real focused guy, Lennie."

"He knows one of the Fergusons, Alvin. The boy who lives in Ottawa."

"Alvin? The artistic one? Don't tell me he's in trouble?"

I thought he was trying to suppress a grin.

"Certainly not," I said. Not really a lie, since Alvin's various arrests happened in the service of Justice for Victims and didn't constitute trouble in its purest sense.

"That's good. He's his own man, all right."

"He's freaking out about this."

Deveau nodded. "Not surprised. They're close, Jimmy and Alvin, aren't they?"

"That reminds me. Do you remember the circumstances when Jimmy nearly drowned?"

His forehead creased. "Vaguely. I think I was at police college at the time. He fell into the pond in the park, didn't he? They thought he was going to die. I remember the whole parish praying for him."

"I don't have all the details. But something tells me it's connected with the state Alvin's in over this disappearance."

Deveau raised his pastel eyebrows. "I thought you were a friend of the family."

"You know families. They don't always like to talk about things."

"I guess not."

"I imagine you've interviewed known sex offenders."

"Standard procedure."

"Could an assault like that happen? Jimmy would have been street-proofed."

"Look, I think we're looking at some kind of accidental mishap. But we have to follow up everything. Can't take a chance. Jimmy was always getting caught in the wrong place at the wrong time. He had a child's judgement. He couldn't understand a lot of stuff, and then he got into these situations. In some ways he was so innocent."

I held my breath. "Was?"

"Sorry, that slipped out," Ray Deveau said. "We've searched the entire region. We're combing the woods. The kid's vanished."

"And no one saw him," I said.

"Not since dusk on Canada Day. Everyone in Sydney knew Jimmy. He had his rounds."

"What do you think could have happened to him?"

"Well, the harbour's right there. Like I said, he wasn't always sensible. Maybe he had something in his hand that blew into the water. Maybe he leaned over to see something. Wouldn't be the first time something like that has happened."

"What did you do to investigate? Did you treat it like a twentysomething guy who took an unscheduled holiday?"

I must have had an edge to my voice, because Ray Deveau jerked back in his chair.

"Sorry," I said. "I didn't mean to imply anything. But most missing persons make the choice to go missing."

"We didn't view it like that. Anything but. This is a close-knit community. We all saw Jimmy almost every day. The situation was treated like a missing child."

"You didn't wait twenty-four hours?"

"Sure didn't."

"But young guys stay over at friends' houses and forget to call home and all that. Sometimes it takes a while for people to realize that they're really gone."

"Not the Fergusons. Like I said, they kept a close eye on Jimmy. I would say at any time the mother and Vince both knew where he was. They drove him places, they were tight. Tracy too, even though she's not living at home any more. If you'd asked me this last week, I would have said they were way too overprotective."

"So when did they report him missing?"

"Same night. He was supposed to show up at his friend's place and spend the evening. Vince Ferguson went to pick him up at ten, and the friend said he'd never arrived."

"His friend didn't think that was strange?"

Ray shrugged. "Kids. Thought maybe he was in some kind of trouble."

"What could Jimmy be in trouble about?"

"He didn't know."

"So by the time they found out it was ten o'clock. And it was too dark to search?"

"We didn't start right away. They didn't call us in until after midnight. The family figured it was a misunderstanding right off the bat. Vince made the rounds of Jimmy's places. The last time anyone saw him was around dusk near Fuzzy's Fries. They were hoping he had met some other friend and forgotten to call them."

"Would he have done that? He was supposed to be so docile."

Ray Deveau shrugged. "He was a kid."

I knew what he meant. "So they called you later."

"Right. Jimmy had a habit of hiding when he was scared or

when he thought he might be in hot water. They figured he'd show up in the morning, but they weren't willing to take a chance. Like I said, Vince checked his likely spots."

"So they were really worried."

"Naturally, the mother was pretty uptight. Vince was ticked off. Tracy was in a panic."

"And you guys took it seriously? I mean right away."

"Oh, sure. The constable on duty was a friend of Tracy's. He pulled out all the stops."

"And then what happened?"

"We had a lot to deal with that night. Crazy stuff going on. But they did the usual. They alerted the guys on patrol. Followed up with the people he had seen. Did their job."

"Hey, I'm not suggesting you didn't. You've done way more than I would have expected, but I'm trying to get everything straight in my mind."

"We were worried too. As people, not cops."

"My initial reaction was to think, so a twenty-one year-old guy didn't come home on a Saturday night. Big deal."

"Jimmy Ferguson is vulnerable. Physically, because of his medication, and also because of his personality. If he was in this town and alive, someone would have seen him."

I decided to follow something Deveau had said. "Pretty unsettling. Not like he'd ever been in trouble before."

A look flickered across Deveau's face. He stared out at the wall behind my head. His neck was flushed enough to make me wonder why. I figured it was a good thing he didn't have to make his living as a liar. I pushed on with my gut feeling.

"Has he ever been in trouble?"

"You know I can't tell you that."

"What do you mean? Innocent question from a concerned member of the public."

"Come on, eh. You're a lawyer."

"So what?"

"You know I can't talk about anything connected with a young offender." Even the tips of Deveau's ears were red. Was he the nicest guy in the world or a crazy-making machine?

"What are you talking about?" I said.

"Think about the terms of the Young Offenders Act. Excuse me." Deveau pushed back his chair.

I said, "Okay, on another topic, did you interview the guests in the hotels overlooking the boardwalk to see if anyone saw anything?"

But I was talking to myself. Deveau must have been able to walk through walls.

As I left the station, an officer standing by the front door looked me up and down. "You sure got Ray Deveau rattled. That's a first."

I could think of only one reason why Ray Deveau would get himself in such a twist. Jimmy Ferguson had some kind of brush with the law when he was underage. According to the Young Offenders Act, those records would be confidential. Sure, the information wasn't available to the public, but I wasn't foolish enough to think that the cops in a small town would erase their memories. That gave them the advantage. I had to ask myself what kind of trouble that perfect angel Jimmy Ferguson had been in. And whether it was connected with his disappearance, and how seriously the police regarded it.

•   •   •

I stopped into the James McConnell Memorial Library and asked about the local paper. Seconds later I was tucked up at a light oak reference table near the large window looking over Falmouth Street with the *Cape Breton Post* for Monday, Tuesday and Wednesday set out in front of me.

The police must have been on the ball, because the paper had an item about Jimmy the morning after he went missing. I was impressed, because there'd also been a hit and run the same evening. An unidentified man had been struck in front of a crowd of stunned onlookers lined up at Fuzzy's Fries. Serious stuff, that. The police would have had to reroute traffic, send over a SOCO team, interview witnesses. Small city like this, they probably would have had to call in some off-duty officers. I had to ask myself, if you put that on top of the extra holiday workload, how much real attention would they have given to Jimmy Ferguson, who was probably going to show up anyway, looking a bit sheepish for staying at a friend's without calling home? You could understand if they'd been a tad perfunctory in their interviews.

Sure, alleged nice guy Ray Deveau talked a good story, but cops have to set priorities. The notice about Jimmy reappeared in Tuesday's paper. This time in the form of a human interest story with a photo of Jimmy, looking more like a model than a lost boy, and a shot of Gussie looking devastated. No one who read the newspaper could have missed the coverage.

Of course, the hit and run made the front page too. Police had not released the name of the victim, still listed in serious condition in the intensive care unit. The scene of the incident, sectioned off with POLICE LINE DO NOT CROSS tape, made an effective shot. Ray Deveau interviewed well. The investigation was progressing. Public would be kept informed. Blah blah.

Witnesses gave quotes. One man who refused to be identified said: "The driver aimed straight for him. Didn't slow down a bit."

Another witness offered: "Shocking, never seen nothing like it. Never touched those brakes."

Someone added: "French fries everywhere."

A woman said: "You could hear the screaming for two blocks."

I felt my throat closing. Paul's crumpled Tercel flashed in front of me, as fresh as yesterday. Paul pinned by the steering wheel as the jaws of life went to work.

This was Wednesday. The morning paper had more on Jimmy. Divers would continue to search the harbour. Police and volunteer search teams were spreading outside the city limits as far as Mira and Coxheath. Police were conducting house to house interviews. Ray Deveau hadn't mentioned that. Vince Ferguson appealed to anyone who knew anything at all about Jimmy to come forward.

No one mentioned the possibility of abduction. Or pedophiles. Or anything else inflammatory.

The hit and run victim had died overnight. Police had not released his name pending notification of family members.

My knees buckled as I got up from the table. I knew what it was like to be the next of kin. If the victim had a wife, five years later, anything reminiscent of that accident would still shake her.

"Are you all right?" the reference librarian asked.

"No," I said and got the hell out.

I must have walked for hours, avoiding the spot where the hit and run took place, even though that would be the logical place to go, since it was so close to where Jimmy was last seen.

I worked to get myself under control. Paul was dead. There was nothing I could do about that. But I could help find Jimmy if I could manage my emotions.

Luckily, I had posters and a staple gun, and the town had plenty of telephone poles.

•   •   •

Gussie's tail thumped the hardwood floor when I walked through the door. Someone was glad to see me.

It was after one, and the Fergusons were well into lunch mode by the time I got back. You could practically count their ribs, and yet every two minutes they were stuffing food into their mouths. I enjoyed being bothered by this. It took my mind off other things. Mrs. Parnell headed next door. Apparently, she had been busy too.

"Things to talk about, Ms. MacPhee," she said. "When you get a chance. You look a bit pale. Are you quite all right?"

"Sure."

"Loretta and Donald Donnie are quite the goldmine of information. Lucky for us that I am enjoying their hospitality."

"Great. I wish I could move over too."

"Ms. MacPhee. You are needed here with young Ferguson."

I opened my mouth to mention that Alvin had also spent the night at Donald Donnie and Loretta's, and no one had their panties in a twist over that.

"Take the opportunity to eat while you have the chance," she said. "We don't know where this thing will take us."

Lunch was a very fine fish chowder and more homemade bread. I didn't say no. Despite the conversation around the table, you could feel the tension in the air. Tracy soon disappeared out the door with another box of posters. Vince drove off to join a team tasked with a second sweep of the Mira area. Mrs. Ferguson was packed off upstairs with a nerve pill.

It was Alvin's turn to dry the dishes and my turn to wash, apparently. I am never permitted to help with the dishes at my sisters' homes. And I never have any dishes to speak of in mine. I don't wash takeout containers. Even as a child people would get me out of the kitchen as soon as they could.

"Fine. All part of the service."

I squirted detergent onto a sponge, picked up the first chowder bowl and ran it under the hot water. "I wanted to ask you something."

"What are you doing?" Alvin said.

"What do you mean what am I doing? What do you think? I'm washing the dishes."

"Like that?" I wasn't sure what he had to be snarky about, since I was pitching in without a complaint. I was on the third bowl now.

"Don't worry about those bubbles," I said. "They'll wipe right off when you dry."

Alvin snatched the bowl from my hand.

"Relax." I picked up another bowl and gave it a quick rinse.

"Step away from the sink."

Normally, I don't take orders from Alvin, but since I didn't want him back into his shell, I decided to cooperate.

He filled the sink with water hot enough to boil an egg and squirted in an excessive dose of lemon-scented detergent. While the sink was filling, he separated the dishes: the glasses first, then the silverware, then the bowls and last, the chowder pot. All lined up nicely on the counter top. He filled the second sink with clear hot water. I could tell he'd done this before.

That was fine with me. I sat on a chair and watched him. When things looked ready to go, he snapped on a pair of yellow rubber gloves. He handed me a dish towel. It looked like it had been ironed.

"You can dry," he said.

I bit my tongue when he had me redo a couple of glasses. I wanted a relaxed atmosphere to explore what Ray Deveau wouldn't tell me about Jimmy Ferguson.

"So," I said, when everything breakable had been consigned to the cupboard, "Jimmy seems to be a real angel."

"Everyone loves him."

"That's nice. You're very close."

I could see Alvin's Adam's apple moving. "Yes."

"You've stayed in touch."

Alvin sniffed.

"Sorry, Alvin. I'm trying to learn about him. Is it too upsetting for you to talk?"

"It's okay, and yeah, I stayed in touch with him."

"And he stayed in touch with you." I tensed a bit, because I didn't want to precipitate another crisis by mentioning Jimmy's postcards.

He nodded, sniffed. I had to reach out and pat his shoulder. Where was Mrs. Parnell when I needed her? At least he hadn't curled into a ball.

"You're a year apart, aren't you?"

"Two."

"I imagine you got into a few pranks as a kid. I suppose Jimmy was always the good one."

Alvin sat down. He rocked back and forth a bit in the chair. For one heartstopping moment, I thought I'd lost him again. "He was always good."

"Come on, Alvin. Everyone gets into a little bit of trouble. Even angels have a little bit of the devil in them."

He rocked a bit harder.

"Not even smoking behind the barn?"

"We don't have a barn. This is a city, Camilla, in case you haven't noticed."

Good. Angry was much better than whimpering.

"Not skipping classes?"

"Jimmy loved school. He was in a special class. That's where he met his friends. He never skipped."

"What about snitching a bit of money from your mother to sneak out to a movie?"

"Jimmy had enough money to go to the movies. He always had little jobs, cutting grass, that kind of thing."

"Maybe he got caught watching dirty movies?"

"What's the matter with you?"

How did Alvin say that without moving his mouth? Ventriloquism was a new skill and one I wouldn't have minded having myself. But, of course, it wasn't Alvin.

I whirled around to face Vince. Tracy stood behind him, her hand up to her mouth.

"I thought you were gone to Mira." Considering the importance of their search, they didn't seem to be able to stay out for long.

"And I said what is the matter with you? Are you crazy?"

"Just reminiscing with Alvin about his boyhood."

Alvin, damn him, chose that moment to let two perfectly shaped tears run down his pasty face.

"I knew it was a mistake to have her here," Vince said.

"It's okay, Vince. She's trying to wear me down. I'm used to it."

I whirled again. "What?"

Alvin said, "It's not like you are too frigging subtle, Camilla."

"So what? I hear that Jimmy likes to hide. Is that true?"

"Gosh," Tracy said, "it sure is."

"Why does he hide?" I asked.

"Lots of reasons, right, Allie?" Tracy said.

"Yeah, he's always done it. He'll hide if he doesn't want to go to the doctor or learn his catechism or whatever. And if he's afraid," Alvin said.

"What's he afraid of?"

"All sorts of things. Sometimes it's a dog. Certain places. Sometimes people spook him," Alvin said.

"Any people in particular?"

Tracy and Alvin looked at each other and shook their heads. Alvin said, "It never makes any sense. He's pretty good at hiding, but you can always find him."

"And you believed he was hiding the night he disappeared."

"Vince did," Tracy said. "He kept checking out Jimmy's favourite places. But now we know Jimmy wasn't hiding."

Vince glowered.

I said, "No one here mentioned that to me."

"Why the hell should they?" Vince said, raising his voice.

"Gee, maybe because I made a journey of over a thousand miles supposedly to help out. Then I learn his family keeps secrets that might shed light on Jimmy's disappearance. Then Vince gets in a snit if I ask questions. It all makes so much sense."

"Secrets?" Alvin said.

"Allie should have had the brains not to bring her here. She's a first-class..."

"But what do you mean by secrets?" Alvin said.

"Shut up, Allie."

"I want to know. What kind of secrets is Camilla talking about?" Alvin said.

"All I have to do is step out of the house, and I discover things no one is talking about here. Issues relevant to this investigation," I said.

A lesser woman might have felt threatened by the way Vince leaned forward. "Nobody asked for your help. We all remember the harm done to Allie during your previous so-called investigations. We don't need you here."

"That's enough, Vince," Tracy said. "Camilla's right."

"What were you going to say, Vince? A first-class...?" I said.

Tracy kept on. "We really should tell the truth."

"The truth is Jimmy is a sweet, damaged kid who wouldn't hurt anyone," Vince said.

"I don't believe I mentioned anything about hurting anyone."

"Let it go, Camilla," Alvin sniffed.

Vince paced. "That's all in the past. No point in dragging every little thing up. It will only hurt Ma."

"What will hurt me?" Mrs. Ferguson said from the door.

"Talking about Jimmy, Ma."

"Don't be foolish. How could it hurt me to talk about our Jimmy?"

The kitchen was getting crowded again. "I thought all you people were out combing the hills," I said.

"Ma's right," Tracy said. "We should tell the truth."

"Of course, I raised my children to tell the truth."

Tracy said. "There's no reason to keep Camilla in the dark."

Mrs. Ferguson said. "In the dark about what?"

Tracy and Vince and Alvin exchanged looks. They did furtive well. A cop would arrest them on grounds they had to be guilty of something.

I stuck in my two cents. "Exactly. What am I in the dark about?"

Vince stared at the tiles. Alvin squinted at the handles on the cupboard doors. Tracy examined her bitten nails.

I said, "Well?"

Tracy stepped toward her mother. "You know, Ma," she said.

"What are you talking about, Tracy? I am mystified."

"I'm talking about Honey."

Vince slammed his fist into the cupboard door. Mrs. Ferguson slumped into the nearest chair. If I hadn't jumped forward to catch her, she might have kept sliding onto the floor.

"We will never talk about that," she said.

Eleven

Well, we were on to something, but I had no idea what. Who was Honey? A person? A place? A snack? The name sure had a powerful effect. The family sat, white-faced, chiselled and intransigent.

Vince ate a couple of Cape Breton pork pies. Tracy got up and made a sandwich. Mrs. Ferguson nibbled a shortbread. Alvin sipped a cup of black tea out of a china cup.

I went for the weakest link. "Alvin. You look pale."

Of course, Alvin would look pale with a sunburn. I know it and he knows it and he knows I know it.

"Time to get the roses into your cheeks, my lad. Nothing like a brisk walk to get the bloom of health back."

His eyes bulged behind the cat's-eye glasses.

"Beautiful day," I said. "Let's not stay here upsetting each other. I am sorry. We should head off and get some exercise."

"Exercise?" he said.

"Yes! Tracy, do you have any of those posters left? I used all mine up, and we have lots of territory to cover yet." Silly question, because boxes of posters were stacked by the back door. The challenge would be finding a telephone pole not already smothered with Jimmy's picture.

"Chop, chop," I said.

Tracy came to my aid. "Plenty more. Do you want me to come with you?"

"No no no no. It's more efficient if we split up. They need you on one of the search teams. Alvin can help me. He'll know the best places."

Gussie wanted to come too.

• • •

"I know exactly what you're up to," Alvin said.

"But it doesn't matter if you know what I'm up to. I'm up to it, and you're going to play along."

"Not a good idea."

"Keeping stupid secrets that impede the search for Jimmy?"

"You don't know, Camilla."

"I do know. I know the police reacted differently from the typical no-show. And I know they are aware of something else with Jimmy. And I want to find out what it is."

"It's not important."

"Listen, I think it is important. Too bad I managed to burn my bridges with my one police contact here, and that cost us. And that's because you people didn't fill me in on the background properly."

"You're always burning your bridges with the police. You can't blame that on us." Alvin's eyes gleamed.

He looked better already. I could see my mistake. All that kindness and tender loving care had exactly the wrong effect on him. He didn't need namby-pamby poor lovely boy shit. He thrives on conflict.

I said, "I can blame it on the whole crowd of you. You are playing me for a fool."

I couldn't hear exactly what he said, and perhaps that was best.

"Here's the key thing," I said. "Ray Deveau told me he

couldn't answer my questions about Jimmy because of the confidentiality provisions of the Young Offenders Act."

Alvin didn't meet my eyes. No surprise.

I said, "The YOA. That tells me something, Alvin."

"It was a mistake. Nothing of consequence."

"Whatever Jimmy did, it was something."

Alvin turned and stapled a poster onto a fence. "But it wasn't true." Now we were getting someplace. "That's what Ma gets so upset about. It was such a disgusting lie. But everybody believed it anyway."

"Look. I've been pretty tolerant, Alvin. But I'm at the end of my patience. If you don't tell me what it is, I'm in the Buick heading back to Ottawa."

"Yeah, right, Camilla. Like you'd quit."

I drew myself up. "It could happen."

"You don't have to issue your ridiculous puffed-up threats. I'll tell you."

"As long as it's in this calendar year."

"Honey is a girl. Jimmy had a big crush on her."

"Keep talking."

Alvin waved his skinny arms. "Well, that's it. No big deal. But, Lord thundering Jesus, you would have thought it was the crime of the century."

"What was?"

"This isn't easy for me, Camilla."

Gussie whimpered in sympathy.

"Try anyway."

"I don't know the whole story. We weren't allowed to discuss it."

I understand not discussing unpleasant matters. I come from the same kind of family. "Okay. Tell me what you know."

"Honey was one of those special girls. Popular. Really smart.

Beautiful. Talented. Always winning awards. Always getting her picture in the paper. You know the type."

I knew, all right. Everyone remembers people like that from their high school class. Thinking about them annoyed me. "Go on."

"When she'd come home from college, Jimmy used to follow her around. He thought she was wonderful."

I waited. After I while, I gave him a nudge. "And?"

"Don't snap, Camilla."

"Sorry, Alvin. But if you want to help your brother, you are going to have to put your emotions on hold and give me some information. When this is over, you can be as upset as you want. But now, cough it up. And don't leave anything out."

He blinked. "One day she was attacked."

It was my turn to blink. "Attacked?" The picture of the beautiful boy in the First Communion picture flashed through my mind. "What kind of an attack?"

Alvin shrugged.

"A sexual assault?"

"Supposed to be. That's what everyone in town was saying."

"Rumours. They spread like the flu."

"The cops came to talk to Jimmy."

"Okay. Did they question him about a sexual assault?"

"I don't know. They took him in to the station. Ma and Vince went later. I was away that weekend. Afterwards, no one in the family would talk about it."

"Why not?"

"I guess I get too upset."

"And why *is* that, Alvin?"

He shrugged his bony shoulders. "I don't know. It's been that way ever since Jimmy and I were kids. Maybe because he almost died because of me." Behind the cat's-eye glasses, his eyes filled with tears.

"Cut that out, Alvin. You were a child. You can't blame yourself."

"Jimmy's brain-damaged. Yes, I can blame myself. That was my fault. And so is this."

"That's ridiculous, Alvin. You were in Ottawa when Jimmy disappeared."

"Doesn't matter. His whole life is my fault."

"That's crazy. How can it be?"

"Because I should have stayed here and looked after him. I shouldn't have moved away. If I hadn't gone away, I would have been here. I would have spent time with him. He probably wouldn't have been by himself on that day."

"Talk sense, Alvin. Even if you lived here, you wouldn't have been with Jimmy every minute. Who would have thought anything could happen to him on the boardwalk? Who would be prepared for that?"

Alvin wasn't paying attention. "It was the same thing with Honey. I was in Halifax. I should have been here then too. This is the third time."

"Stop punishing yourself. Let's get back to this assault situation. When was this supposed to have happened?"

"It was, let me think, eight years ago, I guess."

"So Jimmy was thirteen."

"Right."

"And Honey was?"

"I don't know. Nineteen, probably."

"Somehow it doesn't jibe with what people say about Jimmy."

"I know."

"So let's see if I understand. This was the first time in Jimmy's entire life he'd ever been in any trouble?"

"Well, not the first time."

"What? Not the first time?" I felt like a particularly thick-headed parrot. "What the hell does that mean?"

"It means he had little scraps, but nothing to worry about."

"What kind of things? And tell the truth and don't leave anything out. It's time you started to level with me, Alvin."

He nodded. "The other things were nothing. Like you said. He tried smoking behind the garage. Sneaking a couple of bottles of Vince's Moosehead. Coming home late."

Exactly the kind of things I had suggested to an outraged clutch of Fergusons. "That's it? Big deal."

"Ma and Vince were worried about him. Father Blaise was too."

"Oh, bullshit," I said. "I did all those things and more, Alvin. You probably did too."

"No, I didn't, actually."

"Back to our main feature. Why did the police talk to Jimmy?"

"I don't know."

"Did this Honey accuse him?"

"I don't know."

"Who would know?"

"Ma, I guess, but she's not going to talk about it. I suppose you could ask Vince."

"Yeah, right. What about Tracy?"

"Tracy's like me. They didn't tell her much. Jimmy and I and Tracy were always the little kids and the others were the big kids."

"Frances Ann?"

"She was away at university."

"Okay, I'll talk to Vince. He gets pissed off at me for breathing, so prepare for some fireworks."

"Don't let him push you around."

"Whatever we find out can only help Jimmy."

Alvin was quiet. Perhaps we were sharing the same thought. What if what we learned didn't help Jimmy at all? What if it made things worse?

"Vince will be okay," Alvin said.

"You're a brave person, Alvin."

Hard to know which of the two of us was most surprised by that.

"No, I'm not. I'm a disgusting coward."

"Stop it. I've seen what you do in a crisis." I grabbed him by the skinny shoulders and shook. His earrings jingled.

Several people stopped on the street and stared."Leave that poor boy alone," a tiny lady with blue hair said.

I ignored them. "Since you're already upset, Alvin, why not answer a few more questions. How can I reach Honey?"

"I don't know. She doesn't live in Sydney any more."

Twelve

V ince says he'll talk to you later. But not in the house."

I rolled my eyes. "Forgive me. Is everyone always this dramatic here?"

"That's the Fergusons. Not calm and sensible like the MacPhees."

Touché. That was another glimpse of the old Alvin. "Fine. Vince can pick the spot."

Vince wasn't home, so I was going to be cooling my jets for a while. It seemed like the perfect time to touch base next door. I could see Mrs. Parnell and find out what she'd picked up. Gussie trotted along for the walk.

"Ms. MacPhee. What a relief to see you," Mrs. Parnell was in her glory, sitting in a rocking chair with a full tumbler and a fresh Benson and Hedges.

"And can I get you something to drink now, dear?" Donald Donnie brandished a bottle of Captain Morgan's Dark in a meaningful way.

I shook my head. I needed my wits to deal with Vince.

"How is young Ferguson?"

"Almost back to his normal weird self."

"Wonderful. And word on the brother?"

"Nothing."

"Ah. And yet young Ferguson is coping."

"Seems to be."

"Don't be fooled, Ms. MacPhee. He's probably going through the motions. I've seen it many times before."

"I don't know, Mrs. P. He seems to be getting a bit of his old spark back. I think he's glad to be here." Although I hadn't seen a mouthful of food actually enter Alvin's emaciated body.

"Perhaps. Don't let your guard down. You don't know what might trigger an episode."

"Okay. I remember the postcards."

"Postcards?" Loretta said. Her eyes bugged out behind her glasses.

I looked at Mrs. P. She said: "Jimmy used to send postcards to young Ferguson. He became most agitated when we mentioned them. Related to the shell-shock, obviously."

I was glad I didn't have a drink, because I would have dropped it when Loretta shrieked. "Postcards! I guess so. Did you hear that, Dad? Didn't those boys love their postcards?"

"Indeed, they sure did. That Jimmy used to wait for the mail every day. He'd grab that postcard and hightail it into the house, wouldn't he, Mum?"

"Indeed he would. It was so sweet and sad to see him waiting by the mailbox."

"Who were the postcards from? Pen pals?"

"Pen pals!" Loretta screamed. "They were from Allie, in Ottawa."

"Indeed," Donald Donnie said. "Of course they were, Mum."

"But I didn't realize Jimmy could read all that well."

"Well, maybe he couldn't read his way right through the encyclopedia, but he could manage well enough, couldn't he, Dad? Always reading comic books."

I didn't mention that comic books had pictures in them as well as words. "That's great."

"Indeed, of course, Allie used to print neatly for him and make things easy."

"Jimmy brought them over here?" Loretta and Donald Donnie exchanged looks that could only be described as shifty. I decided to push. "Did he?"

"Well, what else could he do? Right, Dad?"

"Indeed."

"What do you mean?"

"Well, he didn't want *them* to see the postcards."

"You mean the Fergusons?"

"Indeed, who else? You know what they're like."

This didn't seem like any kind of an answer.

"Could you clarify, Loretta?" Mrs. Parnell said.

"I guess it was last year. Vincent was going on about Allie's cards putting ideas into Jimmy's head, wasn't he, Dad?"

Mrs. Parnell and I stared at each other.

"I can't imagine Alvin sending postcards if his family didn't want him to. His mother was on the phone to him all the time. She certainly would have reminded him," I said.

"They probably never told him to stop. But Jimmy was worried about it."

"Indeed. Loretta overheard Vince telling Tracy that Allie's postcards gave Jimmy ideas."

"Wouldn't want Jimmy to have ideas," I said.

"So Jimmy always got the mail first, and he picked up the cards and no one in the family saw them. Isn't that right, Dad?"

"Indeed, seems to be the way."

I said, "So it might have looked like the postcards from Alvin had stopped. But Jimmy picked them up and hid them. Is that it?"

"Well, we don't know for sure. We never asked. But

whenever he couldn't read a word, he brought the card here for us."

"And yet you didn't mention this to the Fergusons?"

"Why should we? We've always been fond of Allie, and if Jimmy wanted to come over here to show us his postcards, what was the harm in it? Those cards couldn't have been more innocent, could they, Dad?"

"Indeed, Mum. No one told us they didn't want Jimmy reading Allie's cards."

Loretta said, "Those postcards were so much fun. Allie has a way with words. He'd tell Jimmy what was going on in Ottawa, big things, exciting things, festivals and art galleries and all about his job and his little apartment in Hull. Sometimes, he'd make up stories, and sometimes he'd tell him about his adventures, all kinds of stuff, even you. I loved to read them, myself."

"Indeed, they meant a lot to Jimmy," Donald Donnie said. "They gave him a view of a world he'd never know about otherwise."

"Alvin kept Jimmy's postcards too," I said thoughtfully. "So they were obviously very important to him."

• • •

After the postcard chat with Donald Donnie and Loretta, I had one less reason to look forward to talking to Vince Ferguson. Even though I had another serious question. When I arrived back at the Fergusons', Vince's car was still not in the driveway.

"Alvin," I said, full of false good humour. "Since Vince is not back yet, why don't we toddle off for another walk."

"We already had a walk. I want to join the search parties."

"Lots of time for that. Let's build on our momentum."

Mrs. Ferguson stuck her head in through the door. "That's a good idea, Allie."

Alvin gave me a poisonous look. He was still sulking when the door slammed behind us.

"Would you like to hear my plan?" I asked.

"I suppose I will anyway, whether I want to or not."

"Glad to have the old Alvin in the land of the living," I said.

I heard no comment from either the old or the new Alvin, so I kept talking. "Let's go visit Jimmy's friends. Retrace his steps on the last day he was seen."

Alvin stared at me. I leaned forward and looked as mean as I could. "If you want to help him, you're going to have to stop feeling sorry for yourself. When we get him back, you can collapse, but I'll be back in Ottawa living my own life, and I won't have to look at you."

"Nice try, Camilla. But you won't be winning the bitch of the year award with that little effort."

"I'll get worse. I'm practising."

"Don't..."

"No, you don't. Don't interrupt. Don't be sarcastic. Don't be negative. Here's the plan. We will retrace Jimmy's steps and see what we find."

"The police have already done that. They've spoken to all his friends."

"So what? The police don't know him like you do." I made sure I used the present tense. "And anyway, they are stretched. They had a hit and run the same night, and they must be investigating that too."

"My family has talked to the police."

"Big deal. How many crimes has your family solved, Alvin?"

A slight smile hovered on his thin lips. "Not many."

"That's right."

"Unlike us."

"Exactly. And I've had it with sitting around doing nothing. Time to kick a little butt, Alvin."

"Got my shitkickers on," he said.

•   •   •

First stop was in the North end of town, a small, blue, two-story dwelling with a crooked front porch. The home of Thomas Young. Thomas turned out to be tiny and anxious. I couldn't tell how old he might be, somewhere between twenty and thirty, I guessed. Gussie was very glad to see Thomas. It was hard to hear over the tail thumping on the porch floor boards.

"Hi, Allie," Thomas said. "Did you find Jimmy?"

So maybe the kicking wouldn't start here.

Alvin swallowed. "No. Not yet."

"But maybe you can help us," I said.

It looked as though we wouldn't get asked in. Fine. I'm not crazy about the smell of cabbage.

Thomas occupied the exact centre of a sway-backed sofa on the porch. He sat, twisting his small hands. I perched on the railing. Alvin slumped on the stairs.

"I hope you find Jimmy soon."

"So do I, Thomas. My name is Camilla." Thomas nodded gravely. "Alvin and I thought you might be able to help us."

"I don't know where he is."

"But maybe if we can ask you some questions, it might help."

A doughy, white-haired woman in a baseball cap stuck her head out the door. "Who the hell are you?"

"That's Camilla, Gran," Thomas said.

"And who the Jesus is Camilla when she's at home?"

I stood up and stuck out my hand. "Camilla MacPhee. I'm a lawyer."

She narrowed her black little eyes. "Lawyer? Get the frig off my property before I take the broom to ya."

"Aw, Gran, don't say that," Thomas said. "She's nice."

"Take the broom to me? What for?"

"I said, get the frig out of here." She reached behind the door and picked up what looked more like a mop than a broom, but it hardly seemed like the time to quibble over semantics.

Alvin stood up. The little misery actually laughed out loud. "Camilla only looks bad, Mrs. Young. But she's harmless in small doses."

"Thank you, Alvin," I said with dignity, considering I was staring into the business end of a mop.

"That you, Allie? Well, look at him, Thomas. Big city boy, now, aren't ya?"

"That's me."

"Home to see what you can do for your ma."

"That's right."

"You always were a good boy, weren't ya, Allie, no matter what anybody says."

"Thanks, Mrs. Young."

"So what's going on with her, then? Lawyer, me arse." She indicated me with a sharp nod of her head.

"That's my boss. She wants to find out what happened to Jimmy."

"Here from Ottawa, is she? Well, isn't that something."

"We're talking to Thomas about what Jimmy did on Canada Day."

"And you think you might find out something useful from our Thomas? Good luck to you."

"Well, Thomas and Jimmy are really good friends," Alvin said. "He might know something."

"We'd all like to know what happened. Getting so you can't step off your porch. Sydney used to be such a safe little town, and now we have every Jesus thing. Hit and runs, disappearances. I'm not letting Thomas out of my sight until things settle down."

"Good idea, Mrs. Young," Alvin said. "You can't be too careful."

"Disappearances?" I said. "You mean more than one?"

"Tell your *boss*, Alvin, that around here we think one is more than enough. Jimmy's disappeared. Not like Ottawa, where a life's not worth a Jesus nickel."

I opened my mouth, then shut it again.

"Did you say MacPhee?" she said.

"Yes," I said.

"Your family from around here?"

"Originally. I was born here."

"Who's your father?"

"Donald MacPhee. He was a teacher when he lived here."

"Of *those* MacPhees. Right full of themselves, if you ask me."

I hadn't asked her. And didn't plan to.

"Camilla's not full of herself," Alvin said, the edges of his skinny mouth twitching. "And I asked her to come here to see Thomas."

"Suit yourself, Allie Ferguson. But don't you scare Thomas. He's been up every night with bad dreams since Jimmy went missing. I'm too Jesus old for this kind of life." She pulled herself back into the house and thundered down the hallway.

I was pleased to note the mop went with her.

It took a minute to refocus. "So, Thomas," I said, "do you remember Jimmy coming by here on Sunday afternoon?"

"I remember."

"What did you do?"

"Nothing much."

"Sat around and talked?"

Thomas frowned. "We didn't talk much. We were trading comics."

"You sure?"

"Yes. We always trade comics."

"So you didn't talk?"

"Not so much."

"Did Jimmy have comics with him?"

"Yes. He took my new X-Men, and I wanted to read it again. He was going to bring it back in the morning, but he never came."

"I see."

"Gran says the X-Men comic is not important compared to Jimmy."

"I'd say Gran's right."

A screech echoed from the cabbage centre of the small house. "You forget about that Jesus comic, Thomas. You got three thousand others to look after."

Alvin said, "That's too bad about the X-Men, Thomas."

"I'm sorry to hear about your comic." I meant that too. "So Jimmy was going to bring the X-Men comic the next day?"

"That's what he said."

"Did Jimmy ever lie to you?"

Thomas's eyes widened. "Jimmy never told lies."

Alvin said. "I guess he wasn't planning on going anywhere. Is that true, Thomas? Jimmy wasn't planning to go anywhere."

"He was coming here. The next day. He said so."

I tried to make eye contact with Alvin. "Okay, and on the day he was here, did he mention anywhere else he might want to go?"

"Canada Day."

"Yes, do you remember where he was going afterwards?"

"Same as always. He came here first. Then he was going to Brandon's."

"But this time," Alvin said, "he didn't get to Brandon's."

"No, Allie. He didn't. I was worried."

"Why were you worried, Thomas?"

"Because Brandon called and said where was Jimmy. Brandon was worried. Then Vince came by and he was really mad. And we don't know where Jimmy went. Nobody knows." Thomas had tears in his eyes.

So did Alvin. So did I. Where the hell was Jimmy Ferguson?

"Jimmy needs his medications. Or he will die." Thomas said.

"Yes, he does," Alvin said. Heroically, I thought.

"And I would like my X-Men comic back."

Mrs. Young stuck her head out of the door again. "One more word, and I'll throw those Jesus comics into the furnace, Thomas."

I glanced at Alvin, but he seemed to be holding up all right. I wanted to understand the triggers that sent him over the edge. Because if it had been me, this intensely sad conversation with Thomas would have done it. But Alvin seemed fine.

Another ten minutes of talking to Thomas yielded no more information. As we stood up to leave, I had one question left. "Did you tell the police about Jimmy's visit?"

"Yes."

"Did you tell them about the comic book?"

"The X-Men? No."

"Why not?"

"They didn't ask me."

I sat down again. "What did they ask you, Thomas?"

"They wanted to know who his other friends were."

"And what did you say?"

"Jimmy was everybody's friend."

"And what did they say?"

"They said, any new friends?"

I glanced at Alvin. "And did Jimmy have any new friends?"

"That's what they asked. Did he meet anybody new at the video store or something? Someone who was supposed to be a secret."

"And did he?"

"I don't think so. He never said."

"Did they ask anything else?"

"Just about special friends," Thomas said.

"You mean, Jimmy's special friends?"

"I was Jimmy's special friend. And Brandon. And Father Blaise."

"That's it?"

"They wanted to know what else Jimmy said. But he didn't say anything else."

•   •   •

We dragged our sorry butts past a new Lexus in the brick-paved driveway. The house was a Georgian-looking dealie in an upscale subdivision high on a hill off King's Road. The home of Brandon, Jimmy's other special friend.

"Brandon shattered his spine in a diving accident. He hit an outcrop. He has some brain damage. Let's hope we can understand him. Sometimes it's harder than others. Sometimes his speech is clear."

"This was a long walk for Jimmy." It had been a long walk for me, and I was used to hoofing it all over Ottawa.

Alvin shrugged. "He loves to walk. Ma and Vince figure it's good for him. He sees lots of people. He stops and talks to them."

That would be worth following up. If Jimmy could talk to people, we could talk to them too.

The doorbell had an expensive peal. Brandon's mother, slender and elegant in trim silk taupe pants and matching top, did not smile when she answered. Gussie didn't get past the door.

We followed the scent of Brandon's mother's exotic cologne to the media room. She still held the automatic door opener to the Lexus. She looked like she was on a quick break from filming a high-end lifestyle show, and it was time for Take Two. On second thought, I decided her face had too much hard edge to make her really likeable on television.

"You have company, Brandon. Alvin Ferguson and a friend. I'll be back in half an hour. Maria's here if you need anything. Don't forget to offer your visitors something to drink."

I figured a warmer woman might have offered Alvin her concern about his missing brother, but hey.

Brandon presided over a room full of electronic equipment, soft carpet, halogen lighting and a whiff of disinfectant. I figured that the motorized wheelchair had set somebody back twenty-five grand minimum. According to Alvin, it was a custom job. Brandon looked like any other freckle-faced, red-headed young man, except for the shrivelled legs and the scar down the right side of his face.

"How you doing, Brandon?" Alvin gave his shoulder a squeeze.

Brandon's lip quivered. It took me a minute to figure out what he was trying to say, but Alvin didn't seem to have a problem understanding.

"I know," Alvin said. "It is too bad about Jimmy."

I strained to hear Brandon's response.

"Yeah, it is hard," Alvin said. "But we haven't given up hope."

I was impressed Alvin could understand the torrent of syllables.

"I don't know where he could have gone. Hey Brandon, this here's Camilla. She's helping us find Jimmy. She wants to talk to you about Canada Day."

I shook his hand. Brandon's left-hand grip was remarkably strong. Despite her apparent need for speed, Brandon's mother hovered near the door of the media room.

Fifteen minutes later, we were no further ahead. Thanks to Alvin's translation, I learned Jimmy normally got to Brandon's between five and six o'clock on Sunday afternoons. As a rule, they would watch two videos that Jimmy had picked out while eating takeout pizza courtesy of Brandon's parents. Brandon didn't read comics. They watched the videos until just before ten in the evening, when either Tracy or Vince came to pick up Jimmy. Sometimes, if Tracy and Vince were tied up, Brandon's father would drive Jimmy home. Once or twice, he'd taken a taxi. But the routine was unvaried. Nothing we hadn't known when we'd arrived.

Brandon's mother interrupted. "Don't forget, Brandon. We had something special planned for Canada Day."

Brandon said something.

Alvin said, "He didn't forget."

She raised her sculpted eyebrow at the response. "Well, you didn't mention it, dear."

"We didn't ask him," Alvin translated. For my benefit, I guess. They both seemed to understand everything Brandon said.

You had to know how to ask the right questions with these kids. And not only that, but you had to ask the questions right.

"Did you have something special planned for Canada Day, Brandon?" Alvin asked.

"Yes," his mother said. "We had a big barbecue planned for the evening. Steak and corn on the cob. Strawberry shortcake. Brandon was terribly disappointed when Jimmy didn't show up. We waited and waited."

Brandon said something.

"You're right," Alvin said. "Jimmy must have had a reason."

"At the time, I was annoyed because Jimmy didn't let us know he wasn't coming. It held up our little party, and I believed he was being thoughtless," Brandon's mother said.

"What time did you expect him?"

"We were going to get started about six. He knew that."

"You said his mother should have called us." This time Brandon spoke clearly enough for me to understand.

She flicked a glance at Alvin. "I assumed he'd changed his plans. And Brandon was so disappointed, it made me really angry at Jimmy."

"I guess I can understand that," Alvin said.

"Jimmy wouldn't miss a barbecue," Brandon said.

"I didn't realize that fully," his mother said.

I strained to understand Brandon. "I told you he called me," he said.

"I should have contacted your family, Alvin," she said.

"Maybe they would have started the search earlier. I feel so responsible."

"It's easy in hindsight," Alvin said, with admirable grace.

"Perhaps. I keep asking myself why I didn't make that call."

That was a good question. "Why didn't you?" I said.

She hesitated. "Jimmy often did foolish things. And he could get himself into a state over silly situations."

Brandon said, "Sometimes thinking isn't Jimmy's best thing."

"That's true," Alvin said.

"I don't think anyone in your family mentioned the barbecue," I said to Alvin.

"They probably didn't know."

"Why wouldn't they? They keep such close tabs on him."

"You have to know our Jimmy."

"What do you mean?"

"Maybe he thought they wouldn't let him come."

"But he always came here, every Sunday and special occasion. Why would he hide it?" Brandon's mother said.

I caught the implication. "So you're saying that Jimmy told lies?"

"No," Brandon said.

"Yes," his mother said.

Alvin kept his cool. "Not really lies. He always gets caught when he tries. He doesn't mention things he should if he thinks he won't get to do something. Or thinks he'll get into trouble."

Brandon's mother pursed her expensive lips. "That's a form of lying."

Alvin shrugged. "It's our Jimmy."

Brandon said something I couldn't make out.

His mother said, "Maybe I do feel guilty." If you went by

the look on her pinched face, she not only felt guilty, and rightly so, but she felt angry at Jimmy for causing it.

"You're going to find him, Allie," Brandon said.

"Thanks, Brandon," Alvin said.

"Did you find out who Jimmy was afraid of?" This time even I understood every word.

Alvin said, "Jimmy was afraid of someone?"

"Yeah."

"How do you know?"

"He told me."

"When?"

"He told me on the phone. When he called about the barbecue."

"What did he say?"

"He said he might come a different way to my house. The boardwalk. He said he saw someone bad from a long time ago, and he said he was afraid." Brandon looked exhausted by the effort of making himself understood.

"But he didn't say who?"

We couldn't mistake Brandon's expression. I had seen that grief on the faces of everyone who cared for Jimmy.

"I told him don't be stupid, don't go on the boardwalk. I told him to come the regular way. I told him to call Vince." Brandon appeared to be struggling for breath. "I told him. Now he's gone."

"Oh, my God," his mother said. "You should have said something."

Tears trickled down Brandon's scarred cheeks. "You would only get Jimmy in trouble."

"Brandon," I said, "help us. Did Jimmy say if it was a man he was afraid of?"

"Just he saw someone bad, and he was afraid."

"And he didn't say what he was afraid of?"

"No."

"Did he say anything else?"

"I can't remember."

"Brandon?" No mistaking the accusation in his mother's voice.

"What?"

"Why didn't you tell me? Really," she said.

Brandon stared at the wall. "Jimmy said don't tell anybody. He said it's a secret."

"Did Jimmy call back?" I said.

"No. And he never came."

"Do you know where he phoned from?" I said.

Brandon looked from me to Alvin to his mother. "He didn't say."

Alvin leaned over and gave Brandon a hug. "Thanks, Brandon. You have been such a big help. We didn't know Jimmy was afraid of someone."

"One more thing, Brandon. Did you tell the police?" I asked.

"They didn't ask me."

Alvin said. "This is important. We will have to talk to the police."

"I'll tell them about the phone call, Allie. But you have to bring Jimmy back."

Thirteen

So we have something to get our teeth into," I said as we schlepped the long walk down King's Road towards the Fergusons'.

"What?"

"Now we need to find out who Jimmy was afraid of."

"How?"

"We know he wasn't afraid of anything when he was with Thomas."

"We think we know that."

"What do you mean?"

"We didn't ask Thomas if Jimmy was afraid of anything."

"Fine. We'll ask him. And we need to find people who might have seen Jimmy on his way from his visit with Thomas to Brandon's place."

"Yeah, maybe. But it was Canada Day, so people would have a different routine. Lots of visitors, tourists."

"We can get a call out through the police and the media."

"I guess we have nothing to lose," Alvin said.

I thought we had plenty to lose if we didn't pick up the pace.

To my surprise, Ray Deveau answered his phone when I called from my cellphone. Even more surprising, he didn't sound unhappy to hear from me and quite pleased to get this possible lead from Brandon.

He said. "Thanks. We'll get on it right away. We'll talk to

Thomas again too and see if he knew anything about this."

"Aren't you going to tell me to mind my own business?"

He chuckled. "Appreciate the tip. Take care of yourself."

"Imagine that, Alvin. A cop who doesn't get pissed off."

• • •

Mrs. Parnell waved at us from the porch next door as we shuffled up the front walk to the Château Ferguson. Even Gussie was shagged out. But I could tell by Mrs. P.'s triumphant expression that she had a juicy bit of intelligence. We headed next door and met her on the porch. She lit a Benson and Hedges and dragged deeply on it. "Donald Donnie and Loretta seem to know a lot about what's going on in Sydney."

"No kidding," said Alvin. "They're the biggest gossips in town. Part of what I love about them."

"One has to admit, it has a certain convenience."

"Don't say that in front of my mother."

"Never mind. It's turning out to be a blessing. Donald Donnie and Loretta think Jimmy had another friend your family didn't approve of, dear boy."

"He did?"

"Apparently."

"They said they had made several attempts to pass the information on to Vince, but he wouldn't even stop to talk to them."

"Vince doesn't like them much."

"He told them to mind their own business and not to bother your mother."

"That's Vince for you."

I said, "We need all the leads we can get."

"Thank you, Ms. MacPhee.

"Who did they say his friend was?" Alvin asked.

"I believe I have this right, someone named Reefer. Is that possible?"

"Lord thundering Jesus," said Alvin.

"What?" I said.

"That would be Reefer Keefer."

"They also said that Dr. Vincent Bigshot Ferguson shouldn't be so high and mighty, since he got into plenty of trouble when he was a nipper."

"Really?" I said. "And then he grew up to be a jerk." Before Alvin could offer the *pro forma* defence for a family member, I asked, "Could this Reefer Keefer be the person Jimmy was afraid of?"

For some reason Alvin thought that was funny.

Mrs. Parnell regarded him fondly. "Apparently not, Ms. MacPhee. But they thought you might want to talk to him on the double, because he's supposed to be leaving town."

• • •

To find Reefer, Alvin, Gussie and I hoofed seven blocks back downtown and then up a three-story external staircase on what once would have been a grand old home of some steel baron. Whoever owned the building might have been a bit unclear on the concept of maintenance. Alvin seemed calm, but as we climbed, I wondered if the staircase might not tear itself away from the house and collapse, tossing us onto the roughly paved yard below.

As we reached the top landing, which furnished in empty cases of Moosehead, KFC containers, Pizza Pizza boxes and a stack of *National Enquirer*s, the door opened.

"Man, what a bummer." The man in the doorway had

shoulder-length wavy brown hair. He was of average height, slender but well-built. He was a ringer for the man from Galilee. He grabbed Alvin in a bear-hug. Gussie ducked.

"Thanks." Alvin managed to preserve his precarious dignity, even with his earrings jingling.

"I'm ripped up, man, really ripped up," Reefer said, his eyes flickering in my direction. "You know, really right ripped up."

"Yeah." Alvin adjusted his cat's-eye glasses. "This is Camilla. She's okay."

"No shit, man?"

"Yes. And we wanted to talk to you before you left town," Alvin said.

Reefer jerked. "Leave town? I'm not leaving town? What makes you say that? No way. I'm not leaving town, man."

I looked around for a suitcase.

Alvin said, "Okay, relax, Reefer. Camilla's a lawyer. Everything you say will have the seal of confidentiality."

This was the first I'd ever heard about this seal of confidentiality, and I would have been interested in learning a bit more about it, but I lost my train of thought when Reefer wrapped his arms around me.

"Glad to meet you, man. Never know when you'll need a lawyer."

I only had to sniff the air to conclude that, in Reefer's case, this could be any minute.

"Come on in, man," Reefer said, peering over the rickety railing at the street below.

Alvin and I lurched into a one-room dwelling.

"Did you see a patrol car? I'm having a bit of trouble with backdraft on the fan. Have a seat," Reefer said.

I looked around. Everything in the place was a throwback to the seventies, including the cushions on the floor. I figured the seventies was the last time the place had been cleaned too.

"I'll stand. We're in a bit of a hurry. Aren't we, Alvin?"

Alvin had moved a guitar, a huge pile of CD jewel cases and a duffel bag and made himself comfortable on the sofa, which also seemed to be a daybed and possibly a desk. "Sit down, Camilla. You won't get anything out of Reefer if you're standing."

Fine. I moved a stack of comics and plunked myself on the floor. "We are retracing Jimmy's movements on the day he disappeared. So we wanted to speak to you," I said as primly as I could from my lowly position. Gussie licked my ear.

"Ah, shit, man. I feel so bad. Ripped up."

"So Jimmy was here?" I said, feeling tricky.

"Sure was. He's here every Sunday. You could count on him. You could use him to set a clock."

"And he was here this past Sunday too? Canada Day? On time?"

Reefer squinted. "On time?"

I wondered how many grey cells were intact behind those heavenly blue eyes. "Yes," I said, "on time."

Reefer scratched his beard. "Hard to say."

"Why?"

"My clock's not working."

I felt a throb in my temple. The type Alvin usually triggers. But Alvin appeared to be asleep. I decided this time thing was an unnecessary detour. "Did it seem like he was on time?"

"Oh, yeah, man. Well, you know."

"So he came here from Thomas's?"

"Must have."

"How do you know?"

The eyes got bluer. And blanker. "What? Oh, yeah, he had that borrowed comic Thomas didn't want to trade. He was excited about it."

"Okay, so after four then. Do you think he went anywhere

before he came here?" I don't know why I said this. The whole situation was pretty surreal.

"Well, hey, man. I don't think so. Jimmy didn't like change. He wouldn't mess with his routine without a good reason. He was on his way to Brandon's. They were going to have some kind of party."

"For Canada Day."

"He was looking forward to that party. A barbecue."

"Did he mention seeing someone he was afraid of?"

Reefer actually blinked. "What would he be afraid of? This is Sydney, man. In the afternoon. And it was, like, Jimmy Ferguson."

"Perhaps if the police show up, you might remember," I said from out of the blue.

Reefer blanched.

Alvin's eyes popped open. "What?" he said.

"What about the seal of confidentiality?" Reefer bleated.

"Oh yes, I forgot about that. So, Reefer, the Ferguson family didn't mention you were on Jimmy's route, and neither did the cops. Why is that?"

A shifty look crept over the Christlike features. "That's weird, man."

"He wouldn't have been allowed to visit you if the Fergusons knew."

Reefer shrugged. "No harm in it."

Alvin stood and swayed. "You didn't give him anything, did you?"

"Aw, come on, Allie. I would never've done that, man."

"You supplied it to everyone else." His tone was calm, but behind the cat's-eye glasses, Alvin's eyes narrowed.

"No way, Allie. Not little Jimmy."

"You better be telling the truth this time."

Reefer crossed his heart. "I never gave him weed or nothing."

Alvin continued to stare, eyes narrowed. A little band of sweat broke out on Reefer's saintly forehead. I had started thinking about this guy as someone who might provide drugs to a child while looking like an illustration from *The Golden Book of Bible Stories*.

"Jimmy came by to see me. He liked to talk. About plans."

In a cartoon, the light would have gone on over my head.

"What plans?" I said.

"Plans?" Reefer said.

"You just said plans."

Reefer looked from me to Alvin and back again. "This was Jimmy. He wasn't too smart about making plans."

Like Reefer could talk about smart. "But you just said plans. What plans?"

"I don't think he could've made plans. Serious ones." Reefer looked imploringly at Alvin. "He would have needed help with plans. Don't you think, Allie? And he'd talk about them. Now that's the God's truth. Jimmy couldn't keep plans a secret from his friends."

I massaged my temple. "Did he make any calls from here?"

"No."

"Are you sure?"

"Yeah. The phone's cut off, eh. That's the truth too. You can check."

I wanted to explore what Reefer might have said that hadn't been the God's truth. But it turned out Reefer had a standing date with his parole officer coming up shortly, and he didn't like to be late.

We left Reefer's personal time warp not much wiser.

Jimmy didn't talk much. Jimmy talked a lot. Jimmy was a good boy who always did what he was told. Jimmy would keep secrets, and Jimmy would hide. Jimmy would sneak off to visit everyone's favourite source of cannabis.

Jimmy had plans. Jimmy didn't have plans. Take your pick.

• • •

"What do you think?" I asked Alvin as we set out again.

"You never know with Reefer. He probably doesn't know himself. Not that much of his original brain is intact, if you get my drift."

"I definitely do. You think he's dangerous?"

"No way. And I think we're wasting time."

"We know Jimmy wasn't frightened when he left, if we can believe Reefer. And we know it was after he saw Thomas because Jimmy had the X-Men comic. Do you trust Reefer, Alvin?"

"As far as I could throw the Buick. But I believe he was telling the truth, as he would understand it."

"So that means that Jimmy saw whoever frightened him somewhere between Reefer's apartment and Brandon's place. Let's figure out who and how. We'll start with the phone. Where could Jimmy have phoned from between Reefer's and Brandon's?"

"Hard to say."

"But let's be strategic. It would most likely be in some kind of corner store or at a phone booth. He probably didn't make the call from one of the big houses near Brandon's."

"Makes sense."

"So let's walk around this area and see if anyone remembers him making a call. It's not like we have anything better to do. What time is it?"

Alvin checked his watch. "Almost six."

"Wait a minute. Six? What kind of parole officer has appointments at six? Son of a gun. Alvin, we've been had."

Fourteen

Ray Deveau was at his desk, still in a good mood. "Reefer Keefer? I'll be damned."

"You better hurry up, because I think he's on his way out of town. It must really piss you off when people try to do your job, but I had to tell you."

After I hung up, I turned to Alvin. "All he said was thanks. That's pretty weird, don't you think?"

"It's different down here."

"Maybe. Hard to believe he's related to Mombourquette."

We painstakingly worked our way up and down Charlotte Street and all of its cross streets, asking everyone we saw if they'd seen Jimmy Ferguson make a phone call on July 1st. More than one person mentioned to us that if they had seen him, they wouldn't have been too stupid to call the police, since nobody could live in that town and not know Jimmy Ferguson was missing.

Others squeezed Alvin's hand in sympathy. We were batting zero by the time we passed Fuzzy's Fries.

Alvin said, "Jimmy loves these fries. They're the best in the world, but Fuzzy only opens when it starts to get dark."

"Do you think he might have called Brandon from here?"

"You can't make a phone call from a chip wagon, so that doesn't make sense."

"You know something? We only asked people who are

around here in the day. Let's come back when Fuzzy's is open and try again. I bet we'll get different answers."

"All right." Alvin looked like a poster boy for discouragement.

"We need to check something out in the meantime," I said. "Let's go. It's not like we have time to waste."

"Where are we going?" Alvin said.

"Where we should have started."

• • •

I didn't spot Vince when we trooped through the Ferguson front door. Some Fergusons were finishing up a dinner of homemade lasagna, salad and rolls.

"Vince is back from Mira," Mrs. Ferguson said. She lifted a fresh stack of sugar cookies from a cookie tray onto a rack to cool.

I didn't ask where he was.

"I should be searching too," Alvin said.

I said, "No, we're doing something useful."

Mrs. Ferguson looked up in surprise. "Are you, Allie? What?"

Frances Ann glanced up from her list and actually snorted. They might as well have whacked him with the cookie tray. Alvin opened his mouth, but nothing came out.

I said, "We're retracing Jimmy's steps and talking to his friends. We're looking for something the police might have overlooked."

"But the police are trained to do that."

"They're stretched to the limit on this with the hit and run too. It would be easy for them to miss something."

"Oh, I can't believe that. That Ray Deveau knows his stuff.

He's extremely intelligent and cooperative."

I stared Frances Ann down. "That and a quarter won't get you a cup of coffee. Criminal lawyers make a good living out of demonstrating what the police overlook or misinterpret or just plain screw up. Drop into court some day and see for yourself."

Frances Ann gasped.

I steamed ahead. "Alvin has excellent judgement and the best knowledge of the community. And he's more intelligent than anyone I've encountered here. In fact, as a result, we've given the police two new leads. And might I add, Ray Deveau was grateful."

Alvin gawked at me, slack-jawed, which didn't help to bolster the case about his intelligence.

I said, "Let's go, Alvin. Upstairs first."

Of course, if I'd been smart I would have had some lasagna and salad before insulting everyone in the kitchen.

•   •   •

"What do you want to pick up?" Alvin said when we reached the second floor.

"Nothing. I don't want people interfering with our strategy."

"We have a strategy?"

"We do now. Our next step is the one we should have taken first. We have been retracing Jimmy's steps on Sunday. And we've found out some very interesting stuff."

"We have?"

"Were you not with me all afternoon? We know he visited Reefer Keefer regularly, and your family would never have permitted that."

"Right."

"So what else don't we know? And why?"

Alvin said, "I hate it when you ask questions like that. How can we know what we don't know?"

"Don't be defeatist, Alvin. Disregard everything we've heard, and start at the beginning."

"But you said we were getting useful information."

"The useful part is everyone has a different perspective. People substitute beliefs for facts. Are you with me?"

"What do you mean?"

"Take Reefer, for instance. No one asked him about Jimmy but us. That's because they believe Jimmy went only to certain places. That belief limited where they thought of looking. Lucky for us Loretta and Donald Donnie like to gossip."

"But Reefer didn't tell us anything we can use."

"Yes, he did. He told us Jimmy talked all the time. So who else might he have talked to? We know Jimmy had the comic, and he hadn't yet run into whoever scared him. Don't forget that. We haven't found anyone who saw Jimmy at that time, but my gut feeling tells me we'll get lucky tonight."

"I hope so."

"The other thing to remember is that everything we have heard so far has been based in emotion. Your family members want to think that Jimmy is good and docile and only goes where he's supposed to, so that's what they believe. Now, Alvin, start at the beginning."

"Where's that?"

"Jimmy's room. Where his day began."

"But the cops and my family must have searched it."

"Maybe. Remember, we'll be looking with different beliefs."

• • •

139

I plunked myself down on the plaid bedspread and glanced around again. The bedside table held an alarm clock, two loonies, a Matthew Good Band CD and a package of Juicy Fruit.

"Alvin, what's missing?"

He scanned the room. "I don't know. Jimmy didn't have a whole lot of stuff."

"What about videos?"

"What about them?"

"Well, apparently he would take videos to Brandon's. I don't see any. Where did he keep them?"

"He didn't own any. He always wanted to watch new ones."

"So then he rented them?"

"Of course."

"No need to look at me like I'm crazy. So he rented them and that means, what, he went to the video store?"

"Where else are you going to rent them?"

"But we didn't go into a video rental place when we were retracing his steps today."

"Does that matter? I'm sure the police did."

"We're getting our own information. We're not counting on the police."

"If you say so, Camilla."

"I do. Now, here's the other thing. Where are your postcards?"

"My postcards?"

"Don't parrot. You kept Jimmy's. Wouldn't he have yours?"

Alvin looked around the room and scratched his head. "He used to tack them up on the bulletin board."

"Do you think he hid them because he wasn't supposed to have them?"

"What are you talking about?"

"It's been suggested that Vince thought your postcards would put ideas into Jimmy's head."

"Ideas in his head. What's wrong with ideas, especially in your head?"

I said, "Don't even think about getting emotional on me. So where do you think the goddam postcards are? Would he hide them?"

It took a full minute before Alvin got a grip on himself and said, "Come here."

He headed to the end of the hallway next to the bathroom. He opened a door to reveal a well-stocked linen closet, nicely organized, with simple, flowered sheets and pastel towels. Alvin hopped up on the first shelf and twisted around. He reached behind the top of the door jamb inside the closet and groped around. He emerged with a light coating of dust on his ponytail and a large black cookie tin. Two seconds later, he brought down another one and sneezed.

Alvin held the first box, and we both peered at the contents. What looked like dozens of postcards. A matching set to the ones Jimmy sent Alvin. Except these featured the Peace Tower, Mounties, tulips, skaters, flags, maple leaves. Our Ottawa shtick. The second one held more postcards and a roll of bills that looked like a couple of hundred bucks.

I was surprised, but Alvin obviously wasn't. "You knew?"

"It's where Jimmy and I always hid things we didn't want people to find. Like extra money. I guess you were right. He didn't want Ma and Vince to read the postcards."

"What wouldn't he want us to read?"

Alvin tightened his grip on the box. "Nothing, Vince."

In my experience, the best defence is a good offence. And offence is my speciality. I stepped forward, tilted my head and looked Vince Ferguson in the eye. "I'm glad you're here. I want to ask you something. Will you excuse us, Alvin?"

I guess it took Vince by surprise, because he followed me into my room.

"Look," I said, when the door clicked shut in Alvin's astonished face. "I don't like this any more than you do. But Alvin doesn't know any of the details of the accusation against Jimmy."

"What accusation?"

"Don't bullshit me, Vince. I'm talking about Honey."

"That foolishness. There was nothing to any of that."

"Look, I don't like you any more than you like me. And I particularly don't like being in a confined space with you. So what? You have a big problem, and keeping stupid secrets won't help."

"Wait a minute, you are an interloper here."

"No, you wait. I can understand why you might protect the family from whatever. And I even understand why you wouldn't want people gossiping. But I am not in this for the gossip. You have a missing brother. I have a life on hold. So the sooner you get your head out of your butt the better."

Vince leaned down and stuck his face into mine. "Don't let us stop you from going back to Ottawa."

"Maybe if you knew what you were doing, Jimmy wouldn't be missing."

Vince turned grey. He sank onto the bed and buried his face in his hands. It took me by surprise. So perhaps that wasn't the best way to get the answers I needed.

"Okay, I'm sorry. I shouldn't imply you were responsible for Jimmy's disappearance."

He raised his head. "Maybe you should." Now it was my turn to keep quiet. "If we'd handled it differently, it might have been better."

142

"Get it over with, Vince."

He took a deep breath before he spoke. "Jimmy was wild about that girl. First, we thought it was cute. He followed her everywhere whenever she was in town. He'd never had a girlfriend. Everyone in the family teased him a little bit, but it seemed so harmless. And she was away at Dalhousie University, except for holidays."

"Teenage boys get crushes."

"He didn't always understand the effects of his actions."

"All right."

"We should have paid more attention. Anything that's ever gone wrong has been because one of us wasn't watching him."

"What exactly did he do?"

"He'd sit on the bench across from her house. He'd follow her home if he saw her walking."

"Doesn't sound too serious to me. He must have been about thirteen. And she was what, nineteen or so?"

"Then he got his hands on her telephone number, and he'd call her whenever she was home from Dal."

"Did she tell him to stop?"

"I think she liked having him follow her around like a dog." Vince managed to malign both Jimmy and Honey with one sentence.

"So she wasn't bothered?"

"Who knows. Her mother called to complain. Ma made Jimmy promise to stop."

"Then what?"

"Then we didn't even think much about it until the night the cops arrived to question Jimmy." It was obvious that Vince was related to Alvin. You had to be prepared to drag everything out of both of them.

"What did they question him about?"

"They said a girl had been attacked. They wanted to know where Jimmy had been that evening."

"And where had Jimmy been?"

"He was at the parish youth club. Later he went for a walk."

"He wasn't doing homework or anything?"

"It was a Friday night. Thanksgiving weekend."

"So he was out, but people couldn't say where?"

"After that, we really clamped down on him and made sure we always knew where he was. I'm not sure how seriously the cops took the youth club thing. It was a big crowd, and Jimmy wouldn't have been the focus of anyone's attention. Anybody could say they went for a walk."

"Okay, but the cops followed up on that church thing?"

"Youth club. Yeah. Later on. Father Blaise said they did."

"But on the night they questioned Jimmy, what happened?"

"They took him to the police station when we were out. Ma and I went over after."

"Why did they take him in?"

"Why do you think?"

"Cut the shit, Vince. What exactly was he accused of?"

"Someone climbed in through a bedroom window and attempted to sexually assault her. The father heard a noise and knocked on her door asking if everything was all right."

"The alleged assault took place right in her home?"

"Yes."

"Her bedroom. Where was it? On the second floor?"

"How should I know? They wouldn't even say who was attacked. They have to protect the victim. But we could figure it out by what they asked."

"So they told you the father scared the intruder away?"

"Everyone knew."

"So once again, I have to ask, why Jimmy? We have a kid

who's never been in any kind of real trouble. All of sudden out of the blue he gets hauled into the cop shop to face serious allegations."

"It almost killed Ma."

"I can understand. But why did they come for Jimmy?"

Vince's voice broke. "Apparently she said our Jimmy tried to rape her."

Fifteen

Once a defence lawyer, always a defence lawyer. I guess you can call it a curse. How would I have handled the investigation into the allegation that Jimmy Ferguson had attempted to rape a girl?

"How did Jimmy know where her bedroom was?" Vince blinked. "You think Jimmy figured it out?"

I liked the way the light dawned on Vince's face.

I went on, "Everyone keeps telling me how Jimmy wasn't the best thinker."

"Finding a bedroom would hardly be rocket science."

"Did you know Honey's house?"

"Every guy in town drove by Honey Redmore's house at least once."

"Redmore? That's the name?"

"Yes."

That sounded familiar, but I couldn't figure out why. I turned my attention to the alleged attack. "How many stories high was the house?"

"Three, I guess."

"Now I'm hearing Jimmy Ferguson was able to figure out which room in a three-story house belonged to this girl and managed to get into the right room without alarming the household. Is that right?"

"That was what they said."

"Would you have known which bedroom was Honey's?"

He stared. "Of course not. I'd never set foot in that house."

"Can you prove that?"

Vince was back on his feet yelling. "What are you talking about?"

"I'd like you to get a feeling for how easy it is to set up suspicions and put a person on the defensive. You with your brains and experience and Ph.D., you're feeling it. Imagine Jimmy. He wouldn't have a hope in hell. So had he ever been in Honey Redmore's house?"

"No."

"Are you sure?"

"Yes. We never would have heard the end of it from her family if he'd been in the house." That was quite a long burst of conversation, for Vince.

"Did they ask how he knew his way around?"

"I don't think so." Vince stared at his hands. "I don't remember that line of questioning. It was a long time ago. Ma and I were practically in a state of shock. We couldn't believe it."

"Did he have legal representation?"

Vince shook his head slowly. "No. We didn't think he'd need it. We thought it was all a mistake."

"It was a mistake, all right, and you people made it, letting the police at that kid without a lawyer present."

"Why would he need a lawyer, when he couldn't be guilty?"

I said, "Read your newspapers if you want the answer to that."

"I guess you're right."

"Was Jimmy charged?"

"No."

"Do you know why?"

"No. We heard rumours, of course."

"What rumours?"

"That Honey refused to cooperate with the police. That she changed her story so they had no case against him."

"Really."

"A lot of people believed Jimmy had tried to attack her."

"And you had no way to clear his name."

"He was a juvenile. You can't even talk about it. It took a long time for things to return to normal in our family."

"So Jimmy got convicted in some people's minds without a trial," I said.

"That's it."

"Would he understand why people were treating him strangely?"

"He was upset that he couldn't see Honey, but he didn't really understand what was going on. It was harder on the rest of us. Tracy was only a teenager. Some of the other girls gave her a rough ride. Some of the boys too. Good thing Tracy can look after herself."

"I guess so."

"After that, we were careful when it came to Jimmy and girls."

"What do you mean? Did anything else happen?"

"No, we made sure Jimmy spent time in productive ways or in visits with friends with an adult in the home. Especially evenings."

"And that didn't bother Jimmy?"

"We didn't make a big deal of what we were doing. Allie seemed to be the one most upset by what happened."

"Alvin was?"

"He was out of town, some school trip. When he found out, he had sort of a collapse. Like you claimed he had with Jimmy's disappearance. He stopped functioning. He couldn't even get out of bed. Then when we thought he was better, he started to get into fights at school. Came home with a bloody nose more than once."

"Really? I've seen Alvin face death and not lose his cool. Now you're telling me on another occasion, he was behaving out of character. Do you know why? Did he learn anything about the attack?"

"I don't see how. He was on the debating team and he had a competition, somewhere that weekend. Halifax, I think."

The debating team. I should have realized. "And when he came back, he found out?"

"That's right. And he fell apart, and that was one more thing for Ma to deal with."

"Maybe it was one more thing for Alvin to deal with. Have you thought of that?"

Vince shrugged. "He's always been high-strung. Since they were kids."

•　　•　　•

"You and Vince were talking an awful long time," Alvin said.

"Time is of the essence, Alvin."

"Yeah, but what were you talking about?"

"More important, right now, I think it's a good time to see what we haven't checked out before."

"It seemed to me like it was a really long time."

"How do I find Father Blaise? I need to ask him a few questions."

"You don't."

"What?"

"Father Blaise is gone. Why?"

"What do you mean gone?"

"He left town."

"In the middle of the search for Jimmy, he actually left town? I thought he cut short his vacation to come home."

"Don't yell at me, Camilla. I didn't leave town."

"Well, I didn't even know Jimmy, and I couldn't leave town."

"But then you don't have a bishop to give you marching orders. So what were you and Vince talking about?"

"Stop harping on that. Where did he go?"

"Vince? Downstairs. They're heading out to search down near Lingan. I'm going to go with them."

"I mean Father Blaise, and you know it. And don't even think about joining one of those searches. I need you for our investigation, which is finally going somewhere. I don't know the town well enough to manage without you."

Alvin assumed a posture of insouciant insubordination. His eyes slanted, his ponytail swung, his nose pointed elsewhere. I knew I couldn't trust him to do what he was told. Great. This was the Alvin I was used to. In a moment of madness I reached out and hugged him. The first time ever. Probably the last too.

"Let's head back downtown, Alvin."

•   •   •

I called Donald Donnie's and reached Mrs. Parnell. I filled her in on what we'd learned and gave her a task. "Find out where the priest went and if he remembers anything about Jimmy the night of the supposed attack. He's bound to know about it."

Then Alvin and I, and, of course, Gussie, were off to hit the video store.

The guy behind the counter had a hangdog expression despite his lovely sky blue hair. I held up Jimmy's picture. "Did you see this man on Canada Day?"

He said, "Man? You mean Jimmy Ferguson?"

"Right."

"He was here. Sorry about that, Allie. Feel real bad."

"You back home now?" Alvin said.

"Doing a couple of summer courses."

"When was he here?" I interrupted.

"Around six, I guess. Give or take."

"And did you tell the police this?"

"The police?"

"Yes."

"No," he said.

"Why not?"

"They didn't ask me."

"Didn't the police interview the staff here?"

"Yeah, but I was off, eh. I just came in to pick up my smokes. Who is she, Allie?"

Alvin said, "It's easier just to get it over with."

I said, "Okay. So when you saw Jimmy, did you notice him with anyone?"

"I don't think so. He came in by himself."

"I guess you wouldn't remember what video he borrowed." I figured the police would have this information, but we could at least catch up to them.

"He didn't get a video."

"He didn't?"

"No, he was looking at them, and then all of a sudden he kind of took off."

"He did? Without a video? You're sure of that?"

"Jeez, yeah. I was headed out, and he almost knocked me over."

"Running?"

"Yeah. Sometimes he did that, you know. He'd get spooked

and take off."

"That's true," Alvin said.

"Did you notice what spooked him?"

His brow furrowed. "No."

"I think it might be important."

"Jeez. I wish I could help."

I leaned forward on the counter. "I wish you could too. In fact, I'm a little pissed off no one else here would have been public-spirited enough to let the police know."

"They probably didn't see him."

"What do you mean?"

"Well, Jimmy was kind of crouched behind those shelves looking for *X-Men.*"

"The comic?"

"No, not the comic, the video. I passed him when I ducked into the back room."

"Okay, show us."

I hadn't noticed the line that had formed behind us, but an in-charge looking guy had and walked over. "Problem?"

"No. They want to know where Jimmy Ferguson was standing when he was in here the other night?"

"He was here?"

"Yeah."

"Nobody told me."

"Jeez, I feel like shit."

"Do what you have to," the supervisor said. "I'll take care of your line."

Buddy with the blue hair showed us where Jimmy had been standing. "He asked me if *X-Men* was in when I went by him. I showed him where it would be if it was in, and he went to pick it up. Gussie was with him too." Gussie's tail drummed on the floor.

"You're right," I said. "They couldn't see him from over here."

"Yeah."

"And while you were walking out, something spooked him, and he ran by you."

"Yeah."

"Was anyone else in the aisle?"

He closed his eyes. "No," he said, after a minute.

"Between Jimmy and the front?"

Again with the eyes closed. "No. And I didn't pass anyone."

"He couldn't see over these racks to the counter or the next aisle."

"I guess not. No, you really can't, eh. Jimmy's about my height."

"But he could see outside."

The three of us stared through the window at the street.

"Yeah."

Alvin said, "So he might have seen someone that frightened him."

I turned to Alvin. "But if someone spooked him, he wouldn't run towards them."

Alvin rubbed his upper lip. "You have to know Jimmy. He doesn't always do the logical thing."

"But the video store was full of people. Surely someone would have helped him. He could have phoned Vince or your mother."

Alvin put his hand on my arm. "You might have done that, Camilla. Or I might have. But Jimmy could panic. If he panicked, he'd run. It wouldn't have to make sense."

I turned to our blue-haired buddy. "Did you notice anyone outside?"

"Jeez. I don't know. I noticed Jimmy, because that was kind

of unusual, you know. But I saw some ladies outside. I don't remember anyone in particular. Sorry, I wish I had."

"It's okay," Alvin said. "You helped a lot."

"Did he make a phone call?"

"Not while I was around."

"Thanks for your help. We have to let the police know what you saw. They'll talk to you too. And listen, let us know if you think of anyone else you saw or remember anyone who was walking by. They might have seen which way Jimmy went, even if they didn't realize it was him."

"Okay. I'll call you, Allie."

"Thanks a lot."

"Listen, it's probably not important, but I saw which way he ran."

"You did?"

"Yeah. He ran down that way."

$$\bullet \quad \bullet \quad \bullet$$

"Now we are going to think like Jimmy. You know him better than anyone in the world, Alvin," I said as we headed down Charlotte Street in the direction our blue-haired friend had pointed.

"Except my family."

"Including your family. I think that's part of it."

"What are you talking about, Camilla?"

"We'll discuss that later. Right now, we're running out of time, so we'd better hop to it. What would Jimmy do if he was in the video store, and he saw someone he was afraid of?"

"He'd hide."

"Okay, so let's assume whoever Jimmy saw was out on the street."

"Right."

"Let's assume it's who and not what."

"Okay."

I had to admit I missed the old Alvin. For all he could piss you off, he was always thinking straight and usually a jump ahead.

"Work with me, Alvin."

"Poor Jimmy," Alvin said.

"Forget the poor Jimmy crap, Alvin. All your affection for Jimmy interferes with your ability to figure out what could have happened to him. We have to use our brains. Dump the emotion."

"I'll try."

"Think. Would he really run out into the same street where the person he was afraid of was? It doesn't make sense."

Alvin hesitated. "Maybe. If he panicked. If he was terrified."

"Remember, forget the emotion, Alvin."

"Right. No, he probably wouldn't have."

"Good. That probably means one of two situations."

"I get you. Either the person was no longer in sight or he might have been in the video store."

•   •   •

Buddy blue-hair seemed reconciled to seeing us again. Maybe he thought it was bad dream.

"I noticed Jimmy because he was crouched between me and the back room, and I passed him twice and he asked me about the video. And I guess because he was looking a bit weird."

"And you didn't notice anyone else in the shop at the time?"

"No one in particular."

"But you didn't tell the police you'd seen Jimmy in here

acting strangely?"

He shuffled. "I feel shitty about that now. I didn't think much about it at the time. It kind of firmed up when you were asking me about him and where he was and who could see him."

"But you knew Jimmy was missing, and you knew you had seen him."

"Well, yeah, but this was hours before he was last seen. I never even thought to call the cops. I heard on the radio people saw him at Fuzzy's. Fuzzy's doesn't open until it starts to get dark."

He had a point.

"And you're sure you saw him before six."

"Don't mind her," Alvin said. "She's from away."

"Cool. And the time is one thing I'm sure of. I was in a hurry to meet my girlfriend. She gets pissed off if I'm late."

"Thanks," Alvin said.

"Hey, Allie, like I said, everyone's sorry about Jimmy."

Sixteen

I called Ray Deveau on my cellphone. Of course, I had to leave a message after the beep. "He'll probably be really steamed about our theory of the person being in the video store. A lot of extra work interviewing the staff again. But our role is to stir things up, get things moving. Right, Alvin? Now where were we?"

Alvin said, "Déjà vu, all over again."

"You know what? I can't remember the last time we ate," I said.

"You ate lunch. At one-thirty."

"My point exactly. About eight hours ago, and since then we've been legging it all over town. Let's hit Fuzzy's."

"I can't eat lately," Alvin said.

"Fine, you can watch. Don't look at me that way. We might pick up some info for the price of an order of fries. I hear they're worth their weight in gold anyway."

The tantalizing fry fragrance filled the air as we joined the line-up. Alvin seemed to know everyone. Although this *was* Sydney, and people would be chatting, whether they knew each other or not. Total strangers talked to me, too.

I worked up and down the line asking if anyone had seen Jimmy Ferguson on Canada Day. After ten minutes of working the crowd, we had nothing but sympathy. Then Alvin got lucky talking to a couple of kids with baseball caps and baggy jeans. "We told the cops, eh. We saw him."

"You guys here a lot?"

"Pretty much in the summer."

"What time did you see him?" I asked, horning in.

"It's okay," Alvin said. "She's with me."

"Seriously?" the first kid said, giving me a look.

"Close to nine, we figured," the second kid said. "That's what we told the cops. Just getting dark. Couldn't have been much later."

The first kid said, "He'll turn up."

The second kid said, "Gotta."

"Was he alone?" I asked.

"Yeah. But, like, there were lots of people around."

"Was he talking to anyone?"

"Just hi and that."

"Did he look scared?"

"I thought he was excited. He kept looking around. Maybe he was scared."

Alvin said, "But he got some fries?"

"Oh yeah, he got fries."

I said, "We're trying to figure out if he made a phone call. We're not sure where he would have gone to make it."

"Hey, that's easy. He made a call from this girl's cellphone."

Alvin said, "What girl?"

"We saw him talking to her for a minute. And then she passed him the phone, and he made this call."

"Did you know her?"

"She was, like, a tourist."

"From the States," the other one said.

"How do you know?"

"We talked to her later. She said she was from Georgia."

"She knew Jimmy?"

"Nah, he just used her phone."

"Is she staying in town?"

"She was with her old man. They were driving to Louisbourg the next day and then back to the States."

"You don't think he was afraid of her?"

"No man, she was one hot babe."

"What did Jimmy do after he used the phone?"

"He headed that way with his fries."

Alvin jerked his head. "Behind the fire station?"

"Yeah, that's where he went. Over that way. In a hurry."

"Thanks, guys. That's a big help."

"Any time, eh. We told the cops."

I said, "Did you tell the police about the girl from Georgia and the cellphone?" They shook their heads. "Let me guess," I said. "They didn't ask."

By this time, we'd reached the head of the line and ordered. The guy in the chip wagon remembered seeing Jimmy, but not when, not where and not anything unusual about him.

"Did he come from the same direction he usually did?"

"The cops asked me that. I looked up, and he was at the window."

"And?"

"If you were planning on asking me if he left the way he usually did, I can't answer that either. I didn't even see him leave." He wiped his forehead, "Sure wish I had. Maybe it could have helped."

If the Fergusons (except for Alvin) could eat non-stop every day, why couldn't I have a bit extra in the course of my duty? I took the largest size fries and went back to tracing Jimmy's movements. I hoped that Ray Deveau could make out the new message I left about the tourist from Georgia and the cellphone, since my mouth was full.

Alvin was standing on the steps of the United Baptist Church on the corner of Charlotte and Townsend, where a small group of people were enjoying their fries. I joined him and looked around.

"This is different," he said.

"You mean eating fries on the church step. Yeah, I guess it is."

"Jimmy always sat here to eat his fries. Unless he was with Ma and Vince. They didn't think you should eat on church steps, even Protestants."

I munched a couple of fries before I said, "Maybe he was watching out for someone. Or something he was afraid of. We can already figure out he made the call to Brandon from here saying he was afraid."

Alvin said. "You know what it was? He got some fries because he would have been ravenous by then, and he was missing the barbecue. He had seen someone that scared him, so he didn't want to take his usual route."

I didn't say anything, because I had another mouth full of fries. I tried to make a face to indicate interest.

"That's it, Camilla. Jimmy was hiding. He just came out to get food."

I swallowed my chip. "Hiding? He really wasn't too well hidden. Everyone could see him, and he ate his chips in front of people."

Alvin said, "You must realize by now Jimmy didn't think like other people. Something would trigger a fear, and he'd be gone. But you could always see his shoes sticking out from under the bed or his shadow behind the shower curtain. Or whatever."

"Right."

"Maybe he thought he was safe in the crowd near Fuzzy's. If

he didn't spot whoever spooked him, he might figure he couldn't be seen either. And most likely that person wasn't around right then. From his point of view, it would make sense."

"Good point, Alvin. What would his point of view have been? Quite a long time had elapsed between running out of the video store and showing up here. Was he being cautious? He approached a stranger to make a call, so he couldn't have been too panicked."

"A girl, though," he said. "He was never afraid of girls."

"What about if..." But my voice was drowned out in a screech of brakes. A beat-up Chevy Nova shuddered to a halt about six inches inside a crosswalk. A sweet little lady gave the driver the finger. She added a few speculations about his parentage.

"Great vocabulary," Alvin said, admiringly.

I said nothing. My mind had shot into overdrive.

"Don't be such a prude, Camilla. She could have been killed."

"That's it, Alvin."

"What?"

"Wasn't that hit and run right here? Near Fuzzy's? Canada Day?"

"I didn't hear about any hit and run."

"It was in the papers. And Thomas's grandmother mentioned it. But now I'm wondering. What are the chances in a town this size, same day, same corner, a fatal hit and run and a missing kid?"

"You mean Jimmy might have seen something?"

"Exactly. What would he have done if he had?"

"It would depend. You never could tell with Jimmy. He might have told someone what he saw. He might hide."

"What's the longest he ever hid?"

"You mean, you think he might still be hiding?" A flash of hope lit up Alvin's face.

"Could be. He'd be really traumatized by something like that. Especially if he was already frightened."

"He might be alive." Behind the cat's-eye glasses, Alvin's eyes shone.

"We have to believe that."

"But he can't be in Sydney. Someone would have seen him."

"Maybe so, but let's try to figure out if he could have seen something, and then work on what might have happened next."

Alvin said. "This is the only hope we've had. Maybe he got out of town."

"Maybe." I headed back toward the chip wagon.

"That accident that happened last week," I said to a guy in line, "did you hear about it?"

"This corner? It can be a freakin' zoo."

"I'm talking about the hit and run. I think you only had one of those. A tourist, I think."

From way down the line a voice piped up. "We saw the whole thing. That poor guy lost his face. Goddam idiot driving."

"I saw it too," someone else said.

"Me too."

"Yeah, young guy, minding his own business. Bad way to die."

Before long I had confirmation. It tied in with what I'd read in the library earlier. Alvin slumped against the telephone pole, paler than death. "You heard them, Camilla. It was a young guy."

"What? Driving the car? Can Jimmy drive?"

"I don't mean that. Camilla. What if it was Jimmy that got hit?"

I stared at him. "That's crazy. Snap out of it, Alvin. And don't go slumping and humming either. Jimmy needs you conscious and thinking clearly."

"It could have been him."

I took the plunge and asked around. "Did anyone notice what the victim was wearing?"

"Jeans and a T-shirt."

"And a baseball cap."

"That's what Jimmy had on. But who identified the victim as a tourist?" Alvin was hyperventilating by this time.

"Half the world is dressed like that. I'm dressed liked that, except for the cap."

"It could have been him. Vince didn't go to the cops until after ten. Maybe they'd already got the wrong name, and they didn't even think about Jimmy."

"Let's not indulge in egregious speculations, Alvin. We can talk to the cops and find out what happened."

Alvin is not a fan of talking to the cops. Even so, he said, "Yeah. You're right."

"I'll call Ray Deveau and tell him it's an emergency. I hate breaking in new police officers."

Ray Deveau picked up the phone at his desk. Life is full of surprises.

·   ·   ·

Deveau didn't yell at us when we met him at the police station. Turned out when the investigating was over for the day, the paperwork began. It was starting to tell on him, judging by the bags under his pale blue eyes. "You've been busy," he said with a ghost of a smile.

"Alvin wants to ask some questions about his brother's disappearance."

Ray Deveau glanced over at Alvin, who was leaning against the wall, looking limper than usual. "You all right, Alvin?"

"What do you think? His brother's missing. He's upset."

"Tell him, Camilla. About the hit and run."

"Alvin wants to know how you established the victim of the hit and run was an unknown tourist and not Jimmy."

Deveau ran his hands through his pale hair. "Oh, boy," he said.

"Save it. This is a legitimate question."

"We confirmed his identity without question. You want to sit down, Alvin?"

"Because," I said, with remarkable reasonableness, "when this man was hit, Jimmy was seen in the same vicinity. When you identified the victim, you didn't know Jimmy was missing. No one is blaming you, Sergeant."

He chuckled. "Well, that's good. But I can assure you both, Jimmy was not the victim."

"Are you one hundred per cent certain?"

"Yes."

"How do you know? He was a tourist. A stranger."

"The victim's name was Greg Hornyk. He was a young teacher from New Brunswick here on his honeymoon. Day two."

"How can you be sure since no one knew him?"

"His wife knew him."

"His wife?"

"She identified the body."

"They said his face was destroyed by the impact."

"She was standing right beside him. She witnessed the

accident. She saw the whole thing happen."

"Oh. But why didn't you have the name earlier?"

"She had to be restrained after the hit and run. She collapsed and hit her head, on top of everything else. The boys hauled her off to the hospital. It was a while before we could make any sense out of her. Then we needed to contact family members."

"They didn't have ID?" This was Alvin.

"As a matter of fact, they didn't. They'd left their valuables back at the hotel desk and their room keys too. They took a few dollars and went for a stroll on the boardwalk to see the Canada Day stuff. Then they decided to get fries. The girl at the hotel desk told them about Fuzzy's. She feels terrible now."

"Wrong place, wrong time," I said.

Ray Deveau said, "It was a tragedy, Alvin, but it wasn't Jimmy."

"Thank you," I said.

Alvin walked ahead of me, loping towards the front door of the station. I turned back to say something to Deveau.

He beat me to the punch. "You two look beat. I'm leaving now. You need a lift?"

"Sure, if you take dogs too."

"Can't do much to my car."

His Taurus was cluttered with kids' toys, paper and a stack of stuff from the dry cleaners, which I managed to keep Gussie from lying on.

As we pulled onto Crescent Street, Deveau said, "Mrs. Hornyk is still pretty distraught. She's gone back to New Brunswick, but she's in a bad way."

"I've been in that situation."

"Right, I gave Lennie a call. He mentioned that," he said. "I know what it's like to lose somebody. So we both realize it's not a good idea to get in touch with her unless it's absolutely necessary. That right?"

"No need now," I said.

"Good."

"By the way, speaking of leaving town, did your guys talk to Reefer Keefer?"

"He's skipped. Must have been right after you left. Thanks for that tip, though. Reefer's not swift enough to stay lost for long. But if you're suggesting him for the hit and run, he doesn't match the description of the driver."

"Reefer?" Alvin snorted. "Way too mellow."

"Get some sleep," Deveau said, as we climbed out of the car.

"You too," Alvin said.

I said, "You told us the hit and run driver didn't look like Reefer. Does that mean you got a good description? I haven't heard one."

"We sure did. And we're on it. Just a matter of time, step by step."

"If you say so," I said.

Seventeen

We were not permitted to drag our weary butts to bed without bringing Mrs. Parnell, Donald Donnie and Loretta up to date on everything that had happened. That seemed to take as long in the retelling as it had in real time. Maybe I rambled a tad because of the generous pair of rum and cokes Donald Donnie pressed on me. Whatever, there's something about having a small, intense crowd hang on your every word.

Alvin had already crashed. Ditto Gussie.

When I had finished the litany of events, the phone call to Brandon, Reefer's departure, Jimmy's peculiar behaviour in the video store and later at Fuzzy's and the odd coincidence of the hit and run, Mrs. Parnell leaned back.

"Well done, Ms. MacPhee. You have covered a lot of territory."

"Yes, in every sense."

"I have less to report," she said, "but I think you will find it interesting, all the same."

"Indeed," Donald Donnie said.

"You found out something? Where?"

"Right here, Ms. MacPhee. Another piece of the puzzle."

"That's true enough, isn't it, Dad?"

"I waited until young Ferguson was asleep in case he was troubled by it."

"Troubled by what?" I sometimes wish Miss Manners would permit one to scream "get to the point."

"Something else Donald Donnie mentioned about Jimmy's accident." Mrs. Parnell blew a pair of triumphant smoke rings.

"And that was?"

"Why don't you tell it, Donald Donnie?"

"*I'll* tell it," Loretta said. "Violet thinks it might explain Allie's reactions."

"Tell it soon," I said.

"What Violet got excited about is what we remember."

"Although, indeed, it was a long time ago," Donald Donnie said.

"Sixteen years. I remember like it was yesterday, whether you do or not, Dad."

I cleared my throat.

Loretta said, "You're getting a bit of a cold there, Camilla. Anyway, Allie came running up the hill, hollering for help and, of course, as you know, no one came out except Tracy, who couldn't have been more than nine. What could she do?"

"Here's the part," Mrs. Parnell said.

"And he was screaming and crying that the big boys were after Jimmy."

"The big boys? What big boys?"

"We don't know."

"And when you got down to the park, did you see any boys?"

Donald Donnie's voice cracked. "All I saw was little Jimmy's face down in the dirty water. I didn't even look for boys. I gave him mouth-to-mouth, and Mum called for the ambulance."

"What about afterwards? What did Alvin say then?"

"Well, that's it, he never said a thing, did he, Dad?"

"Indeed he didn't. Jimmy was in intensive care for a long

168

time. We knew he had brain damage, and the doctors believed he would die. Allie took to his bed. When they questioned him, he couldn't remember a damn thing."

"Of course, you told the police this at the time? Or did they ask?"

"Indeed, we told them. I don't think they believed a word. We didn't see any boys. Allie didn't remember anything. No one else was around."

"And the Fergusons?"

"They were too busy blaming Allie and absolving themselves. They thought he said it to get himself off the hook for leaving his little brother, right, Dad?"

I said, "Well, it's probably not connected with Jimmy's disappearance, but if it's true, it sure explains a lot about Alvin's reactions."

"Right you are, Ms. MacPhee. It's typical of these boys to forget some terrible event and then suffer from flashbacks."

"It might be even worse for Alvin if some other children caused Jimmy's brain injury. But if we know for sure, we can help him deal with it."

"Perhaps," Mrs. P. said. "Perhaps."

At that point I woke up Gussie, and we hiked back to the Fergusons' and the pink ruffled room next to Vince. None of the small pack of Fergusons I encountered inquired about Alvin. They had no word on Jimmy, and at the end of day four that was very bad news.

• • •

It was hard to believe the next morning that I'd had any sleep. My dreams were full of tearing metal, body impacts, videos and vile smelling French fries.

When I opened my eyes, I realized it wasn't the fries. I gave Gussie a push off the bed and crawled out to face the day. Even a shower and shampoo didn't seem to make much difference.

Alvin and Mrs. P. had already arrived from next door for breakfast. Alvin looked daisy fresh as he bustled about in the kitchen. Mrs. Parnell was also full of pep. Gussie had preceded me to the kitchen by a full fifteen minutes and wolfed the last serving of French toast. I muscled my way to the coffee pot. Mrs. Parnell had news.

"Father Blaise is in Ottawa? You're kidding me," I said.

Mrs. Parnell shrugged. "He's attending a conference at St. Paul's University. Loretta and Donald Donnie checked their sources. Father Blaise is on the program and couldn't cancel out. He'll be in Ottawa for a week. That's the best I can come up with. Apparently he was not at all happy to go. He wanted to stay with the Fergusons."

"Well, well, well. Maybe you can find out how to reach him."

"I'm on it, Ms. MacPhee. I'll give St. Paul's a call and see how you can contact him."

"Ready to roll, Camilla?" Alvin said.

•　•　•

We were back downtown before Gussie knew we were gone.

Alvin said. "The shifts probably change for holidays. We should check with everyone who works at the video store to see if anyone remembers who else was in the shop when Jimmy was hiding. If Jimmy ran out and ran down the street, it would be because either the person had left, or was in the video store."

"Or maybe the person walked off in the opposite direction. Or was no longer in view. Or maybe Jimmy panicked."

"Yeah."

"You know something, Alvin, let's pick this stuff off in the order of likelihood. My money's on someone being in the video shop."

Too bad no one in the video store remembered anything. We decided to wait for the next shift. Our blue-haired buddy wasn't working that morning.

I said, "Okay, let's keep going anyway. The second most likely scenario is the person walked in the opposite direction. No?"

"I guess so."

"Let's retrace where Jimmy might have gone."

"We know he ran down Charlotte Street."

When we reached the corner by Fuzzy's, deserted in the daytime, we had three choices. Four if you counted retracing our steps. Alvin couldn't imagine Jimmy doing that.

"Okay, be Jimmy for a minute, Alvin, where would you go?"

Alvin pursed his lips. "Not down Townsend that way."

"Why not?"

"Jimmy was scared of a big German Shepherd that used to live on that block. He wouldn't go past the house."

"That doesn't make sense."

"Look, you told me to be Jimmy. I'm being Jimmy. I'm afraid of the dog that used to live in that house. Accept it."

"Right. Narrows the field. Let's try out the remaining two."

"He was seen on the boardwalk."

"But he was seen on the boardwalk in the evening. If you were Jimmy, would you stay on the boardwalk all that time?"

Alvin thought for a minute. "No, someone would have seen him."

"And he used to hide if he was scared."

"He couldn't hide on the boardwalk. So where would he hide?"

"Okay, Alvin, let's keep walking down Charlotte Street toward the park and keep thinking like Jimmy. Maybe he was trying to get home."

"Jimmy wasn't crazy about this route either."

"Why not?"

"Who knows? But he'd never walk all the way to the end."

We were already part way. "So what would he do? Hide?"

"Maybe. Behind someone's house perhaps. In a garage."

"What?"

We stared at each other. Could Jimmy Ferguson be stuck in someone's garage for more than four days? Accidentally locked in by someone who'd left town?

"If Violet were here, she'd suggest a military strategy," Alvin said.

"Good thinking. Let's split up. You take this side, and I'll take the other."

Alvin said, "No. We're working well together. One of us might notice something the other one didn't."

"Deal." We agreed to start again at the top of the street and to knock on every door. If someone was home, we'd explain we were looking for Jimmy and ask if we could search the back yard, garage and basement. We'd ask if they had seen Jimmy on Canada Day. If no one was home, we decided to overlook the finer points of the law in terms of trespassing.

• • •

"Stop looking so down, Alvin."

"We've been at it for an hour, we're coming up empty and

we're halfway down the street."

"We have to keep slogging. We don't have anything more effective to do."

"I could be out combing the woods with everyone else."

"Go do it, Alvin, if it makes you happy. I'll keep on here."

Alvin stood, staring at his feet.

"Go ahead. If you really think you have more chance to find Jimmy in the woods, that's where you should be."

"You don't have to shout. I thought you might manage a pep talk."

"You want a pep talk? Here it is. Move your butt."

Five backyards, four garages, two sheds and a pergola later, I felt I needed a pep talk myself.

Alvin said. "Jimmy would never go further on this street. Something about it bothered him."

"Fine, we'll finish and try the other direction."

Alvin said, "You know something? I'm being Jimmy. I run down here in a panic and then, I think, hey wait, this is *that* part of the street, and then I think of whatever scared me in the first place about that area, and this makes me panic more."

"So we give a little extra attention to this part of the street."

We were in front of a large brown house with an old-fashioned covered veranda. Alvin rang the doorbell, and I checked the mailbox. I rifled through several pieces of mail, plus flyers from Sobey's and Atlantic Superstore. "Looks like the Smith family has been away for a couple of days, Alvin." A broom, some flower pots and a few gardening tools in a little carrying basket lay on the veranda. Alvin kept ringing, and I stepped to the end of the veranda to check if there was another path to the backyard. By the edge of the veranda, wrinkled and curled, lay an X-Men comic.

"Bingo, Alvin," I said. "Time to call the cops."

"Hey, Camilla, we don't have to. They're already here."

"That's great." I bustled down to the sidewalk. "Officer? Could you come around here? What? Wait a minute. Why the hell should I put my hands on top of the car?"

"Lord thundering Jesus," Alvin said.

There might be worse outcomes than ending up in the holding tank in Cape Breton Regional Police Force's Central Division, but I was hard pressed to imagine them. Plus that goddam fingerprint ink is hell to get off.

·   ·   ·

Ray Deveau was in his usual good humour as he entered the interview room, where I was fuming. He had Alvin with him. He said, "I can't wait to hear your explanation."

"Apparently doing the job the police should have done." With any other cop that would have been a strategic error.

Ray Deveau threw back his head and laughed. "We don't usually get involved in breaking and entering. They must have different methods on the Mainland."

"Very funny. You know we weren't breaking and entering."

"Neighbours saw you going in and out of garages and slinking about in backyards. We must have had half a dozen 911 calls."

"Do I look like I can slink?"

"Under the right circumstance, I'm betting you could."

"Be serious."

Alvin said, "Are you blushing, Camilla?"

"No, but I think I might be having a stroke."

Ray Deveau laughed harder. Finally he wiped his eyes. "It's hard for us not to charge you, considering the number of laws you violated."

Alvin sniffed. He hates getting arrested.

I said, "Go right ahead and charge. It will make good reading. Lets see: Heartbroken brother of missing boy, tired of police incompetence, finds trail and gets arrested in police cover-up."

"Just kidding," he said. "What trail?"

"It will all come out in court."

"Don't get huffy. If you found something, we'd better get on it."

Alvin blurted it out. "We found the X-Men comic Jimmy had with him the day he disappeared. On the veranda where we got arrested. We told those cops who we were and what we were doing. They wouldn't listen. It's still there."

"If it's any consolation, those guys are never gonna make detectives. I'll keep you informed about what happens."

"Better bring us with you. And a scene of the crime tech. Plus you'll need Thomas's fingerprints. I imagine you already have Jimmy's."

"It's a great break. We'll get a search warrant for the property. As a lawyer, I imagine you know about that irritating due process stuff."

Turned out Ray Deveau's good nature did not extend to inviting us to join the investigation. However, he did have us sent home in a squad car, which was easy on the feet.

•   •   •

Loretta and Donald Donnie were overjoyed to be asked about the Smiths. As a bonus, I got some pretzels for breakfast and a Joe Louis for lunch.

"Loretta will check out the street, won't you, Mum?"

"You need a cover," Mrs. Parnell said, her eyes gleaming.

"You don't want to give away our position."

"Don't you worry, I've got a cover all right, don't I, Dad?."

Loretta flipped through the phonebook and began making calls. She was working her way through everyone who lived on the street, asking for donations for something she called the Find Jimmy Ferguson Fund. All the conversations went something like this: "That'll be grand. Donald Donnie will be right along to pick that up, dear, as soon as his arthritis is a bit better. Isn't it a shame about that poor boy? Awful. Awful. Awful. I heard the police have been asking everyone if they saw anything unusual on Canada Day. Donald Donnie thinks they figure it was a kidnapping. What? Today? I can't believe it. A man and a woman. Did they? A ponytail? Dangerous? Really?"

Alvin let out a bleat.

"But what about the day in question, dear? Did you see anything then? No? No sign of Jimmy? Of course, you'd tell the police. No, no, I don't think you're dumber than a cow's arse. Sometimes, we see things we don't know are important. No, that's not what I'm saying."

Five calls later and she hit the jackpot. "The Smiths are out of town, all right. But they're only in Ingonish. We're on to them."

It took another three calls to track down the very same Smiths at their cabin in Ingonish Beach. Loretta had refined her tactic.

"My God, girl," she said, when Mrs. Smith finally came to the phone. "The police are all over your place." We couldn't really make out the squeaks and squawks. "It has to do with that Jimmy Ferguson being missing... God, yes he is. Since Canada Day. Did you not hear about that? It's been all over the radio and television... Well, you heard it now. Yes, it is awful. But listen, the police want to talk to you... Because, his comic book was found on your front porch. They're getting a search warrant. They'll have a scene of the crime officer in your garden and everything. They'll go through your dresser drawers. They'll dig up your garden... Well, dear, no one's accusing you. When did you leave town?... Oh, not until *Monday*... I don't mean anything by that... He went missing on Sunday, Canada Day. They'll want to know if you saw him hiding out in your area. Maybe in your backyard... Go on! Did he?... Was he?... No! And you saw this?... You're right. That is very strange... What? At your door now. Ask them to wait. I want to hear about the..."

Loretta slammed down the phone. "Well, if that's not the living end. She hung up because the Mounties were banging on the door. Isn't that something, Dad?"

Eighteen

Alvin's long, fishlike fingers twitched near Loretta's neck. "We need to know what Mrs. Smith said." I did not say cut the dramatic bullshit, which took some self-control on my part.

"Well, if it's so important, why aren't you willing to wait and hear the story?" By now, Loretta was definitely in sulk mode.

"Everyone would relish your story, Loretta," Mrs. Parnell said. "But it is urgent. Give them the bare bones of it, and you can repeat it, adding all the rich detail, later. While young Ferguson and Ms. MacPhee are investigating, you can call your friend back and find out what the police wanted. I am certain she'll be delighted to tell you." Loretta glowed.

"So," I said. "What happened?"

"She saw him. In her backyard. He seemed to be playing a game with a woman, then Jimmy careened into the roses. Destroyed her prize Peace rose bush and God knows what else."

"A woman?"

"Yes. She said the woman shouted she was sorry, and she'd pay for any damage to the flowers, but she had to get Jimmy home fast. Then Jimmy broke right through the cedar hedge and took off, and the woman took off after him. Mrs. Smith was planning to call your mother when she got back from Ingonish and tell her to replace the rose bush."

"Did Jimmy say anything?"

"She said no, but he was crying, and now she'll never forgive herself. I mean, it was only a frigging rose bush."

We stared at Loretta.

Alvin said, "What woman would have been chasing Jimmy to take him home?"

. . .

Mrs. Parnell took charge of the next phase. Unlike me and Alvin, she commanded respect from the Fergusons. Mrs. Ferguson, Frances Ann and Tracy were stunned. None of them had gone to find Jimmy, much less chased him through a garden, trampling a rose bush before bursting through a cedar fence.

"Chased him? Do you think we're crazy?" Frances Ann said.

"No one would chase Jimmy. He would panic even if one of us chased him." Tracy had tears in her eyes.

"Imagine, then," Mrs. Parnell said, "what would Jimmy do if someone else was chasing him?"

Mrs. Ferguson gripped her throat. "He could have another seizure. Oh, holy mother of God."

Alvin let out that low keening sound.

I gripped his elbow.

. . .

"Poor boy," Mrs. Parnell said, inhaling deeply in sympathy.

Alvin was back at Loretta and Donald Donnie's. Gussie was snuggled up next to him on the sofa.

"I hope he's in control, because he's been the key so far," I said. "Do you hear me, Alvin? Jimmy needs you."

I squinted to avoid the smoke Mrs. Parnell aimed at me.

"Don't go too far in that direction. Remember, Ms. MacPhee."

"Remember what?" Alvin said.

"We figure your spells are connected with Jimmy's accident. And we'll make sure we deal with them after we find him," I said.

"Are you feeling all right?" Mrs. Parnell asked Alvin, after giving me a look that would kill a lesser woman.

Alvin said. "You said something about the accident?"

"Yes. We'll make sure you finally get some treatment for that trauma. But now, hop to it. We have unfinished business downtown."

"Treatment? I don't even remember the accident. We were kids."

"It is quite likely that's why you're collapsing now, dear boy. Even so, you mustn't allow Ms. MacPhee to bully you."

"Move it or lose it, Alvin," I said.

"What does the accident have to do with what's going on now?"

"Probably nothing," I said. "And speaking of now, it's time to go. We'll wait while you get yourself ready. Countdown three minutes."

Outside the bedroom Mrs. Parnell fixed me with another look. "Be careful, Ms. MacPhee. You're playing a dangerous game here."

"No game. He seems to respond well to firmness. I agree with you that he needs help, and we'd better make sure he gets it. Strategically, since the Fergusons listen to you, you should make them get him hooked up with a therapist here. But in the meantime, Alvin has to help himself. That's something Jimmy can't do. If he's alive, he's on his own until we find him."

"Camilla's right," Alvin said, emerging. "We're Jimmy's best chance."

"Good attitude, Alvin. Enough talk. Let's roll."

"I thought you needed to talk to Vince again. He's on his way out."

"Okay, I'll tackle him, and you tell Loretta to get a description of the woman who was chasing Jimmy. Probably quicker than getting it from Ray Deveau."

Vince was already in his car, and he wasn't happy to see me. And even less happy to discuss Honey again. Of course, I didn't give a rat's ass about his happiness.

"How do I reach Honey Redmore?"

"Are you still harping on that?"

"I am."

"Why?"

"Because we haven't found Jimmy yet, and we know there's a woman involved. Maybe that event sent Honey over the edge in some way, and she's getting even. Who knows? It's something to follow up on."

"That doesn't make any sense at all. Honey wasn't the type to go over the edge. Anyway, she doesn't live here. Her family moved away right after the, um, event."

"Where does she live now?"

Body language is easy to read. Vince sat in his car, with his face and body turned away from me. He kept his arms crossed, his eyebrows knit. "I don't know. And I don't want to know."

• • •

Loretta had struck out, but not from lack of trying. The phone in her hand must have been white hot.

I used my cellphone to call P. J. and left a message asking

181

him to practice his research skills and to ferret out one Honey Redmore, whereabouts unknown. What's the point of having friends if you can't ask a favour every now and then?

"Okay," I said to the rest of them, "we've turned up a lot of good stuff. Now we've got to focus, concentrate and strategize."

"Yes!" Loretta screamed from the phone. "Yes, yes, you're kidding, yes, yes, really, yes, okay, that's good, dear." I expect to spend less goddam time in Purgatory than Loretta took to say goodbye.

We all stood up when she finally put the phone down.

"What is it?" Alvin, Mrs. P., Donald Donnie and I said.

"The woman who was chasing Jimmy was...here let me sit down for a minute, and catch my breath." Loretta collapsed in a chair, clutching her chest. "I'm so excited that my heart is racing. It does when I get right worked up. Doesn't it, Dad?"

"Indeed." But even Donald Donnie didn't want to drag this out.

"Every minute counts," Alvin said.

Loretta fanned herself. "Right, dear. A woman, she thinks a tall woman, wearing jeans and a scarf."

"A scarf?" Alvin said. "Who wears a scarf in July?"

"I meant a head scarf."

"Even so."

"Someone who doesn't wish to be identified," Mrs. Parnell said.

"Anything else, Loretta?" I said.

"Well, Dad, Mrs. Smith did mention that she was pretty ugly, but she wouldn't swear to that in a court of law."

"I guess that's something," I said.

"Alvin, is Honey Redmore tall?"

"I don't remember her being particularly tall."

Loretta said, "Honey Redmore?"

I don't know who howled louder, Loretta or Donald Donnie. Gussie howled a bit too.

"What's so funny?" I was more than a bit miffed.

"If you're thinking she was the ugly woman, think again, dear. No one ever called Honey Redmore ugly. Did they, Dad?"

"Indeed, they never, Mum."

"You know her?" I said, realizing as the words tumbled out that, of course, they knew her. This was Sydney.

"Those Redmores thought they were something special. Didn't they, Dad?"

Donald Donnie's face flushed. "Indeed. Did some damage."

I was in a tricky situation. I couldn't ethically reveal the accusation against Jimmy or suggest Honey was possibly the victim of a sexual attack. Or even that she might have falsely accused Jimmy. Turned out I didn't have to worry.

"That talk about Jimmy was absolute bullshit," Loretta said.

"Indeed. As if he'd attack her," Donald Donnie said.

"Plenty of people believed that story, that's the worst part of it. And the Redmore family got a lot of sympathy. Things were tough for them next door. Hard for her to keep her nose in the air after that. Sorry, Allie."

"I imagine," I said.

"So, Ms. MacPhee, you were asking because you believe it's connected to the disappearance of young Jimmy."

"Well, I was really hoping I'd found our ugly woman."

That was enough to set Donald Donnie and Loretta off again.

• • •

Half an hour later, after talking to our blue-haired buddy and other staff, we had to accept that no one in the video store that evening fit the description of an ugly woman in denim. The new guy behind the counter said, "We get lots of ugly women in here. But wasn't anyone like that Canada Day, or I would have noticed."

"He notices all the women," one of his co-workers offered. "And he really likes ugly women, so he would have noticed for sure."

"Shut up."

"No, you shut up."

Bottom line, no ugly women in denim with or without scarves. Alvin slumped all the way home.

"It's a mild set-back on one theory. Pull yourself together," I said. "She was probably outside when he spotted her. Or maybe he saw her on a neighbouring street and ran to the video store to hide."

"But who is she?"

"We'll figure it out. Now I have another idea. Let's bounce it off Mrs. P. and Loretta and Donald Donnie. They've been really helpful so far."

I left a message for Ray Deveau suggesting he follow up on the ugly woman theory, thus saving him the trouble of checking with the video store.

•   •   •

"Okay, let's explore this idea," I said back at Donald Donnie and Loretta's when I had everyone's attention again.

"Go on, Ms. MacPhee."

"We know he was scared of someone, most likely this woman, and that made him late for Brandon's barbecue. Suppose he was already agitated and then, on top of that, he witnessed that horrible hit and run."

Alvin nodded. "That would explain a lot."

"Exactly. So what would happen?"

"He'd flip out."

Loretta said, "He would, wouldn't he, Dad?"

"Indeed, he would. And it will be easy to follow up on, because a lot of people go to Fuzzy's a couple of times a week."

"You think they'd come back after seeing a fatal hit and run?"

"Take more than that to keep people away from Fuzzy's, wouldn't it, Mum?"

"You're making me hungry, Dad."

"The mind boggles," I said, "but, okay, Alvin, let's go back down to that area and see if anyone saw Jimmy right before the accident took place. We didn't really get a clear idea of when he bought his fries. We can follow his steps along the boardwalk and keep thinking like him. We haven't done that with this new theory in mind."

"That's probably a good idea, Camilla. But I keep telling you, Jimmy's not a good hider. So even if he wanted to, he couldn't stay out of sight in this town for that long. It isn't possible. Unless..." He clamped his mouth shut at this point.

I waited. Finally I said, "Unless what?"

"What if this woman is holding him prisoner?"

"Unlikely, Alvin."

"But possible. And if someone is, we'll never find him. Jimmy would never figure out how to outwit a captor."

"Never say never. He seems to have put up a good fight. In this town and this community, it is possible but highly unlikely someone is holding Jimmy prisoner. Admit it."

Alvin said, "What if you're wrong?"

"Forget that. Now we need to work on where he is likely to go. The hit and run is our best lead."

"We already spoke to a lot of people about that."

"Sure, but we were looking at things differently. We didn't ask the right questions. Even though some people saw it, most witnesses wouldn't have been back at Fuzzy's last night. The reports I read indicated the people were really traumatized by what they saw."

"Were their names in the paper?"

"No. That's the problem. We'll have to ask Ray Deveau. If he won't tell us the names, maybe P. J. can find out something for me from a colleague. I'll add it to his list. It will make a nice change from brown-nosing that right wing idiot he's shadowing." I picked up my cellphone and pressed P. J.'s numbers.

Alvin was saved from the need to comment by some sort of fracas going on in front of the Ferguson house. You could hear the racket right through the walls. He went over to check. The door slammed behind him.

Mrs. Parnell looked like she was having dark thoughts on some subject. She didn't even seem to notice when Donald Donnie topped up her glass.

"I feel so useless with these legs," she said. "Last year, I could have done some of the fieldwork for you. I swear this is the last time I'll leave home without my computer."

"You can find a number for this Mrs. Hornyk. You don't need a computer for that," I said.

"But it's ever so much faster. Nevertheless, you can count on me, Ms. MacPhee."

Before I could give her my vote of confidence, the front door burst open. Alvin flung himself into the room. Tears tracked his skinny cheeks. Loretta gripped her chest. Donald Donnie fumbled the bottle of Harvey's Bristol Cream. I jumped to my feet.

Alvin wept. "They found him. They found Jimmy."

Nineteen

Framing the right question was beyond me. Mrs. Parnell alone had the courage to touch Alvin's leather arm.

"Dear boy, is he alive or dead?"

"He's alive!"

"It's wonderful, wonderful news. Don't you be rushing off, Allie," Loretta said. "We want all the details, don't we, Dad?"

"Indeed we do. No one else next door is going to tell us."

"Sit down, dear boy," Mrs. Parnell said. "What has happened?"

"He's in Moncton."

"Moncton? Moncton? How far is that from here? How the hell did he get to Moncton?" I said.

"Ray Deveau just called Ma. Some transport truck driver got in touch with the cops up there a short time ago. Apparently this guy picked Jimmy up in his truck right here on King's Road just before ten that night and took him as far as he was going, which was Moncton. He said Jimmy just appeared on the road. This guy didn't hear the radio alerts, because he only listens to CDs in the truck. Then today he saw Jimmy's face on the TV at some truck stop."

"Take a breath, Alvin," I said. "You're going to pass out."

For once, he did what he was told.

"A victory calls for celebration," said Mrs. Parnell.

"Indeed." Donald Donnie raced across the room with the sherry.

"Isn't that a stroke of good luck about Jimmy," Loretta said. "Of course, next door they'll be saying it's a miracle. They'll be claiming it's because of the rosaries, won't they, Dad?"

I didn't care if it was a miracle or a stroke of luck or a result of the rosaries. As long as Jimmy was alive. "So where is he now? Can we pick him up? He needs medical attention."

"That's the thing, Camilla. Jimmy told the driver he was going to Ottawa to see me. We have to get the hell back before it's too late."

· · ·

"P. J." I said when he answered, "I need your help."

He said, "John Hammond and George Thorogood."

"That's great. I might even get to hear them. Jimmy Ferguson's alive and on his way to Ottawa."

"You're kidding."

"He told the truck driver who picked him up in Sydney he was going to visit his brother, and then he was going to see the sights in Ottawa."

"What? Hey, Tiger, that's great."

"It is, but we're not out of the woods yet. Jimmy's in real danger of suffering more seizures if he doesn't get his medication. It's been five days, and most likely he's been under a lot of stress. With luck he'll head straight for Alvin's apartment. He could be there already."

"Could he find Alvin's place? Isn't it in Hull? I thought this kid could hardly read."

"He can read well enough. And he knows Alvin's address. Jimmy sent postcards to Alvin every week." I lowered my voice. "And he knows about Ottawa, because Alvin used to talk about the city in the postcards he sent Jimmy. If we don't find Jimmy right away, I think the cards will give us a clue about what he'd want to do."

"Good thinking."

"Isn't it? So here's what I'd like you to do. Head to Alvin's place…"

"Which would be where?"

"Boulevard St. Joseph, not far from the Armory on Boulevard Alexandre Taché."

"Okay."

"Trot on over and check for Jimmy. Maybe you should leave your phone number with Alvin's neighbours."

"I do have a job, you know. Between the cat and the birds and this extra assignment, I'm running."

"That reminds me. Did you think to water the prickly cactus? And stop whining. Any self-respecting reporter would be thrilled to get the inside track on this kind of human interest story."

"I'm working on becoming a political commentator, remember? But of course, I'll help with the search for Jimmy."

"It must be hard to tear yourself away from all those political insights. I appreciate the sacrifice you're making, I hope you know that."

"I can read between the lines," he said. "And by the way, that Honey Redmore, are you still interested in her?"

"You're the best, P. J. It's not so urgent now that we know Jimmy's alive and on his way to Ottawa, but it couldn't hurt to get an address and phone number. Thanks. Gotta go now."

I raced off to pack up my few belongings and toss them into the car. Then, in case Mr. Nice Guy Ray Deveau hadn't thought of it, I left Mombourquette a message to fill him in. He'd know what to do.

Despite the rush, Mrs. Parnell had managed to track down

Lianne Hornyk in New Brunswick. I had to hand it to her. Efficiency or what. Of course, she packs light.

Donald Donnie and Loretta had crammed the Buick with dinner: jumbo bags of sour cream and chive chips. Salsa and nachos. Mars bars and Coke. Alvin made sure we had Jimmy's extra medication and puffer." At least we have our vitamins," I said, as we shot away from the curb. Loretta and Donald Donnie stood, pyjamas flapping in the gentle evening breeze.

We didn't wait for the convoy of Fergusons who were busy organizing themselves for the trip to Ottawa. We shot out of Sydney, planning to drive all night.

About halfway to the Canso causeway, I wrinkled my nose. That's when the co-conspirators finally chose to mention that Gussie was along for the ride.

Gussie, they claimed, would help Jimmy get over the trauma.

I wondered what would help me get over Gussie.

• • •

Perhaps it was unwise, considering our need to get to Ottawa fast, but I did it anyway. After Fredericton, I pulled off the highway and drove into a small town. I left Alvin and Mrs. P. at a Tim Hortons restocking essentials.

"We shouldn't waste time." Alvin flicked his ponytail.

"I won't be long," I said. "Have dinner."

"This will add hours to our trip," Alvin said.

"Twenty minutes. Trust me," I said.

I squealed out of the parking lot and around the corner. I reached the front door of the neat bungalow sooner than I wanted. As much as I needed the information, I almost hoped no one would answer.

But someone did. The woman at the door was tiny. I looked down from my chunky five foot three. It didn't take a trained eye to see she'd recently lost a lot of weight. Her tank top hung from her bony shoulders.

"Ms. Hornyk," I said. She stared back at me, her eyes lacklustre.

"My name is Camilla MacPhee. I need to speak to you about an urgent matter." I was surprised to hear the emotion rising in my own voice. "I'll be quick."

She shrugged.

I squeezed into the small dim living room. The most noticeable thing in the room was the proliferation of carnations, lilies, mums, plus a few ferns. Every surface was covered with vases, most of them parked in front of framed photos.

It was obvious she didn't care much who I was and whether whatever I wanted took a long time or not.

She sat in one of two matched chairs in a trendy minimalist design. The gloom exaggerated the deep circles under her eyes. I wondered how long since she'd slept.

"First, let me say how sorry I am about your husband." She nodded. "I understand how you feel. I'll try to make it easy."

"Why does everyone say that? No one understands how I feel."

"I'm sorry."

"I hate that. I always want to tell them to fuck off."

"Point taken. Five years ago, a drunk driver killed my husband. I understand better than most."

This time she made eye contact. "Even that doesn't help me."

"It will be a long time before anything helps."

"How long did it take you to feel normal again?"

"I'll let you know." No point in avoiding the truth. "But it gets easier."

She turned and stared at a ten by twelve colour photo of a smiling bride and groom.

"If you say so. We got married in April. This was our honeymoon. We had to wait until school finished."

"A boy is missing in Sydney," I said. "He is developmentally challenged and probably in great danger." She kept her gaze on the photo. "I believe his disappearance and your husband's death are connected in some way."

She snapped around. "You think this boy killed Greg?"

That had never crossed my mind. "No. But I think the boy may have witnessed the accident."

The dark eyes flashed. "It was no accident."

"You mean someone ran your husband down deliberately?"

"That's exactly what I mean."

I chose my words carefully. "Can you tell me exactly what happened?"

"What difference does it make? You probably won't believe me."

"Why wouldn't I believe you?"

"The police didn't."

"Police don't believe anyone. It's their training."

"This is not a joke," she said.

"Who's joking? It's the way they are. They're used to getting torn apart on the witness stand, having their cases crumble, having people lie and misinterpret things."

"You're saying I'm misinterpreting what happened?"

"I'm saying I'm not the police, and I would really like to hear whatever you can tell me about the hit and run."

"Call it what it is. Call it Greg's murder. Would you like to hear about Greg's murder?"

"All right. Tell me what happened. Then I'll tell you about Jimmy Ferguson. Maybe we can figure out what the hell's going on."

Her nails dug in her palms. "The car hit him. Aimed right for him. It wasn't an accident."

"That can happen with a drunk at the wheel."

"I don't think it was a case of drunkenness," she added. "We are talking about a one-eighty like a Formula One driver could handle."

"A U-turn?"

"Yes. The car was headed away from us and slowed down, and that killer made a perfect U-turn, aimed straight at Greg and accelerated."

"Could the driver have panicked?"

"No," she said, "I told you it was deliberate."

I've found out the hard way that when we try to make sense of death, we often search for guilty parties. Accidents and mistakes leave us struggling to find meaning. It helps to have someone to hate. I know. "I understand the police are treating this as an accident."

"Screw the police. I was *there*. Do you want to hear what I saw or not?"

"I do. You were saying the killer made a U-turn, and it looked like he was in full control of the wheel, then he drove off without stopping."

"I thought you were going to listen. This is what happened. We had come up from the boardwalk to that street that runs along it. We heard the fries were great."

"The Esplanade."

"Whatever. Greg was ahead of me. I was dawdling. I noticed this car driving by at a moderate speed, but the killer was looking around, searching for somebody. You with me?"

You bet I was with her.

"That's when the killer slowed down, made a very controlled turn and then *aimed*, I repeat, aimed right for Greg."

"What did Greg do?"

"Nothing. He was facing across the street and trying to figure out where we should go next. He never saw the car."

"And what did you do?"

"First, I stood there. Stunned. It didn't make sense. Then I thought, that car's going to hit Greg. I ran to push him out of the way." She struggled to control herself. I'm not such a physical person, but I reached out to her. "I think I made it worse."

"No," I said.

"Yes. Greg turned toward me, probably wondering what I was yelling about, and the car hit him."

"It's the fault of the driver. Not yours."

"The fault of the killer."

"Yes. The killer."

"I keep asking myself, what if? What if we'd crossed earlier? What if we'd gone down on the boardwalk directly like Greg wanted? Lots of what-ifs. No answers."

"Look, choosing to cross the street at that moment doesn't make it your fault. It's hard to get your head around that, but it's important if you want to live with yourself. Trust me."

"Cross the street? We weren't crossing the street. We were right on the sidewalk. Greg landed in the street as a result of the impact, but he started on the sidewalk."

"My God. Were you able to identify the car?"

"Dark blue or black, medium-size. Sedan. Nothing out of the ordinary and, no, of course, I didn't get a license plate number. The car was dusty, dirty and you couldn't have read the number even if you had time to."

"You saw dirt on the plate?"

"I didn't. But I heard someone else mention it."

"Did you notice who said it?"

"No. My husband was lying on the sidewalk, horribly injured. I didn't even turn my head to see who was speaking. Only Greg mattered."

I cleared my throat. "After the car hit Greg, what happened?"

"He flew up in the air and banged into the window of the car. I think it shattered. Then he rolled off onto the street. It felt like slow motion. People rushed over. Someone called the police with a cellphone. Everyone was very kind. Trying to help him. Trying to help me."

"And the driver?"

"She reversed and turned really fast. After Greg rolled off the car, the car shot down the road."

"Did you say *she*?"

"Why? Didn't you know?"

"No one mentioned it. It wasn't in the paper either. Did you recognize her?"

"I'd never seen her before. I have no idea who she was."

"Did you see where she went?"

Lianne shook her head. We both were silent for a long time, each in our world of bloody memory.

Finally she spoke. "If you find any way to bring her to justice, I want to be part of it."

"Right. Here's the situation. I am looking for a missing boy. He seems to be on the run from Sydney. One thing we know: he was at or near Fuzzy's Fries on the same day your husband was killed. His name is Jimmy Ferguson. He has brain damage. He's a child in a man's body, sweet and loveable. His family say when he's afraid, he hides. An unidentified woman was seen chasing him in the afternoon. Now with this new information, I'm asking myself if Jimmy saw something, saw the hit and run driver and recognized her as the same woman. He may have run away as a result. It looks like he is still alive, but if he does know who she is, he's in grave danger."

She stared at me, unblinking.

"Or it may be that the same psycho killed your husband and tried to kill Jimmy too." I handed over my copy of the "Have You Seen our Jimmy" poster.

Lianne took the poster and squinted at it.

"Do you remember seeing him around near the time of the murder?"

She closed her eyes and sat quietly for a minute. "No. I didn't see him then. But I saw him earlier in the day. Does that make sense?"

"Can you remember where?"

She shook her head. "No. I'm having a lot of trouble with concentration lately."

"Takes a while to get over that."

"So you think he may have seen something."

"It's the best theory we have. If you do think of something, could you contact me?"

"For sure. It will feel good to be able to help him."

"Yes." I fished out a Justice for Victims card and scribbled my home and cellphone numbers.

"Call me collect if you think of anything, even something far-fetched."

"I will." She handed me back the poster of Jimmy. "Would you like to see a picture of Greg?"

Oh, shit. "Yes."

She stood up and moved to the sideboard with the most vases and plants. She plucked a picture from behind a cyclamen. "This was my favourite shot. Not as good as the professional ones, but I took it myself, and it was *so* him. This is what I have left."

I reached for the framed photo. I saw a slim, good-looking, relaxed young man, short dark hair, big goofy grin. Casual in his T-shirt and jeans. I felt a triple sense of loss. For Greg Hornyk, killed on his honeymoon. For Jimmy, missing and endangered. For Paul.

Now I had something to think about on the long drive back to Ottawa. No one in the police had mentioned that a woman had run down Greg Hornyk, or that it had seemed deliberate. But then, obviously, I hadn't asked the right questions.

Lianne gave me a hug as I left. "Thanks for not saying stupid things about getting over it."

As I walked toward the Buick, I realized I was wobbling. Meeting Lianne had brought home one thing. I was nowhere near ready to have a life.

Twenty

Somehow, when I got back to the Tim Hortons, Mrs. Parnell had managed to get behind the wheel again. This was good, because all I could do was fight the rush of images. I saw Greg Hornyk crumpled by the hit and run driver, dying in his wife's arms. Sometimes Greg had his own face, and sometimes he had Paul's. I saw a terrified Jimmy Ferguson watching this senseless crime with horror, running. The images whirled through my brain.

"Ms. MacPhee," Mrs. Parnell said, some hours later. "Whatever is bothering you after that visit, perhaps you should talk about it."

"I don't know where to start. Why would a woman mow down a total stranger in daylight?"

"Early evening, Ms. MacPhee."

"Dusk," Alvin said.

"But bright enough to see, not pitch dark. Think about it. The place was full of witnesses."

"Do we know for sure this is what happened?"

"No. I bet the police think she's hysterical."

"Did the police discuss it with you?"

"No. Deveau told me not to bother her."

"But you believe her?"

"Oh, yes. I believe her."

Alvin spoke up from the back seat. "So the cops missed the

boat. That doesn't surprise me."

"Looks like it. Although, in fairness, who would imagine such a thing? Greg and Lianne didn't know anyone. They were travelling alone. So it would have been a random attack. The drunk driver theory has appeal in comparison."

"Maybe they wanted to take the easy way out."

"I am no fan of the police, but if you remember, they put plenty of muscle into trying to find Jimmy."

"Not enough," Alvin said.

"But they did get results. That's why we're on the road."

"That wasn't the police." Alvin wasn't ready to believe the police would do anything right.

Mrs. Parnell said, "Their forces were spread thin, and Ms. Hornyk's belief the attack was deliberate would strike them as the emotional reaction of a bereaved woman. I assume they checked out the witnesses. Then the sensible thing would be to seek a drunk driver."

Alvin said. "Bunch of frigging dolts."

"It won't turn out to have been sensible if the killer strikes again," I said. "I think it's all connected. We should try to figure out how."

"Careful, Ms. MacPhee."

I knew she didn't want me to set Alvin off again. I avoided eye contact with her. "Even since talking to Lianne, I keep having flashes of the accident, even though I didn't witness it. The images keep getting mixed up. My husband Paul and this Greg. But also Greg and Jimmy. It's really disturbing."

"Ms. MacPhee," she said warningly.

"Maybe it would be a good idea to pull over at the next rest stop and have this talk," I said.

"I know what you're thinking, but don't worry," Alvin said. "I'm not going to lose it. I've got a grip on myself, for Jimmy's sake."

"Okay, I think we have been looking at this whole sequence the wrong way. We concluded that Jimmy witnessed the hit and run, and that's why he thinks he has to hide."

I looked at Mrs. P. She shrugged, but I knew I was in for an especially smoky ride. I went on, "I think we got that wrong."

"What drew you to that conclusion?" Mrs. Parnell said.

"Do you mind keeping your eyes on the road?"

Alvin leaned forward from the back seat.

I said, "Lianne showed me some photos. Greg Hornyk was the same physical type as Jimmy. Short, dark hair. Slim. Older, but still young-looking. Walking in the same part of town. At the same time."

Mrs. P. said, "From a moving car, it could be easy to mistake him."

Alvin grabbed the seat back. "You mean the killer believed he was running down Jimmy?"

"But it's *she*, Alvin. The hit and run driver was a woman, remember?"

"Lord thundering Jesus."

"Exactly."

"Were they wearing the same kind of clothes?"

"I don't know," I said. "It didn't dawn on me that the killer might have thought Greg Hornyk was Jimmy until after I left Lianne's place."

"Perhaps you should confirm that, Ms. MacPhee, before we get too carried away with this idea."

"Right," I said, reaching for my cellphone and digging Lianne's telephone number out of my purse. I could feel their eyes on me. "Damn," I said.

"What is it, Ms. MacPhee?"

"No service. Ninety per cent of this country seems to be a goddam dead zone."

"We'll find a place to phone. Roll on, troops."

• • •

Mrs. Parnell pulled in at yet another Tim Hortons not too far from Edmunston. It had everything we needed: coffee, food, bathrooms and a telephone booth.

It was well after midnight, and Lianne didn't bother to keep the surprise out of her voice when she answered.

"Please don't think I'm crazy," I said, "but I need to know what Greg was wearing when he was killed."

"What difference does it make?"

"It's important."

"Okay. He had on jeans, Guess jeans to be exact, and a white T-shirt."

"With a design on it?"

"Plain. He didn't like designs."

"And on his feet? Sandals?"

"Running shoes. Nike with the swoosh. And, of course, he was wearing that stupid baseball cap."

"Colour?"

"Dark green."

"Did he have a backpack?"

"Yes."

"What colour was that?"

"Dark green too."

"He wasn't carrying anything else?"

"The bag from the video store."

"The video store?"

"Is that important? We bought a couple of videos to take home. Souvenirs. Big whoop."

"Right."

"Greg said it would be the most excitement we'd get. Guess he was wrong."

"I'm sorry," I said.

I heard the snuffle on the other end. "I would like to know why you are asking."

"You remember I told you about the missing boy, how I thought he'd been a witness."

"The boy in the poster. Jimmy."

"Now I believe the real target could have been Jimmy."

"But I saw that boy's face. He didn't look anything like Greg. No one could mix them up."

"Jimmy was last seen wearing jeans, his white T-shirt, no logo, a navy baseball cap. He had on new running shoes, not Nike but never mind, and he had a backpack. And he had been to the video store. I think the killer saw Greg from the back and figured she was getting Jimmy."

"You said that boy was like a child. That's monstrous. How could anyone run him down?"

"I don't know. But you've helped us get closer to finding out."

"Thank you."

"What for?"

"For letting me help. I feel so useless."

"Been there," I said. "Felt that."

"Let me know if I can do anything else."

"You bet," I said.

• • •

I rejoined the other two musketeers and their stinky dog in the Buick. Now we had something to keep our minds occupied for the rest of the long trip home. Why would anyone want to kill Jimmy?

Except for our regular stops for gas and Tim Hortons for coffee and Timbits, I didn't notice a damn thing through the last of New Brunswick and Quebec, not even the grinding crawl across the top of Montreal. Mrs. P. used her time at the wheel to relive her adventures as a transport driver during WWII, while Alvin seized the opportunity to bond with Gussie. I tried to sort out the junk in my head.

I found myself wondering who Jimmy really was. Was he an innocent, almost saintly child as his mother believed? Was he the loveable kid brother Alvin feared for? Was he the confused, desperately ill burden the rest of the family chewed their nails over? Maybe he was the thoughtless, untrustworthy liar that Brandon's mother thought she knew. Or the former young offender that Ray Deveau refused to discuss. Had he really stalked and attacked Honey Redmore? Was the truck driver who picked Jimmy up in Sydney and then dropped him in Moncton right when he said Jimmy knew exactly where he was going and why?

· · ·

I never thought I'd be excited to see Hull, but eighteen hours is a long time to spend in an enclosed space with Gussie. Especially when Timbits are involved. All four windows were down by the time we hit Alvin's neighbourhood. We'd been pretty lucky with Stan's Buick, and except for random Benson and Hedges ash, a collection of empty takeout containers, a few chips ground into the carpet, and a residual Gussie aroma that a good deodorizer should take care of, it was like new. I planned to leave the windows open in my garage until Stan got back from Scotland. Two weeks should do the trick. I hadn't yet worked out how to handle the mega-kilometres racked up on the odometer without contravening the Criminal Code.

We pulled onto Alvin's street. Mrs. Parnell and I planned to join Alvin when he went into his apartment. Jimmy or not, we figured Alvin needed someone. And a dog, of course.

One is always prepared for a shock entering Alvin's home, but this was different. Even as the Buick purred towards Alvin's building, it took us a minute to understand the scene.

The building was gone. Nothing remained but a few blackened supports. We slid slowly by with our jaws hanging. The second floor where Alvin's apartment had been had vanished. Maybe I only imagined the few sinister wisps of smoke.

Mrs. P. turned the car around and inched back. Gussie whined to be let out. Mrs. Parnell and Alvin stared across at the smouldering building still surrounded by fluttering yellow tape, indicating a police line.

No more toilet in the living room, no more fridge, no more grandmother's tea set, no more talking art works. Nothing.

"Eight families lived here," Alvin whispered. "Eight families."

"Horrific," Mrs. Parnell said. "And the smell."

"Yuck. That dog is going to blow," I said, opening the door of the Buick. Gussie leaped out, gratefully.

Alvin yelled, "Do you want my dog to get killed too?"

"Don't be silly," I said, as Gussie raced off. Alvin and I were out of the Buick in a second, chasing him or her down the middle of the road. Unsuccessfully. What a great game. Gussie turned around and headed back towards the car with the two of us in hot pursuit. Which is when we ran into the not-so-nice policeman.

Twenty-One

Explain it again, *Madame*," the cop said, his eyes flicking from Alvin's bedraggled ponytail and lived-in leather jacket to Mrs. Parnell, who had emerged from the Buick in a swirl of smoke, and then back to me.

How do you explain anything to do with the Ferguson family? Especially to one of those impossibly goodlooking Hull police officers who are always trying to issue a person speeding tickets for no good reason. I gave it my best shot. I told him about Jimmy. I described our trip from Sydney.

"So you see, officer, we got out to chase the dog."

"And why were you parked outside of this building? Do you know anything about the fire?"

"Once again, my colleague, Alvin Ferguson, lives here. We were delivering him home.

"But the street was blocked off, *Madame*."

"I see that, but he lives here and when a street is blocked it is usually still accessible to residents."

"But he is not a resident, is he, *Madame*? There is nothing to reside in."

"True enough, but we didn't know that when we drove in."

Alvin gripped the officer's arm. "My brother might have been here. Have you heard anything about him?"

"Do you mean your brother might have been responsible for this fire?"

"Of course not, but he may have been hurt in it."

Or worse, I thought, meeting Mrs. Parnell's eye.

"Did he have a history with fires?" The officer showed a limpetlike tendency to stick with one bad idea.

I interrupted. "Was anyone killed, officer? Surely we have the right to know."

"No, everyone escaped."

The three of us exhaled in relief.

"When was the fire?"

I could tell he didn't want to tell me in case I tried to rig myself up with an alibi. I have a problem with Quebec cops. I believe the Code Napoléon goes to their heads. "I can find out easily enough."

"Last night."

"It looks like such a disaster, it's hard to believe that anyone got out."

"Some of the residents woke up, and they managed to save each other. They knocked on all the doors and got everyone out." His tone implied no such thing could happen on the Ontario side.

"I gather you consider this deliberate devastation, young man." Mrs. Parnell lifted her eyebrow to indicate she expected details.

I translated. "You've got police tape all over. Was it arson?"

He raised his shoulders, Frenchly. "You tell me, *Mesdames.*"

• • •

The smelly Buick was a problem but nothing compared to the fact that if Jimmy came looking for Alvin, he'd find a smouldering hole in the ground. Unless he had already been to the apartment, in which case, where was he now?

"What is the best tactic, Ms. MacPhee?"

"We can go home and shower. Alvin needs some rest. He's had a terrible shock."

"I can't rest. How can I rest when I don't know where Jimmy is?"

"You do have to rest, Alvin. This must be terrible for you. Even I can tell that. I'll ask P. J. to find out where the residents are staying. He's been a police reporter, he'll know or he'll know who knows. Then we can find out if anyone saw Jimmy here."

"Hardly anyone speaks English, Camilla. That's why I picked this neighbourhood, I wanted to pick up French."

"Great. And did you pick up French?"

"Some."

"How about you, Mrs. P.?"

"I picked up a bit in France during the war."

"So you can work with Alvin on the interviews. I'll get the names and locations of the people who were here, you check them out and find out if anyone saw Jimmy."

"*Excellent.* It will take me right back," she said.

"*Au contraire*, it better take us forward." I like to have the last word.

• • •

I opened my door to a lonesome cat, a flourishing prickly cactus and 54 voice mail messages evenly divided: my sisters sputtering from Scotland, Leonard Mombourquette sputtering from the Ottawa Police Headquarters and P. J. sputtering about blues bands and times.

Mrs. Parnell's cat had already decided to let bygones be bygones and rubbed against my leg in a forgiving fashion. Of course, she hadn't met Gussie yet. I called Mombourquette back and held the phone away from my ear when he answered.

When I could get in a few words, I said, "No, as a matter of fact, I did not cause havoc for the Cape Breton Regional Police Force. What are you talking about, misrepresenting myself?... Well, maybe he did run away, as you put it, Leonard, but someone was stalking him, and a man who looked like him was murdered in Sydney. We figure mistaken identity...It's not important who 'we' is, Leonard, the important thing is Jimmy is probably in the Ottawa area, and he's in danger... Really? Well I'm glad you're aware of that fact and, no, I don't believe the police are idiots. For one thing, he'll be running out of medication and for another, someone burned down the first place he'd be likely to visit... Alvin's apartment building... No, I'm not making that up... It's in Hull. That's probably why you didn't hear about it... Right to the ground... I don't know if he was there, Leonard, but I'm going to find out. In the meantime, what information have you picked up?... Fine, be like that. The entire Ferguson family is on the way to Ottawa, and you are about to discover it was much easier dealing with me. But hey, your choice... Tell me, did Ray Deveau say I caused any problems in Sydney?... I am not a pain in the butt. Did he say that? Did he?"

I hung up first. That's always my preference.

• • •

P. J. came through in record time. He'd located every single one of Alvin's neighbours. Most of the residents of the burnt-out building were staying with relatives. He'd called with addresses for me before I was able to figure out if Gussie was better housed in Mrs. Parnell's apartment with Lester and

"Maybe they wanted something else," I said.

"What would that be? I don't own anything valuable, except the silver spoons, and my landlord didn't know about them."

"I wasn't thinking of spoons, Alvin. I was thinking of Jimmy's postcards. You kept them in that dresser."

"But if someone was looking for Jimmy's postcards, it would mean he knew about Jimmy, and he'd have to know where I lived."

"He or she would. Yes."

"Why would anybody want them?"

"They might reveal what Jimmy wanted to do in Ottawa."

Alvin stared. "But it would have to be someone we know."

"You got it."

Mrs. Parnell was shocked enough to require another glass of sherry. "Certainly that is most disturbing, Ms. MacPhee."

"No kidding. But back to the situation in the apartment. What did the landlord do when he discovered the robbery?"

"Nothing. I gather he and Jimmy cleaned things up. They couldn't really communicate very well, because of the language thing. The landlord wanted to wait for me to decide whether to call the police or report it for the insurance. He thought it might be an art installation."

"Yes. I could see how he would."

"He didn't even know I was away. But, good news, he took some videos of the damage to help me out."

"Great."

"It would have been great, but the videos were in his apartment. They were lost in the fire."

"So scratch that. Did your landlord know where Jimmy went afterwards?"

"Jimmy was going to spend the night in the apartment and wait for me." Alvin's voice broke. "Jimmy didn't know I had gone to Sydney."

Mrs. Parnell cast a worried look at Alvin, but he seemed to be holding up all right.

"Did any of the residents see Jimmy around the time of the fire?" I said.

"A couple of them. They banged on the doors of all the apartments, and they said they saw Jimmy run out into the street. He had a box with him."

"And then?"

"And then apparently he ran away and fought off a couple of people who tried to help him, including my landlord."

"Do they have any idea where he went?"

"No such luck."

"We'd better whisper this news into the furry grey ear of Leonard Mombourquette."

"And then, we must mobilize our forces to find young Jimmy before it's too late." Mrs. Parnell had another sherry to help her mobilization.

"If only we had the postcards. Jimmy might have mentioned something useful," Alvin said. "Maybe that's what he had in the box."

"No. That's a bit of good news. They've been sitting in my briefcase all along."

"And you never mentioned it?" Alvin's eyes bugged out.

First, I hadn't wanted to trigger one of Alvin's states. Then we were in transit. I was about to explain all this when it crossed my mind that I was the only person who had known where they were.

•   •   •

I only stepped back into my apartment to settle Gussie in and to check he or she couldn't open the bedroom door and eat Mrs. Parnell's cat. Or that Mrs. Parnell's cat couldn't open the door to the living room to slash Gussie's nose.

The phone was ringing when I got there. A few minutes later, despite the fact my sister was on the line from Scotland, I was glad I'd answered. I was a lot further ahead after talking to my father.

"Don't thank me," he said. "Of course, I know them."

"Excellent."

"Lovely people, the Redmores. Protestant, of course."

"Oh, well, Daddy. You can't have everything."

"They came from Ontario originally."

"Oh?"

"The father's dead now, of course."

"And Honey?" I preferred to avoid the route of dead fathers and any pre facto guilt that could induce.

"Of course, she's not dead, Camilla. She's a young woman."

"I meant do you know where she lives?"

"I don't know why you didn't look her up in the phone book. I tried to teach you self-reliance as a child."

"What?"

"Self-reliance. When a person stands on their own feet and does things for themselves rather than asking others to wait on them."

"You mean look her up in the Ottawa phone book?"

"Well, where else would you look her up? They all live in Ottawa now."

"All?"

"The son and the daughter. I believe the mother winters in Florida. Those young people have done very well for themselves. The daughter works on Parliament Hill. Apparently she's on the staff of the Minister of...let me think, what is that now. Well anyway, and the son is in the television business. I am sure the mother is very proud of them both."

"Minister of what?"

"Absolutely no need to yell, Camilla. Did I not teach you manners as a child?"

"Sorry, Daddy. Do you remember what minister she works for?"

"Is that important?"

"Yes."

"No memory of that. I've lost interest in politics. At my age, you know. I thought it was interesting that the son had won several important awards for investigative journalism."

"Really. That's great, Daddy. But you don't remember where Honey works?"

"Who?"

"The daughter."

"No. I don't."

"It's okay. I didn't realize she lived in Ottawa. For some reason I expected Toronto or Vancouver, even Halifax. I'll get her number."

"I will be glad to see you showing some self-reliance."

"Thanks, Daddy."

Before I could hang up, my sister Edwina's voice rang firmly into my ear. "Just once could you speak to Daddy without getting him all upset? We're trying to enjoy our trip to Scotland, you know."

"You and me both," I said.

"Stan wants to know how the car is. I told him it was fine, and to stop being so overprotective."

Time to change that subject. I filled her in on Jimmy's disappearance. I used the arrival of a fleet of Fergusons as a diversion. That brought out the general in her. Jimmy must be found. Alvin must be looked after. The Fergusons must be made comfortable at all costs. Think what they were going through, she said. They couldn't be expected to stay in a hotel. As many as needed to could make themselves comfortable at her place, four bedrooms, would that do it? If not, put the overflow at Alexa's and Donalda's. I thought I heard Alexa squeak in the background, but she can fight her own battles. I had all their keys. I wanted to get the hell off the phone before Stan grabbed the receiver to ask about his baby blue Buick. And now I was running a hotel.

P. J. caught me before I left again. He said, "But you're here in town now. You drove non-stop from Sydney and tonight's performances are going to be amazing and you really wanted to go to this. Remember?"

"That was then, this is now. We have an emergency. We are mobilizing our forces. The whole Ferguson family is coming to town. I have to go back to Mrs. Parnell's and see what the plan is. Don't make such a fuss. It's only a couple of concerts. Try to understand."

Only a couple of concerts? I never thought I'd hear myself say anything so foolish. "And, anyway, how come you never told me Honey Redmore lives here?"

"I didn't? You sure? It doesn't matter, I tracked down her home number for you. Don't ask me how."

"You're a bud, P. J. I wish I could be with you tonight."

•   •   •

Gussie was very excited about strolling down the hall to Mrs. Parnell's apartment. When we got there, Alvin and Mrs. P. were also excited. Alvin had some colour in his cheeks. Mrs. Parnell had a full glass in one hand and a Benson and Hedges in the other. I continued to marvel at how she managed that walker.

They had indeed been busy.

Five hundred copies of the "Have You Seen Our Jimmy" poster were rolling off Mrs. P.'s Hewlett-Packard 3100. I didn't think I'd been gone that long, but apparently Alvin had managed a quick run to the stationery shop to get staple guns and more printer paper, plus a vast map of the National Capital Region and a serious box of coloured pushpins. He busied himself taping the map to Mrs. Parnell's living room wall.

"Great news, Camilla."

"We need it."

"I don't know why it took me so long to figure it out. I've been checking the postcards. Look at this one."

I leaned over. Sure enough, Jimmy had written something about Bluesfest in large cursive letters.

Alvin said, "He might find his way to it. I talked to him about it last year and this year too."

"But I didn't think you were at all interested in it, Alvin."

"I'm not really, but I wanted to give him new information all the time and things to think about. So I mention all the festivals and events. Jimmy loves all kinds of music, so I make a big deal about them. I told him the Matthew Good Band was coming."

"I noticed them on the program. But I wouldn't call them a blues band."

"Whatever. They're playing on Youth Night. Jimmy knew who they were. He mentioned them himself in two different postcards."

"Could he find Bluesfest?"

"You can hear the music straight across the river in Hull. So the thing is, you *should* go to Bluesfest, Camilla, so you can look for him. Violet and I are combing through the rest of the cards one more time, and we'll make up a grid of locations Jimmy talked about and make sure people blanket those areas with the picture of Jimmy. My family will work on that too."

Gussie eyed Lester and Pierre and licked his or her lips. Lester and Pierre shrieked. I thought they had a point.

"Young Ferguson will cover his own neighbourhood, as well as the market area and Elgin Street. You could hand out these posters at this music festival, since you have decided to go, Ms. MacPhee. Thousands of people from all over the region will be flocking to it. All ages and types. Someone may have seen him. I shall help get the family settled when they arrive."

"Jimmy left his money at home. How could he get to Bluesfest?"

"I'm hoping he found my cash in the apartment before it burnt. He would have needed some."

"But you didn't have any money. I went all over your apartment for your ID and didn't see any."

"Use your brain, Camilla. It was hidden."

"How would Jimmy know where to find it?"

"We both use the same hiding place. Above the closet door but on the inside."

"But he couldn't know that."

"Sure he would."

"Do you think he'd steal your money?"

"Not a case of stealing. First of all, he'd need money to survive. Second, he'd borrow it, not steal it. He knows he can pay it back."

"Okay. I guess it's good he has money. What else did he say he wanted to see?"

"Well, Parliament Hill, the Peace Tower, the locks, the canal, the market. Even the Justice for Victims office. All the things I told him about." Alvin's ponytail drooped with misery.

Mrs. Parnell's printer was humming again. "Systematically combing the city, that's the main thing. Starting with the most likely areas," she said.

I said, "Systematic is not my best thing. So I've also decided to pursue the Honey Redmore angle."

"I don't know why you're so hot and bothered about Honey, Camilla. None of us has seen her for years."

"You're probably right, but there's something strange about whatever happened with her. It's bothering me. The incident with the Redmores may not be connected to his disappearance, but it's definitely connected to Jimmy. We're better off knowing how."

Twenty-Two

M s. Redmore, my name is Camilla MacPhee. I'm a lawyer with Justice for Victims. I'm doing a bit of research on a somewhat sensitive issue to do with justice for victims and policy implications," I said. "I am sorry to bother you on the week-end, but I think you'd bring a unique perspective to my research. Could you spare half an hour to discuss it? Over a drink perhaps." I was prepared to argue the case.

"Sure," she said. "That sounds very interesting. When would you like to meet?"

"This afternoon?" Almost too good to be true. "Are you okay meeting on a weekend?"

"Better than during the week. It's hard to get away from the office," she said.

"Great. Five o'clock okay?" Five would give me plenty of time to catch up with P. J. at Bluesfest.

"Five it is."

"How about meeting at the Black Tomato in the market? Is that convenient?"

"Sounds good, it's not far from my place," she said. "See you on the patio if the weather holds."

I stared at the phone. Honey Redmore had sounded quite pleasant, although I wasn't so sure how long that would last.

• • •

I found no one who looked like a Honey Redmore in The Black Tomato. I decided maybe something had come up, and maybe I would be cooling my jets for a while. I headed toward the patio and stuck my head outside.

At a table in the shady corner a pretty, dark-haired woman smiled in my direction. I gave her a nod and kept looking.

"Are you Camilla?" she said.

"Yes. Do I know you?"

"I'm Honey Redmore."

"I don't know why, but for some reason, I expected a tall blonde."

"Sorry to disappoint," she said.

"Who's disappointed? I have issues with tall blondes. Now I'm in a good mood."

"I bet there's a story."

"Yep. But it would take way too long."

"I bet I can swap you tall blonde story for tall blonde story." She had a pale heart-shaped face fringed by very expensive shiny hair the colour of good quality coffee beans. She also had huge almond-shaped eyes with serious eyelashes. She looked great in jeans and a T-shirt.

"Buy you a drink?" I said.

"You bet. Corona and lime," she said, smiling. I figured somewhere an orthodontist had died rich and happy. Honey Redmore didn't have much to worry about in the looks department. I had been prepared not to like her. I decided I might have to work at that. It was too bad, because she wouldn't like me much by the time we were finished our cosy chat.

I stuck with coffee. Didn't want to lose my advantage. I decided to wait until the drinks came before I got to the point. "How did you guess who I was?" I said, stalling for time.

"Recognized you from your picture in the papers."

"Oh."

"You got a lot of media coverage last winter."

This bothered me. "You mean I look like those pictures in the paper? Wet or cold or both?"

"Oh look, here's our drinks. In the nick of time too," she said.

My family had videotaped the television coverage of last year's debacle. "I'm not a vain person, but there are limits," I said, resisting the urge to dash to the ladies and check my reflection.

She seemed to think this was amusing. She had quite the glint in her eye, or maybe that was the late afternoon sun glancing off the Corona bottle.

It was time to get down to brass tacks. "The reason I wanted to talk to you was about a young man named James Ferguson."

She put the Corona bottle down with a thump.

"Surprised?" I said.

"Yes. I thought we'd be talking about youth issues and policy implications."

"This is an issue, but a specific one. You know Jimmy Ferguson?"

"Yes. I know Jimmy."

"Good. I have a few questions to ask about him."

She twisted her hands. "Poor Jimmy."

"What do you mean, poor Jimmy?"

"Well, he *is* missing, isn't he?

"Oh, you know about that?"

"Of course, it was all over the news. Police bulletins."

"Really?" I was surprised. I guess Mombourquette had been on the ball about that, or maybe it was the RCMP. Whatever, it was good news.

"And they haven't found him yet?" Her lower lip quivered.

"No," I said. "Not yet."

"There's no way he's going to be all right on his own."

"You mean because of his medical conditions?"

"I mean, he is too innocent and trusting. It's like someone wearing a KICK ME sign."

"You know him well?"

"I used to. When I lived in Sydney."

"How did you meet him?"

She laughed. "It was Sydney. You don't have to meet people. You automatically know them. Everyone knew Jimmy. He had his little routes, and you would run into him all the time."

"Did you have a good relationship with him?"

"I was always glad to see him. He got so excited about things. If someone had sent him a letter. Or whatever video he was about to watch. Sometimes he was excited about school. I've been worried sick all week."

"All week? When did you find out he was missing?"

She stared at me. "Well, you really couldn't be in town that weekend without knowing something was going on. It was all over the media. The radio was having call-ins about him. The newspaper ran his picture. They ran appeals on television. This is not the sort of thing you get in Sydney."

"Sydney? You were there?"

"Yes."

That was a shock. "But I thought your family lived here."

Another smile. "We are allowed back, you know. My brother wanted to connect with an old school buddy, and my mother and I flew in to meet him. My mother still has friends in Sydney. We hadn't been back since my father died. Then we left town late in the evening of July 1st and headed for Baddeck. We spent a couple of days going around the trail, then we drove to Halifax and flew home."

"Did you see Jimmy on Canada Day?"

She shook her head. "No. We were trying to catch up with people. The whole day was taken up racing from house to house. People can't get enough of you. They want to feed you and make you drink and all that good stuff."

"Tell me about it."

"I figured you'd recognize the behaviour."

"Sure do. Back to Jimmy Ferguson. You're sure you didn't see him?"

"Absolutely. I would have loved to have seen Jimmy. When I heard the news, I racked my brain to see if I could remember spotting him. I wasn't even sure I'd recognize him after all these years. He must be in his twenties now. Even when we were going around the trail, the radio kept broadcasting these appeals for information over and over. It was on every TV station in our accomodation. We were all quite agitated about it, but none of us saw him."

"Did you speak to the police?"

"Why would I speak to the police?" Was it my imagination or was Honey Redmore the slightest bit rattled?

"Didn't mean to upset you."

"I am not upset."

"Sorry." Like hell I was sorry. Something was not right, and I planned to dig and push and unsettle until I found out what it was.

"It's okay. I was disturbed about him being missing, that's all."

"And yet you didn't speak to the police."

She gave me a look that showed the spine she would have needed in that high-powered job with the ear of the Minister of whatever the hell it was.

"I understand there was an incident with you and Jimmy several years ago."

The bottle slipped from her hand and shattered on the cobble-stoned patio. Corona splashed my bare legs. The little slice of lime skittered under the next table. The smell of beer filled the air.

Every table at the patio was filled, and every person there whipped around to stare at me, it seemed. I figured no one could believe that pretty little Honey could have a clumsy accident.

I lifted my intact mug to set the record straight. The server scurried over to get the broken bottle shards out of the way.

"Don't worry about it," she told me. "It happens. Would you like another one?"

It was another five minutes before the patio was swept up and Honey had her replacement Corona. The server gave Honey a sympathetic look. I guess she figured Honey was covering up for klutzy old me, and wasn't that nice of her.

"Sorry about that," Honey said. "And the day was going so well up to that point."

I said, "I'd like to talk about an incident several years ago. Something to do with a situation between Jimmy Ferguson and you." She shook her head. "In your home."

"No."

"Some kind of an attack, I hear."

"There was no attack."

"Assault perhaps."

"No."

"Look, I am a victims' rights advocate. I understand how difficult this would have been for you, particularly since you liked Jimmy. I am sure it was traumatic and upsetting, but the fact is Jimmy does not function intellectually as an adult, so he could easily misread situations. I need you to tell me exactly what happened."

"Nothing happened."

"Please," I said. "Work with me here. Jimmy's out on his own, without his medication, which you will know if you are following the news on him. He's already most likely done himself more physical damage, and he'll be dead soon if we don't find him. If we can understand his behaviour, perhaps it can give us some leads about what he might have done that led to his disappearance."

Her hand was tight around the Corona. "I wish you'd listen to me. No attack. No assault. Jimmy Ferguson never did a thing wrong to me. Never."

"But I've been told the police took Jimmy into the station after something happened between you and him."

"Trust me. Nothing happened. Why are you asking about this?"

"But the police did take Jimmy in for questioning. Not that they will talk to me."

"They took him in for questioning?"

"Yes. For hours. Without legal counsel, I might add."

"I didn't know about any of that."

"Didn't they take a statement from you?"

"No. They didn't."

"But they must have. That doesn't make sense."

"Well, they didn't. And that's because there was nothing to take a statement about. I repeat. No assault and no attempt at assault and nothing that could have been construed as assault or attempted assault. Am I making myself clear?" Her cheeks blazed.

"Really? And yet they took him in for questioning. Why was that?"

"I don't *know*. This is really upsetting," she said. "I thought I'd put it all behind me."

"Put what behind you? You just said nothing happened."

"There were rumours. In a town like Sydney, where it seems there's only one degree of separation from everyone, gossip can spread like a virus."

I rubbed my temples. "Do you mind just telling me what might have kick-started the rumours, and then I could stop upsetting you."

"Okay. The rumour went all over town that Jimmy had attempted to rape me. Some of the rumours went further and said he'd succeeded. Other people said he'd been arrested and charged. I even heard he'd been sent away."

"What was behind the rumours?"

"Nothing Jimmy did, that's for sure. How could he have been arrested for attacking me if no one asked me a thing about it?"

"And the police never talked to you?"

"Please believe me."

"And life went on as before?"

"Not really. I had a lot on my mind at the time. I was very upset when I heard the rumours. Of course, some of them were really nasty."

"Yes?"

She gripped the new Corona bottle. "Some people suggested I might have teased him, then turned on him when he tried to take it further. Others seemed to believe Jimmy was a ticking time bomb."

"Jimmy was damaged by these rumours."

"I'm sure he was. And so was I. Everyone was diminished by them."

"The police never should have taken Jimmy in. Something's

wrong about this story. Something's missing," I said.

"Did you speak to them?"

"I tried, but there are issues with the Young Offenders Act, so they weren't going to talk. Now I see that even hauling him in was a travesty of justice."

"The whole thing was a travesty."

"That doesn't make any sense. But I can see why they'd have to investigate any accusations."

"I hope this is the last time I have to repeat this. I did not make any accusations."

"Even his brother said Jimmy had a crush on you."

"He often sat outside the house and waited for me. I liked him. And I never led him on. And he never did anything that was out of order. He was very sweet."

"And you continued to socialize with him?"

"No, I didn't. My father died quite suddenly, and we moved from Sydney very shortly afterwards. Of course, the rumours were upsetting, so I kept to myself. I didn't really have any occasion to see him after that time." I opened my mouth, but she interrupted me. "But I would have had time for Jimmy. You can believe that."

The funny thing was, I did believe it.

"One more question," I said. "If you didn't complain to the police about Jimmy, who did?"

Honey looked like she'd been smacked with a solid right hook. "If you'll excuse me, I have to go now." She stood up, tossed a twenty onto the table and headed off across the cobbled courtyard at a brisk clip. I figured that was the end of what might have been a beautiful friendship. And I knew I'd hit paydirt.

Twenty-Three

The meeting with Honey Redmore hadn't used up the hour I'd allotted to it, so now I had time on my hands before I was to meet P. J. I had the Buick, and I was close enough to Elgin Street to strafe Mombourquette to see if he'd learned anything about the fire in Alvin's building. You always have to sneak up on Mombourquette, or he disappears into some dark recess with a flash of the tail.

Of course, it was a Saturday in July, and anyone with a life wouldn't have been at their desk. I was betting Mombourquette didn't have a life. Particularly with his partner on three weeks leave.

Amazingly, the cheerful wave to the desk Sergeant outside Criminal Investigations got me a nod. "Must be a party going on."

I couldn't imagine that. I stuck my head into Mombourquette's office, anticipating that he would recoil as usual. I did the recoiling.

"How ya doing?" Ray Deveau said.

My mouth hung open.

Mombourquette said, "Close your mouth, it's bad enough you smell like a brewery."

"Lennie said you might drop in. Good to see you." Deveau got to his feet and shook my hand warmly. Words failed me.

"Gracious as always," Mombourquette said.

"I'm surprised," I managed.

"Looking for Jimmy Ferguson. It's my case. Time's running out. And now we know it's more than a runaway situation."

"Doing his job. Without any help from you," Mombourquette said.

"Actually, Camilla was great. Always one step ahead. Made a big difference to us. Opened up quite a few possibilities."

"Really? How many laws did she break in the process?"

Deveau gave that big, booming laugh. "We lost count, but back home we're not as tight-assed about that stuff as you Mainlanders."

"Yeah, right. What do you want, Camilla? We're about to leave."

Deveau grinned. "We're heading out for a bite to eat, and maybe a drink. You want to join us?"

"She's busy," Mombourquette said.

Lucky me, I found my voice at that point. "Love to paint the town red with you guys, but, sadly, I have a date."

Deveau's grin faded. "That's too bad."

"Especially for the date," Mombourquette said.

"I want to talk about the fire at Alvin's place. Who's the point person on the Ottawa force for the Jimmy Ferguson case? I know it isn't you, Lennie, but I figure you can get the information to the right desk."

"Have you found out something?" Deveau said.

"Why can't you be more like your civilized cousin?" I asked Mombourquette.

Mombourquette flashed his incisors. "Get to the point, if you have one."

"I'd like to know if you've heard from the Hull guy whether that big fire on St. Joseph was arson. That was Alvin's place, and Jimmy Ferguson was in the building the night of the fire."

"You're kidding."

Mombourquette turned a paler shade of grey. "We weren't aware of that. There weren't any fatalities."

"Just lucky, I guess. Have you seen the place? Nothing left. A charred hole in the ground. Neighbours saw Jimmy running away from the building. So, at least, we know he was alive after the fire."

Deveau said, "I knew I could count on you. Do you have names of people who might have seen Jimmy?"

"I gave them to Alvin. He's staying at Mrs. Parnell's." I wrote down the number. "I think they're all French-speaking."

"And me stuck with a name like Deveau. *Quel dommage.* How will I cope?" Always chuckling, that man. I wondered if all that good humour would get on your nerves after a while. "You want to give me your number?" he said. "I might need to check in and share information."

"Sure," I said. I wrote my cell number and home number on the back of my card and handed it to Deveau. I enjoyed the expression on Mombourquette's face. "I'd better get yours too, Ray. I'm heading for Bluesfest tonight. Alvin thinks that might be a place Jimmy would go."

"I'll call you. I'm staying at Lennie's."

I was proud of myself. I didn't say a word about tails, whiskers or holes in the wall.

• • •

Even the threat of rain doesn't dampen the spirits of a crowd at an outdoor festival. Great if you feel like fun. I didn't expect to keep Jimmy out of my mind long enough to enjoy the shows fully. Particularly with P. J.'s mood.

"Okay, you can stop fussing. I'm here now." I followed P. J.

through the special Clubhouse entrance and onto the Bluesfest Grounds.

"I can't get over it. You missed Blue Rodeo last night and all the afternoon stuff today."

"Cool it, P. J. Remember, you never heard of any of these people before. You like alternative rock, remember? If it's too big for the garage, you lose interest."

"Funny, Tiger."

Even with the special entrance, I picked up the buzz from the crowd. Close to twenty thousand people merged and surged on the site, heading to one of the four stages or the Compact Music tent to buy CDs. People bought souvenirs, festival chairs, beer. Music swirled all around, and people moved their bodies to the sound. Even me. I couldn't keep the shoulders or the hips still.

This was the first time I remembered being at a Bluesfest without having to carry a blanket or chair to sit on. Our Clubhouse passes guaranteed chairs that you didn't have to carry, great views of the stages and our own Clubhouse porta-potties.

"Wouldn't want to line up with the hoi-polloi," I said.

"Don't knock it, Tiger. You'll be glad not to be standing downwind of twenty guys after they've had a couple of beer."

He had a point.

We passed the Gospel Tent, which was practically swaying to the beat of the music inside. We zigged and zagged towards the Main Stage, on our way to The Louisiana Stage. Acres of grass were covered with low festival chairs, plastic lawn chairs, folding camp chairs, picnic blankets and canvas armchairs with beer holders. If I took a guess, many of the people would have been pushing fifty, but kids spilled around, lying on blankets, working on puzzles or quiet games.

I sniffed the air and got a whiff of illegal herbs. If Alvin had been there, he would have approved.

I wasn't one hundred per cent sure this was the place to be. After all, Jimmy Ferguson wouldn't be hiding out in one of the Clubhouse tents. And while the views would be great and the sound even better, it lacked the scouting opportunities I'd have in the milling crowd. On the other hand, we would be making tracks between Clubhouse tents if we were going to catch the performances I'd picked for the evening. Dr. John at the Louisiana Stage, followed by John Hammond up the hill at the Acoustic Stage, and the big Main Stage performance, George Thorogood and the Destroyers.

P. J. didn't mind me doing the picking, which was wise on his part, but he wasn't thrilled to have me handing out posters to everyone we passed either.

"I can't believe you put your telephone number on them, Tiger. Why not just write your name on the bathroom wall?"

"Funny."

We settled into chairs in the Clubhouse by the Louisiana Stage, and I made myself comfortable. P. J. got us drinks (I said anything but Corona), then headed off to score some appropriate food. I'd handed out a dozen more "Have You Seen Our Jimmy?" posters to the other people in the Clubhouse by the time he got back with Blackened Chicken Salad for me and BBQ Brisket Po Boy for P. J.. The band was late, as usual. At an outdoor festival with four stages, no one should be too surprised if performances run late, or bands have last minute substitutions. In spite of it, everybody stayed mellow.

P. J. said. "This is about relaxing and cutting loose. Right?"

"I can't really cut loose until we find Jimmy. You'll have to relax for both of us."

"I think I'm going to do that," he said. "Nicholas is taking the weekend off to take care of personal and spiritual matters."

"Nicholas? Excuse me while I throw up," I said. "You're on a first-name basis with Nicholas Southern now?"

"You don't know the guy, and you let your knee-jerk liberal prejudices close your mind."

"That's me, pinko commie all the way. You're letting bad values slip in by osmosis. I thought you guys in the media were supposed to keep an open mind."

"More open than yours. In fairness, the guy has good ideas and values. He made a ton of money by working hard and using his brains, and he's got real leadership qualities. At the same time, he's an urban guy, not a hick. Don't snort, Tiger, it's not flattering."

"Hard work? The guy makes over a hundred million in a dot.comedy, and you call it hard work? Blind luck and a knack for pulling a fast one is more like it."

"Come on. He built a company and sold it. Someone valued it enough to buy it."

"Oh, yeah. I bet they're real happy now. Where is that company? Oh right, in the toilet. But *Nicholas* still has the big bucks. How many shareholders would like to tar and feather him?"

"*Caveat emptor.* You know that, Tiger."

"No kidding. But you know something, P. J. I don't like what's happening to your politics."

"Seriously, you have the same views as Nicholas does on people taking responsibility for their own actions, on criminals serving sentences that match the seriousness of their crimes. A lot of the things you go out on a limb for are the same principles he has."

"Next you'll suggest I could vote for someone like him. Be

careful unless you want your mouth washed out with soap."

"You and whose army? What are you doing?"

"Sorry, I thought I saw someone."

"Jimmy?"

"No such luck. It's someone else from Sydney. And I've got to track him down."

"What? We just settled in. Where you going?"

I didn't hear any more since I had scrambled out of the Clubhouse tent, trying to catch up with a jeaned backside as it vanished into a sea of people.

• • •

"I'm sorry, P. J., but I had no choice."

"You were gone forty-five minutes. You missed Dr. John, who is someone I actually enjoy. Who the hell were you chasing?"

"I was chasing after a certain Reefer Keefer from Sydney. One of the people Jimmy spent time with the afternoon of his disappearance. He's a small-time dope dealer, an ex-con, and I guess some kind of musician. Oh, and a liar. Anyway, he slithered away."

"I gathered by the fact you don't have a prisoner that you didn't catch him. How come you're limping?"

"I tripped over a tent wire. At least I got close enough to see he had a blue wristband, so we know he's got a pass for the whole festival. He's probably planning to be here every day. So that's someone else we're on the lookout for. Besides Jimmy, of course."

"You are."

"Don't tell me you're not keeping an eye out for Jimmy."

"Of course I am, but I don't even know what this other

guy looks like."

"He looks like your Lord and Saviour in faded blue jeans."

"Don't mock me. Come on up to the Acoustic Stage, we might be able to catch the last bit of John Hammond. If we're lucky."

I wondered if Jimmy would be at the Acoustic stage and decided with the complex program and huge crowds it was as likely as anywhere else. You could have a good time anywhere.

"Don't rush, P. J. These things always run late."

•   •   •

By 9:30 I had distributed every one of my Jimmy posters, had had four false spottings of Reefer Keefer and, for reasons that didn't seem sound in retrospect, had consumed two more beer.

P. J. and I settled into the Main Stage Clubhouse to wait for George Thorogood and the Destroyers to make their appearance. P. J. gave me a little pep talk about personal responsibility and the potential effects of societal change on our soggy economy.

I yawned, pointedly.

"Laugh all you want, Tiger, but this guy is on to something. I think he really could end up with a new political party people would be proud to join. He's got a definite appeal to younger voters."

"By any chance, P. J., have aliens eaten your brain?"

"Plus Nicholas Southern has integrity, which is undervalued."

"Certainly undervalued by reporters, which you seem to have forgotten you are."

It takes more than that to get P. J. off a high horse. He droned on for the next little while, even as the band set up on the stage. Once we got comfortable, the effects of several nights of lost sleep, my frantic hour-long race around Lebreton Flats, the two beers and P. J.'s channelling of Nicholas Southern's right wing ravings combined. In the middle of a show with one hell of a decibel level, my head flopped back, and I started to saw logs.

I will regret that to my dying day. There's no such thing as just a concert when you're talking George Thorogood.

•   •   •

This is Ottawa. We have noise bylaws. As Alvin had mentioned earlier, you can hear the Bluesfest clear across the Ottawa River in Hull, so the whole thing shuts down by eleven o'clock. P. J. and I waited until the last possible minute before we joined the throng flowing towards the parking lots. I knew many people would be heading off for after hours concerts, but all I could think of was my bed.

"I can't believe you slept through that," he said, as we wove our way towards my place. "It's not even possible. You're like the date from hell. First you want to fight over politics, then you snore."

I didn't say anything. My eyes were closing again. They popped open when he pulled up in front of my apartment.

I said, "Did you really think this was a date?"

"Like I said, from hell. We have all day tomorrow to try again and see if we get the hang of it."

•   •   •

I stumbled through the foyer to the elevator. On the sixteenth floor I tiptoed past Mrs. Parnell's place. For once, she wasn't in her doorway, and no sliver of light showed under the door. I figured if she had good news or really bad news, she and Alvin would let me know. I wanted to pitch head first into my bed. Therefore, the sight of Vince Ferguson sitting on my sofa at midnight was the emotional equivalent to having a piano dropped on my head.

"What are you doing here?" I said.

"I have to stay somewhere." He was peevish as always. "Not my idea. Violet insisted."

I blurted, "But you're supposed to be at my sister Edwina's."

"Everyone else is at your sister's. I got into town about twenty minutes ago. I drove straight here by myself. I'm beat. Allie is out somewhere, so Violet told me to settle here. Allie's on her sofa tonight. I'll head out tomorrow. It's not like you didn't stay at our place."

I guess Vince had drawn the short straw. Me or the street. He probably had to think long and hard before making his decision.

"Fine. You get the sofa."

By now I'd been jolted wide awake. Worse, I would have to wear bedclothes, something else to be resentful about. As I was about to toss my Bermuda shorts into the hamper, I spotted the splash from Honey's spilled Corona. That reminded me. Maybe it wouldn't be a wasted night after all. Now I had an opportunity to ask a few tough questions of Vincent Ferguson, Ph.D.

Of course, I had to get dressed again first. I knocked on my living room door before coming out and telling a big lie. "I'm glad you're here, Vince. I'm sure Alvin appreciates it too. He's pretty exhausted."

"Aren't you helping him?"

Typical Vince with that accusing tone in his voice. "That's not the point. Naturally, I'm helping him." More than you are, I thought. "Remember, Jimmy might not want to be found."

"I don't see how he can evade you, if you're all really making an effort."

Sure, like he hadn't evaded Vince and his mother in Sydney. A moment of silence fell before I played the offensive. "Speaking of evading. How about you fill me in on one bit of information. You said Jimmy had been questioned in connection with the alleged assault on Honey Redmore." Dead silence. It wasn't like I'd invented the story. "I understand the assault never happened."

"Correct. I told you that."

"But you also told me Jimmy was questioned by the police."

"What does this have to do with anything? We've been all over it. It's old news."

"Bear with me, Vince. So he was questioned."

"Yes. And released."

"Look, we both accept the assault never happened. I spoke to Honey Redmore, and I believe she's as outraged as you are about Jimmy being questioned."

"You spoke to her about it? You've got a lot of nerve."

"I suppose I do, although I don't know why that should bother you. But the fact is the police did interview him."

"Listen, we are going through a very difficult time here since Jimmy disappeared. We don't need you upsetting people even more."

"Guess what. I don't give a shit if people get upset. You are not the only one feeling the impact. Your own brother, Alvin, has been in a state of near collapse, and I don't see anyone in your family giving a thought to how he's doing, although I hear that's nothing new. Mrs. Parnell is seventy-nine years old, and she thinks he's worth dropping everything for. I don't even have time to go in to my office to get my own work done, so stop with the goddam stonewalling and tell me what happened."

I was expecting a slammed door but actually got an answer.

"I told you. They interviewed him about breaking into the Redmore house."

"Not assault."

"I don't think so."

"What exactly did they ask him?"

"I don't know. It was all over by the time I got to the station."

"What did your mother say it was about?"

"She wasn't present during the interview. She arrived when I did."

"What? Was anyone in your family with him?"

"Not until afterwards."

"But the police couldn't interview someone like Jimmy on his own. It's not even legal. He would have needed to have an intervener."

"I think they slipped up because of the seriousness of the events."

I said, "You mean they took it seriously because the complaint came from the Redmores. It's a small place, and the Redmores were well-known and respectable."

"So are the Fergusons. They said they had to check it out. They had no choice."

"Fair enough. I guess they have to follow up on complaints. But what were they checking out? Honey Redmore made it very clear there had been no kind of assault on her person."

"Did she?"

"Yes. She was adamant. You said she claimed Jimmy tried to rape her."

"She did say that."

"But I believed her. She seemed genuinely upset that Jimmy had been questioned."

"Not so sure that's true."

"Knock it off, Vince. What the hell happened?"

"That's all I want to say."

"You'd better say a bit more than that. I want to get to the bottom of this. I can't believe the police didn't give your family some indication of why Jimmy was brought in."

"They did."

"Quit acting like a jerk. Get it over with. What did they say?"

"They said it had been a break and enter with violence, I believe that's the term, and that they had to follow up."

"What violence are we talking about?"

"They said Jimmy had been in the Redmore house during an incident, and the Redmores had chased him away."

"But Honey said there was no break-in."

"I talked to the police. A couple of the officers were classmates of mine. They felt they had no choice, considering what happened."

"But seriously, even if Jimmy had been in the house, was that the end of the world? Did he break a window or something? What did he say to you?"

"He said he didn't do anything."

"My family is from Sydney. I know it's a friendly community. People drop in to each other's homes all the time and are made very welcome. Especially Jimmy. Everyone seemed to like him, and he dropped in to see friends all the time. Is it possible Jimmy believed he could walk into Honey's place because she was his friend?"

Vince hesitated. "That's what I thought. He might have got

the signals wrong. But Jimmy said he never went into the Redmores' place. Jimmy can get the facts wrong, but you can always tell if he is trying to lie. He's the worst liar in the world."

"So it looks like he was never in the house, but the family said he was."

"Yes."

"Why?"

"I don't know. But the Redmores were outraged, and they wanted charges pressed. According to my sources, they were quite insistent."

"I wonder what happened?"

"The worst part of it is what took place afterwards."

"Afterwards?"

"When the fuss started, Mr. Redmore actually chased Jimmy right over to George Street and tried to apprehend him."

"Would Mr. Redmore have known who Jimmy was?"

"Of course."

"Even if Jimmy had broken into the house, why would he chase him? Why wouldn't he call your mother?"

"I don't know. But if he had, maybe he'd be alive today."

"What?"

"He had some kind of cardiac event while he was chasing Jimmy. He collapsed and was taken to hospital. They said it was brought on by the stress of the chase."

"And he died?"

"Shortly after. He never really recovered after the first collapse. He had some emergency surgery. Angioplasty or something, and I guess it was too little too late."

A heart attack triggered by the incident that never happened. No goddam wonder Honey had been upset by my line of questioning.

"Ma tried to talk to the family. We felt awful about whatever Jimmy had done. We wanted them to know he would never mean any harm."

"And what did they say?"

"No one in the family would talk to her. Mrs. Redmore walked right by Ma after the funeral and wouldn't say a word. The brother actually told Ma he thought we should have Jimmy locked up forever."

"My God."

"Ma was in pretty bad shape about that."

"But did Honey herself say anything?"

"We never laid eyes on her. She went back to Halifax right away."

"So was it only Mrs. Redmore who was upset?"

"And the brother."

"Something pretty weird about the whole thing. I can't quite put my finger on it, but it's got to have some connection."

"There's no connection. It's history. We'd like to forget the whole thing."

"Honey didn't say anything about blaming your family. I got the impression she was quite fond of Jimmy."

"Try to do something useful."

"I'll do whatever I have to. I want to get Jimmy back, safely, and to help Alvin recover."

"Alvin? Jimmy's the one we need to think about. We can't let Alvin's bid for attention take away from the search."

"You listen to me. Alvin has done more than the rest of you put together. If you spent a bit more time being family to him instead of always trying to cover your asses, maybe he wouldn't need attention."

"Don't tell me how to deal with my family."

Tough talk, considering whose sofa his butt was parked on.

"Here's another news update. I will tell you anything I want and I will ask any question I want until we get to the bottom of what happened to Jimmy. Try stonewalling me again and watch the fireworks."

It seemed as good a time as any to march back to my bedroom. Gussie made an attempt to come with me, which was not such a good thing. Gussie scratched and whined until I relented and opened the door. "You can't stand him either," I said.

Mrs. Parnell's cat would have to cope.

Twenty-Four

In the morning Vince was gone, leaving sheets neatly folded on the sofa. Mrs. Parnell told me Alvin had left already, after five hours sleep. He was scouring the city for Jimmy with the rest of his family. I turned down the suggested eye-opener and took Gussie for a constitutional which put a whole new spin on why I am not a dog owner. On the upside, the walk was long enough to help me plan the day. The main plan was to hook up with P. J. and head to Bluesfest with another pile of posters. I'd start by talking to Security, then work the grounds using my head, not just my ears.

Mrs. Parnell was settled in my living room when Gussie and I got back. Apparently, I'm the only person who can't walk through walls. She had brought a thermos of coffee, so that made everything all right. I filled her in on what I'd learned about the Redmores.

"Something rotten somewhere," she said. "So you'll be interrogating this Redmore woman again today about the father?"

"I left her three messages this morning. I wish she'd return my calls."

"Perhaps I can track her down."

"I've got a lot to do. And this is a big day and night at Bluesfest. After tonight, no events are scheduled until Matthew Good plays for youth night on Wednesday. We need to find Jimmy well before that. If we're going to locate Jimmy at Bluesfest, it has to be today," I said. "If you can find out where Honey Redmore works, I'll head up to her office on Monday. My father said she's on staff in some Minister's office."

"I would imagine she is trying to avoid you."

"Maybe, but so what? We don't have forever to figure out what's going on here. And I think that as a taxpayer, I should have access to those government buildings."

"Give me a bit of time. I may be an old soldier, but I want to make a contribution."

"That's great, Mrs. P. You keep at that. Pretty soon, I want to make a quick trip over to Gadzooks to make sure Alvin hasn't lost his new job."

"Excellent idea, Ms. MacPhee. Young Ferguson has already paid a big price here. Perhaps it's survivor guilt. I've seen that often enough in my career. The boys who came back and lived out their lives felt they didn't deserve to live after their comrades had fallen."

"I can understand that. But Alvin wasn't in a war."

"These things don't come from nowhere. There is a lot we don't know. But remember from what Donald Donnie and Loretta were saying, he was devastated by Jimmy's accident. Devastated but unharmed."

"I believe you. And I'd like to know more about the boys they talked about. The Fergusons never even mentioned them. Let's keep digging, Mrs. P."

• • •

Deveau called me before I called him. Cross off another thing on the list.

"Reefer Keefer," I said, before he got in his two cents worth.

"What?"

"Reefer Keefer."

"Most people say hello, but suit yourself." I could almost hear his grin.

"Ha ha. This is serious. I saw Reefer yesterday at Bluesfest."

"Here? Really? That's amazing."

"I'll keep an eye out for him again today. I'll be checking out the grounds."

"Maybe I should come along with you."

"Sorry, my date hates it when I detect."

There was that chuckle. "A drink then."

"Sobriety calls," I said.

"But few are chosen. By the way, Lennie's had contact with the Hull side. Looks like they're pretty sure the fire at Alvin's place was arson."

I took a deep breath.

"I'll keep you posted," he said.

"Thanks, Ray. That's gotta be connected with Jimmy."

"Sure looks like it."

"Something to think about."

"See you later," Deveau said.

I hope so, I thought. I really hope so.

•   •   •

When we hit the Bluesfest site along with the surging Sunday crowds, P. J. was back to his normal mellow self. Even though I made it clear I was going to talk to Security before we did anything else.

"I should have done this yesterday."

"No problem," he said. "I filed my story by deadline, so I get to take the day off like a normal human being. I'm off the hook until tomorrow."

"The Great Right Hope in church all day, is he?"

"Don't be like that. He's in Kingston, meeting with some potential supporters who aren't ready to show their colours, so the event's not open to the public. Tomorrow I'll cover his luncheon speech in Montreal. Quebec's been a hard sell. Then he'll be getting mentally prepared for the big interview on *Face Off* on Tuesday."

"Prepared how? Getting a complete personality transplant?"

"Come on. I keep telling you, underneath, he's a decent guy."

"I liked it better when you were young and cynical. Here's the deal. No politics today. None."

P. J. sulked after that, but I paid no attention, because I bumped into at least a dozen people I'd known from school or university. All of the women looked at P. J. speculatively. Who could blame them? He was pretty cute with that curly red hair and the little gap between his front teeth, which you could see when he stopped pouting. Too bad he was such a pain in the ass about this political thing.

The last classmate, whose name escaped me, yanked my arm and pulled me over to give me a garlicky whisper. "He's so cute. But does his mother know he's out?"

"Funny." P. J. had turned thirty on his last birthday. Frankly, I didn't think five years was such a big deal.

"You go, girl," she said. "How *old* is he?"

"Nineteen. But he's had a hard life."

I kept an eagle eye out for Reefer Keefer all the way to the security HQ. No joy.

"Who do you want to hear after this?" P. J. said.

"It doesn't really matter to me. The important thing is to

make the rounds and hand out these posters of Jimmy."

"How about catching Mumbo Jumbo Voodoo Combo first? Then we can work our way around from stage to stage."

"Whatever." The weather was clearing, and it was Sunday, so probably we'd be dealing with close to thirty thousand people. We'd be busy with the posters no matter where we were.

You could spot the security guys a mile off: black baseball caps, clean cut, stoic. We tracked down a honcho not far from the Main Stage. I passed over the picture of Jimmy and ran through the background on him.

"Yeah. Right. The kid from Nova Scotia. We're up to speed on that. We got a hundred of our people on the lookout. Not that they haven't got plenty to do, but the guys will really want to help with this. And we got a couple thousand volunteers. They've been informed about him too."

"Have the police been here already?"

"Cop from down East. Like I said, we're up to speed."

"That's good. So while you're on it, do you mind keeping an eye out for a guy that looks like Jesus Christ?"

"The Christ guy. Yeah. We're already on that too."

As we left P. J. said, "Maybe you should work on your people skills."

"I'm on edge. This kid could be dying. Will die. If Jimmy's around Bluesfest, I've got to make my time pay off."

"What are you going to do if you don't find him today?"

"Tomorrow I'll track Honey Redmore down at the office, because she's not answering my calls. By the way, do you know where she works?"

"Forget it. You'll never get past security. Anyway, the best way to catch her is after work hours. Try six thirty or seven, D'Arcy McGee's pub on Sparks. She drops in a couple of evenings a week."

"That's great, I've got plenty to do tomorrow during the day."

"No guarantees she'll show, but anyway, you could try talking to her brother."

"Why? Do you know her brother?"

"You mean, you don't?"

"Knock it *off*, P. J."

"He's the rising star. Television. *Face Off*. Come on, Tiger. Get with the program."

"I don't watch TV, you know that. I've never seen *Face Off*."

"It's got serious audience ratings and a lot of clout. Remember, I just told you Nick is going to be interviewed by Redmore on Tuesday. It'll be like the dance of death. Redmore is a real hardass when it comes to anything right of Mahatma Gandhi. You want holier than thou, Will Redmore's your man."

"I like him already."

"Watch it once and see if you still agree. Redmore's a shark. Big good-looking guy, mean as hell. Limousine liberal."

"You're worried about your pet politician. Maybe if his feelings get hurt, he won't have the moral strength to put the screws to welfare moms and street kids."

"I won't dignify that with a response, Tiger. But personally, I'd like the interview to be fair. Redmore would shred his mother on camera if it would boost ratings. And the tactic works."

"Good fodder for you as a reporter, though. Admit it."

P. J. chose to keep silent rather than incriminate himself. That was okay, I had plenty to listen to. My feet were tapping.

• • •

By Sunday evening, it felt like we'd combed every inch of the grassy commons, traversing the nearly ten acres a half-dozen times and back to P. J.'s car three times for posters.

Criss-crossing Bluesfest means pushing against crowds, tripping over blankets, squeezing in between lawn chairs, stretching on tiptoes to see over heads. I checked all the lines outside the johns. If Jimmy was around, sooner or later, he'd have to pee.

I got a few remarks the third time I walked up and down the rows.

"As dates go," P. J. said, "this must be among the more unusual."

"Who's that guy coming out of the john at the end of the line?" I said. "Never mind, false alarm."

Every second male at Bluesfest had on a T-shirt and jeans and a high percentage of them had short, dark hair. Ditto baseball caps. I must have tapped hundreds of men on the shoulder only to say, sorry, my mistake, I thought you were someone else.

I had sore feet, beer breath and a sunburnt nose. P. J. looked like a tomato with hair.

"Give up, it's getting dark," he said. "Let's get a seat in the Clubhouse for Jonny Lang."

"First I want to check the Compact Music tent. I should have given those guys some posters. Maybe they saw him."

"I thought he didn't have any money."

"Alvin thinks he might. You know what, you should do something about that burn. Does it hurt?"

"Na."

"Liar. You better get something for it."

"Thanks, Mom."

"You know what, after this, I thought of something. I saw a

picture of Jimmy on a camping trip. Don't they have a campground right over the hill? I never even thought about it. I was concentrating on other stuff. Let's check it out tonight, if you're up to it. "

"I guess I'll look like an idiot tomorrow. With a flame-red nose."

I barely managed not to say that he already looked like an idiot. That was before he turned green. "You okay, P. J.?"

"No."

"What's wrong?"

"Oysters. I knew I shouldn't have had oysters," he said and dashed back to the nearest Clubhouse can.

Twenty-Five

I jumped at the sexy whisper in my ear. The CDs I was holding went flying. I grabbed at them before they fell onto the grass and got trampled.

"Sorry," Ray Deveau chuckled, "I guess I thought you were fearless."

"Oh, I'm getting my heart rate up."

"Thought you had a date."

"Gone home. Apparently I make him sick." I handed over the money for three CDs, Jonny Lang, John Hammond and Dr. John. Why not? Sooner or later, life might be normal, and I'd want to hear what I'd missed.

"I see a pattern here," Deveau said. "So, do you want company?"

"Sure. Big show's about to start. Almost everyone will be at the Main Stage. Maybe between us, we'll see Jimmy in the crowd. Later, I'll check the campgrounds over the hill."

"Save your time. We checked it out today. No sign of him. Left instructions and the photo at the check-in too. But we can try again if you want. Better safe than sorry."

"No point. We're running out of time, and we have plenty to do without going over old ground."

"What do you have in mind?" I was starting to like that chuckle.

We hit every one of the late night clubs. It must have been after two by the time we'd burned through Café Toulouse, T-Rex, The Bytown, Labatt 7 Bar Blues and finally The Rainbow. I was having trouble sorting out who was playing where and when. Good thing Deveau was the designated driver. After our second stop, I'd made the switch from suds to Perrier, or he'd have been the designated thinker too.

I learned a bit as we went. His wife had died of leukemia three years earlier, he was proud of his daughters aged eleven and thirteen and if they hadn't been at music camp, he wouldn't have been in Ottawa. I also learned that he was using his own time to follow up on Jimmy Ferguson.

To my surprise, I found myself hoping he didn't have a girlfriend. We handed out posters wherever we went. The late night crowd didn't seem too troubled by the idea of the missing kid. Until we passed the poster to a couple of denim-clad girls at The Rainbow.

The short brunette squinted at Jimmy's image. "Hey look, isn't he the guy we saw on Dalhousie yesterday?"

Her friend nodded. "Yeah. That's him. But I think it was on George near the flower stalls."

"Or York maybe."

"Let's have your names and phone numbers," Deveau said. Must have been very coplike, because the two of them melted through the crowd like ice on a summer sidewalk. "Sorry," he said.

"Why didn't you yell 'I'm a cop. Everyone put your hands up. It's time for the strip search?'" I said.

Naturally he chuckled.

"At least I know where to head tomorrow," I said.

"Got news for you. It's tomorrow now."

•   •   •

Wakey wakey came way too early. I staggered to the bathroom, dislodging Gussie and Mrs. Parnell's cat. I tried to remember exactly what had happened when Ray Deveau had brought me home. The throb in my temples got in the way of my brain activity.

The latter part of the night was less than a blur. When had I said goodnight? Had we said goodnight?

I remembered sitting on the sofa with Gussie emitting something stunningly noxious, and I remembered Deveau suggesting I stay away from Cajun food. His chuckle was the last thing I remembered. Then through the fog, a dim recollection of a chaste goodbye at my door. That was good news. After five years of celibacy, I would have hated to fall off the wagon and not remember it.

It's a good thing Mrs. Parnell doesn't knock. My head might have imploded.

"Greetings, Ms. MacPhee. Found time for a bit of R and R last night, I see."

"Relentless and research."

"Excellent. Although, I realize girls will be girls. I was young myself once."

I let it drop. "Can you get hold of Father Blaise today? And I'll need the address of every hostel or shelter that might take in a kid like Jimmy. Concentrate on the market area. A couple of young women last night seemed to recognize him from that part of town."

"Consider it done, Ms. MacPhee. I believe it was Wellington who said, 'Endeavour to find out what you don't know by

254

what you do'."

"Before my time, Mrs. P." I carefully closed the bathroom door and groped for the Tylenol.

It was ten-thirty before I turned on the radio to catch the news.

Top story: The body of an unidentified male had been found on a deserted downtown side street. Police were treating it as a hit and run.

•   •   •

Mombourquette did not answer his phone. Deveau had not called yet. As far as I knew, P. J. was covering the rubber chicken schtick in Montreal. He didn't answer his phone either or return sympathetic messages. I called everyone I could who might know about the body. I had a good plan to bullshit my way into the morgue when the phone rang.

Deveau. Not chuckling. "Have you heard?"

"Jimmy?" I felt a wave of grief for a boy I'd never got to meet.

"No, thank God."

I collapsed onto the sofa, throat aching.

"But you can stop looking for Reefer Keefer."

•   •   •

However miserable I felt crawling through the Byward Market in the thirty degree Celsius heat working my way through Mrs. P.'s list, I figured P. J. might have been worse off if he'd trekked off to Montreal to observe Nicholas Southern address disaffected conservatives who would be willing to kick in two hundred and fifty smackers a plate for the privilege of hearing him rant. I hoped the oysters were long gone. Wherever and whatever, he didn't answer his cellphone, and he still wasn't returning his calls.

Of course, when you start combing through the shelters, it gives you a bit of perspective. So my Monday was wasted with no sign of Jimmy anyway. I had a headache. Big frigging deal. I had a home, food, relatives who cared enough to badger me. And I had Mrs. Parnell's cat and Gussie to keep me company.

I was shocked to learn how many kids were on the street. Sometimes fleeing savage homes. Sometimes drawn by drugs and bad companions. By the time I'd checked the Youth Shelter, the Mission, the Shepherds of Good Hope and the Food Bank, I was feeling pulled down by the sheer weight of human misery. If I'd run into Mr. Pull Up Your Socks Southern, I would have pulled up his frigging socks all right. Through his ears.

No one remembered seeing Jimmy. I figured that might be good news, but the people I talked to figured otherwise.

The last worker said, "Good-looking kid, he wouldn't last long on the stroll here. Hope you find him soon."

One more reason to worry.

• • •

It was well after six when I slid into the cool confines of D'Arcy McGee's pub on Sparks Street. If something political was happening in a watering hole in Ottawa, it would be happening there. I had to admire the irony that the only sitting Canadian politician to be assassinated was celebrated with a trendy drinking spot.

Honey Redmore, looking gorgeous, was locked in an intense discussion with a tall, good-looking man. He seemed familiar, but I couldn't place him. Since his suit must have set him back over a thousand, I took him for one of the seasoned lobbyists who inhabited the place. What was he promoting? Booze? Cigarettes? Chemicals? I guess we've all got to make a living, but some of us draw the line.

I waited until she headed for the ladies room. No place like the ladies room if you burst into tears. "Hi," I said, following her through the door, "fancy meeting you here."

"Oh," she said, like she'd seen something with six legs sashay across her tablecloth.

"Crazy weather," I said.

"Sure is." She headed for the stall.

"That Corona. They say you don't buy it, you only rent it."

"Excuse me." She reached for the door and probably thought that would end our conversation. She thought wrong.

"I have a question. I can wait if you'd like."

Her nostrils flared. A woman of spirit, the lovely Honey Redmore. "Ask your question."

"It has to do with Jimmy Ferguson."

"Stop harassing me. Jimmy did nothing. Nor did I."

"You didn't tell me your family called the police. You didn't tell me your father died chasing Jimmy down the street."

She collapsed against the door frame.

"It's tough, but the sooner you level with me, the sooner I'll go away," I said positively. "Your family insisted on having Jimmy Ferguson charged with breaking and entering. They talked about violence."

"If that's true, which I sincerely doubt, then my family was mistaken."

"The Fergusons, an admittedly biased source, claim the police questioned Jimmy for hours, without a relative present, because of pressure."

The pretty chin was wobbling now.

"If Jimmy did nothing, why would your father chase him? If he believed Jimmy assaulted you, why wouldn't he simply call the Fergusons? They'd have been over in a shot."

She stared at the floor and swallowed.

"I realize we're talking about your father's death, but now we are dealing with another potential tragedy. Jimmy Ferguson will be dead soon. You need to tell me: Why did your father chase Jimmy?"

"I don't know," she said.

"You're sticking to that story? Then you haven't seen the end of me."

That must have been a tough prospect, because she elbowed me in the ribs and ducked out the door.

"Look," I said when I had cornered her again. "Please tell me what you suspect. Something happened, and I know it's relevant. Make it easy on yourself."

I turned as the big guy in the million dollar suit with matching face joined us. The face was not smiling.

"Something wrong here?"

"It's okay."

"You look upset, Hon."

"I'm fine."

"Everything's hunky dory," I said.

"You sure you're okay?" I didn't like the look he gave me.

"We're fine. We'd like a little privacy here," I said.

"No, we wouldn't," Honey said.

"I only need a minute."

"I do not want to talk to you," Honey said.

Loud enough, I thought. A few heads turned our way. The big guy moved off. I decided to press my advantage. "A misunderstanding with tragic consequences, but what triggered it? Which reminds me, are you aware that Reefer Keefer died last night?"

She looked startled. "That's dreadful. But I don't see a connection."

"Oh, there's a connection, and I'll find out what it is."

I felt a tap on my shoulder and whipped around to tell the million-dollar man to go to hell. I found myself nose to chest with someone who might have been a bouncer.

"I've been thrown out of far better places than this," I said as he frog-marched me through the door and deposited me on Sparks Street. The D'Arcy McGee is such a great pub. It was too bad I wouldn't be allowed back.

• • •

"Some would say it serves you right, Ms. MacPhee."

"Not to my face they'd better not."

"Point taken."

"I don't really have much choice."

"One does what one must." She followed that up with a solid serving of Harvey's Bristol Cream in my glass.

"Exactly. And it's impossible to dig around the death of a parent without causing some discomfort."

"Are you certain, Ms. MacPhee, there's something to dig for? Surely, the sudden loss of a father would cause anyone to choke up."

"Possibly. But she didn't really choke up originally. She was very open. She told me Jimmy Ferguson had not assaulted her. She was quite emphatic. So what did he do? Did one of his friends do something? Maybe Jimmy was in the wrong place at the wrong time."

"So you are asking yourself if anything really happened."

"Something happened all right. I figure Honey Redmore is protecting someone."

"From you?"

"I don't know."

"Protecting Jimmy perhaps."

"I believe she *wants* to protect Jimmy from a false accusation. But that doesn't explain it. The police didn't press charges against Jimmy. That can only mean they had no evidence."

"I suppose that's fair enough," Mrs. Parnell said.

"I'd agree with you as a rule. It's intended to protect the young person, but here it's doing anything but."

"I am surprised, Ms. MacPhee, that Sergeant Deveau hasn't spilled the beans. Considering his late night visit."

Does the woman miss nothing? "He's doing the proper thing, legally and ethically. People get slapped with charges if they violate the confidentiality provision. Rightly so. But it's goddam inconvenient right now."

"Not the sort of thing that holds you back as a rule, is it?"

"Of course, it is. I am very law-abiding. Don't bother to snort like that, Mrs. P. Anyway, there has to be something else at work in that weird story. Ask yourself, if your father died because of something someone did, why would you want to protect that person?"

"I take your point," Mrs. Parnell said.

"So who would you want to protect?"

"You mentioned Jimmy's friends."

"Right. Let's look at them. Brandon couldn't get around in his wheelchair, and Thomas is so fragile, I can't imagine it."

"What about Reefer Keefer?"

"Better. I don't think Honey would go out on a limb to protect him. She didn't react much when I told her he was dead. But she certainly got upset about Jimmy."

"Speaks well of her."

"Let's think about it. Who in your experience would someone want to protect?"

"In my experience? A colleague or a superior officer," Mrs. Parnell said.

I sat up straight. "You know something? I think that's it."

"A superior officer? But Honey was a civilian. Or have I missed something?"

"We all have superiors. Even civilians. Even adolescents. Teachers. Coaches."

"Hmm. Let's follow up. And if something happened with someone like that, it might explain why the family decided to move so quickly after the father's death. To get her away from whomever."

"Yep. Makes sense. There would have been rumours. Maybe I can get one of the Ferguson girls to find out what's what. Vince is worse than useless."

"Let me call Loretta and Donald Donnie," Mrs. P. said. "I'll check with the Ferguson girls too, unless you want to. They'll probably be arriving at your sister's soon. Young Ferguson tells me they had quite a full day combing the city."

On my way out the door, I said, "No Fergusons for me tonight. I feel like death, and I haven't fed your cat."

"Or walked your dog," she said.

"Wait a minute. I thought of something."

"What is it, Ms. MacPhee?"

"It's another reason to talk to Father Blaise. He's done a lot of work with the youth club. Even though the Redmores aren't Catholic, he probably knew all these kids."

Mrs. Parnell's forehead creased. "He hasn't returned any of the messages I left at St. Paul's."

I checked my watch. "Too late tonight, but I'll flush him out tomorrow."

I walked Gussie before I took my third shower of the day. I opened a tin of Miss Meow for Mrs. Parnell's cat. I found some leftovers for my dinner. Gussie looked so pathetic I put the dish on the floor. I scrounged some peanut butter and crackers. The three of us shared a companionable meal while my hair dried.

Twenty-Six

At ten o'clock that evening, Ray Deveau showed up looking beat, but wearing clean chinos and a pale blue short-sleeved shirt, pressed. He looked freshly showered and shaved. I noticed a hint of lime aftershave. It offset the dark smudges under his eyes.

Over a cold beer on my sixteenth floor balcony, watching the Ottawa river glitter in the moonlight, I learned more about Reefer Keefer's fate.

"Hit and run again," Deveau said. "Ottawa guys are keeping the details quiet."

"Does it sound like the one in Sydney?"

"Yup. They've found the car. Stolen shortly before."

"That tells us something."

"What?"

"First of all, logic says it's the same killer."

"Probably right."

"It follows that the same person was in Sydney on July 1st and in Ottawa last night. Correct?"

"Narrows it down to a hell of a lot of people. Dozens at least."

"I doubt dozens of people had some close connection with everyone in this case."

"That's true. There's me, of course."

"Cute. What kind of person would use a car as a weapon? A

career criminal? A hit person?"

Deveau narrowed his eyes. "A coward. A bully."

"That's what I think. Sorry, but it seems to leave you out of the equation."

"What a relief. By the way, did I tell you I just learned they found the car that killed Greg Hornyk?"

"Really? Whose car?"

"Belonged to another tourist. Stolen downtown. They found it abandoned in the airport parking lot. No prints, no nothing. They're looking for anyone who saw it dropped off. So far, no luck."

"No surprise," I said. "But on the same topic, you must have had a lot of dealings with Reefer over the years."

"Yeah. He was one of life's great losers. But he didn't deserve to die like that. It shook me up to identify the body. I never get used to the morgue."

I figured that was a good thing. Somehow, during our conversation our resin chairs seemed to have drifted closer together. Our knees were now touching, and neither of us jumped away. I tried not to let that get in my way.

"One question, Ray. Bear with me. It's relevant."

"Ask away."

"The Redmores. Now when Jimmy was accused of whatever it was he was accused of that you can't talk about because of the YOA …"

"Take a breath, Camilla."

"Right. Since the father didn't accuse Jimmy, because he was unconscious, and Honey didn't accuse him, I'd like to know who made the accusations to the police. Was it Will Redmore? And if so, what did he say?"

"You know I can't say what he said."

"Yeah, yeah. The accusation against a youth. But I'm not

going there. Since the accusation seemed to be found to be totally ungrounded, not that anyone ever made that clear to the Fergusons, it seems to me I can inquire about who made it, since it wasn't one of the two alleged victims."

"It seems to me you can't."

"All I want to know is how the brother presented it to you? Was he outraged?"

"Very tricky. I admire your spirit."

"You do not."

"But it won't get you anywhere."

"I'm just trying to get a fix on how the brother could have made this mistake."

"Forget it."

"Oh, that reminds me, was Will Redmore ever in trouble for bullying as a kid?"

The look on his face was all the answer I needed, even though he tried to cover it. He tapped my nose playfully. "What part of the Young Offenders Act did you skip in law school, Camilla?"

"Thanks, Ray. I owe you big-time."

"Well, I can think of ways to repay me."

Chuckle, chuckle.

• • •

P. J. called after Deveau left. I filled him in on my day touring the shelters, the update on Reefer Keefer, my adventure at D'Arcy McGee's and my twin theories about Honey protecting someone and Will being a bully. I even complained about the elusiveness of Father Blaise and the presence of Vince Ferguson. I expressed more sympathy for his tummy troubles.

I may have forgotten to mention Deveau's visit.

• • •

Mrs. Parnell stuck her head out of her door as Gussie and I emerged from the elevator the next morning.

"No joy," she said. "Donald Donnie and Loretta came up empty. Not a single rumour about Honey Redmore and a teacher or a coach. My contact made a few calls. Honey was on a few school teams but wasn't any kind of serious sporting person. No boyfriend who could have triggered the incident. I think we might have hit a brick wall with this line of investigation."

"Good news on that front," I said. "We've been looking at the wrong wall."

"Nice oblique statement, Ms. MacPhee. Do come in and elucidate."

"No time. But I believe the connection could be Honey. This was her first trip back to Sydney since shortly after her father died. Vince told me that Mr. Redmore's death was triggered by chasing Jimmy Ferguson from the house."

"That is horrible, Ms. MacPhee."

"Yes, but I suspect the truth is a bit different."

"Let us hope so."

"Jimmy might still have been upset if he spotted Honey in Sydney, even though she may not have seen him. Plus there's something fishy about that brother. I'll be pushing a bit there."

"Ah, so Jimmy may have remembered that terrible day he was chased and arrested. Some stimulus triggered his panic, as Jimmy's disappearance triggered it in young Ferguson. I agree. The stimulus could easily have been catching sight of Honey. Most likely, that is why he is on the run."

"Right, up to a point, Mrs. P. For sure, Jimmy could have

266

panicked if he'd seen Honey. Maybe he would have been afraid of the brother coming after him. Maybe he worried about being hauled to the copshop again. And who knows what nasty things he heard after Honey's father died. If we didn't have these two other deaths, I'd be happy to put it down to that. The Fergusons could go on the air and tell Jimmy he won't be punished in any way. But we do have two hit and runs. Cops think it's the same killer. And if you ask me, Honey doesn't wish Jimmy any harm, but she's protecting someone."

"Interesting deductions, Ms. MacPhee."

"Something's going on. I could see it in her body language. There's some secret she doesn't want to get out. I figure Honey thinks the stakes are pretty damned high."

"Ms. MacPhee, are you suggesting some kind of abuse?"

"It wouldn't be the first time something like that has happened."

"Does anyone in the family seem the type?" Mrs. Parnell exhaled speculatively.

"I know from working at Justice for Victims that there's no obvious type."

"And you believe she's keeping some secret."

"And maybe worse than that. Maybe she's protecting a murderer. Let's not forget that the hit and run victim, Greg Hornyk, looked like Jimmy from a distance."

"So we are dealing with someone who means business."

"You bet. A person who has killed, perhaps to cover up that very secret. My point is, another member of the family might have spotted Jimmy on Canada Day and decided to take revenge for the father's death. Perhaps it was the brother, still angry after all these years. Maybe the sight of Jimmy triggered his rage."

"For one thing, I thought Honey Redmore assured you her

family knew Jimmy was innocent. For another, I understand our hit and run driver is a woman," Mrs. Parnell said.

"Okay, there are still a few details to work out. But we do know Mrs. Redmore blamed Mrs. Ferguson after the father died. I'd like to talk to Honey and get some more answers."

"Why don't you?"

"Something tells me I won't be able to reach her for the rest of my life. Of course, I'm not the only bear in these woods."

"I don't know her, so I am at a disadvantage."

"I wasn't thinking of you."

"And poor young Ferguson is liable to go off the deep end."

"You're right. I wasn't thinking about him, either. Stay tuned, Mrs. P."

•   •   •

"You have to do it, Vince."

"She won't even remember me."

I didn't dignify that with an answer. Vince Ferguson might be a pain in the butt, but he was a dark, brooding handsome pain, and he had played sports. He wouldn't have been that much older than Honey. The chances were very good that Honey would remember him all right.

"Sound her out about the brother," I said.

"Her brother? Will?"

"Yeah. What do you know about him?"

"He was hot stuff around town for a long time, and then he grew up and went away, and now he's a big deal in Ottawa, last I heard."

"Some kind of current affairs guru, I guess. Television," I said.

"Figures. But I remember him thinking he was God's gift

and throwing his weight around a bit when he was a teenager."

"Right."

"He was one of those assholes you hope will get what's coming to them."

"Maybe he did."

"Nope. I just told you his career's in high gear."

"And he's older than Honey?"

"He must be about thirty."

"Was he living in Sydney during this so-called incident with Jimmy and Honey?"

"No. He would have been gone a long time. He left when he started university. He would have been out working by the time of the alleged assault. Honey was home from Dal for a visit with her parents."

"Didn't you tell me it was Thanksgiving weekend?"

"Yes. So?"

"So her brother might very well have been there too."

"Maybe. I didn't encounter him."

"But that does make sense."

"What are you talking about?"

"Honey is protecting someone. What more likely person than her own brother?"

"But what would she be protecting him from?"

"What do you think of this for a theory? Brother Bigshot is home and sees Jimmy Ferguson outside his home. Maybe he knows Jimmy has a big crush on Honey. He's a bully. Maybe he decides a boy with brain damage shouldn't be hanging around his perfect sister."

"I'm listening."

"What if he tries to scare Jimmy, and in the course of it, his father comes along and gets the impression Jimmy has done something to Honey."

"Sweet Jesus."

"Exactly. So the father chases Jimmy in a rage and collapses with a heart attack."

"He never regained consciousness."

I said, "So he's dead because of something the brother did."

"The mother and the brother call the police, and the police hassle Jimmy and then the father dies. But Honey doesn't know what happened. And by the time she finds out, it's too late."

"She can't say anything."

"That's right. She would have been in a horrible position. She knew Jimmy was innocent, but if she explained what happened, she would be implicating her brother in her father's death."

"She'd never be able to tell the mother," Vince said.

"You got it."

"It would make a big difference for Ma to know for sure Jimmy didn't do anything to cause Mr. Redmore's death."

"I can imagine."

"She never really got over it."

"Right. Since you're here, you should talk to Honey."

"As much as I would like to know what happened back then, I think we have Jimmy's disappearance to deal with first."

"It's all connected somehow."

"How?"

"Honey and her mother and her brother were all in Sydney on Canada Day."

Vince's jaw dropped.

"Didn't you know that? Their first visit since they moved. I can't believe it's a coincidence that's the day Jimmy disappeared."

"What do you think happened?"

"We're going to find out. All you have to do is wait outside her office until she comes out for lunch."

•   •   •

The more I thought about it, the more I wanted to get a good look at Will Redmore. To see but not necessarily be seen. And I had an idea where and when.

P. J. was less than thrilled.

"I need your help again."

"I'm always glad to help you, but I'm up to my ears with Nick. The man never sleeps. Breakfast meetings a speciality, but only after he's done his five-kilometre run."

Good grief, now Nicholas Southern was Nick. What next, honey bunch? I let it go. "We all have problems, P. J. But this one's serious. You got anything on Will Redmore?"

"Well, I've heard some of the Yankee networks have been taking a look at him."

"I meant is there any dirt on him?"

"Is that what you think I do? Go around digging up dirt on people?"

"Save it for someone who doesn't know how you earn a living."

"I don't know much about him. He shows up as a dream date at a lot of the Ottawa socialite fundraisers. I think he was involved with the sports scene a while back. Does a bit of hobnobbing with some of the people in half a dozen lobby groups. If he's mixed up in something unsavoury, I haven't heard about it."

"And you would, wouldn't you."

"Ottawa's a real small town when it comes to spreading the dirt around after someone digs it up."

"Right."

"What impact would a scandal have on a career like his?"

"Hard to say. Sometimes scandal's good for ratings. What kind of scandal?"

"I don't know. Say some kind of youthful indiscretion. A false accusation against a helpless person."

P. J. said nothing.

"You there?" I asked after a while.

"It sounds like you have something specific in mind."

"Put away your pencil. This is pure speculation on my part. I think I told you Honey Redmore and her family were in Sydney the day Jimmy disappeared."

"You think there's a connection?"

"Something happened a few years back with Jimmy Ferguson and Redmore's father. Something I think that a rising media star might not want out in the open."

"Are you making a specific allegation?"

"Speculation only, but I want to get a good look at this guy. Where's he interviewing Nickypoo? And when?"

"Nick has a major fundraising luncheon at the Château at noon. I'm on my way now. The interview's later. At two. On site."

"Will you be there?"

"I see where you're going with this. I can get you a ringside seat, but you've got to promise not to bring me any grief. The interview show is live on the news channel, and then air again taped late night."

"Good. I knew I could count on you."

•   •   •

"You think the brother engineered the accusations against Jimmy, Ms. MacPhee. How dreadful. Imagine doing such a thing."

"I think the full story might be even worse. I want Alvin to get a look at this turkey."

Mrs. P. tracked down Alvin for me and handed me the phone.

"What do you want, Camilla?"

"I want you to meet me at the Château. You should see this Will Redmore guy."

"Honey's brother? What for?"

"A major hunch. It could be our big break. Meet me there about ten to two. He's shooting an interview there. If I'm right, it will be worth the time."

"But I don't even know him."

"He'd be quite a bit older than you. He must be about thirty now. You don't remember him from around town?"

"Not by name. I'd have to see his face."

"That's the idea. He does a public affairs program called *Face Off.* Does it ring a bell?"

"I don't have a television set. I mean, I didn't. I guess, now I don't have anything. You told us a woman was driving the hit and run car?"

"That's what Lianne Hornyk said. Other witnesses as well."

"You don't think it was Honey?"

"No, I don't. But that's just based on talking to her. Maybe she fooled me."

"You're right," he said. "She's not the type."

"We should check out Will Redmore while we have the opportunity. One-fifty, Alvin. Be there."

After Alvin hung up, I turned to Mrs. P. "You'd better come along too."

She raised her eyebrow. "Why, Ms. MacPhee?"

"Because I'm putting two and two together. I've been pulling together a lot of strands that might be connected, even if we can't see how yet. I have a hunch there's something to what Donald Donnie and Loretta said about boys in the park when Jimmy was injured. If Will Redmore did what I think he did to implicate Jimmy, it was so vile, it couldn't have been the first evil thing he'd done in his life. And it won't have been the last. He must have had plenty of practice. Vince remembers him as a bully. I want to see if Alvin recognizes him as one of the boys from the park. It's a crazy long shot but worth taking. And if my hunch is right, it could be rough on Alvin. That's why I want you with him."

"I fear for young Ferguson. Nevertheless, we must not shirk our duty, Ms. MacPhee."

Mrs. P. remained grim-faced from the time we left her apartment until we nosed the Buick into the parking lot at the Château Laurier. With her disabled parking pass, we snagged a prime spot near the door.

• • •

You could hear the racket from inside the hotel as Mrs. Parnell and I made our way up the long incline at the rear entrance to the hotel from the parking lot. We took our time. Mrs. P. was using her walker, and a lot of people swished past us on their way out of the hotel. People in high-powered suits. You could smell the money as they passed.

Mr. Nicholas Southern was able to draw a crowd all right. I felt a wave of dislike for this wealthy, selfish creep who, in my humble opinion, practised the politics of meanness. Adding to his sins was the fact he seemed to be winning over the loyalty of P. J. Not that I had much use for any of the existing political parties, but I couldn't see our budding relationship surviving the discussions that would ensue.

The crowd had moved from the large room, where the luncheon had been served, to the hallway. Behind them a small army of hotel serving staff were removing towers of clinking coffee cups and dessert plates from the now empty tables.

P. J. was waiting by the door of the ballroom. Mrs. Parnell nodded grimly at him.

P. J. said, "I've been making inquiries, and as far as I can tell, Redmore is squeaky clean."

"Not what I want to hear."

"Why don't you tell me what this is about? Then maybe I can do a better job of digging. I have to tell you though, except that he's a bit of a heartbreaker for the women in town, I'm not getting even a whiff of bad stuff about this guy."

"This is now, I want then."

"Out with it. What do you know that I don't?" said P. J.

"I have to know that you're not going to do anything with it until the time is right."

"Do anything with it? I couldn't do anything with it if my life depended on it. This assignment is chewing up every minute of the day."

"Okay. I have a hint from an unnamed source, Redmore was involved in some bullying incidents when he was underage. Possibly Jimmy's accident was caused by bullies. I have a hunch that's the link we're missing."

"Oh, great. A hint. A possibility. Stop the press."

Mrs. Parnell leaned forward on her walker. "Once a bully, always a bully."

"I'm inclined to agree," I said. "I think he falsely accused Jimmy Ferguson of assaulting his sister. Redmore would have been in his early twenties then, but Jimmy was only thirteen. He got hauled to the copshop. Redmore's father died chasing

Jimmy after the brother made the accusation."

"Even if that turned out to be true, Tiger, I can't get a story out of it because of Jimmy's age at the time."

"Think about it this way. Suppose you were an ambitious, ego-driven man on your way up and suppose, for some reason, you thought people would find out about your false accusation against a helpless boy like Jimmy. Would that give you a major motive to run someone down in the street?"

"Sounds far-fetched to me."

"The false accusation happened, P. J. The father died. Jimmy's missing. Will Redmore's a ruthless man going to the top. I might be missing some of the details, but I promise you, help me fill in the blanks and you'll have one hell of a story. It will make your holy roller Southern pale by comparison."

"Holy shit, this could really be something big."

"Not that you've never told a lie before, but I want your word you won't break any kind of story until we have Jimmy safe."

"You can trust me."

"Now I wonder where Alvin is?"

"Alvin? Are you crazy? I can't get you all in here."

"Sure you can. Looking forward to it, P. J."

Twenty-Seven

I am not a fan of whizkids from high tech or of muckymucks from business or of angel investors, although Justice for Victims sure could use one. I was surrounded by a sea of self-interest and Harry Rosen suits. Rubbing shoulders and catching up, slapping backs. Or checking their Rolexes and striding purposefully for the parking lot. But no sign of Alvin.

"What a shame. Alvin's missing the new dawn of Canadian politics. Oh, well, maybe he'll catch the next one."

"Maybe it's for the best, Ms. MacPhee. Since you feel it might upset him to see this bully."

P. J. interrupted. "They're almost set up for the interview. Let's go in now."

I stepped inside the banquet room and glanced around. Television cameras were angled at the far end of the room as technicians plotted the best shots of the dais, where two leather chairs sat facing each other. Nicholas Southern was already sitting in the chair on the right, perfectly natural. He adjusted the perfect knot in his perfect pale blue silk tie. He was good-looking, I suppose, if you like young, blonde, trim, wealthy, would-be politicians with chiselled chins and styled hair. There's nothing like a hundred and fifteen million in the bank to bring out the best in a fellow.

As I watched, a tall broad-shouldered man headed for the second chair. None other than Honey Redmore's tablemate from the D'Arcy McGee. He walked with a surprising amount of grace for such a big bruiser. A thin young woman with spiked black hair and black nails hovered over the two, dabbing the last touches of make-up to their faces. The chairs were positioned to lend the appearance of an intimate chat between friends, while at the same time giving the camera guys a fair shake.

I followed P. J. and Mrs. Parnell along the side aisle to the second row, where P. J. had secured four reserved seats.

"This will be something. Will Redmore comes from a small "l" liberal point of view, and he's got killer instincts. He'll go for the jugular. He'll be hammering at Nick's integrity. This is a make or break media event for us. The doors are closed now. I guess Alvin will miss it."

"This 'Nick' thing makes me tired. Whatever happened to 'I'm stuck with this rightwing asshole and it's going to ruin my summer'?"

"You can't hate Nick when you get to know him, Camilla. That doesn't mean I buy all of his politics. But he's turned out to be a decent person. Despite the money …"

"Easy money."

"Who cares. It's his, and he's choosing to make a difference with it. He has integrity. I think he could end up presenting a real alternative to the existing right."

"And now you don't want to see him chewed up by Redmore?"

"Be serious. I'm a reporter. We live for blood. A 'good news' story is no story at all. Nick is making the choice to be a heavy duty political player. He's got to be able to take the heat, or he's toast. Either way, good story."

"I thought he'd already made it."

"Redmore's the acid test. Watch the interview."

"I'm surprised Southern's people don't insist on a cushion or something so he doesn't look so insignificant next to Redmore."

"Believe me, they thought about it. But they knew the press would find out and make him a laughingstock. Remember Dukakis in the U.S.?"

"Would you make a laughingstock out of it?"

"Yeah, I'd have to comment, whether I wanted to or not. My job is to find the soft underbelly. But I think they're striving for a David and Goliath effect. I'll comment on that."

"Good thinking. Looks like they got it."

"Just be quiet, and don't cause any disruption. Promise?"

Someone shushed us.

"Of course. What would I gain?"

"I know you. Even the very slightly improved Camilla is liable to make trouble."

"Trust me. I just want to take the measure of Will Redmore. Considering he may be responsible for three deaths, including his father's."

"I want to hear more about that theory," P. J. said. "Now turn off your cellphone. Right now."

Another shush.

We sat back for a captivating half-hour and watched Will Redmore lay one verbal trap after another for Nicholas Southern. Southern managed to hold his own. I could see how P. J. might want to take sides. Southern was the underdog in this interview, although he handled himself with charm and grace under fire. Voters hate a sign of weakness. If I didn't loathe everything Southern stood for, I might have felt sorry for him.

Redmore was almost big enough to make two of the reedy Southern. Obviously, there was no love lost between them. It looked like Redmore would pick Southern's delicate bones clean.

For all my small-l liberal leanings, if I'd had to chose between these two turkeys, I would have lined up with Southern. Of course, I knew more than I should have about Redmore.

It didn't take a lot of watching to figure out that Redmore would be ruthless in getting whatever he wanted. His performance convinced me he was quite capable of setting up Jimmy Ferguson. The interview concluded with questions left unanswered, but that wasn't one of them.

We stood up and started to move to the side. I hugged the back wall in an out-of-the-way spot. It was time to get the second half of what I came for.

"Get as many shots as you can, Mrs. P." I said. "We can show them to Alvin later."

She raised her digital camera with the zoom lens. She did a nice swoop of the supporters just out of range of the television cameras and the hangers-on in the front row. Then she focused in on Will Redmore as he moved down the aisle.

For one second, Will Redmore looked over. It gave me a spine-stiffening sense of how Nicholas Southern would have felt under that gaze.

I turned on my cellphone. It rang immediately.

"Where were you, Camilla?" Alvin shouted, when I answered. "I have him. I found Jimmy! Spotted him on Clarence Street. Just luck."

A wave of relief swept over me. My knees wobbled. So did my voice. "You found him? Is he all right?"

"He's scared. He's hungry. He needs a bath. But he'll be okay. Do you have the Buick?"

"I do."

"We're in the market, outside a coffee shop on Dalhousie near Cumberland."

"Call an ambulance. Get him to the hospital. Right now."

"He doesn't want that."

"He needs to be seen by a doctor."

"Look, I'm not going to push him. You know about Jimmy. He wants to see the Gallery. If we don't, it's just going to add to his stress. We'll have our little visit and then we'll get him to a doctor."

"That doesn't even make sense. After everything he's been through? Doesn't he want to rest? To see the family?"

"Yeah. He wants all that. I told him about the Gallery in my postcards, and he wants to see it. And he couldn't find it on his own. And he won't settle down until he does. So I'm going to take him there, whether it sounds crazy or not. He's pretty tired and he's still jumpy. I'd feel better if we took him by car. Will you drive us?"

"What about his medication?"

"I had some on me. Everyone in my family's carrying Jimmy's medication. You know that."

"You're sure it's the best thing?"

"Why not? You've been after me to go."

"Don't be facetious. Mrs. P. and I will pick you up as soon as possible. In the meantime, can you try and find out what happened to him in Sydney?"

"It's still too upsetting for him. I'll wait until his medication kicks in, Camilla. He's safe now. We'll get the story when the excitement dies down."

"You're right. I've got to get a grip."

I hugged Mrs. P. and I hugged P. J. I hugged three complete strangers. I hugged a camera technician. I drew the line at hugging Nicholas Southern, but I did nod at him as he walked by. Which was something.

"P. J.," I said, "they found him. They found Jimmy! You'll never believe where we're going now. Is that crazy or what? I'm so glad it's over."

I noticed that, across the room, I had all of Will Redmore's attention. His eyes fastened on us. Thank God I didn't have to worry about that any more. Jimmy was safe at last.

As we walked by Redmore, I said. "Remember me? I plan to be your undoing."

Hey. Sometimes it just feels right.

• • •

If you ever want to get out of a parking lot fast, don't park your big honking Buick by the hotel door when half the new money in town is rolling its Jaguars and Mercedeses and Lexuses through the parking gates at half the speed of an old glacier.

I left messages for Deveau and Mombourquette.

"Such wonderful news," Mrs. Parnell said when I hung up. "What a relief."

I handed her the phone. "Yeah. But Alvin will be having a bird because it's taking us so long. Do you want to get him and tell him we'll be there eventually?"

She was already keying in the number. They chatted happily while I gave a few moguls the finger.

• • •

Jimmy looked bedraggled and smelled worse. Streaks of dust lined his handsome face. Even his hair had dust in it. He grinned at me when Alvin introduced us. Well, we all had goofy grins. Mrs. Parnell's eyes seemed suspiciously wet.

"We've been worried about you, Jimmy. You must have been scared after that fire. Where did you stay?" I asked, as he settled into the Buick.

"Tell her, Jimmy," Alvin said.

Jimmy said, "Aw, come on, Allie."

"You'll never guess where Jimmy slept the last two nights."

"Under a bridge," Jimmy said, with some pride. "Some girls told me about it."

"That explains a lot," I said.

"There were lots of ducks. And even some swans. They let you feed them. You'd like that, Allie."

"Sure would, Jimmy." Alvin's voice was tight.

"Are you okay now?" I said.

"I am. It was scary, and I'm glad to see Allie. We'll be safe here, won't we?"

"Yes. You can come back to my place or Mrs. Parnell's. We'll all make sure you're okay. We're glad Alvin found you."

"It was just luck," Alvin said.

"We're lucky, aren't we, Allie?"

"Yeah, Jimmy. We're lucky now."

"But I left my stuff under the bridge. Can we go get it afterwards?"

"What stuff?" Alvin said.

"What bridge?" I said.

"Of course we can," Mrs. Parnell said.

Alvin pointed. "Look, Jimmy. There's Gadzooks Gallery."

• • •

There was a tow-away sign in front of the gallery. It probably didn't bother most of the customers. I guess if you can afford those immense glass sculptures, your chauffeur could drop you off to browse and come when you snapped your fingers.

I let the gang off in front of the door and found the first parking spot which was halfway up the hill. I was grumbling when I got out of the car. I passed a wizened panhandler shuffling up the incline.

The panhandler gave us a dusty grin, showing at least four teeth. "I hope things get better for you, Missus," he said.

"You too." I fished out a loonie from my pocket. Even though I prefer to give directly to the Food Bank or the Mission. Even though I knew the panhandler might just as easily head to the liquor store instead of the Loeb for fresh vegetables. I have a roof over my head and more food than I need, even if it is in cans. And I have to look at myself in the mirror. I was glad to get that good wish, even from a rumpled old stranger who had troubles of his own.

I'd missed the expression on René's face when the three dusketeers walked through the door of Gadzooks, but he hadn't recovered his composure when I arrived. No wonder. Alvin still had tear-tracks down his cheeks. So did Mrs. Parnell. Who knows. Maybe I did too. It was quite obvious Jimmy had been living on the streets. A couple of clients escaped through the door.

Jimmy turned around and around, touching every elaborate glass construction in the gallery. "This is so beautiful, Allie. Look at all the things."

"Sculptures, Jimmy. Glass sculptures."

"They're beautiful, just like you said they were. Like magic." He reached up to touch the spectacular outcroppings of a three-part sculpture that towered with spiked shards of glass.

"Yes, they're like magic."

"No wonder you said this would be the best job ever, Allie." Alvin glanced my way. "Sorry, Camilla."

"Hey. I can handle it."

René didn't look like he could handle it.

"We want to thank you," I said, "for your understanding as Alvin dealt with this incredible crisis with his brother."

"Is this the boy they were talking about on television and radio? I heard the appeal for information about your brother on television." He leaned over and whispered to me. "Was another brother killed?"

"That turned out to be a mistake. I want to apologize. But now everything has turned out well. Alvin's been through hell, but he'll snap right back and be in to work in no time."

René glanced at Alvin. If I read the expression on his face right, he didn't think Alvin would ever get back to normal. I could see his point, but I knew better.

"You can't believe the resilience this young man has. I owe him my life. What more can an employer want or say? At any rate, he'll be back on the job by Monday, I'm sure. We'll be sure to mention where he works in any media coverage of Jimmy's story, won't we, Alvin?"

I grinned at Jimmy, who had made his way to the very back of the gallery, smiling and touching, smiling and touching.

"Lord thundering Jesus," Alvin said.

"Now, Alvin." I wanted just enough warning in my tone to keep him suitably polite.

"Look out!" Alvin grabbed at Jimmy.

"Troops, hit the dirt and roll," Mrs. Parnell yelled. "Cover your heads."

I turned to see the front end of Stan's Buick flying towards the plate glass window. Only René stayed on his feet, gaping in disbelief. The rest of us hit the floor, rolling towards the side of the room.

When the last shards of shattered glass tinkled on to the floor, we raised our heads and stared.

It was too late for the splendid glass statues. Too late for the Buick. And, unless he was very lucky, it was too late for René Janveau.

Twenty-Eight

The ambulance carrying René had just shrieked out of sight, and I was picking glass out of my hair when Mombourquette showed up. He looked around Gadzooks and shook his head.

"I guess you call this a crash course in Modern Art, eh?"

"What a wit," I said.

Mombourquette was just warming up. He turned his beady eyes to the Buick. The front was in the middle of the Gallery, and the tail end just protruded through the window. "Remind me never to lend you my car."

"With all due respect, Lennie, *I* didn't drive that car through the window."

"Why is it you two just can't stay out of trouble?"

"Stay out of trouble? We were visiting an art gallery. I fail to see how even you can construe that to be getting into trouble."

He pointed to the Buick. "Exhibit A."

"This is Alvin's new place of employment," I said sadly.

Mombourquette flashed his incisors. "And already it's trashed. That's setting some new kind of record."

Ray Deveau appeared in what was left of the door, red-faced and out of breath. "What do you mean, some new kind of record?"

"He doesn't mean anything."

"I mean when you get these two together, you're gonna have

broken glass, cars crashing, gunshots, people getting killed, that sort of thing."

I said, "What a kidder. Come on, Mombourquette. There's a café across the street. Let's go get some cheese."

"I don't know who's worse, her or him," Mombourquette said. "They've cost the taxpayer more than a few bucks, let me tell you. So what was this glass thing before Stan's Buick ran through it?"

"It was a Josef Weinburg," Alvin said weakly from the floor. "Worth sixty thousand dollars."

"Really? Worth a bundle, was it? Maybe your new boss will have to dock your pay for the next while."

I couldn't remember Mombourquette ever blaming Alvin for anything before. Usually I was the villain. Alvin deserves to be picked on from time to time, but this was definitely not one of the times.

"Alvin was not to blame. Jimmy insisted on coming here. He was trying to do the best he could to keep Jimmy calm until his medicine kicked in."

"And this is the best he could do? So, Camilla, Ray tells me you're causing trouble for him too."

Deveau said, "Knock it off, Lennie."

"Listen, enough of this crap, Leonard," I said. "We have been victimized here. You guys should get off your butts and talk to Will Redmore. I don't know how, but I know goddam well he's behind this."

I picked up my cellphone and called P. J. to give him the same opinion.

Alvin said, "Where's Jimmy?"

We raced to the door. We checked the street, looked behind the garbage cans in the alley, circled the block, called Jimmy's name. Alvin ran frantically through the neighbouring streets, his ponytail swaying wildly.

But Jimmy Ferguson was nowhere to be seen.

• • •

A half-hour later, there was still no sign of him. Mombourquette was unamused and Deveau was confused, P. J. was unavailable, and Vince Ferguson, when he finally showed up, was furious. He seemed to speak for the rest of the family who milled about, wailing.

"What were you thinking taking that boy anywhere but to a hospital?"

"I called you, Vince. It's what he wanted," Alvin bleated.

Vince's comments were unprintable. That turned out to be a strategic error on his part. Mrs. Parnell pulled herself up to her full height and unleashed a tongue-lashing I will remember for a while.

"You don't deserve this boy," Mrs. P. said whenever a Ferguson opened its mouth. Alvin was sunk on the floor, back to the wall, face in his hands.

"Did you manage to waylay Honey Redmore at lunchtime?" I asked Vince.

"Of course I didn't. First of all, I don't dance to your tune. Second, I was looking for Jimmy. Third, had I found him, I wouldn't have exposed him to danger."

Vince was exposing himself to danger at that point, but Deveau got between us and pulled me away.

Outside the gallery, media trucks vied with ambulances and police cars. All you could see were flashing lights. Glinting off the shimmering piles of glass. Reflecting off the deep gloss of the crumpled Buick. A SOCO made his way toward the scene.

I turned to Deveau who was scratching his head. "It made

sense at the time for Alvin to bring Jimmy here, you know."

"I don't even know what to say. It's unbelievable."

"The worst thing is, the killer might have a better idea how to find him than we do. Unless Mombourquette pulls him off the street."

"They have an all-points bulletin out. Don't worry. They'll get him."

• • •

Mrs. Parnell did not believe she was in need of medical attention for shock. She looked a lot more chipper than she had before the Buick shot through the window. Alvin, on the other hand, was bleeding.

"We will all go looking for him," I said, "but not before you two see a doctor. Don't argue."

Deveau had a rental. Once Alvin had accepted his need for stitches, Deveau drove us five blocks to the Sandy Hill Health Centre walk-in clinic. I explained the logic behind my theory to Deveau and Alvin.

Alvin said. "I don't remember any boys in the park. I don't recall anything about that day. Except Jimmy going to the hospital in an ambulance and everyone crying."

"Donald Donnie and Loretta remember it. Clearly. It puts a different spin on things, doesn't it?"

"Are you all right, dear boy?" Mrs. Parnell said.

I stuck to my guns. "It could have been an attack."

Alvin nodded. "If it's true, then I didn't cause Jimmy's accident. It would mean I didn't leave him alone to play in the water. I ran for help. It's a terrible thing to say, but I almost hope it is true, that there were boys. I always thought it was my fault. I never knew how I could do such an awful thing to my little brother."

"And your family let you think that," I said under my breath.

"Too bad I missed my chance to see this guy at the Château. Maybe it would have triggered a memory," Alvin said to my surprise.

"You will get a chance to see Redmore because Mrs. Parnell got some great shots with her digital camera."

"Unfortunately, it was in the Buick," she said. "It's gone now."

"You checked?"

"I did."

"You mean you checked after the car went through the window?"

"Of course."

• • •

Deveau watched my face intently. Not a sign of the mellow man I'd come to like some much. "Hard to believe the things kids can do sometimes," he said.

"We've got a couple of things to follow up on, and I don't think they're at the top of the list for the police here. But they will make a difference. Will you help us?" I figured this was a major test.

Ray Deveau passed with honours. "Wouldn't miss the opportunity. Lennie might not like it, but that's not my problem."

"We need you to track down Father Blaise. I think he's got information we need."

I liked the idea that I could surprise Deveau.

"Really?" he said. "Shouldn't be too hard."

"He's attending something at St. Paul's University here. But he hasn't returned Mrs. Parnell's calls. You take care of that, and I'll confirm something about the first hit and run."

While we waited for Alvin to get his stitches, I called Lianne Hornyk. Like everyone else in the world, she had voice mail.

I left a crisp message, telling her we had a lead, and repeating my cellphone number twice in case she'd lost it. I asked her exactly what made her think it was a woman driving the car that ran down her husband.

When I looked up, I found myself facing a reporter from *The Citizen*, one of P. J.'s buddies, a woman with shaggy black hair and a dangerous grin.

"Did P. J. rat us out?" I said. Usually I like her a lot.

"Can't reveal my sources. Want to give me an interview?"

She was blocking the entrance. Although she did have a great grin, it wasn't enough to get a story out of Deveau. "No comment," he said pleasantly, revealing his cop training.

Mrs. Parnell wouldn't have broken under torture. Alvin might have blurted out information, but luckily he'd gone in to get his stitches. I'd also suggested a sedative, but not every doctor does what I say.

That left me for the interview. But I didn't plan to have the papers get the scoop on Will Redmore before the cops did their jobs.

"I've promised P. J. an exclusive. It's the least I could do for him. I guess you could say he encouraged me to enter *The Citizen*'s Bluesfest contest, and I won those two Clubhouse passes."

"What?"

"I won them. Tell you what. When this is over, even if P. J. gets the scoop, we'll see you get a worthwhile interview. How's that? But we'd like to be alone now. We're under a lot of strain."

"What contest are you talking about?"

"*The Citizen* contest. The draw for the Clubhouse passes. I won it. I really wouldn't have entered if P. J. hadn't pushed it, so to speak."

"First I've heard of this contest. Are you sure?"

"Of course, I'm sure." I showed my wristband.

All of a sudden, I wasn't so sure. What the hell was P. J. up to this time?

•   •   •

Our reporter had given up and departed seeking more cooperative types, and Deveau was driving us home when the call came through from New Brunswick.

"Camilla? It's Lianne Hornyk here. You asked what made me think it was a woman who killed Greg? I have thought a lot about it. The car was speeding towards us, of course, but I got a good look at the person driving. I couldn't see the colour of her hair because she was wearing one of those expensive scarves tied over her head, you know, that French design, tied like she was a movie star from the early sixties. She had sunglasses on. The bad news is, because of the scarf and the sunglasses, I couldn't ever really identify her... What else can I tell you? She was thin and elegant. Sort of Hepburnish. She even wore gloves... I hope this helps, but I don't see how it can. I gave all the information to the police, but I don't think they thought it would do them much good. You can imagine why."

I could.

"Hermès," Alvin said when I passed on the information. "They're called Hermès, those scarves."

I said, "Whatever."

"Ms. MacPhee, I believe we have a strategic problem with

the idea of Mr. Redmore being the hit and run driver."

"I know what you're going to say, Mrs. P. The man's like a well-dressed mountain. No one would ever mix him up with a woman."

Alvin said, "Not even in a car? Wearing a Hermès scarf and sunglasses to hide his face?"

"No. Not even wearing a tent. The guy must have been a linebacker in college. He's got hands like patio slabs, and it would be obvious to anyone."

"So that means it couldn't have been him."

"All it means, Alvin, is that there's something we still don't know."

Alvin said, "Anyway, we can't think about that now. We have to get out and find Jimmy."

At that point, Deveau butted in. "Look, you've all been through a rough experience. You need to go home and get some rest. You were almost killed today, and you need to look after yourselves. You might consider getting cleaned up too."

"Jimmy comes first," Alvin said.

"The Ottawa cops are out in force. I checked with Lennie. They've put extra foot patrols in the Market and other key spots. They've issued a major media alert. They'll probably do a house-to-house in the area near the Gallery. And they're calling for volunteer searchers. I'll head back as soon as I drop you off. I'll keep you in the loop. They'll find Jimmy."

"What if he's hurt? There was glass flying everywhere. He could be injured. His medication would have barely kicked in. After all he's been through, this last shock could trigger a seizure."

Mrs. Parnell took Alvin's arm. "Dear boy, your family are also checking the hospitals. They'll be on the lookout. It will all end well."

I didn't say anything. I wasn't convinced.

Deveau drove us home and insisted on coming up. Once we were in my apartment, he said: "I'm heading back downtown. But I want you to listen to me. You just finished picking glass out of your head. Alvin's experience would put most people in the hospital. Mrs. Parnell talks a good story, but she's eighty years old."

"Seventy-nine."

"I think you get my point, Camilla. Someone's playing a very dangerous game, and we don't know what it is. Make sure you three don't do anything foolish."

"Absolutely. I think the best thing we can do is sit tight and use our brains."

• • •

Mrs. Parnell was serving up Harvey's, purely for its medicinal value. I declined. So did Alvin. Gussie, sensing a wounded spirit, snuggled in. Mrs. Parnell's cat chose me instead. Lester and Pierre shrieked indiscriminately.

"What kind of woman would wear a fancy French scarf on a holiday in Sydney?" I said.

"Hermès, Camilla," Alvin said. "You're right. They set you back a couple hundred dollars."

"I know the ones you mean. Gold, swirly designs. My sister Edwina got one on her thirtieth anniversary trip to France. That's my point."

"You mean not everyone in Sydney would have one?"

"Exactly. But more important, if you're looking at a speeding car, how could you know someone was wearing imported silk or just a K-Mart imitation?" I said.

"I probably could," Alvin said.

"Well, that doesn't surprise me. But I couldn't. Do we think Lianne can?"

"There's something about them. You can spot the real thing a mile off."

"So there's the other angle. Who's going to be walking around looking like that? In July? With gloves yet."

"Be serious, Camilla. No one."

"That's my point. You'd be extremely noticeable in the casual crowd around Charlotte Street, done up as Audrey Hepburn, even without the gloves."

Alvin's eyes gleamed. "Everyone would be trying to figure out who you were."

"If they could stop laughing long enough."

"Exactly. It's a disguise."

"Obviously."

"Bear with me. Ask yourself, why would the person want to be disguised."

"Let me think. Maybe because fatal hit and run is illegal?"

"Sarcasm does not become you, Alvin. The person didn't want to be identified. Does that mean she *would* be recognized?"

"She might be someone well-known around Sydney, you mean."

"Exactly."

"That would include Honey Redmore, even though she's been gone for years."

"And even more to the point, it indicates the person who killed Greg Hornyk had an intended victim. I think she planned to kill Jimmy and she decided in advance to put the scarf on and the sunglasses and the gloves."

"But you don't think it was Honey."

"I find it hard to believe, although this whole thing's been hard to believe. It's easier to picture the brother trying to eliminate Jimmy, as the person who could finger him, not only as a childhood bully, but also an adult who makes false accusations. He's still a bully, only now he has a network audience."

"But like you said, the guy's practically a giant. Anyway, Honey also knew Jimmy didn't do anything. So wiping out Jimmy doesn't even make sense."

"Yes, and that's my other point."

"What?"

"The only person who would have a reason to kill Jimmy is a person who actually thought Jimmy was responsible for Mr. Redmore's death."

"But you've explained that Honey and her brother both knew it wasn't true."

"Yes. But I'm betting the mother didn't know."

"That Mrs. Redmore was like a hound from hell afterwards. She practically attacked Ma in broad daylight right on Charlotte Street."

"Indicating an unstable and vindictive personality."

"You said it."

"But an elegant, well-dressed woman, who would probably own a whatdoyoucallitscarf."

"Hermès. And yes."

"What does she look like?"

"I haven't seen her for years, but she looked like an older version of Honey. Not so pretty, but the same physical type."

"And people would recognize her on the street in Sydney."

"Not everyone, but there'd be a good chance."

Mrs. Parnell raised her glass. "At last, it is beginning to make sense."

"Some of it is. It certainly could explain why Greg Hornyk

was killed. But it doesn't tell us why Jimmy would go into hiding. Would he have been afraid of Mrs. Redmore?"

"Probably not, but remember with Jimmy, it's not always logical. Maybe he saw the brother with her and remembered the bullying. They were all there."

"You forget a woman chased Jimmy that afternoon," Mrs. Parnell said. "If that was Mrs. Redmore, he most certainly would have been fearful of her after that."

"That's true," Alvin said.

"But it doesn't explain who torched Alvin's apartment building. Or who killed Reefer," I said.

"If Mrs. Redmore lives here, she could have done it," Alvin said.

"Maybe. But how would she know where you lived? How would she know Jimmy was there?"

"And would she have driven the Buick through the Gadzooks window?" Mrs. Parnell puffed thoughtfully.

"How could she know we were at the Gallery?" Alvin said. "She couldn't."

"Holy shit," I said. "She sure could have. Her son knew. He could have called her. He was there when we said we were picking up you and Jimmy. We don't even know what she looks like. Maybe she was in the audience. She wouldn't have had to know where we were going. All she had to do was follow us."

"It certainly took long enough to get out of that garage," Mrs. P. said.

"Too bad we don't have a witness," Alvin said.

I thought back. "Maybe we do."

• • •

Deveau showed up at my place again at six with pizza and a

sheepish look. Mrs. Parnell and Alvin and I were planning our next strategies. I seemed to be the only one who found his visit surprising.

We wolfed the pizza, leaving hardly any for Gussie. It's amazing how hungry you get dodging death.

"Well, that was great. Thanks, Ray. Now tell me, do you want to help me track down a witness?"

"Actually, I want to get over and talk to Father Blaise."

"Father Blaise? He finally called back?"

"No. Didn't I tell you? What's the name of your big hospital? Anyway, he's there. ICU."

"The General. And you did not tell me. What's he there for?"

"I thought I told you. Are you sure?"

"Of course, I'm sure."

"Okay, I know what happened. I found out from Leonard, but when I heard your car crashed into that Gallery and then Jimmy got away again, I guess it just flew out of my mind. It's a tragedy. But it's not like Father Blaise was directly related to the case."

I let that pass. "Did he have a heart attack or something?"

"I went over to St. Paul's, and they told me he'd been hit by a car the night before last."

"Holy shit," I said. "You don't think that's related? That would make four instances where someone's using a car as a weapon."

"My God. I can't believe I missed that connection. I thought it a case of an old man in a strange city getting hit by a car. I don't know if it was a hit and run." No chuckle from Deveau as he picked up his cellphone. "We've got to get over and talk to him."

Alvin, looking haggard and dejected, headed out to join the

family. "Say hello to Father Blaise. Tell him we're looking for Jimmy."

Mrs. Parnell said "I'll smoke out that Redmore creature while you're gone. I'll check what Donald Donnie and Loretta have to say about her. We'll see if we can get a photo of her somewhere. And we'll get them to show it to the woman in Sydney who saw Jimmy being chased in her backyard."

"Mrs. Smith."

"Precisely. We can also send a copy to the young widow, Ms. Hornyk."

"Terrific. I'll be off."

• • •

Deveau and I were halfway down the hall when the elevator doors dinged open. P. J. emerged and turned in our direction.

"Oh," he said, looking at Deveau and then back to me. "I was late getting your message. I thought I'd drop in and see if you were all right."

"Never better. By the way, I had a fascinating chat with a colleague of yours about *The Citizen's* Bluesfest contest."

P. J. paled. "Oh, I can explain. When we're alone. But anyway, I have this tape of *Face Off.* I thought since Alvin missed it, he might watch and see if he recognizes Redmore."

"I'll take that," I said. "You're in a hurry to get out of here."

"I am?" P. J. had that expression he gets when I've caught him in a lie, and he hasn't figured out how to weasel out of it. Yet.

"Trust me." I didn't feel like sharing an elevator with him. I'd watched the little liar slither off before it occurred to me he'd kept the tape.

Deveau chuckled, but I wasn't smiling.

Twenty-Nine

We struck out big-time at the General. Not even Deveau's official cop status was enough to get us past the nursing station at the ICU.

The only thing that moved us forward was a call from Mombourquette. Mombourquette didn't want to talk to me.

"You were right," Deveau said afterwards. "It was another hit and run. Another stolen vehicle. The woman at St. Paul's didn't even mention it yesterday."

"Maybe they didn't know. Where did it take place?"

"I didn't even think to ask. If the person can attack in Sydney and Ottawa, I guess he can get around."

"He or she," I said.

"Father Blaise was my parish priest when I was growing up. I knew him from Youth Club. He's a funny old duck, but he's always been the kindest person in the world. He did everything for us kids. We had team sports, drama, art stuff, discussion groups. He put a lot of young people back on the right track. It was a shock to hear he'd been hit."

"Logic tells me he has something to do with the case."

Deveau scratched his head. "I don't see how Father Blaise could be involved in this mess. With Reefer Keefer, of all people. Reefer's hardly a church-goer. The whole thing is crazy."

"There has to be some connection. Would Reefer Keefer

have been in the Youth Club?"

"Sure. Father Blaise could spot a troubled kid. Reefer was always off the rails, but in small ways. I guess I can talk about that, since he's dead. I remember him as a teenager when I was first on the force. He would have ended up in a juvenile facility if Father Blaise hadn't stepped in."

"What about bullying?"

"Reefer? No way. Nothing like that. No violence. He'd be playing hooky, smoking dope, breaking into garages, minor stuff. He once had a fine crop of weed growing in the field behind the church. Father Blaise sought out that kind of kid and found things to change their path. I think he had Reefer in the choir and the drama group. If I remember correctly, the guy had a great voice. What a waste."

"Well, he sure struck out with Reefer."

"Not for lack of trying. Father Blaise is a good person. I've been a cop for eighteen years, and I think I'm a pretty good judge of character."

"No one said he was guilty of anything. It never occurred to me he was involved. I only wanted to talk to him about what happened to Jimmy way back, to see if he could shed any light on it."

"We may never know. Mombourquette just said they don't think he'll pull through. "

"None of this makes sense."

"And because none of it makes sense, we have no way of knowing who else the killer might target. Everyone involved might be in danger."

I said, "We know for sure Jimmy is."

"I was thinking about you."

• • •

Deveau was driving along Smythe Road on our way back from the hospital when the metaphorical light went on over my head.

"Bridges," I said.

"What?"

"Jimmy said he spent the last couple of nights under a bridge. We just drove over the Rideau River. There are bridges over the river in the area. Overpasses too that a person can hide under. Some of the homeless people live there. Do you want to pull over?"

"You don't think they would have searched them already?"

"Probably not this far from downtown. But there are lots of ducks, and Jimmy mentioned ducks.

"Great idea. Perfect time. He might be heading back to sleep."

"Right. But it's getting dark."

"It's almost nine. Let's go to a Canadian Tire. I think we can find one before they close. How about if you figure out which bridges to check out while I pick us up a couple of flashlights."

• • •

Three hours later, with midnight looming, we were pretty well ready to give up. If there were people sleeping under the bridges, we hadn't run into them yet.

"Maybe not such a brilliant idea," I said.

"Worth trying. I don't have a better one."

"Let's try one more spot," I said as we followed the bicycle path along the Rideau near Algonquin College and under the Queensway. "It's not really a bridge. It's where the Queensway passes over the Rideau. I used to ride past here on the bike path."

"No problem. You think there's a chance?"

"Kids hang out under here, but you never see them in the day. You often see bundles and abandoned stuff. I used to think it would be a good spot for runaways and hitchhikers. And it's easy to get to. A bit far from downtown, but Jimmy's used to walking. Can you hear the ducks? There are swans too on this part of the Rideau, and Jimmy mentioned swans."

We parked the rental in the lot by Algonquin and headed down the slope to the path. Trees cast long shadows and obscured the highway briefly. With the soft chirp of crickets and the call of a lovesick bullfrog, it was hard to imagine we were a five-minute drive from Parliament Hill.

"This is something," Deveau said.

"It is. On the other side is the National Capital Commission bike path system. Goes for umpteen miles."

"Maybe I'll bring my daughters up for a visit, and we'll try that sometime," he said.

I thought I might like that.

There was a bit of light from the Queensway and a black glimmer from the shallow Rideau which ran under the highway. Every now and then I heard the startled quack of one of the many ducks. Near the far bank we could just make out three sleeping swans, heads tucked under wings. Then we were under the highway. Ugly graffiti bloomed on the concrete walls, hundreds of cigarette butts cluttered the path. Bits of broken glass blinked in the beams from our flashlights.

"Not what you'd call romantic," Deveau said.

Our flashlights shone on the concrete supporting walls. No sign of anybody.

"Point the lights up. Sometimes you can see where someone is sleeping up in the openings between the supports and the concrete ceiling."

"Tell me you don't come here by yourself in the night."

"Of course not, but during the day I used to notice sleeping bags sometimes."

Fifteen minutes later, on the far side of the river, we shone our lights on a cardboard box tucked almost out of sight. Deveau climbed up and passed it down to me. Inside was Alvin's grandmother's pink flowered china tea set and eight silver spoons.

"Looks like Jimmy was here. What a stroke of luck."

Deveau said, "I guess these had sentimental value to both those boys."

"Most likely. I'd feel a lot better if Jimmy was here now."

"Me too. Why don't we wait and see if he shows up again?"

I liked the way this guy's mind worked.

Two hours later, we called it quits, picked up the box, and headed for the car. But not before Deveau had a word with the Ottawa cops and told them to keep an eye on the place.

•　•　•

My alarm went off four hours after I hit the pillow. When I pried my eyes open, I had one thought in my mind. Witness. I needed to find a witness. I stumbled out of bed.

It gave me quite a shock to bump into Alvin as I groped for the coffee filters in the kitchen. It's not easy facing Alvin first thing in the morning, particularly when you have a throb in your temple, and he has a bee in his bonnet.

"We have to talk," he said, as I gripped the counter.

"Not before I have coffee." That was part of a long list including not before I get dressed, not before I brush my teeth, not before I remember my name and not before I walk that stinky dog.

"I made coffee. It's almost ready. I've figured out who it is."

"Who what is?" I pulled out the coffee-pot and stuck my cup right under the drip.

"The person who knew everything."

"What are you talking about?"

"Someone knew when I found Jimmy. Someone knew Father Blaise was in town. Someone knew Jimmy was in the campground."

"I thought he was under a bridge."

"Later. After my place burnt, he said he bought himself a tent at the Canadian Tire downtown and camped in the lot by the Bluesfest, but then someone came in the night and he heard them asking around for him. He said he just managed to grab his stuff and run. That's why he didn't have any money, he blew it on the tent."

"This is the first I've heard of it."

"He told me while we were waiting for you and Violet to pick us up and take us to Gadzooks."

"Right. Gadzooks. Surely the dumbest thing I've ever done. But how could anybody know? About that."

"Think about it, Camilla."

I rubbed my temple.

"You told P. J. Jimmy was staying in my apartment. Violet heard you."

"Don't joke when I have a headache."

"Just because he's your boyfriend."

"He's not my boyfriend. He's just P. J."

"Did he know about the postcards?"

I stared. "Alvin, he's our friend. You don't believe he could be involved."

"He was out of town on July 1st. He couldn't come to my party."

"That's hardly a crime." Charlottetown. How far was Charlottetown from Sydney?

"He could have been in Sydney. Easily."

I thought about it. Half the country seemed to be running back and forth. "But why would P. J. go to Sydney?"

"He knew the Redmores. Both of them."

"Yes, but from here. They're big news in this town."

"He's a wiry little guy. Put a scarf and gloves on him and…"

"Talk sense." I felt sick. Everything fit into place. He'd been awfully casual about his mother's heart attack scare. Why hadn't he wanted me to send flowers to his mother? Because there was no heart attack?

I turned at the rustle at the door. Mrs. Parnell stood there, leaning on her walker. "I am sorry, Ms. MacPhee, but I must support young Ferguson here. It looks bad for your friend."

My hand shook, and the hot coffee soaked through the front of my housecoat, burning my skin. It didn't matter.

"But why? What motive could P. J. have?"

She said. "We must consider the possibility he was the second boy in the park."

Will Redmore, the first boy. P. J. Lynch, the second boy.

"Alvin do you remember P. J. in the park?"

"I don't remember any of it. So that won't help one way or the other."

"We are speculating about the boys in the park. We have no proof. And P. J. grew up in Ottawa, in Westboro. I know that."

"People move, Camilla. How many Cape Bretoners do you know in Ottawa? How many that came and went back and came out again? Probably some of them grew up in the West End."

"It may make sense, but I don't believe it."

"Perhaps that is what he is banking on, Ms. MacPhee."

Alvin said, "Did you tell him you saw Reefer here?"

I thought back to my sighting of Reefer at Bluesfest. The night P. J. left early because the oysters didn't agree with him.

"Did you tell him about the two boys in the park? Because if you did, we're all in danger."

"I must concur. Who knew I had taken pictures with my digital camera? Who knew enough to steal it from the Buick?"

It was hard to imagine a darker moment.

"Who heard we had found Jimmy? And we were taking him to Gadzooks?" said Alvin.

"What do you really know about P. J., Ms. MacPhee?"

Not for the first time, I found it hard to maintain faith in my buddy. Especially since I knew he was such a liar.

• • •

An hour later, Deveau nosed the rental into a Byward Market parking lot. We started our long prowl through the crowded market streets, past fruit and vegetable vendors, flower stalls, crafts, tables of maple products, Indian dresses, wooden clocks, you name it. We were on the lookout for a dusty drunk with four teeth and a real positive attitude. Deveau liked the market, particularly the smell of fresh strawberries. It took an hour before we hit pay dirt, partly because he kept stopping to sniff and sample.

"You're unusually quiet," he said.

"Stuff on my mind. We'll just keep looking."

For some reason, Deveau decided to buy me a sunflower.

"Why?" I said.

He gave me a funny look. "No reason. But you know what, while we're here, maybe I should get a bouquet or a plant for Father Blaise. I checked this morning. He was still in the ICU yesterday. They thought he'd be there awhile. He hadn't regained consciousness. The people from St. Paul's said he was lucky to be alive. Apparently he landed on some garbage bags, and that helped to break his fall. A woman walking her dog spotted him and called 911."

"Was it a hit and run?"

"Looks like it. He was on the sidewalk. The driver didn't report it. They think it was hours before he was found."

"I sure hope he makes it. Any other information from the locals?"

"On another topic, yeah. Turns out your ex-Buick was hot-wired by someone who knew what they were doing."

Sometimes your luck turns. As we paced back and forth outside the Château Lafayette, the ancient watering hole in the market favoured by poets and panhandlers, waiting for Mombourquette to call back, the object of our search stumbled out and flashed me a smile like an old friend. He doffed an imaginary hat. "Oh, Missus, I hope your day went better."

"Actually, it didn't. My car shot through the window of the Gallery at the foot of the hill."

"Was that your car now? I guess it was. I saw that. Lot of excitement. Like the movies."

"Too much excitement for me. Since you saw it, I need to know, did you see anyone around the vehicle after I left?"

My new friend seemed to be eyeing Deveau cautiously. Even though Deveau was discretion itself. Eyes open, mouth shut.

"Is this fella here a cop?"

"Does he look like a cop?"

"You can always tell, Missus. Don't ask me why. It's not nice to say."

"It doesn't matter."

"I wasn't panhandling."

"Of course not."

"He can't arrest me. I knows my rights."

"Hey, trust me. I just want to know if you saw anyone around that Buick before it shot down the hill."

"I'm not going to court."

"Off the record. As a favour to me."

"I don't want to talk in front of the cop."

"Fine. Go away, Ray."

But Deveau did not go away. He stuck his hand in his pocket and pulled out a ten. "Consider it a favour to me too," he chuckled.

"I didn't see no one."

"You didn't see a woman? A weird looking lady. Wearing gloves. And a scarf. And sunglasses?"

"No, Missus. No one like that."

"Well, did you see a woman near my car?"

"No, Missus. No women at all. I would of wished them a good day. They like that."

Right. Money talk. "Okay, what about a man? A big guy?"

"Like him, you mean?" He pointed to Deveau.

"No, no. Let's say he's medium. I mean did you see a big guy?"

Deveau laughed, but that might have been because I was puffing myself up and working on a Will Redmore facial expression.

"Sorry, Missus. No one like that."

I was out of questions. "Thanks, I hope your day gets better too," I said.

All four teeth showed. "It just did, Missus." He had Deveau's ten to thank for that, and he'd already begun his slow hustle down the street.

Deveau and I had walked two blocks back to the parking lot and had just reached the rental when I remembered the lesson learned talking to Jimmy's friends in Sydney. If you don't ask the right questions, you don't get the right answers.

I was out of breath when we caught up to our new friend as he trotted through the door into the LCBO on King Edward and Rideau. I engaged him in conversation as he picked up a litre bottle of Entre-Lac Dry Red.

"Did you see anyone near my car just before the so-called accident?"

"I might have, Missus." He cast a longing look at the rows of bottles.

Deveau dug out another ten. Funny, I hadn't remembered kissing a frog.

"What did you see?" My teeth were beginning to hurt from the effort of not screaming.

"Just a fella."

"The big guy?" I puffed myself up.

"No, Missus. I told you I didn't see a big fella."

"What. Did. He. Look. Like."

"He was kind of puny. Not that much to look at. Nothing much else I can say." He lifted off another bottle of red and cradled it like a new baby.

Ask the right questions, I reminded myself. "Did he have red hair? Blonde? Dark? Was he bald?"

"I have no idea, Missus." He'd managed to inch to the cash register as we talked.

Deveau said, "Why don't you remember his hair colour?"

"I would've, I guess, but I couldn't see it because of his hat."

That was all we got out of him, but I thought it was twenty dollars well spent.

We stood outside the LCBO, and I stared at my feet. It was

time to fill Deveau in on the suspicions about P. J. No choice.

"You waited long enough," he said.

"They just came up with these speculations this morning." I heard the defensiveness in my own voice.

He rubbed his chin. "A couple of hours. Could make a difference."

"Look, for what it's worth, I don't believe it. It will turn out to be a weird coincidence. Somehow I think that Redmore found out the same information. Certainly I told Honey plenty. I'll try to figure out the rest."

"I can check with the guys back home. And we have to let the local guys here know there might be something."

"I thought you might talk to Mombourquette."

"Will do."

"And make sure you tell him I don't believe it's P. J. Not even a little bit."

Thirty

Back at Mrs. Parnell's, the war room was booming. Vince was there, as well as Tracy and Frances Ann. Mrs. Parnell had morphed into General Patton at his finest. Even Vince was on his best behaviour.

Mrs. Parnell signalled me to meet her in the kitchen. Once there, she lowered her voice. "I don't want to upset the Fergusons, but there's no joy from Sydney. Loretta talked to Mrs. Smith. She remembers Mrs. Redmore well. And Honey. Apparently they attended the same church. To make a long story short, she's absolutely certain neither one was the woman chasing Jimmy in the backyard."

Back in the living room, the mob was getting restless. Alvin sat poised on the edge of the black leather sofa, several large bags from Radio Shack at his feet. Mrs. P. picked up a laser pointer and beamed a red dot at a series of blue Xes on a large chart taped on the wall. Lester and Pierre shrieked support. Gussie grinned.

"Damn, I forgot to bring the cat," I said.

"Sit down, Ms. MacPhee. We are planning our deployment to isolate and contain Jimmy Ferguson."

"Really."

"You will be an essential part of our strategy."

"What exactly are you planning?"

"Pincer movements."

"Of course."

"Don't mock, Ms. MacPhee. Surely you didn't think we were sitting on our backsides while you did the investigating?"

It was one of those questions best not answered. "Tell me what you're planning."

"Young Ferguson here is convinced his brother will come to the youth night concert tomorrow."

"The Matthew Good Band concert. Jimmy really wanted to go. It was the main thing he wanted to talk about when I found him yesterday."

"You think he could get in without being spotted?"

"We hope to find him early on, but he may be able to slip by us."

"The whole family's going to be there."

"What if he sees you? Will he run away?"

"We'll take a leaf from the killer's book," Mrs. Parnell said, pointing to a pile of red baseball caps.

"The Ottawa police will be combing the place," Deveau said.

Alvin paled. "That's the worst thing you can do. Ever since you guys hauled him in, Jimmy's afraid of cops in uniform. He kept hiding from them when he was on the run. If he sees cops, he'll take off, and we won't find him until it's too late."

I said, "Okay, stop hopping around, Alvin. I'd be the last person to deny the police can be kind of ham-handed."

Deveau looked kind of hurt, but I couldn't help that.

"Precisely, Ms. MacPhee. That's why we have a better plan."

I said, "But they don't need to be in uniform. They could give us some plainclothes officers and we could..."

"Hear us out." Mrs. P. flashed her pointer.

I sank down on the leather sofa and listened.

"As soon as the subject is spotted and his location

confirmed, Platoon A will advance from behind these hills to the East and move in a westerly direction."

"Who's platoon A?"

"That's me," said Alvin. "I'll be moving in a westerly direction."

"Platoon B, that would be Vince, Tracy and Frances Ann, will come from the North. And platoon C will be moving forward obliquely from the Southwest and…"

"Let me guess who Platoon C is."

"Please resist the urge to interrupt, Ms. MacPhee. You will play your part."

"Platoons A, B and C will remain in contact through Command Central."

Ah. No need to ask.

"And how will these communications be managed?"

"Bring out the materiel, dear boy."

I watched as Alvin produced boxes of walkie-talkies. It might have felt like Christmas if we hadn't been so worried about Jimmy.

"They're easy to use, Camilla," he said. "They work up to three kilometres. We just need to get our codes arranged."

"That's right," said the field commander, putting down the laser pointer just long enough to jam a fresh Benson and Hedges into her cigarette holder. "Everyone will get one, and we will use them to co-ordinate our approaches."

Gussie's tail beat a tattoo on Mrs. Parnell's hardwood floor.

• • •

"Don't feel bad about it," I said to Deveau, as he left my apartment some time later. "I'm sure if you're a good boy, they'll let you be Platoon D."

He chuckled. "I'll be there with the local guys. They're not as dopey as you think. They'll be undercover."

"But he's bound to know you."

"Not a chance. He might recognize your Keystone Cops down the hall, but I guarantee, he won't spot me."

"Mysterious. But good, I suppose."

He leaned in a bit. "What about you, Nancy Drew? Will you be keeping an eye on your so-called date, the liar?"

• • •

The rest of Wednesday was a nailbiter. We spun our wheels around town, combing bike paths, peering under bridges, easing our way through shelters and parks, hospital waiting rooms, walk-in clinics, the Food Bank, the Shepherds, the Sally Ann, the Rideau Centre, the food courts and vacant lots, the back alleys and the tawdry strip of tattoo parlours, junk shops and sleaze on Rideau where the street kids hung out.

All without a glimpse of Jimmy.

"Sorry to be the one to tell you," Deveau said, "but the Ottawa guys hauled in your friend."

"They're holding him?"

"Questioning. So they tell me."

"I better get over there. I don't believe P. J. could be involved in this. No matter how it looks."

"You wouldn't be the first person to be fooled by a con artist."

By the time I got to Elgin Street, Mombourquette had finished the questioning. P. J. passed me with his head down as he walked out the front door. For some reason, he wasn't speaking to me.

We had a lot riding on the Matthew Good Band concert.

The Ottawa cops had planned to ring the area. Deveau was their secret weapon. After all, he knew Jimmy, and chances were good he could recognize him even in the unlikely event Jimmy managed to disguise himself.

The unofficial team, led by General Violet Parnell-Patton, was assembling HQ, collecting walkie-talkies and practising their roger over and outs. I got my marching orders, walked Jimmy's dog, fed the commandant's kitty, picked out my baseball cap and sunglasses and paced.

Nothing much would be happening at Bluesfest before nine-thirty, when the band tuned up. At eight-fifteen, I figured I had nothing better to do and nothing to lose. Everyone else seemed to have some kind of important and urgent task.

That gave me time to skip to the Ottawa General and try to see if I could slip in and see Father Blaise. I took the sunflower.

I grabbed a cab to the General. Lucky I had twenty dollars in the pocket of my jeans for the fare, because we had pulled up in front of the main door before I noticed I had forgotten my backpack at home. That's the state you can get in when someone who is more than just a friend might be something very different.

I had no cellphone either, but then you can't use a cellphone in a hospital anyway. I had my housekeys with my serious Swiss Army knife, but that didn't help. They don't make a Swiss Army knife with a cellphone. Maybe they should.

"That's right. I am Father Blaise's niece," I said, making every effort not to look shifty-eyed. I wasn't sure where this would rate on the scale of sins. "We're so glad to hear he has regained consciousness. Mom can't get out of the rest home to see him. I represent the family."

Lucky this niece got a round-faced, chatty nurse. "You're fortunate. He's conscious now. He'll be glad to see a family member."

Father Blaise gazed nearsightedly at me, mystified. "Niece?" he said. "How lovely, a new niece."

"Oh, dear," I whispered to the nurse. "His memory's not good at the best of times. I hope the accident doesn't make it worse."

"My memory's better than yours, I'll bet," Father Blaise whispered. He lay like a grey lump in the bed. With the bandage around his head and no sign of his glasses, I wouldn't have known him.

Good thing the plump, cheerful nurse was already making her smiling way to check on another patient.

"White lie," I said. "We need to talk. It's a matter of life and death for Jimmy, and they only let family in."

"You're that MacPhee girl," he said, weakly.

"Looks like you had a rough time, Father."

"Nice chance to slow down," he said. "We all need a break every now and then."

Adversity brings out the best in some people.

"Father, I need your help. Jimmy Ferguson is still missing. I think it has to do with one or more incidents that happened in the past. So I'm really glad to hear your memory's so good."

"Go on." That gave me a shiver. How many times have I heard those words in confession?

"The first incident was the accident in the park when Jimmy

nearly died. We have reason to think he might have been injured by bullies. Does that mean anything to you? Would you have any idea who those bullies could have been?"

"I'd shake my head, no, but it hurts when I shake."

"Fair enough. Then surely you remember the accusation against him and Honey Redmore."

"I certainly do. Disgraceful talk. Not that it was public, but small towns have their weaknesses."

"He was supposed to be at the Youth Club."

"It doesn't matter where he was. He has his flaws, don't we all, and he could be foolish, but I know in my heart he could never, never have done what they said."

"Thank you. I have a question about the boy who might have made the allegation, Will Redmore. I know he isn't Catholic, but you may have known him."

"Oh, yes, I remember Will."

"Do you think he could have been a bully? Or capable of lying about the accusation that Jimmy assaulted his sister?"

"That's very serious. I couldn't speculate. I knew him. He was a bit of a hellion in his early teens. I won't say what he did, but his parents got him away from certain bad companions and packed him off to boarding school. I don't remember which one, but it did the trick. He certainly settled down. He turned out well, successful, high profile, good son, that's what counts." Father Blaise seemed exhausted with the effort.

"Just a couple more questions, Father." My heart was pounding. But you gotta do what you gotta do. "Did you know a boy named P. J. Lynch? Red hair, freckles. Gap between his teeth? He's thirty now. About the same age as Will Redmore. A bit older than his sister."

"No, I'm sure I don't know that boy. No. Not one of mine."

"Thank God. And you can't tell me anything more about

Will Redmore?"

"No. We mustn't judge children because of their early behaviour. Adolescents are very fragile and easily influenced. They need a chance to prove themselves. Will turned out fine. And so did his friend."

"Friend. What friend?" Oops. A bit too loud.

"What are you doing? This is a desperately sick man, you can't upset him." The plump, cheerful nurse stood behind me with her hands on her hips. I guess her initial opinion of me had changed.

"Tell me what friend, Father."

"The other boy that was always in trouble. He was always the ringleader, in my opinion."

The nurse said, "You'd better leave." She grabbed my arm. I shook her off.

I leaned over Father Blaise's bed. "What was his name, Father?"

"He turned out fine too. I saw him last week, just before I left on my holiday." Father Blaise's voice began to trail off. Softly.

The nurse called for help.

"It's good, you know, when the things we do pay off. Sports, drama club, those things can change a boy."

"His name, Father. Life or death."

"A long time ago that boy. So angry when he first showed up at the Youth Club. Setting fires. Stealing cars. Roughing up other children. But he certainly came to life on the stage. He could transform himself. It was marvellous. It's what drama is all about. Gave him the polish he needs for public life. It helped him to deal with his anger."

Two burly orderlies appeared.

"He's still angry, Father. He killed Reefer. He ran you down.

We need to find him before he kills Jimmy Ferguson."

The orderlies picked me up, one by each elbow. I tried to grab for the bed, then the doorframe.

"No, no. You must be mistaken," Father Blaise said, his eyes half-closed. "He turned out very well. I'm sure he'll get elected."

Holy shit.

I didn't actually need security to speed me on my way. I was ready to race out the front door of the hospital so I could use my cellphone to call Mombourquette, Deveau, Alvin, Mrs. P. Everybody. But, of course, I didn't have my cellphone.

Or money for a payphone.

Or money for a taxi, for that matter.

Thirty-One

The cab driver was pretty irritated as he accompanied me to my apartment. Some people lack a highly developed sense of humour. His mood did not improve when Gussie, the mildest of dogs, took an instant dislike to him.

"Thank you, Gussie," I said when I shut the door after the cabby had fled with my last twenty. "You're like a secret weapon."

Gussie's tail thumped.

"In more ways than one," I said.

•   •   •

I called Honey Redmore from Mrs. Parnell's number. There's more than one way to deal with Call Display.

"Tell me," I said when she answered, "did your mother lose a Hermès scarf in Sydney?"

"How did you know that?" she said, before she caught herself. "I have nothing more to say to you. One more call and I'll take legal action."

"I'd say you'd better be careful who you line up with here. Legal action plays both ways. Since you are choosing to protect people, you may find yourself in the hot seat with them. Your choice."

While I spoke to Honey, Mrs. Parnell got busy. "Pictures of

Nicholas Southern and Will Redmore? Of course, I can get them off the web," she'd said.

"Good. We need to show both of them to Alvin. Fast."

"It will only take a minute."

"P. J. was in Prince Edward Island with Southern on June 30th when he got called back here because of his mother's heart attack. I need confirmation Nicholas Southern was in Sydney on July 1st, officially, or otherwise. And I'll need Southern's bio, if you can find one."

Mrs. P. kept her computer and colour printer humming, while I made calls. I had just left messages with Mombourquette, Deveau, Alvin and P. J. when she slapped a sheaf of paper in front of me.

She'd pulled up some good images of Southern and Redmore from the web. "Thanks, Mrs. P. We'll show them to Alvin. Maybe he can identify them as the boys in the park."

"We see their faces splashed all over the media. It is hard to imagine young Ferguson wouldn't have recognized them."

"Maybe. But it was a long time ago, and the context is so different. And Alvin follows the art scene, not politics."

"I'll keep trying to find out where Southern was on Sunday."

"Thanks, I'll check the bio."

"I printed out a couple of them. Try the long version."

"Holy shit."

"What is it, Ms. MacPhee?"

"It's all here. Nicholas Southern lived in Sydney among many other places for a while as a young teenager. Then he moved with his mother to Calgary at sixteen. What else? Business degree on full scholarship. Active in drama and politics at university. Bless you, Mrs. P., and bless Father Blaise too."

"If I may say so, I believe these are slim grounds to accuse a public figure of these heinous crimes. But, who am I? You are the lawyer."

"And I'm building my case."

Of all the other people I needed to speak to, only Deveau returned my call. His timing couldn't have been better.

"How well do you remember the alleged assault on Honey Redmore?" I said. "Just answer. Don't give me any bull about the YOA. I'm asking you how well you remember it."

"Well enough."

"Do you recall if there was anyone else in the house at the time except for the family and possibly Jimmy?"

"Jeez. You don't ask much, do you?"

"Answer me."

"I think there was another guy there. A friend of the brother. He didn't get involved, though. Just backed up the story."

"Nicholas Southern," I said.

"The software guy on the political crusade? What about him?"

"Was he there?"

Silence. Silence from cops, even nice ones, can be a good sign.

"Did you know him in Sydney? My source says he got into plenty of trouble as a kid."

"I remember him."

"Don't get slippery. Answer this question. Was he in trouble with the law as a juvenile?"

"Come on now. We've been all through this."

"Fine. You could tell me where he lived. That wouldn't violate any laws."

"I don't see what difference it would make, but he and his mother had an apartment on Charlotte Street."

"Near the park?"

"What of it?"

"Okay. Now I'll talk. You listen. Here's what I think happened. Nicholas Southern and Will Redmore are buddies. A couple of smart kids with chips on their shoulders and nasty dispositions. Get in a bit of trouble in school. They push the younger kids around. Rough them up. Maybe get noticed by the cops. You with me?"

"I'm not breaking the law."

"Good. So one day, things get out of hand, and a child is injured seriously. The child is Jimmy."

"No one ever suggested those two kids were involved with that."

"That's part of the problem. There were no witnesses. Jimmy's too damaged, and Alvin has blocked everything out. It looks like they got away with it."

"Go on."

"But it wasn't the only thing they did. There were other things, small fires, thefts. Sooner or later, they're in trouble. Redmore's parents clamp down on him and ship him off to boarding school. But Southern's not from money. His mother connects him with Father Blaise and his Youth Club. Father Blaise sees the kid has promise. He gets him into drama and other things, and first thing you know the little bastard has a scholarship to university and a ticket to success. A happy ending for everyone but Jimmy."

"A lot of speculation, Camilla."

"But it's all falling together, isn't it?"

"Maybe."

"Here's another idea. What if Nicholas and Will touched base again, ran into each other somewhere, Dalhousie maybe. Nicholas comes for a visit for Thanksgiving. His mother's out west, and he's finishing up at Dal. So is Redmore."

"That's really far-fetched."

"What's far-fetched about it? Two guys from the same town, who were friends as children, and I read your silence before as a 'yes' to that, these guys reconnect at university and one visits the other. Big deal. Hardly the *X-Files*."

Deveau cleared his throat. He hadn't managed a single chuckle during this phone call.

"Are you with me?"

"Yes."

"So, let's say during this visit, Jimmy Ferguson is waiting to see Honey. Maybe he sees these two guys together, and maybe some memory is triggered. Maybe Southern gets nervous that Jimmy will tell people what he did. Or maybe Redmore does, and they decide to create a distraction. Or maybe, once a bully always a bully, and the bully found an opportunity to pull a really vile trick on a former victim."

"Go on."

"Only it goes really wrong, and the father dies. Maybe that's what created the tension between Redmore and Southern. The stakes are way up. But neither one can let the cat out of the bag, because they're both guilty of something the public won't take lightly."

"Career limiting," he said. "In a big way."

"No kidding. Does it answer a lot of questions so far?"

"I hate to admit it."

"A lot of things are starting to crystallize. Try this for a theory: Southern was in Sydney the day Jimmy disappeared. So was Redmore. So was Honey."

"I'll call Sydney and see if someone can review those old files. No guarantee we'll find anything useful."

"Right. Why don't you check this out? I suggest that you ask Honey yourself."

"Do you think she was part of it?"

"I find it hard to believe. I liked her. Even if she didn't like me much. But a woman was driving the car, both times. Mrs. Redmore must be in her early sixties. We know she held Jimmy responsible. Maybe she could have been driving the car that killed Greg Hornyk in Sydney. Somehow I can't see her rolling out of the Buick and sprinting away from Gadzooks. That would have to be a younger woman. Honey fits the physical profile."

"But you said Honey knew Jimmy wasn't to blame."

"True. Even so, she's close to her brother. Maybe he could weather accusations of childhood bullying, but his career wouldn't survive framing an innocent kid for an incident that led to the death of his father."

"I'm sorry, Camilla. I can believe those guys were involved, but I've met Honey, and it just doesn't ring true to me."

"Yeah well, maybe I haven't figured all the angles yet. But I'm getting there. Anyway, this whole topic upsets her. That's good. You should be able to get her flustered. My guess is she'll let something slip."

"She didn't let things slip when you talked to her."

"I didn't ask her the right questions. You have the background now," I said.

"No, you're the one who believes this. You should talk to her. Make the accusation to her face. I don't want to jeopardize the case if it comes down to that. Not that I believe it will."

"She won't talk to me, but you're the police. You can easily ask her if Southern was there on the Thanksgiving when Jimmy was accused. Ask her in person. Face to face. See what happens. While you're at it, you should interview Father Blaise. They might let you in to the ICU now. He knew both these kids. I believe he saw Southern on Canada Day. If you can get in, you can find out where and we can see how it fits in with what we know so far."

"Camilla?"

"What?"

"There's so many holes in your story, I don't know where to start counting."

"I'll be busy filling in those holes. While you're talking to people, you might fill in some of them yourself."

"I know you believe you're on to something, but I have to tell you, as a police officer I can't go out on that limb. This is pure conjecture. I'm sorry."

"Ray, you're here to look for Jimmy. You can't take a chance. You have to follow up."

"Sorry."

"You don't really have a choice."

"You just put the finger on your reporter friend, and now this is a complete about-face. I'm not going to badger Honey, and I am not going to harass a frail old man in intensive care. Try to get used to the idea."

"Sure. I'll get used to it. And, Ray?"

"What?"

"Don't call me, I'll call you."

I may have slammed the phone down. Mrs. Parnell raised her eyebrow and her glass of Harvey's in a sympathetic salute.

"Sometimes, Ms. MacPhee, discretion is the better part of valour."

"Yeah, well, discretion is not my best thing. And it's too late for that now. What am I going to do? We're really out of time."

"You can't blame Sergeant Deveau. He doesn't know you well."

"And he won't be getting to know me any better."

327

"Let us be strategic. Who can talk to Honey?"

"I need to think about that."

"Have a look at this while you're thinking. I found a bit more background on our Mr. Southern. Mostly the theatrical stuff. Do you notice anything?" Mrs. Parnell shot a little jet of smoke in my direction.

I said, "Just a write-up mentioning some of the activities this Southern person was involved in." I stared at the article. It appeared to list every activity Nicholas Southern had ever taken part in. As far as I could tell they were all innocuous. "I'm surprised they don't list sleeping seven hours a night and flossing his teeth as achievements. Are these people paid by the syllable? What are you driving at, Mrs. P.?"

"I thought you might find the theatrical history illuminating."

"You're kidding, right? And am I supposed to be really impressed that he once drove a tour bus for a summer job?"

"Examine it closely, Ms. MacPhee."

I took my time, but after two rereads, I wasn't wiser. "Out with it," I said.

"Look at those performances. *Some Like It Hot. Victor Victoria. La Cage aux Folles.* What was different about them?"

"Sorry," I said, "I'm not getting this. Oh. Shit. How could I miss that?"

"Precisely, Ms. MacPhee."

"Men dressed as women."

The last piece of the puzzle. "Father Blaise said he really got into his roles. Shone on the stage."

• • •

Dogs are not allowed at Bluesfest. So it took a certain amount of ingenuity to get in with Gussie. I already had the sunglasses. Gussie did a great seeing eye dog routine. I thought the white cane would come in handy anyway.

Youth night at Bluesfest was something new. The Matthew Good Band was supposed to pull in younger crowds. A quick glance told me the tactic had worked. It was like another species. I looked around at the surging mass and saw ten thousand reasons why I was not a youth. Body surfing was only one of them.

Lots of the youth had cellphones. I hoped they were having better luck with them than I was. Deveau didn't answer his. Mombourquette didn't answer his. Alvin didn't answer his. Mrs. Parnell didn't answer hers. I blamed the goddam walkie-talkies. I didn't have one of those.

P. J. didn't answer his phone either. I hoped he wasn't in the slammer.

I kept leaving messages as Gussie and I wove our way through the crowds. Gussie sniffed jean legs and pulled here and there. "Find Jimmy, Gussie," I said. Not that Gussie understood a word, but if Jimmy was near, Gussie would know.

I looked around desperately for Platoons A, B and D. No luck.

Like any band worth its salt, the Matthew Good Band wasn't going to start on time. It was already dark when the tuning up on stage started. Dark enough to make the search through the crowd tricky. Even with my sunglasses off, half the crowd would have had the same basic description as Jimmy.

Mombourquette was the first to answer his phone.

"I guess you feel like a dope," he said, "dating a crazed killer, and let's not forget trashing Stan's Buick."

"Sorry to disappoint, Lennie, but it's not P. J."

"Listen, we didn't have enough to hold him. But we'll get him."

"Get this. It's not P. J. I never really believed it. The person you want is Nicholas Southern."

"What? The politician? Are you fucking nuts?"

"It may sound crazy, but hear me out. This guy's whole political platform is built on each person taking responsibility for his own actions. He's always howling about the need for law and order and let's lock up those bad guys forever. Now it turns out he was a kid in trouble with the law. If word gets out he's not squeaky clean, the media will take him down. Think piranhas."

"Even supposing that's true, no way the guy's juvenile records will get out to the press. So if you think we're going to hassle a would-be politician who's in the news every friggin' day, you'd better think again. Next you'll be telling me here's three good reasons to arrest the Pope. I haven't forgotten your boyfriend, Camilla."

"I didn't tell you to arrest P. J."

"You know what, Camilla? You cause everything bad to happen."

"Where's Deveau? I need to talk to him."

"I don't know where he is. Get off my phone."

Deveau still didn't answer his own cellphone.

P. J. did pick up on my third attempt. I guess I shouldn't have been surprised that he wasn't interested in my theory. Or anything I had to say. There's something about a dial tone that speaks volumes.

I settled for joining the milling throng, craning my neck to check for Jimmy Ferguson among the thousands of excited young people jockeying for position near the Main Stage.

Suddenly Gussie yanked so hard on the leash that I fell to

my knees. I struggled, but found myself dragged away from the Main Stage. Gussie began to lope away from the crowd with me attempting to get control. Gussie's lope grew to a gallop, and we tore up the hill towards the Acoustic stage. Gussie was obviously aiming towards a figure running ahead, dodging and tripping.

Another person streaked along after the first. Neither one wore the red baseball cap designating Platoon A, B or D. I knew the first runner was Jimmy. I was just as certain that the second figure was Nicholas Southern.

Up the hill the huge swooping sail of the Acoustic tent dominated the view. There was nothing and no one near it. A bus with images of a band was parked off to the side, probably packed with sound gear. Maybe there would be musicians or roads near it. Maybe there'd be help there. On any other night, the hill would have been packed with people, but tonight, they were all clustered by the Main Stage. The security people would be working that area, keeping the kids from leaping onto the stage, keeping control. No sign of them in this area.

I ran like hell to reach Jimmy. Gussie helped. I shrieked Jimmy's name. But by this time the band had launched into its opening number and the crowd was screaming louder.

I gasped raggedly as we tore up the hill, tripping on rocks, divots, paper cups. Racing to head off the killer. Far ahead Jimmy Ferguson tripped and turned a terrified white face behind him.

My hands shook as I pulled out the cellphone and dialled 911. The dispatcher knew who Jimmy Ferguson was.

"There are police on site. Send them to the Acoustic tent."

"I can't hear you."

"The Acoustic tent," I screamed.

"You'll have to speak louder."

Gussie yanked hard, and I fell flat on my face. I dropped the cellphone and the cane as I clung to Gussie's lead.

Jimmy had vanished. So had Nicholas Southern. There was nowhere they could be but in the Acoustic tent. Gussie pulled, I followed. Up onto the stage.

I yelled a message meant for two sets of ears. Even this far from the Main Stage, the band was clear and loud.

"Nicholas, leave Jimmy alone. You can't kill us all."

"Don't be so sure," came the voice behind me.

I froze but managed to say," But why?"

"Because I have something important to do. I am going to make a difference in politics. I am going to the top. And I am not going to let you little pissants stop me. You're in my way, and you're not important. Hello, Jimmy."

I whipped around, expecting Jimmy but seeing only the empty stage. The sky exploded. A sharp blow to the back of the head will do that. I don't remember falling off the stage, but I must have hit the wooden stage stairs head on.

Hard to say how long I was out. When I staggered to my feet, the stage was empty. Blood seeped into my eyes. No sign of Jimmy. Gussie was gone too. I pushed my way up onto the stage. The floor and sides were painted dead black, so I clattered around in the dark, tripping over the onstage cable covers.

I tried to control my breathing and listen. I thought I heard whimpering, ragged breathing nearby.

Jimmy? Should I call his name? If he answered would that alert Nicholas Southern?

We are each responsible for our own actions. Fair enough, Nicholas, but which actions? If I drew attention to Jimmy, would that draw Southern to him too?

There has to be a plan. Think, think.

I wasn't sure of the shape at the back of the stage area. I felt my way around, trying not to miss anything. My head swam. Silver dots danced in my eyes. Cover the area. Left to right and back. Doesn't matter if you go over some ground again.

Right to left. Left to right.

Wipe blood off face with sleeve.

Right to left. Left to right.

Why not a scrap of light?

Slowly, painfully, I crept until finally, I felt the warm, trembling body. Heard the terror in the sob.

"It's okay, Jimmy," I whispered. "We're going to be all right. This time it will be all right."

I only wished I believed it.

Gussie licked my hand. From somewhere to my left, I heard the roar of an engine.

Police? No.

A truck? A fire truck maybe?

I knew what it had to be. My heart sank. Nicholas was back. With the bus.

The floor shuddered as the bus hit the supports of the tent. I wasn't sure how stable those tent posts were. Jimmy shook.

"Come on, guys, we're getting out of here," I yelled.

The next slam of the truck must have caused the structure to sag. I heard the high whine of the bus. What, in reverse? Then a loud pop as the cable anchoring the structure snapped. The heavy vinyl sail sagged. The metal studs groaned. More snapping from outside, and then the whoosh as the vinyl tent roof sank slowly to the stage. I fought for breath.

The bus rammed the side again and again. Was he crazy? Did he think no one would see him knocking down the Acoustic tent with a frigging bus?

It appeared that he did.

What difference did it make? We were dead anyway.

My keys dug into my leg as the heavy canvas and supports pressed our bodies down. We were trapped. What good were keys with no door and no way out? It was almost funny.

Wait. Think.

I felt until I found the Swiss Army knife. Struggled to find the right blade. Not the corkscrew. Not the goddam stupid little scissors. The knife blade. Struggled to open it. Pushed with all my might to cut through the vinyl without breaking the blade.

Outside, the slow crush of the bus continued. Back and forth. Southern had nothing to lose at this stage and everything to gain by wiping out Jimmy and me. Finally, I managed to work a medium sized split in the canvas. A speck of light appeared. I sliced, pushed, forced the hole larger.

The bus hit again with a thunderous crash. The rest of the supports were going.

"Get through, Jimmy," I yelled. "Push. Get through."

We tumbled through and out onto the hillside. I had Jimmy by the collar. I'd be goddamed if I'd let him get away again. A yelp told me I had Gussie's tail.

We rolled.

No one heard. But someone saw. The bus rumbled toward us, down the hill. Zigging. Zagging.

Somewhere through the racket and the pain in my head I heard voices. People. Banging. Shouting. People reached out.

"Jimmy! Jimmy."

"Oh, shit, are they dead?"

"Holy Mary, Mother of God."

I heard the crackle of walkie-talkies, voices, loud voices. Someone lifted me.

"Help Jimmy," I said, staggering around.

I heard Deveau's voice. "Jimmy's okay."

"And Gussie?"

"Gussie too."

"Good."

"How about you? Gonna make it?"

"Yes. Where's Nicholas Southern?"

"Where he should be."

I thought I knew what he meant by that, but I can't say it bothered me.

In the background, unbelievably, the music played on.

Thirty-Two

J immy's EEGs and neurological tests show some damage, probably caused by a lack of medication and the immense stress of his ten days on the loose. We can only assume he suffered several seizures. Only time will tell the long term impact. The phrase the doctors use is cautious optimism. Who knows how much help he'll need to get over his ordeal, but his family will make sure he gets it.

On a sad note, the brave and loyal Gussie seems to trigger distress in Jimmy now. A one-way trip to the Humane Society seems an inappropriate reward.

The media had a field day with the fall of the wonder boy, Nicholas Southern. Bit by bit, we are still piecing together what happened. We can only speculate that somehow Jimmy reacted in a panic when he first saw Southern in Sydney. Southern was quick enough to figure out why. I believe Southern thought he'd better nip that little PR problem right away. Perhaps someday Jimmy will be able to tell us if he recognized Southern as the bully or merely panicked without knowing why. Alvin thinks he might have reacted to Southern's voice. Whatever it was, Southern wasn't going to take a chance on word getting out. The one fact we are sure of: Nicholas is a much bigger story as a dead crazy than he ever was as a wannabe politician. Calls for stronger laws are loud and clear. Nicholas Southern would have approved.

P. J. got the scoop, and the scoop behind the scoop. Bad boy grows up and pretends to be good boy. Makes a lot of money. Fools lots of people. No names mentioned.

I knew giving P. J. the tip-off to interview Father Blaise about seeing Nicholas Southern in Sydney would add drama along with the story of the attack in the park. P. J. got some serious sound bites out of Donald Donnie and Loretta too. He even got some mileage out of an interview with René Janveau bemoaning his shattered Gadzooks Gallery. The heavily bandaged René made for a first-rate photo op too.

In the end, I was proud of P. J. His feature story revealed his own inadvertent role in keeping Southern up to speed on Jimmy's whereabouts and our tactics through seemingly idle chit-chat. He didn't go easy on himself.

We're still not clear how much Honey Redmore knew about Southern. There's not much chance we'll ever prove Will was the second boy in the park. Alvin's statement based on photos would be flimsy in court. Contact from the Redmore's legal representative put a serious chill on that angle of P. J.'s coverage. But it's funny how word spreads with journalists.

I'm not sure if things will be okay between P. J. and me. Ever. Some accusations you shouldn't believe for a minute about a person. He knows it. I know it. And there's not much I can do but wait and see.

Father Blaise went home to Sydney in a wheelchair, and he'll probably stay in one for the rest of his life. He's still as sharp as ever though, and he has helped to clear up some of the confusion about what happened. According to Deveau, Father Blaise has a clear memory of seeing Reefer Keefer arguing with Nicholas Southern in downtown Sydney on Canada Day. The local cops have equally clear memories of Reefer using embarrassing information about people as a source of supplementary income. That would explain a lot.

The ballistics test showed that Mombourquette's bullet was the one that stopped Nicholas Southern. It's administrative leave for him until the SIU report comes back. If he had a life, he might enjoy that. But he doesn't.

Alvin's referral for therapy has come through. I thanked my doctor. Let's hope it does the trick. Mrs. Parnell found him another apartment in Hull, which he has already begun work on decorating. He will be back at Justice for Victims. I will cope.

Deveau remained in town for the last four days of Bluesfest. I sat next to him through James Brown, Wilson Pickett and Little Feat. I spent the shows in a haze of painkillers. There's something to be said for drugs and music. Sunglasses too, if both your eyes are black.

He stayed over at my place. In case I had a medical crisis in the night. Or had a nightmare. Or needed scrambled eggs in the morning. Or something.

He has a warm heart and cold feet. I believe there's a song about that. At any rate, I guess he's not with me for my looks.

Today is July 16 and Deveau has to go back to Sydney. His kids are coming home from music camp. He has a life. He has a job. He's out of holiday time.

Mrs. Parnell has weathered it better than anyone. But then, war becomes her.

For me, I've been told to take it easy. I think Gussie and I will do that. Mrs. Parnell's cat will have to stop sulking one of these days. I keep my feet up and stay on hold with the insurance company over the Buick.

The Fergusons have decided that I'm a good guy after all. They've taken to calling me collect twice a day. I have invested in Call Display. We now have seven days left until the rest of the MacPhee family returns from Scotland. The technical term for that will be Armageddon.

Mary Jane Maffini is a lapsed librarian, former co-owner of the Prime Crime Mystery Bookstore in Ottawa and author of the Camilla MacPhee series (the other books are *Speak Ill of the Dead* and *The Icing on the Corpse.*) She was a 2001 double nominee for the Crime Writers of Canada Arthur Ellis Awards for best short story. Her quirky characters have appeared in *Storyteller Magazine, Ellery Queen's Mystery Magazine, Over My Dead Body, Chatelaine* and *On Spec*, as well as in the Canadian crime anthologies *Iced, Best of Cold Blood, Menopause is Murder, Cottage Country Killers, Fit to Die* (RendezVous Crime 2001) and *Over the Edge.* "Cotton Armour" in *The Ladies Killing Circle* won the Arthur Ellis Award for best short short story in 1995, and she was a 1999 finalist for best first novel for *Speak Ill of the Dead.*

She is currently president of the Crime Writers of Canada, a member of the Ladies' Killing Circle and is working on more Camilla MacPhee novels.

The Camilla MacPhee Mysteries

Speak Ill of the Dead

Camilla MacPhee is the black sheep of her perfect, blonde family, although she runs a law office specializing in Justice for Victims of violent crimes. However, her uneasy association with the world of crime takes a bizarre turn when a vicious, vindictive fashion columnist with underworld connections named Mitzi Brochu is crucified in a downtown hotel room. The problem is that Camilla's best friend Robin was on her way to meet the victim, and has become the main suspect.

ISBN 0-929141-65-2 $9.95 U.S / $11.95 in Canada

The Icing on the Corpse

It's now forty below in Canada's capital, but Camilla is feeling the heat. When a savage serial batterer goes on the rampage looking for revenge against his former girlfriend, the terrified woman turns to Camilla for help. But a sudden change of fortune causes her client to really feel the chill. Camilla wades into the investigation, now one of murder. Soon everyone connected with the case is either cooling their heels behind bars or trying to avoid cold storage in the morgue. Camilla's really skating on thin ice looking for this killer—literally.

ISBN 0-929141-81-4. $10.95 U.S / $12.95 in Canada